*TH*

As much as he wanted to deny it, that was the full and puzzling truth. Her blue eyes and determined smile seemed to hover in the black of night, turning the darkness into light.

The aching need to kiss her pretty, pink lips almost overwhelmed him. The desire to stroke her gloriously long, gloriously blond hair was too much to bear.

"Oh, Elizabeth." He whispered her name in the dark. Was it really true? Were a woman's wild driving habits really an indicator of what a man could expect in bed?

What if they were? Lord, almighty! Wouldn't that be something?

She could have all the say she wanted over her body, but he wanted it, dammit, wanted her more than he'd wanted any woman in his life. . . .

# Ribbons in the Wind

*Margaret Brownley*

A TOPAZ BOOK

TOPAZ
Published by the Penguin Group
Penguin Books USA Inc., 375 Hudson Street,
New York, New York 10014, U.S.A.
Penguin Books Ltd, 27 Wrights Lane,
London W8 5TZ, England
Penguin Books Australia Ltd, Ringwood,
Victoria, Australia
Penguin Books Canada Ltd, 10 Alcorn Avenue,
Toronto, Ontario, Canada M4V 3B2
Penguin Books (N.Z.) Ltd, 182–190 Wairau Road,
Auckland 10, New Zealand

Penguin Books Ltd, Registered Offices:
Harmondsworth, Middlesex, England

First published by Topaz, an imprint of Dutton Signet,
a division of Penguin Books USA Inc.

First Printing, November, 1996
10  9  8  7  6  5  4  3  2  1

 REGISTERED TRADEMARK—MARCA REGISTRADA

Printed in the United States of America

*To Daniel,*
*who has an affinity for "wild" women*

# Chapter 1

"A man would rather take his chances with a husband-hunting spinster than a woman driver."
*Women at the Wheel*
Circa 1915

Three elderly nuns dressed in black habits stood piously guarding the boarding gate at the Syracuse train station, and gently prodded passengers to "Save the poor."

Coins were dropped into the collection box with gratifying regularity and donors rewarded for their generosity with the promise of a "special place in heaven." Those who rushed by without so much as a glance received a resounding "Bless you, child."

No one got blessed more sincerely than Jimmy Hunter. Holding on to his white Panama hat, he raced in and out of the crowd, dashed around a cart filled with steamer trunks, jumped over a crate of squawking chickens, and made a death-defying leap to grab hold of the polished brass handrail of a moving Pullman. With practiced ease, he pulled himself onto the passenger car just as it picked up speed. Grinning, he tipped his hat to the startled nuns behind him, then ducked through the narrow door, disappearing inside.

His worn carpetbag firmly in hand, he made his way down the swaying aisle.

The majority of male passengers were already hidden behind the bold headlines of the morning newspapers.

A pretty young woman wearing a stylish high-crown hat cast an approving eye at Jimmy. Next to her a tightly corseted woman held her knitting needles close to her ample bosom, and nudged her young charge with her elbow. Paying her chaperon no heed, the younger woman continued to flutter her eyelashes at Jimmy with shameless disregard for propriety. Finally, her disapproving companion shrugged and resumed her knitting, the needles clicking furiously.

Balancing himself as best he could, Jimmy tipped his white straw hat politely as he passed, bringing a blush to the face of the younger woman and a glimmer of respect to the older.

He lifted his carpetbag to the luggage rack overhead and took the only seat available, next to a rather stout man with a sweeping mustache. The man's portly build required Jimmy to sit in his seat at an awkward angle so as to avoid physical contact as much as possible. The hazy, not to mention odorous, cloud of blue smoke coming from the man's cigar made Jimmy's throat tighten in protest.

The passenger looked up from his paper and studied Jimmy over the stump of his smoking cigar as if he resented the half seat Jimmy occupied. Jimmy braced himself for a verbal battle and was surprised when the man clamped down on his cigar and spoke in a friendly voice. "I say there, young man, didn't you speak at the Inventors Exposition? You're the son of Kate and Jonas Hunter. You're, eh ..." He snapped his fingers, trying to recall Jimmy's name.

Jimmy cleared his throat and acknowledged the man with a congenial nod. He was used to living in the shadow of his illustrious parents. Secretly, though, he'd hoped his latest speech would help distinguish him in his own right as a pioneer in the field of electricity. "Name's Jimmy Hunter. Don't tell me you're a fellow inventor."

"Rye Crankshaw's the name. No doubt you've heard of me?"

The name didn't ring a bell, but it seemed impolite to say so, especially since it wouldn't take but a slight shove from his seatmate to send him sprawling into the aisle.

Jimmy pulled off his hat and held out his hand. "I'm very pleased to meet you, sir."

Crankshaw pumped Jimmy's hand like a thirsty man with a dry well. "Where are you heading?"

"Hogs Head, Indiana. Perhaps you've been there? It was one of the first towns to make electricity available to its private citizens. Eight-five percent of our houses have electricity as their main power source." If he had his way, every house would be wired. But some old-timers were still resistant to change. He never could understand why anyone would opt for a kerosene lantern over an electric lightbulb.

"Is that so?" Crankshaw sounded impressed and Jimmy warmed to him. "Sounds like an interesting place. I'm afraid I haven't traveled as much as I would like. But that's about to change." He leaned closer, forcing Jimmy to lean over the armrest and into the aisle. Crankshaw reeked of imported cigars, bootlegged whiskey, and that part of the city condemned by pulpit-pounding clergymen. "I'm entering the cross-country Model T Ford race."

Jimmy had heard talk about the race at the Inventors Exposition. "That's mighty interesting. Have you ever raced before?"

Crankshaw waved his cigar through the air. "Never." His dark eyes sagged at the corners beneath his straight eyebrows. "But this race will focus attention on the importance of the automobile."

"So you don't think automobiles will go the way of bicycles?" Jimmy asked. A fair number of people were of the opinion that automobiles were merely a passing fad.

"Not on your life. For one thing, it's cheaper to

operate a car than care for a confounded animal. An automobile only costs twenty-five dollars a month. That's a hell of a lot cheaper than the forty dollars it takes to feed and care for a horse."

"You've got a point there. But I don't mind telling you these self-propelled vehicles have caused a lot of controversy in Hogs Head. The horses in the livery stable are so spooked the owner has to keep them tranquilized."

"You can't mix cars with horses. It's either one or the other. Mark my words, these modern automobiles are the wave of the future." Crankshaw flicked the ashes from his cigar onto the floor. "Think of the advantages. Without all that disease-breeding manure on the streets, we'll have cleaner air. We'll also have less traffic problems. You can park two automobiles in the same space needed for a single horse and wagon."

"They definitely take up less space," Jimmy agreed. "But the noise factor is appalling. I would certainly hope these gasoline-driven automobiles are put to rest in favor of electrical cars." He personally drove an electric runabout, a car that was odorless and noiseless and with the development of a more efficient battery would be far superior to any gasoline guzzler.

"You get no argument from me in that regard. Space-wise, I suppose it doesn't make a whole lot of difference. It still amazes me how an automobile can turn around in the middle of town without causing a traffic jam." He nudged Jimmy's arm with his elbow. "Another thing, a car can't kick or bite and it only eats when it's on the road." He laughed at his own joke, then added, "There's a twenty-five-thousand-dollar reward for the first motorist to make it from Buffalo to Seattle."

Crankshaw's excitement was catching. It was the kind of excitement that had been missing from Jimmy's life in recent months. Now that the electrical works was such a large and important part of Hogs Head, it required a full-time manager. Jimmy had precious little time left from his daily responsibilities to work on his beloved experiments, and he missed the excitement of trying out new ideas. "Twenty-five thousand dollars." He let out a low whistle. "That much, eh?"

"That's not all. The second-place driver gets fifteen grand and the third place, ten. It's a publicity stunt, of course. What isn't, nowadays? Mr. Ford is trying to draw attention to our nation's disgraceful roadways. Once we get more paved roads, I expect automobile sales will skyrocket."

"I expect they will," Jimmy agreed, though it seemed a person could hardly travel a mile, anymore, without seeing at least one or two Tin Lizzies, as Model T Fords were affectionately called by an adoring public, and considerably more in well-populated towns. Model T's were fast becoming the vehicle of choice for people living in rural areas, where streets were not only unpaved but in many cases nonexistent.

"What would you do with all that money?"

"Do? Good heavens, lad. I could do anything I wanted. I could travel, see the world, and hopefully talk that independent widow lady, Myra Tucker, into taking a second husband. Nothing else I've done has worked with her. The way I figure it, winning that race will make me rich and famous. What woman in her right mind would turn me down then?" He winked. "Got any prospects lined up?"

Jimmy laughed. "Not me. I like my freedom. I'm not the marrying kind." Heavens! Every time he so much as kissed a woman, she started getting all possessive and emotional, demanding to know why he wasn't calling on her every day or sending her flowers. Imagine living like that.

"I remember saying those very words when I was your age, lad." Crankshaw studied Jimmy for a moment. "Do you know anything about the mechanics of a gasoline automobile?"

"I've torn down a few engines. In fact, that's how I put myself through school. Why do you ask?"

"I need a mechanic. The one I have is too green for my peace of mind, not to mention a royal pain in the ass. He's got more physical ailments than there are body parts. You strike me as a bright young man. If you agree to work for me, I'll see to it that you get a generous cut of the prize money. What do you say?"

Jimmy was tempted. It wasn't often a chance like this came along. But the truth was, as manager of the family-owned Hunter Electrical Works, he couldn't afford to be away from home for much longer. Besides, he wasn't much of a gambling man. Nor was he keen on the idea of driving cross-country in one of those smelly tin can rattletraps with an internal combustion engine. Driving across town in his mother's touring car was enough for him. Still, he regretted having to pass up the offer. "Sorry I can't help you out. But I'm due back in Hogs Head."

"Too bad." Crankshaw shrugged. "It doesn't hurt to ask, though." He chuckled. "You won't believe this, but one of the drivers is a woman."

"You don't say?"

Crankshaw blew a cloud of cigar smoke. "Don't you think it strange a woman would sign up for an automobile race?"

Jimmy coughed and waved the smoke away. "Women do all sorts of things nowadays. My mother's an inventor and my aunt . . ." He stopped. His eccentric aunt was difficult if not altogether impossible to describe.

"But this is different. This woman actually thinks she has a chance of winning."

"Maybe she'll surprise you."

Crankshaw let out a loud guffaw that brought a disapproving glare from a matronly woman passenger across the aisle. "Not by winning, she won't! Her name is Elizabeth Davenport, and I'm here to tell you she's a bold and brash woman the likes of which you've never seen. Not even those confounded suffragettes can compare."

Jimmy wasn't sure he'd heard right. "Excuse me, sir. Did you say Elizabeth Davenport?"

"Yes, that's the one. As I was saying, she has no business driving an automobile, let alone entering a race. I tell you, she hasn't got a chance in high heaven of making it to the first checkpoint." Crankshaw narrowed his eyes. "Don't tell me you know her?"

"I'm not sure." It surprised Jimmy to find that the mere mention of the name Elizabeth Davenport had such an effect on him, even now, twenty years after he'd last seen his childhood playmate. Even more astounding, his heart was beating so fast it was hard to catch his breath. "I once knew someone by that name, but it was a long time ago. It's probably not the same person."

"Probably not." Crankshaw shrugged, stuck his cigar back in his mouth, and went back to his newspaper.

Amazed at the coincidence of the lady motorist having the same name as his little childhood friend, Jimmy gazed out the window. The train sped past woods and farmlands, hills and lakes. The sky was the color of molten steel, contrasting sharply with the rich green countryside. But the colors blurred together much as the memories of the past.

*Elizabeth Davenport.* It couldn't be her! Jimmy's Elizabeth had been sweet and gentle. Why, there hadn't been a bold or brash bone in her body. That alone was enough to convince him the woman driver was not the same Elizabeth Davenport who had haunted his memory for all these years.

He tried putting the matter out of his mind, but once the memories were triggered he couldn't seem to stop them. The clickety-clack of the train didn't help, for it only reminded him of another train, another journey, and how the Elizabeth Davenport of his youth had sat in the baggage car of that westbound train, crying her poor little heart out.

It was the unforgettable memory of her inconsolable sobbing that made Jimmy turn back to his seatmate. "I really don't think it's the same Elizabeth Davenport I once knew. She was, how should I say it? Very emotional."

Crankshaw folded his newspaper. "All women are emotional. That's why they have no business on the road."

Jimmy smiled to himself. Crankshaw had no idea how lucky he was that Jimmy's mother or aunt wasn't around to hear his biased comments. "Would you mind describing her?"

"What?"

"You know. The color of her hair. Her eyes. Does she wear eyeglasses? How old would you say she was?"

"I'm afraid I can't be much help to you there. I've never met her personally, you understand. I only know her by reputation." He glanced around to make certain no one was listening to their conversation, then spoke in a hushed voice. "I heard tell that she pushed the mayor of San Francisco into the mud."

"No!"

"That's not all she did. She spent time in jail for writing an obscene book."

"Obscene?" This was definitely not the same Elizabeth Davenport he'd known in his past.

"Do you think a woman who writes obscenity can be trusted behind the wheel of an automobile? It's been my experience that a woman who's wild in bed is wild on the road."

Jimmy had not considered the possibility that a woman's capacity for passion predicted her driving ability, but it was an intriguing thought. He was nowhere near an expert on women, though not for lack of trying. For all he knew, a woman's bedroom antics could indeed determine her driving ability. He only hoped the same wasn't true of males. He considered himself a cautious driver, but he sure as hell wouldn't want anyone to think he was equally as careful or dull in bed.

Crankshaw fell silent, leaving Jimmy's mind to wander. Soothed by the gentle swaying of the train and the comforting thought that *his* Elizabeth Davenport was probably safely married by now, with a half-dozen blond-haired, blue-eyed children in tow, he laid his head against the white cotton antimacassar and dozed off. *Don't cry, Elizabeth. Please don't cry!*

He woke with a start as the train gave a sudden jolt. A suitcase flew off the rack overhead. A woman screamed.

"Good heavens!" Crankshaw gasped. "What was that?" He craned his head to look out the window.

A harried-looking porter rushed down the aisle, his slender frame barely filling his crisp blue uniform. "Please stay in your seats. We've had to make an unexpected stop." He adjusted the shiny stiff visor of his blue broadcloth hat. "A train has derailed up ahead. I'm afraid we'll be delayed."

"Delayed?" Crankshaw's fleshy jowls shook with impatience. "What do you mean, delayed? For how long?"

The porter paused by Jimmy's side and leveled his gaze at Crankshaw. "It looks like we could be delayed several hours at least, sir."

"Good heavens, lad! I don't have several hours." Crankshaw motioned for Jimmy to move.

Jimmy rose. "Where are you going?"

"I'm hitching a ride into town. We're only about two or three miles outside of Buffalo. The race is due to start at noon. If I hurry, I should make it in plenty of time."

Jimmy stood in the aisle while Crankshaw reached overhead for his battered suitcase and walking cane.

Still shaken by the effects of hearing Elizabeth's cry in his brief but haunting dream, Jimmy made a quick

decision. "Would you mind if I accompany you? Since
there's going to be a delay, I may as well wait in
Buffalo for the afternoon train. That way I can see
the start of the race."

"Don't mind at all. This is history in the making.
But do hurry or we'll be late." Crankshaw plowed
down the aisle like a runaway tractor, swinging his
cane and bellowing orders. "Coming through. Clear
the aisles."

Following in his wake, Jimmy doffed his hat and
offered apologies to the other passengers, who didn't
take kindly to Crankshaw's rude behavior.

Once off the train, they hiked the short distance to
the dirt road and hitched a ride into town on the back
of a hay wagon that moved too slowly for Crankshaw's liking.

"Can't your old nag muster up a bit more steam?
If it weren't for my bum leg, I'd get there faster on
foot."

"If it weren't fer old Sugar Baby's four bum legs, I
dare say she could, too," the farmer drawled.

The sky was overcast, and though the ground was
still muddy from the early morning rain, the sun was
making a gallant effort to break through the fast-moving
clouds.

At long last they reached a large open field outside
of Buffalo that was normally reserved for carnivals,
circuses, and medicine shows. Ten black Model T
Fords were parked haphazardly in the freshly mowed
field, their tall boxy bodies as bright and shiny as polished black jade. The brass windshield mountings and
acetylene-gas headlamps of the older models gleamed
in the filtered rays of a peek-a-boo sun.

Brass accessories had been replaced in the newer
models by black-painted steel. Steel accessories had
become such a status symbol, one of the car owners
had painted over the less desirable brass accessories
to give his car a more modern look. One by one the

black canvas tops were lowered and buttoned down to take full advantage of the warming rays of late spring.

Crankshaw led Jimmy to his open-air Ford. A placard marking the car as number three was attached to the dummy door on the left side of the vehicle. Fastened to the rear was a sign that read SEATTLE OR BUST.

The driver was required to climb over the dummy door on the driver's side, or use the single door on the companion side and slide across the button leatherette seat. "So, what do you think of my flivver?" Crankshaw caressed the gleaming black fender of his Model T with his fat fingers and rubbed his pudgy hands together like a man about to begin a long-awaited feast.

"It's a beauty," Jimmy said and meant it. The boxy cars were generally considered homely, and had been likened in appearance to a gawky knock-kneed adolescent. Jimmy, however, thought the design functional. Crankshaw's automobile had been maintained perfectly, inside and out.

"That it is," Crankshaw agreed. He piled his suitcase and cane into the backseat, and stepping onto the running board on the companion side, slid across the seat. With a wink, he demonstrated the tilting steering wheel he'd had specially installed to accommodate his bulk. Jimmy was impressed. There was no end to the possibilities.

A dark-suited race official wearing a four-in-hand tie stood on a makeshift podium, lifted a megaphone to his mouth, and began introducing the drivers. "Driving car number seven is Howard Fastbender."

The crowd cheered and a man dressed in a natty checked suit with a red bow tie greeted the cheers with arms raised over his head. He then donned a full-length duster to protect his clothes from road dust.

Crankshaw bit down on his cigar. "The man is a former pickpocket and racketeer. You can bet your bottom dollar he's up to no good."

The race official's voice rose again. "And driving car number one is Sir Phillip Higginbottom."

Sir Higginbottom toasted the cheering crowd with a bone china teacup. A short man with a long, aristocratic nose that gave his profile an arrowlike appearance, he wore a tweed cap and shiny white spats.

A look of disdain crossed Crankshaw's face. "He's a bloody Englishman who keeps insisting we're driving on the wrong side of the street. Have you ever heard anything more ridiculous in your life?"

Crankshaw had equally uncomplimentary things to say about each of the drivers in turn. "Billy-Joe Mason, ha! He should go back to his cattle ranch. And what the hell does that Staggs fellow think he's doing? The last time I bumped into him, he was being carted away in a paddy wagon for spying."

Jimmy's eyes widened. "He's a spy?"

"Of course not. But he sent Teddy Roosevelt a box of moose droppings to protest the man's Bull Moose party. You know the government; they can't tell the difference between a spy and a crackpot. Whatever you do, be careful around him. He's always taking photographs. I tell you, it's not normal. It's got to be a fetish."

As if on cue, Staggs disappeared behind his camera and snapped a photograph of the cheering crowd.

Crankshaw shook his head in disgust. "What did I tell you?"

The race official announced the other names in quick order. "Cabby O'Brian."

Crankshaw snorted. "The man couldn't find his way out of a paper bag."

"And in car number six, Clyde Stonegate."

Stonegate wore a black suit and a shiny stovepipe hat.

"Be careful around him," Crankshaw cautioned. "He's an undertaker. If you fall asleep in his presence, you're likely to wake up six feet under."

Ten drivers were scheduled to drive in the race, but

the race official announced the names of only nine. Jimmy wondered if this meant Miss Davenport had been disqualified.

Crankshaw called over to his mechanic. "Crank her up, Sparky."

Sparky was a wheezy bone-thin man with pale watery eyes and a puffy red nose. He didn't look strong enough to manage his next breath, let alone muster up the fortitude necessary to crank up a Model T.

"He's allergic to gasoline fuel," Crankshaw explained. "If you ask me, it's a damned nuisance."

"I can imagine," Jimmy said, sympathizing with the mechanic. "That's one of the reasons I think electric cars are the coming thing."

"You could be right, lad." Crankshaw pulled on his leather helmet, adjusted the dust flaps over his ears, and fastened the strap tight beneath his double chins. "My offer still holds."

"Thank you, but as I told you, I'm due home." Jimmy held out his hand. "Good luck to you, sir."

Crankshaw shook his hand. "Thank you, young man. Give my best to your parents." He turned on the spark and adjusted the gas levers.

The mechanic sneezed as he bent in front of the car and turned the L-shaped crank in a circular motion. As Jimmy had anticipated, the man struggled with the crank. He stopped a time or two to mop his forehead before resuming the task. Crankshaw had good reason to worry.

Finally, the engine snorted and growled, then started with an angry roar. Luckily, Sparky managed to pull his arm away in time. The backward kick of the crank could break a man's arm quicker than a bucking horse could throw him.

Crankshaw beamed and rubbed his palms together before pulling on his fur-lined leather gauntlets. He planted his hands firmly around the vibrating steering wheel. The automobile sputtered like a pot boiling over on a cookstove.

Model T Fords had a tendency to advance forward even in neutral. In Jimmy's estimation, it was one of the serious drawbacks of the much-touted planetary transmission.

At the first sign of forward movement, Jimmy rushed to Sparky's side and together they pushed against the front grille to keep the automobile from taking off.

Crankshaw gazed at them over his steering wheel, his cigar clamped in his teeth. "See that? There's no holdin' her back."

Bent at the waist, Jimmy fought to hold the car steady. How he hated these rattletraps. The noise was deafening and the fumes strong. "Put your emergency brake on."

The emergency brake helped, but such forceful vibrations could probably bounce a house off its foundation.

Crankshaw slid the strap of his goggles over his head. The goggles were tinted orange to reduce road glare and fitted to keep the dust out of the driver's eyes.

Jimmy kept the automobile from moving while Sparky took his place on the leatherette companion seat next to the driver. The poor man sneezed before donning his own protective gear.

The race official shouted through a megaphone. "Gentlemen. The race will commence in six minutes."

"What? What did he say?" Crankshaw yelled.

"Six minutes!" Jimmy yelled back, holding up six fingers. He waved Crankshaw on and jumped out of the way.

Crankshaw lifted a hand in farewell and drove off.

One by one, the Model T's roared past the cheering crowd and pulled up to the starting line, all but drowning out the brass band that played a lively medley of Sousa marches.

Only one car remained on the otherwise empty field. At first Jimmy thought it belonged to one of the race officials. Then he noticed the placard attached to the door. For some reason car number ten had not yet taken its place at the starting line.

A closer look revealed an array of brightly colored ribbons attached to the back of the gleaming Ford. They flapped in the breeze like the switching tails of grazing cows. And it was the bold-colored ribbons that told him he had found the infamous Miss Elizabeth Davenport.

# Chapter 2

"A woman motorist doesn't need help getting into trouble—but she'll get it anyway."

*Women at the Wheel*
Circa 1915

Elizabeth Davenport sat in her shiny Model T Ford, listening to the engine idle, tapping her fingers impatiently on the brass-spoke steering wheel. Where was he? Where was that wayward mechanic, Cummings, who was supposed to have reported for work two days ago? She needed to get to the starting line, and soon! *Ooooooh*. If she ever got her hands on the man!

Thanks to that irresponsible scalawag of a mechanic, she'd been forced to prepare her automobile for the long journey ahead without any assistance. It had taken her twice as long as she'd anticipated.

Race fever had spread like wildfire through Buffalo, and the town had gone berserk. The numerous saloons and hotels had been packed for weeks. Crowds gathered nightly outside the nickelodeon to debate the virtue of each motorist. Tempers had flared and wagers were placed. The jailhouse had never been so crowded.

The names of those drivers favored to win were posted outside Ray Baldenbushes's barbershop and received top priority from local shopkeepers, the owner of the town's filling station, and the blacksmith, who doubled as a mechanic.

Elizabeth's name was not among those posted and therefore she was the last to be served. In many cases she had to take whatever supplies were left, and because she'd had to drive all over town looking for a fuel can in which to carry an emergency supply of gasoline, she'd barely made it to the fairgrounds in time to check in.

She did a mental tally of the supplies she'd purchased. A wooden box was strapped to the foot-wide running board, filled with such necessities as a tire pump and tow rope, a canvas bucket, several cans of oil, a block and tackle, tire chains, and of course a five-gallon can of gasoline. Though she went through her list several times, she was certain she'd forgotten something important.

*Ooooooh.* Just thinking of what she'd gone through because of her irresponsible mechanic infuriated her.

Was it asking too much for the man to show up on time? Because of his flagrant disregard for his responsibilities, she had been forced to run herself ragged with last-minute preparations. She'd wasted valuable time—time set aside to study her maps and to prepare herself mentally for the grueling trip ahead.

She fingered the chatelaine watch worn on a ribbon around her neck, adjusted the pillow at her back, and tried not to panic. The man had been unavoidably delayed. That's all it was; he would arrive any minute now. She just knew he would. Yes, indeed. Any minute.

The problem was she didn't have too many more minutes to spare. The race official had just sounded the five-minute warning.

Without a mechanic she'd be disqualified and all her hard work would be wasted. So would her chances of winning that twenty-five-thousand-dollar prize!

Without the money, her plans for building a residential home for orphans and unwanted children would be thwarted, perhaps this time for good. Her original plan had been to invest the money earned from her best-selling book into the project. Considering the book had been declared wanton, she'd earned quite a bit of money.

What a pity she had been forced to spend so much money defending herself against an obscenities charge. Had she been able to put the funds toward building her home, she wouldn't have had to resort to entering a race where she wasn't wanted, and probably had as much chance of winning as a dead mule.

Yet what choice did she have? By the time she had been released from jail, any money she'd earned from her book had been thoroughly depleted and her reputation was in ruins. She was censored by the church, and her loan applications had been returned with a tersely stamped REJECTED across the form.

She had actually been convinced her dream would never be realized. But it was when things looked the darkest that she was blessed with a stroke of good luck—or at least that's how it had seemed to her at the time.

She happened to be sitting on a wooden bench in Central Park, next to a gentleman perusing the *New York Tribune*. Shamelessly reading over his shoulder, she spotted the advertisement for the Model T Ford race. The man looked startled when she suddenly tore the article out from beneath his very nose. Not taking the time to explain, she'd rushed back to her publisher's office on Fifth Avenue.

Her editor's name was Clyde Hoversmith, a humorless man who had rejected her latest proposal. He'd told her she could write a second book to complement her first, but she could not write criticizing orphan trains. *The old mule!*

Elizabeth knew Mr. Hoversmith's wife had supported the Children's Home Society for years. But it had never occurred to her that her publisher would consider any book written on the subject of orphan trains off-limits. Sheesh. Just because the Children's Home Society happened to be one of his wife's favorite charitable organizations was no excuse for him to be so hard-nosed dead set against a book that suggested reforms.

Elizabeth had hoped to write a book as successful as her first, without as much controversy. It annoyed her that Mr. Hoversmith had such little regard for her personally that he would insist she write another book certain to land her back in jail.

Upon reaching her publisher for the second time that day, she'd walked right into Mr. Hoversmith's office without waiting for the receptionist to announce her. "I'll write a book about a woman race car driver."

It was clear from the bland look he gave her that he'd not been all that impressed. "Absolutely not, Miss Davenport," he said in that pompous tone of his. "Either you write a follow-up to your first book, or you find yourself another publisher."

Never one to give up, she'd boldly declared, "I'll write a follow-up, but only on the condition you also let me write my driving manual."

Hoversmith glowered. Writers were supposed to write, not make conditions, but she knew the lure of her follow-up book being next year's top-selling book was too great to pass up, and he finally agreed.

Then began the usual haggle for money. She'd asked him outright how much he intended to pay her and he had the audacity to offer her "The same as last time. A hundred dollars."

The nerve of the man! Last time she wasn't a best-selling author and she'd pointed this out loud and clear.

"And it remains to be seen if you are this time," he'd replied.

She recalled with amusement the look on his face when she'd asked for a five-hundred-dollar advance. Why, his bushy eyebrows had disappeared clear into his hairline. "That's outrageous!" he'd thundered. "Two hundred."

"Four." They'd settled on three hundred and fifty

dollars. It wasn't enough to buy a new Model T Ford, but it was enough to fix up the rather unpredictable Model T she'd purchased a year earlier from a little old lady in Rochester, who blamed her nervous disorder on the "dang-tooting tin can."

What little money was left over after paying for automobile repairs and the entry fee would have to cover Elizabeth's expenses across the country. That was just one of the reasons she was now so infuriated; she had drafted a check in good faith to that scoundrel of a mechanic!

With only four minutes left until the race was scheduled to begin, she gripped the leather steering wheel until her knuckles shone white. It was humiliating. She'd be the laughingstock of the country. She could see the headlines now: WOMAN DRIVER FAILS TO LEAVE STARTING GATE.

*Ooooooh.* If she ever got her hands on that mechanic, she'd not be responsible for her actions.

She was warned in advance that this Cummings fellow had a weakness for moonshine whiskey, but she had no choice but to hire him. Few mechanics would chance harming their reputation by working for a woman driver, especially one who'd only recently been released from jail on an obscenities charge.

He was the only mechanic desperate enough or drunk enough or maybe even crazy enough to take the job.

She'd watched with sinking heart as one by one the other drivers zoomed by to take their places at the starting line. Now she sat on the big open field all alone.

The race official's voice boomed through the megaphone, but she could barely hear him over the sound of her idling motor. "Gentlemen! Three minutes left. Two minutes, fifty-six seconds. Fifty-one."

Frowning in annoyance, she glared through her goggles in the general direction of the race official, who was little more than a blur. She narrowed her eyes but she still couldn't see him clearly. The driving goggles were no substitute for the eyeglasses she generally wore.

Never mind. She didn't need to see him to know he resembled the wrong end of a donkey. He had steadfastly refused to acknowledge her and hadn't even extended the courtesy of introducing her with the other drivers. Well, she'd show him. She'd show them all. She scanned the field ahead, straining her eyes in every direction. That is if her scoundrel of a mechanic ever showed up. *Dear God. Where is he?*

Then she saw him. He was younger than she had imagined based on his correspondence, probably somewhere between his late twenties, early thirties.

Much to her relief, there was no swagger to his walk, nothing that would suggest he had been on a drinking binge. If anything, he walked with a quiet confidence, as if he were out for a Sunday stroll. Lord almighty, he was even dressed in what surely must be his sparkling white Sunday go-to-meeting suit—with a white Panama hat, no less.

What in heaven's name did he think this was? A tea party? Did he not hear the official giving the final count? See the other automobiles at the starting gate? Think it odd that hers was the only automobile left in the prerace area?

She slid over to the companion seat and, grabbing hold of the top of the divided windshield, stood up. Windmilling her right arm, she motioned frantically, finally getting his attention. "What's taking you so long, you fool?" The car was vibrating so much, her words came out sounding garbled, as if she were talking underwater, but there was no mistaking her angry tone of voice.

The man looked startled and glanced around as if he thought she might possibly be talking to someone else. Sheesh! He was obviously what young people nowadays called a jelly bean. "You're the one I'm talking to!" she crackled.

The man pointed a finger to himself and mouthed the word "Me?"

"Yes, you! Now get over here!"

He quickly closed the distance between them. It was about time. Obviously, he thought working for a woman was going to be a lark. Well, he would learn soon enough that she wasn't about to stand for his slacking off.

He stood in front of her rumbling automobile, and though the Model T allowed her to tower over him, she was nonetheless surprised by his height. She guessed him to be well over six feet tall, with wide shoulders and a broad chest. He didn't look like any mechanic she'd ever met.

"Excuse me, ma'am." It was necessary for him to raise his voice to be heard over the coughing, hiccuping sound of the engine. "I was wondering ..."

"There are no excuses!" she snapped. She was tired of being treated as a second-rate citizen because she was a woman. "Get in the car!"

"I beg your pardon?"

"You heard me. Get in the car! At once. Or I'll have your fool head. Now do as I say or you'll not receive another penny from me!"

The mechanic's startled gaze took in the shapeless though practical overalls she'd purchased from the men's section of the Sears, Roebuck mail-order catalog, and apparently decided she meant business.

"Well ... I ... If you insist. . . ." He ran around to the companion side and wasted valuable time by climbing into the car like some English-bred gentleman.

She made a sound of disgust, then pressed her foot hard against the gas pedal. The car lurched, hesitated, lurched again like a frog leaping from one lily pad to another, then with a sudden, not to mention alarming, burst of energy, sped forward. Oh, yes, indeed, before this race was over, all the good citizens of Buffalo who had made her life miserable this last week would change their tunes!

The crowd of spectators turned into a blurry streak as Elizabeth zoomed past.

Keeping her mouth clamped shut and her eyes narrowed in concentration, she zigged around a block wall and inadvertently drove through the bandstand. Screaming musicians jumped out of the way and the pompous-looking race official fell off his soapbox into the mud.

Though Elizabeth glanced back to make certain he wasn't injured, she didn't feel sorry for the man. It served him right for excluding her during the introductions.

As she barreled toward the waiting Model T Fords, the mechanic seated beside her held on to the door with both hands. He had turned a ghastly shade of white and his eyes were as big as saucers.

Narrowing her eyes at the rear bumper of car number seven, she nodded in grim satisfaction. Before this day was over, her mechanic would know she meant business!

# Chapter 3

"It's common courtesy to assist any horse and buggy you have the misfortune of running off the road."
*Women at the Wheel*
Circa 1915

The earsplitting, potboiling rattletrap had shot forward like a metal cage tossed through the air. Jimmy gasped in terror and held on to the door frame like a flea clinging to a scratching dog.

The woman drove like the devil on wheels. She left behind a trail of havoc before coming to a tire-squealing, rubber-burning stop a mere inch and a half away from the rear bumper of car number seven.

Had it not been for the laminated safety glass, Jimmy's head would surely have gone through the windshield. As it was, the crown of his Panama hat was crushed flat as a pancake and his head slammed against the glass like a rubber ball against a brick wall.

This Davenport woman was obviously out to kill him. Well, he had no intention of hanging around long enough to give her a chance to succeed. Desperate to escape while he still could, he rose from his seat and lifted one leg over the door frame.

"Where do you think you're going?" she demanded.

"Anywhere you're not."

"Oh, no, you don't! You're not getting out of it that easy." She sank her fingers into his arm like a regular wildcat. "You and I have an agreement and I intend to see you keep it."

It was hard to see much of her face. Her eyes were hidden behind man-size orange-tinted goggles and her hair was covered by a leather driving helmet. But he didn't have to see her face to know she was half a bubble out of plumb. "I have no idea what you're talking about. Until a few moments ago, I had never met you and ..."

He was interrupted by the sharp cracking sound of a gun. With amazing speed, Miss Davenport released his arm, grabbed the steering wheel, and pressed down hard on the gas pedal.

The race had begun.

Pinned to the stiff leatherette back of the hardsprung seat by the force of gravity, his one leg hanging over the door frame, Jimmy held on to his flattened hat and stared out of the windshield with horror-filled eyes.

He didn't know that a Model T was capable of going so fast. He drove an electric automobile which, in comparison, was considerably slower, a thousand times quieter, and rode as smoothly as a duck gliding across a pond.

Miss Davenport literally flew over a ditch and barreled at amazing speeds across an empty field, stirring up clouds of dust and forcing the loose-jointed wheels into every angle imaginable.

The car hit each and every rut, lurching up and down, and listing side to side like a ship in a wind-tossed sea. Finally the vehicle made a sharp turn and veered onto the road again, well ahead of the other cars.

Under less trying circumstances, he might have admired such a bold and dangerous move, but today he could only wonder what other death-defying tricks she had up her sleeve.

"I must insist you pull over at once and let me out." He raised his voice to make himself heard. Despite the cold north wind that blew off Lake Erie, beads of perspiration dotted his forehead.

A relatively straight stretch allowed him enough time to mop his brow with a handkerchief before she made a dangerous maneuver to keep car number two from passing them. His body bouncing several inches into the air, he grabbed hold of the door with both hands to keep from flying out.

When she made no attempt to stop, he raised his voice. "Miss Davenport! I must . . . oops . . . insist you . . . watch out! . . . Stop the car at once! Yeow!"

He covered his face to keep from having to watch her plow into the back of a gasoline-driven tractor. When it appeared she had miraculously managed to miss it, he spread his hands wide and peered between his fingers. "In the name of God, will you slow down!"

She swerved around another horse and wagon. "Are you going to sit there and complain all the way to Seattle?" She sounded downright peevish.

"Let's get something straight. I am *not* going to Seattle. I have a train to catch and if you don't stop the car and let me out this minute, I'll have you arrested for kidnapping."

"Listen, mister, I don't know how much moonshine you've had today, but I don't have time for this. I have a race to win."

"Since you're more likely to spend time in jail than win a race—watch out!" She skidded sideways around a man and his mule, and gasping in relief, Jimmy waited until she steered the car back on course before continuing. "I think it would be best for all concerned if you simply pull over and let me out." When she failed to react to his threatening tone, he threw up his hands. "All right . . . yeow!" He took a deep breath. How she missed that telegraph pole, he would never know. "I'll make a deal with you. You let me out here and I won't press charges."

She stared at him through her goggles. "Are you

out of your mind? You know what the rules of the race are. Without a mechanic, I'm disqualified."

"Look out!" he cried, directing her attention back to the road.

She swerved just in time to miss a brown-and-white cow standing in the center of the road. The cow escaped, but the same could not be said for the poor farmer who had been riding along the side of the road in his horse-drawn wagon as if he didn't have a care in the world.

Elizabeth squeezed the black bulb of her air horn, emitting a shocking sound. *Ah-oog-ha!* The farmer's gray-dappled horse reared back in panic, then bolted. The next thing Jimmy knew, the Model T was in an all-out race with the horse and wagon.

"Dang it!" the farmer shouted angrily. "Can't you see my horse is out of control?"

"What do you want me to do about it?" Miss Davenport shot back. "The car's out of control, too!"

Jimmy had managed to reclaim his seat after being thrown to the floor. "Step on the brake!"

"I *am* stepping on the brake."

"That's the gas pedal!"

Miss Davenport lifted her foot off one pedal and slammed it against the next. The car spun around in one direction, the horse and wagon in another. Miss Davenport was so busy watching the farmer, she inadvertently stepped on the wrong pedal again and plowed across a newly planted field.

"Stop!" No sooner had Jimmy given the command than he was thrown against the cherrywood dashboard, and it was only fast action on his part that kept him from hitting his head against the windshield for a second time.

"Dammit! When I say stop, I mean stop slowly."

"I'm sorry," she said, and she actually sounded sincere. "Are . . . are you all right?"

"Let's just say I'm in better shape than that farmer

back there. Now, back up. No! Don't back up. Turn around. No, don't turn around. Stay here!"

Jimmy scrambled out of the car and, fearing the worst, ran to the spot where he'd last seen the wagon. A grizzled man stood at the bottom of a ravine looking madder than a bull seeing red.

The horse had come unharnessed and was safely grazing a distance away. "Are you all right, sir?"

"Dang it, do I look all right?" the farmer sputtered. "If I ever get my hands on the dang-fool woman driver, I'll string her up by her ankles and fill her so full of buckshot, she'll think she's a sieve."

Jimmy glanced back at Miss Davenport, who stood by the car watching him through her amber goggles. What the farmer proposed was a tempting thought. "I think you can climb out over there."

"I'm not leavin' my wagon."

Jimmy glanced at the wagon. It didn't appear to be damaged. "Hold on. We'll get it out." He cupped his hands around his mouth so Miss Davenport could hear him. "I need some rope."

He laid his suit jacket on a log and rolled up his shirtsleeves. Already he was covered from head to toe with road dust. He'd have to change before boarding the train, that is if he ever got to the railway station.

Miss Davenport ran up to him, a coiled rope draped on her shoulder. He was surprised at how small and delicate she appeared when she wasn't behind the wheel. Why, the terror-on-wheels was almost pint-size, the top of her head barely reaching up to his shoulders. Her small frame looked lost in the oversize blue denim bib overalls that crisscrossed in back. Belted fetchingly at the waist, the overalls were rolled up at the cuffs to accommodate her short stature.

*Wild in bed, wild on the road.* Startled by the thought that suddenly popped into his head, he quickly grabbed the rope.

"Is he all right?" she asked. Without the usual loud

range, her voice was surprisingly soft, almost musical
in tone, with none of the earlier rancor.

"He will be. The question is whether you'll be all
right once he gets near you."

The man-size driving goggles covered nearly half
her face, making it impossible to see much more than
her rosy bow-shaped mouth.

A wisp of hair had escaped her leather driving cap.
Her hair, the rich golden color of sunlit honey, jolted
him. For a fleeting moment he considered the possibility that this was the same Elizabeth Davenport he'd
known in his childhood.

He then recalled what Crankshaw had said about
her pushing a mayor into the mud and writing an obscene book. This, combined with his own startling ob-
servations, made him immediately discount the idea
as preposterous. Nothing could convince him that his
dear sweet Elizabeth would grow up to be so brash
and bold.

"What's takin' so long?" the farmer yelled. "Do
you think I have all day?"

Jimmy tossed an end of the rope down the ravine.
"Tie this to the wagon," he called. He turned to Miss
Davenport, and raked her over with a frown. The
woman was trouble and he best not forget it. Whether
or not her behavior in bed corresponded to her driving
habits was none of his concern. "Do you think you can
drive over here without creating further problems?"

Muttering beneath her breath, she turned and
headed back to the flivver. He couldn't make out a
word she said, but judging by the way she flitted her
head and swung her arms, he would bet she wasn't
reciting his virtues.

No, thank God, this wasn't *his* Elizabeth. The one
he'd kept in his heart and his soul was special and
dear to him, and he was greatly relieved to know that
the sweet memories he'd cherished all these years had
not been jeopardized by the bold, brash stranger bearing her name.

*I'll always take care of you, Elizabeth.* He'd only been seven when he'd made that promise. Yet to this day, he carried the guilt of knowing that somehow he had let her down. His only hope was that his childhood friend had been adopted by a loving family.

His thoughts were interrupted by the realization that the Tin Lizzie was barreling straight toward him. Fearing for his life, he was about to join the farmer in the ravine when she abruptly made a U-turn and stopped.

Cursing beneath his breath, he tied the other end of the tow rope to the rear bumper, just below the porcelain brown-and-white New York State license plate. "Drive forward. Slow ..." He eyed her anxiously. "You do understand the word slow, do you not?"

She gave her head an indignant nod, and he imagined sparks of fire shooting out of her goggles. "Of course I understand!" she snapped.

Not sure he could trust her, he stood on the top of the ravine and called down to the farmer. "Is the rope in place?"

"Course it's in place, dang it!"

Jimmy wiped his brow and said a silent prayer. "All right, Miss Davenport. On the count of three. One ... two ..."

The car shot forward with unbelievable speed. Before Jimmy's startled eyes, the wagon flew out of the ditch, whizzed over his head, and sailed over the Model T before crashing to the ground. Splintered boards scattered in every direction. One wagon wheel rolled back down the ravine. Another flew up and was caught in the gnarled branches of an old walnut tree.

Miss Davenport screeched to a stop and gazed openmouthed at the scattered wagon parts.

The farmer emerged from the ravine, huffing and puffing and stomping his feet in a rage. "Now look what you and that ... that mechanical louse have done. Of all the idiotic, stupid, asinine ... !"

Jimmy felt terrible. "I can't tell you how sorry I am."

"Sorry? What the hell good is that gonna do me?"

"We, eh . . ." Jimmy reached inside his jacket and pulled his gold Elgin pocket watch out of his vest pocket, letting the two-stranded gold chain dangle in midair. The watch was the only thing of value he had with him. "This will help compensate you for your losses."

The farmer grabbed the watch, but his disposition showed no improvement. "Git out of here," the farmer yelled. "And don't let me see either one of you agin." With that he picked up the shotgun that had flown out of the wagon as it sailed through the air and fired off a round of warning shots.

Jimmy ran toward the Model T and vaulted over the door like a rabbit down a hole. "Go!" he yelled, and for once he found no fault with Miss Davenport's tire-squealing start.

His approval, however, lasted only as long as it took them to drive out of shooting range. Once the danger was over, Jimmy took strong exception to the way she weaved from one side of the road to the other. Great thunder! Was it possible the woman was constitutionally unable to drive a straight line?

"Watch out!" he shouted when it looked as if they were going to plow straight into a tree. "Look where you're going!"

"What's the matter with you?" she demanded. "You act like you've never been in a fuel-propelled vehicle before."

"What's the matter with me?" He pulled his gaze from the road and stared incredulously at her. "What's the matter with *you*?" This time his voice wavered as the left rear tire ran over a fallen log.

"There's nothing the matter with me!" she informed him. "Your job is to keep the car running. I'll do the driving."

"Keep the car . . ." He gritted his teeth and for the

first time noticed her pert freckled nose beneath the
oversize driving goggles. What a pity that such a pretty
nose and mouth were wasted on a stubborn and irritating woman. "Listen, lady. I would consider it my
contribution to mankind to see that you and your car
are forever banned from public roads. Meanwhile, I
think it only fair to warn you, I intend to bail out at
the very next stop."

"You can't do that," she said, her chin lifted in
defiance.

"Oh, no? Just watch me!" He folded his arms across
his chest and glared out the windshield. He didn't
need this aggravation in his life. He'd sooner ride in
a car with a blindfolded hog. He and Miss Davenport
would come to a parting of the ways at the very next
stop. Make no mistake!

Unfortunately, the next stop was in the middle of
nowhere, with no sign of civilization for as far as the
eye could see. Come to think of it, he hadn't seen any
of the other racers for miles. Jimmy wasn't even certain he and Miss Davenport were on the right road.

Despite his warnings, Miss Davenport had managed
to drive the car into what had appeared on the map
as little more than a creek. Jimmy decided that either
the mapmaker had suffered a serious lapse of judg-
ment or the area had experienced a record rainfall in
recent weeks. Of course, there was always the possibility they were hopelessly lost and this was actually
some uncharted river.

"Now look what you've done." Disgusted, he
reached into the backseat for his carpetbag, dug out
his Everstick invisible rubbers, and fitted them over
the soles of his shoes. He climbed out of the car and
promptly sank ankle-deep into the mud. He lifted one
foot out of the mud and then the other and made his
way around the car. The two front wheels were under
water. "It's a wonder you didn't get us killed."

Amazingly enough, Miss Davenport looked more

indignant than sorry. "Well, it wouldn't be a problem if they would build a decent road through here."

"That was a decent road, Miss Davenport." In fact, it was the only graded road they'd driven since leaving Buffalo.

Sputtering and fuming to himself, he realized the half rubbers offered no protection against the ankle-deep mud. Seating himself on the running board, he pulled off his shoes and socks, rolled up the cuffs of his dusty trousers, and lowered his bare feet into the muck.

Model T's were built to be relatively lightweight. Actually this was a mixed blessing. Had the car weighed more, it might have made the sharp turn. Hands at his waist, he glanced around and spotted an old wooden wagon that was tipped on its side.

He pulled a few rotting boards off the wagon and wedged them behind the back wheels. While he worked, Elizabeth sat behind the wheel, watching him like an employer with a new hireling.

"All right now. I want you to steer straight." He bit back the urge to ask her if she knew how to steer straight. He'd found out the hard way it didn't pay to insult her driving, however much she deserved it.

He blew on his hands, rubbed them together, and proceeded to push the car back along the planks and up the hill. The icy water bit into his flesh and his toes turned red, then blue. The wind blowing off the Great Lakes sliced through his pants and shirt.

After he'd rolled the flivver back to the road, he scraped the mud off the front and checked for damage. The axle was slightly bent, but with a little luck, it shouldn't cause a problem.

He placed a hand on the starting handle and gave it a few brisk turns. The motor sputtered a few times before catching.

Teeth chattering from the cold, he washed off his feet and pulled on his shoes and socks. Not only was he chilled to the bone, he was hungry and in no mood for Miss Davenport's shenanigans. It made him nervous the way she gripped the steering wheel and stared at the road straight ahead as if she were a hunter about to bag a prized target.

He walked to her side and, straddling his legs so as to avoid the mud, leaned his elbow on the doorsill. "Move over!"

She regarded him through her goggles. "What?"

"I said move over. I'm driving."

"You'll do no such thing." She thrust her chin out stubbornly. "This is *my* automobile. I'll do the driving. Your job is to keep the car in mechanical repair."

He leaned over until he was practically nose to nose with her, and stared through her goggles. For such a small-size woman, she had the largest blue eyes he ever did see. Judging from what little of her face was visible, he'd say she was mighty pretty. Too bad she had the personality of a snapping turtle. "I told you before and I'll tell you again, I have no intention of continuing in this race. Had you not kidnapped me . . ."

"I did not kidnap you!" she declared. "I simply made you live up to your promise."

He opened his mouth to argue, but thought better of it. Instead, he glanced around him, trying to decide what to do. He was tempted—sorely tempted—to drag her out of the car. But even someone as annoying as Miss Davenport couldn't persuade him to resort to anything vaguely resembling violence. He was a peaceful man, accustomed to conducting himself in a peaceful manner, however much he was otherwise tempted.

Still, he suspected it would be safer for her and certainly safer for him if he simply took off down the road on foot. The problem was they were miles from the nearest town and it would be dark in a few hours.

"Well!" she called. "I haven't got all day."

He narrowed his eyes upon seeing a glint of sunshine in the distance. It looked like an approaching vehicle. His spirits picked up. "Then don't let me keep you, Miss Davenport." Doffing his flattened hat, he reached for his carpetbag and walked away from her. Unable to contain his relief, he stood in the middle of the road and impatiently paced back and forth.

Miss Davenport lifted her voice to be heard over her engine. "What do you think you're doing?"

He was all too glad to tell her. Oh, yes, indeed, he was. And he would have told her a few more choice things had he been inclined to go against the teachings of his dear adoptive parents. "I'm hitching a ride out of here. From this moment on, Miss Davenport, you are by yourself."

# Chapter 4

"In an effort to quiet an old rattletrap, it's sometimes tempting to let him drive!"

*Women at the Wheel*
Circa 1915

Elizabeth was tempted to let the man go his own way.
Heaven knew he'd caused her enough trouble. First
he'd arrived late for the race, without so much as a
word of apology. Then he'd done little else since leaving Buffalo but complain about her driving. Why, the
old rattletrap hadn't been quiet for a moment!

*Slow down. Watch out. Stop!* What did he think this
was? A Sunday drive? He'd made her so nervous she
could hardly think straight. No wonder she'd missed
that last curve and wound up in a stream.

Still, he was the only mechanic she had. The truth
was, for all his faults, she needed him. It was a disturbing thought. She hated having to depend on anyone, let alone an irresponsible, pompous, know-it-all.
But she didn't have much choice in the matter. If she
showed up at the first check-in without a mechanic,
she would be disqualified as surely as night follows
day.

She watched the man pace back and forth in the
middle of the dirt road. A lock of brown hair had
fallen across his smooth, tanned forehead. A handsome devil he was, to be certain, but handsome is as
handsome does.

"Are you going to leave me out here by myself? Alone and stranded?" she called, desperate enough to play on his sympathies. If he had any.

He turned, a look of disbelief on his face. He did have nice eyes. It fascinated her the way his eyes changed colors, shifting between sky-blue and turquoise. Sometimes—depending on the state of his nerves—his eyes turned midnight-black, and then she was even more intrigued.

His nose, straight and softly flared, complemented his firm, sensual mouth, which she imagined did, on occasion, actually curve upward, not down. Ah, yes, indeed, he was a handsome devil. What a shame he was such an irresponsible cad!

"Well, are you?" she demanded.

"You don't have to stay here. The next town's not that far. The way you drive, you can easily reach it before dark. If you'd rather, you can follow us. Just do me a favor and try not to run us over."

Elizabeth glared at him. "You'll be sorry. You just wait and see. I'll report you to the authorities. I'll file a complaint with Mr. Henry Ford. I'll name you in my book. I'll ..." On and on she ranted, telling him in a single breath just what she intended to do.

Jimmy stood, feet apart, staring at her, completely astonished. Never had he met such a woman!

The other car rounded a bend, drowning out her voice. Relieved and convinced his problems were about over, Jimmy waved his hands over his head, trying to catch the attention of the driver. Jimmy was almost positive it was one of the other competitors, and moments later he spotted the placard flapping against the driver's door confirming it.

Car number seven barreled straight at him, with no sign of stopping or even slowing down. At first Jimmy remained in the middle of the road, thinking the driver, whose name he recalled was Fastbender, hadn't yet spotted him. When it became obvious that Fastbender had no intention of stopping, Jimmy jumped out of the way just in the nick of time.

Laughing with glee, Fastbender swerved around Miss Davenport's car, honking as he passed. "You'll never make it to the first check-in, Miss Lizzie," he jeered.

Elizabeth stuck her tongue out at the driver and, forcing her lips to vibrate, made a most unladylike sound of derision. Jimmy had never heard a more pronounced raspberry in his life, and to think it had come from the lips of a woman.

Loud laughter faded away as car number seven followed a curve and disappeared.

Jimmy stood, hands at his waist, shocked by the man's unsportsmanlike behavior. "The man tried to run me down!"

"Mr. Cummings . . ."

Something snapped inside him. "My name is not Cummings! Do you hear? It's Hunter, Hunter, HUNTER! Jimmy Hunter."

She studied him through the lenses of her driving goggles, but it was obvious by the stubborn set of her mouth, she didn't believe him. "Sheesh. You don't have to yell."

"It would appear, Miss Davenport, I do have to yell. Nothing else seems to penetrate that thick skull of yours!"

"If you weren't Cummings, you wouldn't be here!"

He crossed the road and stood directly by her car, glaring through the orange lenses. "I'm here, Miss Davenport, because *you* kidnapped me."

"I did not kidnap you."

"We'll let the authorities decide that. Meanwhile, it looks like we're stuck with each other." As irritated as he was with her, he was far more disturbed by the driver of car seven. Indeed, he felt a sense of utter outrage.

What in the name of heaven was going on here?

Did people in automobile races normally act so out of control and discourteous?

"What a mess you've gotten me into. If it weren't for you, I'd be on the train this very moment, bound for home." He paced around in a circle.

When she made no comment, he glanced back at the car. Much to his surprise, Miss Davenport sat quietly in the driver's seat, her head on the steering wheel. Surely she wasn't crying? Not her. Not the bold, brash woman who had put him through hell?

He felt suddenly protective of her, though heaven knew why. She'd kidnapped him and taken him on a hair-raising ride. She had come close to having him riddled with buckshot and practically bounced him out of his seat at death-defying speeds.

It was incredible to think that in the space of only a few hours, he'd had more brushes with death than he'd experienced in his entire life. He'd be within his rights to pull her out from behind that wheel and drive off without her!

If only she didn't look so forlorn and lost. Something softened inside him. Poor woman. It couldn't be that easy, competing with a bunch of rude and obnoxious men. No wonder Miss Davenport behaved so unreasonably. Who could blame her?

Feeling charitable, and strangely protective, he started toward her, but before he reached her side, she lifted her head and managed to look every bit as formidable as she had earlier. He stopped in his tracks.

His instincts had been correct. This was not the Elizabeth Davenport he knew in his childhood. That one had been soft and sweet, gentle and caring. Any physical resemblance the girl in his past had to this maniacal road hog was purely coincidental.

If he had a sensible bone in his body, he would start walking and have nothing more to do with her. And if it hadn't been for the driver of car number seven, he would have done precisely that. But he could

hardly ignore the alarming fact that Fastbender had
nearly run him down. Having no intention of letting
the driver get away with attempted murder, Jimmy
intended to report him to the proper officials at the
first opportunity.

Determined to right the terrible wrongs that had
been done to him, he spun around and reached for
the crank. Giving it a mighty turn, he jumped out of
the way when the engine turned over and leaped over
the door and into the seat of the passenger's side not
a moment too soon.

With Miss Davenport it was all or nothing. She was
either at a standstill or going full speed. He'd barely
had time to settle in his seat when she shot off like a
cannonball, horn blaring, wheels squealing, dust spiraling up behind them. You'd think they were being
chased by an angry mob, the way she took off.

He closed his eyes and said a silent prayer. He was
hungry and tired and his body felt battered. He wasn't
sure how much more of this abuse he could endure.
With Miss Davenport at the wheel, a Model T Ford
could shake the hell out of a person faster than a
roomful of preachers.

As if she'd guessed some of his thoughts, she nodded toward the backseat. "There's food in that basket." He glanced at her in disbelief. It was clearly one
of the most welcome things she'd said to him all day.

"Why the hell didn't you say so before?"

Jimmy grew more irritable with each passing hour.
Normally a calm man, his nerves were frayed and his
patience worn thin. As if they hadn't had enough
problems already, one of the tires had gone flat and
then the radiator had sprung a leak. It took a whole
pack of Wrigley's beechnut chewing gum to plug the
holes in the hose, but the water still leaked out the
radiator. He finally purchased some fresh hen eggs
from a farmer, mixed the yolks and whites together,

and dropped the mixture into the radiator. The hot water cooked the eggs, which then clogged the holes.

But no sooner did he solve one problem when another took its place. It seemed to him they were always either broken down or lost.

Jimmy had always admired Mr. Henry Ford. But after following the race route for these last few hours, Jimmy's opinion of the man began to change. Mr. Ford had purposely mapped out the race to go through as many small towns as possible so that even the smallest and most out-of-the-way communities would see the benefit of his four-cylinder wonder and would therefore want to improve the roads.

It probably sounded like a sensible idea on paper, but in practice it was a nightmare. The ten Model T's were expected to travel miles off the beaten track, motoring down roads that no self-respecting mule would travel. Then after navigating through endless little one-horse towns, the drivers had to backtrack to the main highway.

Jimmy was convinced that at the rate they were going, the drivers would die of old age before reaching Seattle. The chance of Miss Davenport making it to the end seemed especially remote, since ninety percent of the time she was lost.

They had spent the better part of the last hour driving in what appeared to be circles. Jimmy was positive they'd passed the same water tank three times.

"Oh, look!" Miss Davenport said. "Over there." She swerved suddenly, crashing through a wooden fence and landing smack-dab in the middle of a cemetery behind car number six.

Not wanting to get into another argument, Jimmy bit back the urge to point out that the cemetery had a perfectly functional gate through which to drive. Instead, he waved to the undertaker turned motorist, who managed somehow to drive wearing his stovepipe hat. "I say there! Do you know the way to the main road?"

"Just follow me!" Stonegate called back. "Don't you just love old cemeteries?"

Through the cemetery they roared, past every confounded burial plot. Mr. Stonegate kept stopping to point out an interesting grave marker or to send his young mechanic scrambling to read an epitaph or check out the quality of marble. It wouldn't have been so bad had Mr. Stonegate not felt obliged to share this information.

"Damn!" Jimmy muttered. What the hell did he care whether a marker was Italian or Royal Blue Vermont marble?

"Mr. Stonegate hopes to win the race so he can buy his own cemetery," Miss Davenport explained.

"At the rate he's going, he's going to need it," Jimmy said, growing more irritable by the minute. Finally Mr. Stonegate checked out the last of the gravestones, and he zoomed out of the cemetery and led them back to the main road.

It was midnight by the time Miss Davenport rattled into the little town of Erie. With squealing tires and burning rubber, she stopped in front of the Erie Arms Hotel, the first official check-in point.

"Dammit!" Jimmy grated, his nose against the windshield. "Can't you learn to stop gradually?" He climbed out of the car and stretched. His legs were stiff, his backside sore, and his clothes in shambles. No words existed that could adequately describe the pounding sensation in his head.

If he never rode in another motorcar, it would be too soon for him. Normally he embraced every new contraption with enthusiasm, but after today, he was inclined to agree with the people who stubbornly maintained these newfangled automobiles would never replace a horse and buggy.

Walking with a stiff-legged gait, he followed Miss Davenport into the hotel. An old leg injury was acting up, but no more than the other parts of his body. He felt like the losing soldier in hand-to-hand combat.

He grimaced, thinking of the sight the two of them made, their faces covered in road dust, Jimmy's suit now almost black in color. Miss Davenport still wore her helmet, but she'd removed her goggles, which left white circles around her big blue eyes. She looked like a polecat without its mask.

As soon as they walked into the lobby of the hotel, a sleepy clerk yawned and rose to his feet. Jimmy gave him their names and the clerk eyed Miss Davenport in utter disbelief. "Thought you'd dropped out of the race."

Miss Davenport looked surprised. "Why would you think that?"

The man shrugged his shoulders. "Just thought what with being a lady and all, you'd find the roads a mite too rough for your liking."

"I would say the roads are a bit too rough for anyone's liking," Jimmy muttered. "How do I go about making a formal complaint?"

"Oh, I'm afraid you'll have to come back in the morning."

"Why can't I do it now?"

"The race official in charge of taking complaints won't be back till morning. All I'm supposed to do is record the time you arrived. Now . . ." He glanced at Miss Davenport. "If you would be kind enough to sign here, we can complete our business."

Miss Davenport took the fountain pen from him and signed her name. The clerk nodded. "Your official check-in time is twelve-oh-three. The rules state you can not leave town until a full twelve hours after you arrive."

Jimmy raised a brow. "Twelve hours?"

"It's the only way Mr. Ford could get the various towns to cooperate. Some felt that if the drivers were forced to spend time in each town, they would be more inclined to follow the rules of the road in the populated areas. Mr. Ford agreed. He didn't want anyone speeding through towns."

"Imagine anyone speeding," Jimmy said wryly.

"Or driving recklessly," the clerk added.

"Ah, now there's an interesting concept," Jimmy said.

"Of course, once you get to St. Louis, everything changes. From that point on, you can drive around the clock all the way to the end of the race." The man shrugged. "You can bet your life there'll be a few rules broken along the way."

Jimmy arched an eyebrow. "No! How shocking! Breaking the rules, you say? Why, that's terrible!"

Missing the irony in Jimmy's voice, the clerk leaned forward in earnest. "Some of these drivers will do anything to win the race. Anything. Now if you will put your time of arrival on the blackboard next to your car number, I'll stamp your passport and we can all go to bed."

Jimmy walked over to the blackboard and picked up a piece of chalk. Miss Davenport was the last to check in. Two cars had been scratched from the race. The closest car was three hours ahead of them. That made sense. Jimmy had made the mistake of dozing off for a moment and Miss Davenport had somehow turned off the main road. They'd ended up on an old cattle trail. Because they had put on so many extra miles, they had run out of gas and would never have made it into town had he not siphoned fuel from an old gasoline tractor.

After dropping the chalk back into the lip of the blackboard, Jimmy walked outside to the car and reached into the backseat. The acetylene headlamps had run out of carbide, and what little light filtered from the hotel failed to reach the backseat.

He felt in the dark for his ruined straw hat and carpetbag. His belongings in hand, he headed back to the hotel as fast as his sore leg and aching back would allow.

"Wait!" Miss Davenport chased after him.

Grimacing, he turned. He was out of patience.

"Now what, Miss Davenport?" It was too dark to see her face, but she had removed her helmet and the light from a distant lamppost played against her blond hair. The stirrings of a distant memory held him in its grip. *Don't cry, Elizabeth. Please don't cry.*

"Where are you going?"

"Where am I going?" he asked incredulously. "It's after midnight. I'm tired and I'm going to bed."

"What about the automobile?"

"What about it?"

"It's the mechanic's responsibility to stay with the vehicle. Someone could sabotage it. Then where would I be? How do you expect me to win a race without an automobile?"

If fury could produce steam, he'd have enough steam coming out of his ears to travel back home to Hogs Head unaided. "If I told you once, I've told you a hundred times, I'm not your mechanic. And after I get through reporting you to the race official first thing in the morning, you won't need a car, Miss Davenport, because you'll be disqualified."

"Disqualified?" She sounded so shocked by the idea, he could only shake his head in amazement. Was she so foolish as to think her behavior would go unreported?

"But why?"

"Why? Why!" He was shouting, but he didn't care. "For driving like a maniac. For kidnapping an innocent bystander. For attempted murder . . . For . . ." On and on he went, listing each and every one of her many transgressions. "Are there any questions?" he asked finally, surprised at his own fury. Never had he known himself to be so out of control.

"No," she said softly.

No? Just no? He couldn't believe his ears. Relieved, though somewhat baffled that she would so easily accept her fate, he turned. He was too tired to give a damn about the Model T Ford or its erratic driver. "Good night, Miss Davenport." He walked away stiffly, but rather than reveling in having given her a thorough and much deserved tongue-lashing, he felt as guilty as a mother leaving her newborn babe. Lord, who could explain it?

He slowed his step. Maybe he had been a bit too harsh. It couldn't be easy to be the only woman in a cross-country race. And it was unfortunate that her mechanic, Cummings, didn't show up. He supposed that would have made any driver act crazy.

He was just about to change his mind about reporting her when he heard the unmistakable sound of air rushing through vibrating lips. The woman was obviously sticking her tongue out at him and giving him a raspberry!

What nerve! Never had he been so insulted in his life. A raspberry, of all things! And from a woman.

Incensed, he picked up his pace and grimaced in pain. Damn fool woman. How dare she? Oh, yes, he meant every word he'd said. He would report her, all right, along with car number seven. By the time he got through, neither one of them would ever drive again!

# Chapter 5

"The quickest way to learn the traffic laws is by accident."

*Women at the Wheel*
Circa 1915

Elizabeth's body ached all over. Curled up on the hard leather seat with only a thin woolen blanket to protect her from the cold damp air, she couldn't sleep.

She longed for a proper bed, but didn't dare leave her vehicle unattended. It was a good thing, too! She'd forgotten to put the emergency brake on and the car had rolled forward, heading straight for the window of Curly Joe's barbershop! Lord love an orphan, it was a miracle she'd managed to stop the car in time.

Besides, she wouldn't put it past one of the other drivers to pour sugar in her gas tank or to otherwise damage her motor.

Not that it mattered, she supposed, what with her mechanic threatening to jump ship. What was the matter with the man? Accusing her of the most heinous crimes. Kidnapping, for goodness' sake. Attempted murder!

Although she never saw him drink the entire time she was in his company, she suspected that his past alcoholic binges had affected his brain. What else could explain his wild accusations and irresponsible behavior?

It wouldn't surprise her in the least if, at that very

moment, he was in the local tavern drinking his fool head off. It irritated her that he was having a good time while she was cramped on the front seat of her car like a tangled kiss-curl.

She stretched her arm behind her to rub her sore back and banged her head on the brass handle of the door. Muttering under her breath, she tried turning over and only succeeded in knocking her knees on the steering wheel. Despite the obstacles, it was worry more than discomfort that kept her tossing and turning.

Entering the race had been all she'd thought about since reading the announcement in the newspaper. She had filled in the application on that very same day, signing her name, E. Davenport, and mailing it post-haste to Mr. Ford. Then she'd waited impatiently for a letter or wire of acceptance.

Mr. Ford had planned the race as a way to make the politicians aware that the nation's roads had not kept up to the times. Citing the fact that Model T Fords were not only economical, but dependable enough for traveling long distances, Mr. Ford maintained that with proper roads, cross-country touring would become increasingly popular. The founder of the Ford Motor Company imagined families driving hundreds of miles on holiday just to visit one of the nation's many national parks—a luxury few could enjoy at present.

He struck Elizabeth as a man with great wisdom and vision. Ah, but he was still a man, and it was obvious by the look on Mr. Ford's face when she'd walked into the Buffalo hotel where he was staying while he firmed up final plans, that he'd never considered the possibility of a woman entering his race.

Fortunately, she'd arrived at his hotel prepared to argue her case. Armed with statistics she'd gathered by posting herself in front of a well-established grocery in Manhattan and counting the number of women who wheeled vehicles to market, she presented a compelling case for allowing a woman driver to enter the race. Of course, Mr. Ford had no idea that over fifty percent of the *wheeled* vehicles were not horse-drawn buggies or automobiles, as he was led to believe, or even bicycles, but baby carriages, or go-carts as they were more commonly called.

From this unscientific and admittedly biased study, she determined that seventy-eight percent of all wheeled vehicles were operated by women.

Mr. Ford was duly impressed. "I had no idea!" he exclaimed. "Why haven't my merchandising people informed me of this?" he wanted to know, and had indeed thundered this very question into the candlestick telephone in his room while she waited for his decision.

No one believed it when he announced the names of the drivers and her name was included. Headlines screamed the news. Journalists took Mr. Ford to task for allowing such a travesty to occur. Some critics proclaimed the very nature of an automobile made it an unsuitable vehicle for women's unpredictable temperaments.

None of the critics took into consideration the number of women already driving automobiles, of course, or the fact that a woman had already driven one coast-to-coast.

Elizabeth couldn't understand what the fuss was about. Driving across the country was nothing compared to what that amazing "woman aviator in trousers," Harriet Quimby, had done. If a woman could fly a biplane, certainly driving an automobile was a cinch.

Elizabeth had originally entered the race solely for the money. Twenty-five thousand dollars would help her build her home for orphans. That was still her main consideration, though no longer her only one. She now wanted to prove all her critics wrong in their contention that women had no business behind the wheel of a car.

She also wanted to prove something much more

personal. The race followed the same route as the
orphan train that had taken her from New York to
Oregon when she was but a frightened child of seven.
Never would she forget the helplessness she'd felt on
that train. Helplessness had turned to humiliation
when she was hauled off at every stop and made to
stand in front of the locals. Strangers heartlessly
squeezed her legs and arms to determine her work
capacity. Her hair was checked for lice and her teeth
for decay. No one seemed to care that she was terri-
fied by their rough, probing hands and unkind comments. Most farmers were more interested in boosting
their work crew than increasing their family size.

As humiliating as this had been, nothing compared
to the years that followed, when she was subjected to
the most horrible abuses at the hands of the man who
eventually adopted her, Mylar Carson.

She was little more than twelve when he'd first had
his way with her, and after that, things had never been
the same.

Whenever the urge hit him, he'd grab her roughly
by the arm and take her behind the barn. He then did
unspeakable things to her. At first she fought him, but
she soon learned that any resistance on her part only
made him angry, and this would inevitably prolong
the ordeal.

Eventually, she learned to separate her mind from
her body. Forced to lie on the hard, cold ground, she'd
stare up at the colorful ribbons tied to a post overhead, marking the snow lines of winters past, and pretend she was as free as the ribbons in the wind. Her
mind became a bird that could, at will, wing itself
into a wonderful and safe haven where no one could
touch her.

Her mind became a way to escape in more ways
than one. She became obsessed with learning to read
and write. She devoured Shakespeare and all the popular authors of the day whose books she could get
ahold of. Sometimes, while staring at the ribbons in

the wind, she would silently recite poetry or sonnets,
concentrating on the beauty of each word.

It wasn't until she ran away at the age of seventeen
that she knew what it was like to have charge of her
own destiny. It was at that tender age she'd vowed no
man would ever touch her again. Not ever!

And to this day, no man had.

She had a score to settle, and thanks to Mr. Ford,
the means by which to settle it. More important, she
had a chance, a slim one perhaps, but a chance nonetheless, of seeing her dream become reality.

She hoped to find the means by which to build a
series of homes across the country. No child should
ever have to go through what she'd gone through.
And no one, not even a wayward mechanic, was going
to stop her from doing what she'd set out to do.

First thing in the morning she intended to report
the man to race officials. By the time she finished with
him, Mr. Cummings or Hunter—whatever his name—
would regret the day he'd ever met her.

She could hardly wait to see the look on his handsome face when he found out his work as a mechanic
was over for good.

Sighing, she turned over, banging her knees once
again, and closed her eyes. She prayed for one night
free of the nightmares that continued to plague her,
even now, after all these years away from Mylar. Just
one night! After a long while, she felt herself sink into
a vivid blue sea, the very same color as her wayward
mechanic's eyes.

She was suddenly startled into wakefulness, surprised to find herself thinking pleasant thoughts. She
lay perfectly still, trying to capture the dream again.
It shocked her to realize she'd been dreaming about
Mr. Cummings-Hunter. In her dreams, he had kissed
her, and his lips were as sweet and soft as April rain.

Kisses sweet and soft? What an odd notion! Heart
pounding, she tried pushing the memory of the dream
from her mind. A man's kiss didn't feel soft. It felt

brutal and harsh, and tasted vile. It humiliated and
degraded. It . . .

Her body trembled so much, she could hardly think.
She closed her eyes tight and tried to envision the
ribbons that were tied to the back of the car. When
that didn't calm her, she sought desperately to recall
the words to her favorite sonnet.

The words wouldn't come, no matter how much she
tried to recall them. She swallowed hard but couldn't
hold back the hot tears that stung her eyes. For some
reason the dream frightened her more than any of her
nightmares. For it had awakened feelings inside that
were new and strange to her. Feelings she wished
would go away and never return.

She was free now and intended to stay free. Mylar
Carson had robbed her of her youth and any chance
of a normal life. She'd always known that, had learned
to accept it. She could live without a husband. Lots
of women did. She had her work and that was enough.

She lay inside her Model T Ford and ruminated on
spending the rest of her life alone. Only now did she
fully understand how very much her adoptive father
had taken from her.

After many lonely hours, shivering in the small
cramped confines of her Model T Ford, she finally fell
asleep, only to be awakened a short time later by a
noisy rooster greeting the early morning sun.

She sat up and blinked her eyes against the glare.
Warm rays broke through a tiny opening in the clouds,
touching the nearby church steeple with fingers of
golden sunlight.

Spotting a rain barrel next to the general store, she
grabbed soap and a towel from her suitcase and hurried across the cobblestone road. The water was cool
and refreshing as she scrubbed her face and arms.

She dried herself off, keeping her gaze firmly fixed
on the Erie Arms where her mechanic had headed the
night before. It galled her to think of him sleeping in
a hotel room with all the comforts of home.

*Oooooooh,* the man made her so mad. Complaining about her driving. Neglecting to assume a mechanic's responsibilities. Giving her that "holier than thou" look every time he had to pull her car out of some predicament.

The moment this race was over, she had every intention of consulting a lawyer and hauling Cummings into court. That would show him she meant business. That would prove to him that even a contract made with a woman was binding by law!

She thought of all the ways she intended to get even with the man. But while revenge would be ultimately satisfying, nothing she could do to him in the future would help her with her present difficulties.

If the man truly meant to desert her, then she had only until noon to hire another to take his place or she would be disqualified.

She stood in the center of town, hands at her waist, and glanced around. It was still early and the street was deserted, but the clanking sound of a job press rose from the nearby printing plant of the local newspaper.

Given the number of horses and wagons in the livery stables, and the appalling lack of automobiles, there probably wasn't a fit mechanic to be found. Like it or not, Mr. Cummings-Hunter was very possibly her best bet.

She stared at the hotel with narrowed eyes. What would it take to change Mr. Hunter's fool mind?

Jimmy rose early as was his custom and, after shaving and dressing, wandered downstairs to the hotel dining room and ordered a hearty breakfast.

Afterward, he obtained a railroad timetable from the desk clerk and headed for the race booth in front of the hotel just as car number nine left town.

A race official sat behind the booth reading the morning newspaper. A balding man with a squinty look, he glanced up as Jimmy approached.

"Excuse me, sir. My name is Jimmy Hunter."

The man pulled a piece of paper out of his leather portfolio and scanned down the list. "Hunter? I don't see any Hunter listed."

"I was actually mistaken for a Mr. Cummings."

The man brightened. "Ah, yes, here we are. What can I do for you, Mr. Cummings?"

"Eh ... that's Hunter. Jimmy Hunter."

"Oh. You are a mechanic, are you not?"

"No, I'm an electrician. Now how do I make a complaint? I was told last night I would have to wait until this morning."

"Oh, dear. Another complaint. It seems to be the morning for complaints. Sir Higginbottom just registered a complaint against his mechanic, Mr. Chin, for packing only green tea. You'd think the two would have more important things to argue about, wouldn't you?"

"Yes, you would. Eh ..."

"Then Mr. Stonegate lodged a complaint against Mr. Staggs for taking a photograph of him in a cemetery. He said it was disrespectful of the dead."

"This is all very interesting but ..."

"Then Miss Davenport ..."

"Miss Davenport! And what, may I ask, has she got to complain about?"

Taken aback by Jimmy's sudden outcry, the race official cleared his voice. "She said there is a breach of contract between her and her mechanic. Then Mr. Mason complained ..."

Jimmy placed both hands on the booth and leaned toward the race official menacingly. "I don't care what the other drivers have to complain about! Now are you going to take my complaint or do I have to go to the sheriff?"

The man tugged on the lapels of his suit coat and looked indignant. "I can assure you, young man, that I am quite capable of handling any and all complaints as long as they are pertinent to the race." He pulled

an official-looking document out of his portfolio and
produced a fountain pen. "Now if you would be kind
enough to describe the nature of your complaint."

"I would be happy to." Jimmy straightened and
glanced around to make certain no one was eaves-
dropping. "I was kidnapped."

The pen stopped. "Kidnapped, you say? Good
heavens! By whom?"

"By Miss Davenport."

The official let his gaze travel up the entire length
of Jimmy's six-foot-four height, then narrowed his
gaze in disbelief as he leveled his eyes in the direction
of Miss Davenport's Model T Ford. "Are you talking
about *that* Miss Davenport?"

Jimmy turned to follow the man's pointed finger.
Sure enough, Miss Davenport was bent over the open
hood of her Model T and making a terrible racket.
Jimmy shuddered to think of what she was doing to
the poor engine. "That's the one."

Despite the baggy overalls she wore, her womanly
curves were most disturbingly evident. Jimmy let his
gaze wander lazily over her soft rounded hips and tiny
waist before he turned back to the official, who was
staring up at him in disbelief.

Not that Jimmy could blame him. The woman was
no taller than five foot three. A strong wind would
probably blow her away. Nevertheless, a fact was a
fact.

"I must insist Miss Davenport not be allowed to
continue the race."

"I'm afraid I don't have the authority to make that
decision," the official said. "I can only disqualify
someone who is breaking the rules as established by
Mr. Henry Ford himself."

Palms on the table, Jimmy leaned toward the official. "Are you saying that kidnapping is not an infraction of the rules?"

"See for yourself," the man said, handing him a list
of rules. "Do you see any mention of kidnapping?"

Jimmy quickly read through the list. If kidnapping wasn't grounds for disqualification, then he would find something that was.

At first glance, it seemed as if there was a rule for just about everything. Only designated drivers were allowed behind the steering wheel. Broken parts could be fixed but not replaced, though there were a few exceptions. The serial numbers of designated parts would be checked at the end of the race. His gaze lingered on rule number eight. *Drivers must exhibit good sportsmanship.* Ah ha!

"Do you see anything that applies to Miss Davenport?"

"I most certainly do," Jimmy replied. "Rule number eight. She stuck out her tongue and made a strange sound with her lips." He lowered his voice. This was humiliating enough without everyone knowing. "A raspberry. She gave me a raspberry."

The race official looked puzzled. "Would you mind demonstrating?"

Jimmy was taken aback by the request. This was ridiculous; she'd kidnapped him, *for chrissakes.* Didn't that count for anything? "All right, forget Miss Davenport. I want to lodge a complaint against the driver of car seven."

"That would be Mr. Fastbender."

"Yes, well, Mr. Fastbender tried to run me down."

"Run you down, you say? Good heavens, where were you standing?"

"In the middle of the road."

"Oh, dear. I believe standing in the road is against the law. If you would be kind enough to read rule number twelve."

Jimmy let his gaze drop to the paper in his hand. *It is forbidden for anyone to block the road.* He threw the list back at the man and spoke through clenched teeth. "The man tried to kill me."

"But you were standing in the way. You said so

yourself. Now as for Miss Davenport sticking out her tongue . . ."

Distracted by the sudden sound of loud voices behind him, Jimmy turned. Miss Davenport and one of the race officials stood toe to toe, nose to nose, jawing at each other like a couple of angry magpies.

"Is that your complaint?" the race official asked, seemingly unaware of the altercation that was beginning to draw a crowd. "That Miss Davenport did something strange with her tongue?"

Jimmy bit back his irritation. "No, that's not my complaint. My official complaint is that Miss Davenport kidnapped me and Mr. Fastbender tried to kill me. Do you understand? Oh, never mind." Unable to ignore the angry voices any longer, he turned and stepped off the wooden sidewalk and onto the shiny cobblestones. What the hell was Miss Davenport riled up about this time?

# Chapter 6

"Just when you think you know where you're going, the road curves, sending you in the opposite direction!"

*Women at the Wheel*
Circa 1915

Jimmy tried to peer over the rather sizable crowd that had gathered around Miss Davenport's vehicle. Another race official had joined in, and the noisy confrontation had now escalated to the point of stopping traffic.

Though Miss Davenport and the two men were shouting back and forth, it was difficult to understand what the argument was about. Jimmy moved closer, threading his way through the mob of curious bystanders.

Suddenly Miss Davenport pointed in his direction. "There he is!" she shouted. Plowing her way through the crowd with the two officials at her heels, she charged toward him.

Jimmy didn't know whether to run in the opposite direction or to wave a white flag.

"It's about time you got here," she said accusingly. To the others she said, "See, I told you I had a mechanic."

"Are you Cummings?" the shorter of the two men asked.

"As I have explained to Miss . . ."

"Of course he's Cummings. Who else would he be?"

The two officials looked Jimmy up and down, shook their head in what appeared to be sympathy, and walked away.

"Now see here," Jimmy began. He'd had enough of this woman to last a lifetime. Aware that the crowd was still watching Miss Davenport with open curiosity, he took her by the arm and walked her behind the hotel where they could talk in private.

With a firm grip on her arm, he whirled her around until her back was flat against the trunk of a sycamore tree. She glanced over his shoulder as if she sought a way to escape. "Oh, no, you don't, Miss Davenport!" He placed his hands against the trunk, trapping her within the confines of his steel-rigid arms.

"Now listen and listen good." It suddenly occurred to him that it was the first time he'd gotten a close look at her without either driving goggles or road dust obscuring her face, and he was startled by what he saw.

She was the prettiest woman he'd ever set eyes on. A ring of golden lashes circled eyes as blue as a mountain lake. Her hair, seductively tousled and the color of spun gold, framed her delicate features, tiny wisps blowing across her forehead. He knew instinctively that the warm golden color was not the result of the peroxide craze that had turned a nation of brunets into blonds in recent months, but was as natural as the sun.

Never had a hellion looked more angelic, even with the dark look she gave him. If he didn't know better, he'd think she was frightened of him. Miss Davenport frightened? That was a switch!

Nevertheless, he dropped his arms to his side and stepped back. He'd never used physical force with a woman in his life and he didn't plan on doing so now. But rather than stay as he'd hoped, she dashed off.

Cursing, he gave chase. Amazingly fleet-footed, she led him away from the hotel through a nearby park. But he was faster, or at least his legs were longer, and he captured her by a deserted bandstand, pushed her up against the wooden building, and pressed his body against hers, preventing further escape.

They both gasped for air, glaring at each other like two angry bulls fighting for territorial rights.

"I am not now and never will be your mechanic!" he managed at last. Having said his piece, he dropped his arms to his side and stalked away.

"See if I care!" she shouted after him. She then made what was now becoming an all too familiar raspberry sound.

He was no longer shocked, but he was plenty incensed. Curling his hands into two fists by his side, he strode angrily toward the hotel. As soon as he collected his belongings and checked out, he would head to the train station and purchase his ticket back home to Hogs Head, Indiana.

For all he cared, Miss Davenport and those big blue eyes of hers could go to hell!

Miss Davenport stood waiting for him when he arrived at the train station. Even from a distance, it was easy to see she looked remarkably composed. It was obvious from the way she stood, chin held high, legs apart, hands at her waist, that she was ready for combat. He groaned to himself. He should have known she wouldn't make it easy for him.

Since she stood between him and the gate to the train, he had no choice but to walk toward her. Her hair was no longer loose around her shoulders, but had been carefully braided and pinned wreath-style upon her head. She met his eyes without flinching, her face, her whole demeanor, posed in grim determination. Gritting his teeth, he braced himself. He tightened his hold on his carpetbag before stepping onto the platform. He didn't have time for this.

The conductor clung to the side of the train. "All aboard!" Steam escaped from the impatient locomotive and the last of the passengers scrambled into the waiting Pullman.

"Five thousand dollars," Miss Davenport said.

He stopped dead in his tracks. "What?"

"I'm prepared to pay you a five-thousand-dollar bonus from the prize money. That's above and beyond what I've already agreed to pay you."

He was curious as to what she had agreed to pay her mechanic, but he wasn't about to ask. "No deal." He made a move to walk around her, but she blocked his away.

"Ten thousand."

"The answer is no!"

"All right." He made the mistake of thinking she had finally accepted defeat, but instead she came back with another offer. "Fifty percent of the winnings. But not a penny more."

"I wouldn't get back in that car if you offered a hundred percent. Now would you kindly step aside?" When she refused to move, he pushed passed her and walked quickly toward the nearest Pullman.

She caught up with him just before he stepped onto the train. "Please don't leave me."

Something. The plaintive sound in her voice, perhaps, or the haunting familiarity of those blue eyes of hers, made him hesitate. He turned around to face her.

She stood in a circle of sunshine, and suddenly he couldn't breathe. Without her goggles and away from the car, she looked fragile as a flower, soft as a spring rain. But she was none of those things, he told himself. It was an illusion. A trick! She'd do anything to get her way.

"My train is about to leave."

"Please," she pleaded.

For some reason he was having an awful time matching the woman in front of him with the maniacal road hog who had made his life hell. "I'm due home," he said, not wanting to make this any more unpleasant than necessary. "I have responsibilities."

"But you can't just leave me," she said. "We made a deal, and I think it only fair that you keep your word. You know that without a mechanic I'm automatically disqualified from the race. We have an agreement!"

"I don't know what kind of an agreement you think we have. But as I told you before, I'm not—"

She frowned with impatience. "I know, I know. You're not Mr. Cummings and you're not a mechanic."

Now they were getting somewhere. "The truth is, I thought I might know you. That's why I came over to your car yesterday."

Her luminous blue eyes widened and he was suddenly having a difficult time thinking. He knew he had something to do, but for the life of him he couldn't think what that something was.

"Know me? How?"

He hadn't wanted to explain all this, especially now that he realized she wasn't his childhood friend. Still, he could hardly deny the fact that her present predicament was partly his fault. Had he not shown up at the last minute, she would never have started the race in the first place and had her hopes raised. No wonder she was so reluctant to accept the truth. The least he owed her was an explanation.

The whistle blew again, and bells clanged. Jimmy glanced over his shoulder. The train was beginning to inch forward. "This probably sounds ridiculous," he said. Walking to keep up with the moving Pullman, he talked quickly. "But I once knew someone by the name of Elizabeth Davenport." With one hand on his head to keep his newly purchased hat from flying off, he was forced to run to keep up with the train. Miss Davenport ran with him.

"She and I lived at the same orphanage in New

York. The last I saw of her, she was on the westbound train—"

Miss Davenport stopped suddenly and, clutching her stomach, fell to her knees. Thinking she was injured, Jimmy dropped his carpetbag and rushed to her side. "Good heavens! Are you all right?"

She nodded. "You caught me by surprise, is all."

"Surprise? How?"

She gazed up at him and the blue of her eyes stirred memories of softness within him.

"I was on one of those orphan trains," she said, searching his face.

"You ... you were?"

She nodded. "Hunter ... Hunter. I'm not sure ... The name doesn't ring a bell."

He felt a crushing disappointment, until something occurred to him. "My name was Moresall back then." It had been so long since he'd used his birth name, he'd almost forgotten that Hunter was the name he'd taken when Kate and Jonas had officially adopted him. "Jimmy Moresall." When she showed no recognition of his name, he decided she couldn't be his former playmate. She would remember his name, wouldn't she? Remember him?

"What did you look like back then?"

He had to think. "I don't know. I guess my hair was pretty much the same color. I walked on crutches and ..."

She grabbed his arm, her mouth rounded in a perfect O. "Jimmy," she whispered softly. "Is it really you?"

He stared at her in disbelief. "Elizabeth?" *My Elizabeth?* "Is that you?"

She nodded slightly and touched her fingers to her lips. For several minutes they could only stare at each other in utter disbelief. The train gave one last whistle before pulling away from the station completely, but neither Jimmy nor Elizabeth noticed.

Then suddenly she laughed, and as if some barrier had been removed, they both started talking at once.

"I always wondered what had happened to you....," he began.

"I never forgot ..."

"Remember how you ... ?"

Falling silent again, they stared at each other. She shook her head in amazement, and he glanced upward as he did on occasion when something happened that defied explanation.

"You go first," she said.

"No, you."

She bit her lower lip. "I do remember you, Jimmy. You were so kind to me. I remember how you held my hand and told me not to cry."

Jimmy felt a tightness in his chest as he studied her lovely round face. Would her hair—her beautiful, golden hair—feel as soft today as it had felt all those years ago? "I've never forgotten you, Elizabeth. I never forgot hearing you cry in the baggage car. I wanted so much to help you, but I didn't know how."

"You did help me, Jimmy. All those years that followed ..." A shadow crossed her face and the glow in her eyes faded as if someone had turned off an inner light.

Stooped on one knee, he lifted his hand to her cheek. He had done this very thing in the past, touched her, caressed her, but with the innocence of a child; today he touched her with the knowledge and awareness of a man.

Perhaps that would explain why she so quickly drew back, but it didn't explain the look of horror or maybe even repulsion on her face.

Never had a woman looked at him in such a way. Never had a woman made him feel so unworthy. Stunned, he stared at her, feeling as though he'd been slapped. He dropped his hand to his side. "Elizabeth? I wasn't going to ... to do anything. I was just so glad to see you, I never meant ..."

"I know," she said quickly. "I'm still in shock, that's all." She gave him an awkward smile, but her hands remained clasped together. "You were always very kind to me. I can't tell you how much you helped."

"You helped me, too," he said. "You were the only one who didn't laugh at me, even when I deserved to be laughed at."

Shaking her head slightly as if to shake away the past, her face brightened and the dark look faded away, though it continued to puzzle him. "I never thought you deserved to be laughed at, Jimmy. Not even when you tried to climb into my bedroom window and fell into the fish pond."

Jimmy grinned. He'd completely forgotten about the incident. "You have to give me credit. Not too many people try to climb a tree on crutches."

She giggled, and for an instant it seemed to Jimmy that the years were suddenly erased and they were thrown back in time. All too soon, the smile died on her face and she regarded him thoughtfully, as if searching for the boy he once was and discounting the man he'd become.

"Does this mean you'll be my mechanic?" she asked. The beautiful blue eyes that had haunted him since he'd last seen her at the age of seven now tortured him. For he saw things in their shadowy depths he didn't want to see, didn't want to name, didn't want to know existed.

He brushed his hair with his fingers. "I told you why I can't be your mechanic."

"Please, Jimmy. I want to win this race! I *have* to win this race."

He rose to his feet and took a step back. That's when he realized he'd missed his train. But at the moment he was too overwhelmed at having found Elizabeth after all this time to care. "Win the race! You shouldn't even be driving. Why, you could have gotten us both killed."

"But I have a driving license," she said, as if this made the possibility of killing him legal.

He wasn't the least bit impressed. Some places, like Milwaukee, issued licenses to anyone who was eighteen and had two legs. Judging by Elizabeth's driving, it couldn't be much harder to get a New York license.

"I'm sorry, Jimmy. Really I am. I'll drive more carefully in the future. I promise. But if I drop out now, my plans to build a home for orphans will be ruined."

"What home?"

Quickly she told him about the children's home she planned to build. "My plan is to make a place for orphaned children to live until a suitable home is found for them. Anyone interested in adopting a child would first have to go through a rigorous screening process. Once I prove my idea a success, I intend to see that orphan trains and . . . and"—her eyes flashed angrily—"those barbaric viewings are a thing of the past!"

As if surprised by her own vehemence, she took a deep breath before continuing, this time in a calmer voice. "I can't give up now. I won't. A lot of children's lives are at stake. Please, Jimmy. Please say you'll help me."

He walked around in a circle, looking up at the sky. Guilt for leaving her on that train all those years ago was even stronger now than before. Something horrible had happened to her. He could see it in her eyes, in her face. In the very way she dressed and held herself. Why else would she hide behind leather helmets and goggles—and men's baggy overalls—as if she never wanted anyone to get too close to her.

It sickened him to think of Elizabeth being paraded through depots, being probed and inspected like cattle at an auction. No wonder she had pulled back earlier from his touch.

He hated to think of how he'd allowed himself to be rescued from the train all those years ago. How he'd left his little friend to face the future alone. But nothing he'd done in the past compared with the choice he faced at present. He'd walked away from her once, but could he really walk away a second time?

He rubbed his chin and tried to think rationally.

He wasn't a mechanic.

Ah, but it didn't take a mechanic to know a Model T engine. These automobiles were so simple that in most small towns, blacksmiths doubled as mechanics.

All right, so the mechanic part was a lame excuse, but he was due back home in Hogs Head to manage the family's electrical company and that was no lie.

Still, another week or two wouldn't make that much difference, would it?

"Please say you will, Jimmy."

"Oh, all right," he said, reluctantly. He dreaded the thought of another day in that rattling steel trap, but it was for a good cause, and perhaps it would help alleviate some of his guilt.

"Oh, Jimmy!" She bit her lower lip. "I can't tell you how happy I am."

Embarrassed by the look of gratitude on her face, he looked away. After deserting her when she needed him the most, he was more deserving of her anger than her gratitude. He glanced back at Elizabeth's Tin Lizzie, which was still parked by the hotel. The crowd was gone. "We'd better get Old Ironsides ready."

"Old Ironsides?"

He shrugged. "It's as good a name as any. Let's just hope she's every bit as indestructible as the real thing."

"Old Ironsides," Elizabeth repeated. "I like it." She jumped to her feet. "Let's get started. We have only three hours left until noon." She walked away hurriedly, forcing him to run to catch up.

"Wait!" He grabbed her by the arm, forgetting her earlier reaction to his touch. This time she stiffened visibly, and he knew he hadn't imagined the fear he saw in her eyes moments before. Puzzled that he had such an effect on her, he quickly released her. It was hard, but he managed to quell the urge to take her in his arms and make her understand he never meant to harm her. "I'm sorry ... I ..."

She recovered quickly, but stepped out of reach. "What is it, Jimmy?" she asked matter-of-factly.

He narrowed his eyes and studied her, but saw only impatience on her face as she waited. "I said I'll be your mechanic, but some changes need to be made."

"Changes?" Impatience turned to baby-blue innocence.

"Yes, changes. From this moment on, you will drive only on designated roads. Do I make myself clear?"

"Yes, but ..."

"And! You will never, ever drive faster than the speed limit, whether or not a speed limit exists. Is *that* clear?"

"Yes, but ..."

He had her attention and wasn't about to give an inch. Her life was at stake. Hell, *his* life was at stake. "And furthermore, you will learn to stop and start the car gradually, and you will never, NEVER ..." He listed every possible infraction that she had managed in the course of a single day to commit at least twice.

"No more than eight miles per hour through town," he continued. "And you must always, *always* signal your intentions to the driver behind you." At last, satisfied he had covered every possible traffic situation, he folded his arms in front of him like a schoolmaster dealing with a wayward student. "That's the deal. Take it or leave it."

She gave a careless shrug, as if they had discussed something as benign as a sunny sky. "I'll take it." She turned and streaked toward Old Ironsides like a torpedo.

Following close behind, he had a sinking feeling inside. He hadn't made a mistake, had he? Agreeing to be her mechanic?

# Chapter 7

"Love makes the world go round, but so do detours."

*Women at the Wheel*
Circa 1915

By the time he reached the flivver, Elizabeth was already trying to pry a flat tire off the rim. "I'll take care of the car," he said, taking the crowbar, or iron ham bones, as most car owners called it, in hand. "You better get us something to eat for the road. Oh, and pick up some of those chocolate wafers. You know, the ones with the cream inside."

"Do you mean Oreo biscuits?"

"Yeah, those are the ones. Also a couple of packs of chewing gum. If I don't get this radiator fixed, we're going to be needing a lot of gum. Be ready to go by noon."

He watched her disappear into Popper's grocery across the way. What an appealing sight she made, her slender waist and soft rounded hips giving the oversize canvas overalls an intriguing and ultimately feminine shape. He shook his head. It was hard to believe. She really was Elizabeth Davenport.

*His* Elizabeth Davenport.

Who would ever think he'd have the opportunity to keep the promise he'd made to take care of her all those years ago?

Determined to do everything in his power to help

her, he turned his attention to the Model T. One of
the colorful ribbons caught his eye. He lifted it gently
and stroked the smooth satin finish with his thumb.
He recalled the time he'd sat in the drafty baggage
car all those years ago, stroking her long silken hair
as she sobbed.

Shaking away the image, he released the ribbon and
hunched down beside the right rear tire.

Changing a tire was no simple matter. It was easier
to rebuild an engine than to change a tire. After wres-
tling the tire off its rim, he pulled out the tube,
roughed up the rubber, and patched up the hole. He
finally managed to get the tube back onto the tire, but
not without a battle. He then attached the rubber tire
back onto the wire-spoked wheel frame and fit the
frame onto the axle.

Car number seven whizzed by, driven by that mur-
dering fool, Fastbender. He was the sixth driver to
leave town after having satisfied the twelve-hour layover requirement. Elizabeth's car would be the last.

Jimmy glared after the driver, raising his fist. The
man had tried to kill him. If Fastbender actually won
the race, Jimmy would protest—he swore—even if he
had to go all the way to Mr. Henry Ford himself.

Glancing at the church clock, he finished pumping
air into the tire. He doubted they could make up for
time lost on the previous day. The best they could
hope for was not to lose additional time.

He lowered the jack, then worked on the engine for
the remainder of the morning. He'd worked on a lot
of motors while still in college, but never had he seen
one in such poor condition as Elizabeth's. He ground
the valves until they were seated more accurately,
cleaned the carbon deposits off the cylinders, and replaced a cracked porcelain spark plug casing. He managed to get the local blacksmith to fix the hole in
the radiator.

Jimmy then refueled the car, filtering the gasoline
through a sieve lined with chamois until the fuel ran

clear. Finally, he washed and polished the car until it gleamed like black obsidian.

When at last he cranked up Old Ironsides, the four-cylinder, twenty-horsepower engine sounded like a fleet of old wagons on a frozen road, but it was definitely an improvement over how it had sounded previously. Satisfied, he turned off the engine and, grabbing the empty gasoline can, headed for the filling station.

Elizabeth was already behind the wheel by the time he returned to the car. He attached the spare fuel can to the running board, then walked to the driver's side and leaned an arm on the door frame.

"Would you be willing to shake hands?"

Her eyes shimmered in the sunlight. "What?"

"We have an agreement. I'll be your mechanic and you'll drive carefully. I want to make sure it's legal."

"Oh, of course." She held out her hand. It felt small in his and trembled slightly. She pulled away before he barely had time to shake it. "I can't tell you how much this means to me, Jimmy. With you as my mechanic, I can't help but win."

He smiled and gazed longingly at her pretty pink lips. He suddenly had the urge to do more than just shake hands with her. "It's going to take a lot more than just keeping Old Ironsides here running."

"I know. And you're absolutely right. From now on, we do everything just the way you say."

He grinned. This was the Elizabeth he remembered. Sweet and soft. Eager to please. He congratulated himself for the way he'd handled things. How brilliant of him to lay down the law. Making her promise to drive responsibly was ... well, to put it modestly, sheer genius. Yes, indeed. Elizabeth Davenport was a reasonable, sane, not to mention beautiful woman, who simply needed a strong male influence to settle her down.

"Are you ready?" he asked.

She reached for her goggles and driving gloves.

"Ready." She gave him a beguiling smile and his heart turned over and purred like a well-oiled engine.

Feeling like a million dollars, he walked around to the front of the flivver and grabbed the handle of the crank. It took several full revolutions before the four cylinders filled the air with a mighty roar and asserted their full authority.

His arm jerked painfully by the kickback, he cursed, then hopped into the car. "Wait!" Out of habit, Jimmy reached for his pocket watch before recalling that he'd given it to that gun-toting farmer. He glanced back at the church clock and waited until the minute hand moved slowly past the noon hour. To leave even a second too soon was grounds for being disqualified.

Elizabeth lowered her goggles and grabbed hold of the steering wheel, her pretty mouth poised in thoughtful contemplation. Jimmy considered this a sign she was determined to drive in accordance with their agreement.

At exactly three minutes past noon, he dropped his hand. "Go!"

The car bucked forward like a bronco bursting out of its pen. It hesitated for a split second, then took off like the same bronco with its tail afire. Jimmy cried out as he was thrown forward against the dashboard, then back in his seat.

Before his astonished eyes Elizabeth Davenport had reverted back to Miss Tin Lizzie, queen of road hogs and the patron saint of speed demons.

"Yeee-ow!" Jimmy held on to his hat and tried to keep from flying out the door as she shot past the astonished race official, took a turn on two wheels, and sped out of town. "Dammit! You forgot to signal. Slow down. Watch out."

"What?" She shouted to be heard over the engine and the wind. "What did you say?"

"I said slow down!"

"How do you expect me to win a race if I drive slow?"

"We have an agreement!" he yelled. "Now either you slow down or I'm leaving."

"But you said I had to drive slow through town. You said nothing about open road."

"Stop, dammit!"

She slammed her foot against the pedal and Jimmy came perilously close to ending his days as a splatter on the windshield. It took him a moment to recover, another moment to compose himself. He took a deep breath and reminded himself that Elizabeth really was a sane and reasonable person.

"Now," he began, fighting for control, "you will very slowly—SLOWLY, I said!—give it a little gas."

She wisely did as she was told, and the car did a strange little tippy-toe type of thing, moving forward like a ballerina with three-hundred-pound hips. "Now a little more gas." They started to rumble forward. "That's it. Now stay at this exact same speed."

She eyed him incredulously, but said nothing. For the next couple of miles, she maintained what he considered a reasonable speed, given the condition of the road, and managed to stay on the road at least eighty percent of the time.

"All right, this is open road. You can pick up speed." Jimmy kept his eyes on the speedometer, though it really wasn't necessary. He could guess how fast they were going by how the Model T reacted.

At ten miles an hour, the lamps shook; at twenty miles the fenders vibrated; his bones rattled as soon as the speedometer registered twenty-five miles, and at thirty miles an hour, his teeth chattered.

The road leading to Cleveland followed Lake Erie's shoreline. Jimmy wished they could have stayed on that graded road, but the race course made a detour that took them past rolling hills, through lush fruit orchards, and by peaceful dairy farms. They drove through several small communities on roads that were little more than cow trails, and indeed, in one small town, they had to wait for a farmer to move his herd before they could continue on their way.

Five miles outside of the little town of Ipsen, they spotted car number four parked on the side of the road. Jimmy checked his notes for the driver's name. It was the man known as Staggs.

"Stop," Jimmy said, and too late added, "Slowly!" His palms flat against the dashboard, he lifted his voice. "Sir, do you have a problem?"

"I have a hole in my radiator, but my mechanic has it under control. Isn't that so, Casper?" His mechanic, a young man of about eighteen with a long, narrow face and a mop of curly brown hair, lifted his head from the engine and waved.

Staggs continued, "It's mighty kind of you to inquire."

"Have you seen any of the other drivers?" Jimmy asked.

"As a matter of fact, I have. Sir Higginbottom was having a cup of tea back aways. I swear that's all the man does is drink tea. The cowboy was pulled over with a flat tire and that Fastbender fellow had to be towed to a blacksmith shop. I got a great photograph of Stonegate. His Model T was wedged between two grave markers. He had to remove his fenders to free it. I say, would you like me to take your photograph?"

"That's not ..." Jimmy began, but Elizabeth interrupted.

"Oh, please do!"

"Very well." Staggs grabbed his tripod and set up his polished mahogany camera in front of Old Ironsides. The camera, a Conley double extension, came equipped with an automatic shutter and extra-long bellows made from red Russian leather. The bellows made it possible to photograph small items at close range.

"I got a photograph of Crankshaw talking on the telephone to his lady friend." Staggs chuckled to himself. "I don't know what she was saying, but he sure was red." Jimmy sat tapping his fingers impatiently on the door. Staggs took forever to set up his camera. At this rate, they would never reach the next checkpoint.

Staggs moved the tripod back and forth, checked the sun, held his thumb up as if measuring the distance between them. "Ready?"

"We've been ready," Jimmy growled. He and Elizabeth froze in a ridiculous stare that, along with their dust-covered faces, made them look like a couple of worn wooden Indians in front of a tobacco shop. One minute ticked by. Two. Jimmy's patience was at its limit. "What's taking you so long?"

"You can't rush art," Staggs explained. "You have to wait for the right moment. Hold on, now. Here we go." He squeezed the red bulb.

After the photograph was taken, Staggs lugged his equipment back to his car.

"Thank you!" Elizabeth called as she pulled away with squealing tires.

"Slowly!" Jimmy shouted, mopping his brow with a handkerchief.

Shortly after they left Staggs, the driver by the name of Billy-Joe Mason pulled behind them and, with a loud and discourteous blast of his trumpet horn, signaled his intention to pass.

"Oh, no, you don't!" Elizabeth hit the gas pedal hard and the two cars raced neck in neck on a road that was barely wide enough for a single horse and wagon, let alone two fuel-powered vehicles.

Old Ironsides shot over mounds and bounced over gullies, shaking Jimmy from one side of the cab to the other like dice in a gambler's hand.

"Dammit, Elizabeth! Let him pass! We have plenty of time to catch up to him later. . . . Yeow!"

The road made a sudden sharp turn. Unfortunately, Elizabeth kept going straight. She crashed through a wooden fence, barely missing a duck pond, and collected a week's worth of laundry off a clothesline.

Blinded by a pair of men's long johns, she plowed
through the open door of a dilapidated barn.

Chickens flapped their wings and squawked, scattering feathers as freely as falling snow as they raced out
of the way. The car stopped, but not before hitting a
stack of baled hay.

Muttering to himself, Jimmy pulled a fresh clean
pair of ladies' bloomers off his head and a man's flan-
nel shirt from his lap. He stood up and pushed away
the bales of hay that had tumbled onto the car. "Dammit! I told you to stop."

"I did stop."

"Well, you took your own sweet time."

"You told me to stop gradually and that's what I
did."

"Gradually? Dammit, the time to stop gradually is
not when you're about to plow through a barn!" His
voice was two octaves higher than normal. "That's it.
Enough is enough." He climbed out of the car, kicked
a milk can out of the way, and grabbed his carpetbag
from the backseat.

"Where are you going?"

"Home!"

"Jimmy, please . . ."

"Don't start, Elizabeth. Enough is enough. From
now on you're on your own."

He spun on his heel and stormed away. Nothing on
this earth was going to persuade him to get back in
that car with that crazed woman.

Nothing!

He stalked out of the barn as fast as his legs could
carry him. He was so incensed, he damned near failed
to notice the barrel of a shotgun pointing straight at
him.

# Chapter 8

"The tires of a motorcar are almost as much trouble to maintain as a husband—and are not nearly as useful."

*Women at the Wheel*
Circa 1915

The shotgun that was aimed at Jimmy's heart was impressive, but no more so than the incensed farmer whose finger was on the trigger. He was a big, strapping man, his scarred face mean enough to make a freight train leave the tracks in favor of a dirt road. "Just where daya think you're goin'?"

"I'm heading west," Jimmy replied, determined not to give the man cause to pull the trigger. "To Hogs Head, Indiana."

"You were gonna steal chickens and don't say you weren't."

"Believe me, I have no interest in stealing your chickens. I—" The blast was loud enough to be heard two counties away. Buckshot breezed by Jimmy's head.

Shaken, he stared at the farmer in disbelief. "What's the matter with you?" he stormed. "You could kill someone with that thing!"

"Ain't nothing the matter with me, boy. I'm just exercising my right to fill trespassers full of buckshot." He moved the barrel of his gun until it again pointed at Jimmy.

Jimmy wasn't about to stand around and let the man exercise anything, especially his trigger finger. "I hope you don't take this personally, sir, but I plan to do a bit of exercising myself." With that, he took off like wildfire, his feet barely touching the ground.

The farmer was close at his heels. "Come back here, you scoundrel. I'll teach you to steal. . . ." Another blast sounded and it looked as if the farmer had no intention of giving up the chase.

When it seemed as if all were lost, the all too familiar but welcome *ah-ooh-ga* sound of Old Ironsides's horn filled the air. Jimmy glanced over his shoulder in time to see the startled farmer take a dive headfirst beneath the water trough, his shotgun flying upward.

The farmer escaped, but not a moment too soon. Elizabeth zoomed around the trough like a charging bull, barely missing him by a hair. Jimmy was never so happy to see anyone in his life.

Racing alongside the zigzagging car, he grabbed hold of the door frame and heaved himself onto the running board. With his carpetbag still in hand, he dived inside the cab headfirst, his legs sticking straight up like the prongs of a pitchfork.

He waited until they were miles away from the gun-toting farmer before asking her to pull over.

"What?"

"You heard me."

She came to a screeching stop. Without a word, he climbed out of the car and grabbed his belongings.

Elizabeth scooted across the front seat and climbed out after him. They stood facing each other, their gazes locked in combat. "Where are you going? You can't leave me."

He could leave her, all right. He should have left her the day before when he had a chance. But, no! He had to play Mr. Good Samaritan. No more!

Forcing himself to take a deep breath, he tightened his hold on his carpetbag. "We've been together for little more than twenty-four hours," he began, his quiet, controlled voice belying the rampaging fury inside. "And already I've been shot at twice. Twice! I'm sorry, Elizabeth, this isn't working out."

"All right," she said, matching his calm, precise tone. "Desert me. See if I care." With a huff, she climbed behind the wheel and pressed her foot onto the gas pedal. She left him behind in a cloud of dust.

"Good riddance!" he yelled after her. He watched until he could no longer see the ribbons flapping behind her, could no longer hear the putt-putt of the engine, could no longer see her small, determined frame behind the wheel.

He scratched his head and glanced around at the serene pastoral countryside. It was hard to believe that only a short time ago he was running for his life!

A brown cow stood quietly chewing her cud. Bees hovered around a clump of clover. Birds twittered merrily.

Ah, peace and quiet at last. He raised his head and inhaled the sweet smell of spring before starting along the lonely dirt road.

He hadn't deserted her. Of course he hadn't. Given her determination and resourcefulness, she would soon find herself a mechanic and finish the race. She didn't need him.

And he most certainly didn't need her.

Elizabeth blinked back the burning hot tears that blurred her already myopic vision. She gripped the steering wheel tightly with both hands. She was going only ten miles an hour, but any attempts on her part to go faster were thwarted by the deep ruts in the road left behind by last winter's harsh weather.

Lord love an orphan, she couldn't believe it. Who would think that the little, skinny, freckle-faced boy who had crept into her room so many years ago to make her laugh, and who had comforted her in that dreadful baggage car, had grown up to be such a handsome though ultimately annoying old fuddy-duddy!

What a pity.

Never mind. She'd show that Jimmy Hunter. She'd win the race without his help, without anyone's help, that's what she'd do.

So what if she was disqualified for not having a mechanic? The publicity alone should land her enough financial backers to build her orphans' home, whether or not she won the race. Besides, it would be worth it just to see the look on those judges' faces—on Jimmy's face—when she crossed the finish line. And this time she wouldn't be sitting in any old baggage car, crying her eyes out! Oh, no, not her.

She'd cried all the tears she ever intended to cry. She had no intention of wasting time on that now. With iron-willed determination, she swallowed hard, bit back the irritating moisture in her eyes, and, despite the terrible condition of the road, pressed down hard on the gas pedal.

Two hours had passed since Elizabeth had driven off. Jimmy's throat was parched with thirst and his stomach was growling from hunger. He'd followed the road for miles, hoping to find a creek or stream, but so far hadn't seen a drop of water anywhere.

Seeking a reprieve from the hot sun, he sought shelter beneath a grove of aspens.

Mopping his forehead with his handkerchief, he stared down the road, searching for some sign of a farmhouse or town. A flash of color on the road ahead caught his eye. Curious, he abandoned the shade to check it out. A bright pink ribbon lay curled on the road.

Recognizing it as one of the ribbons from Elizabeth's car, he picked it up and was immediately startled by a vision of big blue eyes.

Regret hit him like a ton of bricks; guilt taunted him. He grimaced and looked up at the sky. He had nothing to feel guilty about. He'd tried his utmost to help her. Hadn't he? If only she hadn't been so damned stubborn. . . . Pity the man who ever tried to tame her.

On impulse he stuffed the ribbon into his pocket. One never knew when a bright pink ribbon would come in handy.

He walked another mile or so down the road before noticing the sun reflecting off some shiny object in the distance. He picked up his pace, shading his eyes with a hand as he walked. Was that an automobile up ahead? He certainly hoped so.

He ran the remaining distance, waving his hat over his head and calling out, "Hello, there."

He slowed his pace, then stopped. A Model T Ford was parked on the side of the road, all four of its tires flat as yesterday's pancakes. The bright-colored ribbons that trailed down from the back bumper told him that his troubles were far from over.

His instinct was to turn around and go back in the direction from which he'd come. And if he had one sensible bone in his body, that's exactly what he would have done. What any sane man would have done. But he couldn't abandon her under the present circumstances. God, he'd never forgive himself.

It wasn't until he reached the disabled flivver that he saw her. What a sight she made, hunkered by the right front wheel, her lips pursed prettily. Wisps of blond hair blew in her face as she struggled with the iron ham bones.

He crossed his arms and leaned against the frame of Old Ironsides, casting a shadow across her path. She gazed up at him, her eyes dark with resentment and accusations. "Don't say a word," she warned, scowling furiously.

"I wouldn't think of it," he said with a lazy drawl. Actually, it was harder to keep from laughing than talking. Suddenly, the whole thing struck him as absurd. What in the world was he, a normally sensible man who took great pride in plotting his every move

well in advance, doing out here in the middle of
nowhere?

Then something caught his attention. He hunched
down and picked up an inch-long Pennsylvania nail.
The ground was covered with them.

Elizabeth dropped the iron ham bones. "A little gift
from Mr. Fastbender."

Jimmy sat back on his heels. "Fastbender did this?"

"He was waiting for me when I made the turn."

Jimmy shook his head in disbelief. He hated knowing that someone would purposely do such a vengeful
thing. He nodded toward the two spare tires. "Those
aren't going to do you much good."

"I thought maybe I could find a way to patch the
other two." She walked over to the running board and
pulled the patching kit from the toolbox.

He checked the two rear tires. He supposed it was
possible to patch the holes, but he doubted the repairs
would last long, especially given the poor condition of
the road. All four tires were worn thin in places, probably because of the bent axle. His only hope was to
patch the tires and hope to find a nearby farm, perhaps around the next bend.

He flung his carpetbag into the backseat and rolled
up his sleeves. "I'll take care of the tires if you get
me something to eat."

Elizabeth looked about to argue, then apparently
thought better of it. Without a word she relinquished
the crowbar to him and started digging inside the picnic basket in the backseat.

It took nearly two hours to change and repair the
tires and pick up all the nails that were scattered
across the road. "Go slow," he cautioned her after
cranking up the engine. "And try not to drive in the
potholes."

Luckily, they found a farm less than a mile down
the road.

"Stay here," Jimmy said. "I won't be long."

Elizabeth watched as Jimmy walked up the long

drive, past a mud wagon and vegetable garden, to the door of the wood-framed farmhouse.

She sat impatiently tapping her fingers against the steering wheel. Ten minutes stretched by, then fifteen. What was taking him so long? She had no idea why they'd stopped at the farm in the first place. It seemed to her the tires were working just fine. They were losing valuable time.

She was half tempted to take off without him, but of course she wouldn't. If it hadn't been for him, she would still be stranded on the road. Never had she been so glad to see anyone in her life as she was to see Jimmy. Even if he did give her that "all-knowing" look of his. Sheesh!

At last Jimmy emerged from the house, carrying a metal pail and a gunnysack.

Curious, Elizabeth climbed out of the car and regarded him with hands on her hips. "What do you have there?"

"Warm molasses and chicken feathers." He grinned at her. "It's an old trick I learned a few years back. This vulcanizes the tires much better than straw or even carbon."

Reaching into the sack, he pulled out a handful of feathers and dumped them into the bucket. "This works like an adhesive." He set the pail on the ground and stirred the mixture with a stick. After the feathers had been thoroughly blended into the molasses, he lifted the hand pump from the running board, poured the mixture into the canister, and began pumping it into one of the bald tires.

"We'll have to pick up a new pump at the next town," he said. After he'd finished pumping the sticky mixture into the two worn tires, he tossed the pump onto the heap of junk and headed for the water pump behind the farmhouse.

He primed the pump and washed his hands. He then ducked his head under the stream of cool water.

Elizabeth handed him a towel, then washed the road dust from her own face and hands.

She didn't welcome the thought of more hours on the road. What she longed for was a nice hot bath and a soft bed.

Jimmy handed her the towel. "That should do it," he said. He spun around and headed back to the car. "Let's go."

She watched him stroll away as if he hadn't a care in the world. How she hated knowing that he planned to leave her at the first opportunity. If only . . .

Angry at herself for wishing for things that could never come true, she trudged after him. Let him leave, if that's what he had his heart set on doing. See if she cared.

Oh, but she did care; she hated to think this was true, but she couldn't deny it, however much she wanted to. She didn't want him to leave. Not ever. And if she could think of a way to make him stay with her until the end of the race, she would be the happiest person in the world.

For the next twenty miles Elizabeth managed to drive without incident. Silently, Jimmy took full credit. Apparently a woman was capable of holding her own on the road as long as she had a man by her side watching her every move.

Though he was greatly relieved that his life was no longer in jeopardy, he was nonetheless worried; he hadn't seen a signpost for miles. They had picked up the much touted Lincoln Highway earlier. The newly paved road stretched from New York to San Francisco. Red, white, and blue bands had been painted on telephone poles to mark the road, along with a white letter L.

However, the highway was still incomplete, and they were constantly being rerouted through a confusing maze of detour signs. They hadn't seen a sign since the last detour and that had been at least ten miles back.

Catching a glimpse of Lake Erie through the thick grove of trees, he pulled out the map and spread it across his lap. The shaking and jostling of the car made it difficult to read, and it took him a while to find what he was looking for.

"If we continue at our present speed without any unscheduled stops, we should make it to the next town in little more than an hour." He glanced at her. "That should give us plenty of time to purchase new tires before the shops close. Maybe we'll even find a blacksmith to straighten that axle. I think the bent axle is wearing the rubber thin."

An hour. Not sure she could last that long, Elizabeth stifled a yawn. Lord love an orphan, she was tired. Her eyes felt as heavy as two paperweights. Her arms, her back, even her behind ached.

A rabbit dashed in front of them. In an effort to avoid hitting the little furry creature, Elizabeth swerved and drove over the splintered remains of a deserted wagon.

Two loud bangs momentarily drowned out the noisy engine. Old Ironsides spun like a child's top before coming to a stop.

For several stunned moments, neither Elizabeth nor Jimmy moved or said a word. Elizabeth sat holding on tight to the steering wheel, trying to make sense of her surroundings. Her first horrifying thought was that the sticky warm moisture dripping from her face was blood.

In a moment of panic, she pulled off her goggles and stared in confusion at the gooey substance on the lenses. It wasn't blood. It was . . . molasses and chicken feathers. She gasped as she looked down the front of her. She was covered with the sticky stuff!

"Isn't this just peachy!" Jimmy grumbled.

Her mouth dropped open at the sight of him. His clothes were covered in sticky goo. What an unbelievable mess! Why, she'd never seen anything like it in all her born days.

He climbed out of the car and stood with his arms stretched out to his sides. He looked like a scarecrow that had just been targeted by a flock of crows. But he didn't look as bad as Old Ironsides. Nothing could look that bad. The hood, the windshield, the sides, the interior—everything—was covered in molasses and feathers.

Groaning in dismay, Elizabeth pulled off her helmet and tossed it out of the car. "Now it's all my fault!" She sputtered, trying to spit the feathers out of her mouth. "You were the one who got the bright idea of filling the tires with molasses. . . ."

"If you had stayed on the road . . ."

"If you had . . . Oh, never mind!" She climbed out of the car and grabbed her suitcase from the backseat.

He eyed her with a look of suspicion. "And just where do you think you're going?"

"I'm going to clean up and then I'm going to . . ." She stopped upon hearing a crunching sound beneath her foot. She had inadvertently stepped on her spectacles. *"Ooooooh!* Never mind!"

# Chapter 9

"Fill tires only with clean, wholesome air!"
*Women at the Wheel*
Circa 1915

"Sheesh! Of all the stupid, asinine ...!" Muttering to herself, Elizabeth traipsed along a narrow path. Unable to think of words strong enough to express her anger and frustration, she clamped her mouth shut and dodged through an opening in the bushes that led to a narrow strip of deserted beach. The sparkling blue-green waters of Lake Erie stretched for as far as the eye could see, but she was in no mood to enjoy the scenery.

Since starting on this trip, it had been one thing after another. Nothing, however, compared to this latest disaster.

She set her suitcase in the sand and glanced around. A mild wind was blowing and choppy waves pawed the shoreline like cats toying with a mouse.

The cove was hidden from the road by a heavy growth of trees and bushes. Assured of her privacy, she worked the straps of her overalls down her arms, using only her fingertips. What a mess! The molasses had soaked through the fabric all the way to her undergarments.

She had no choice but to take off all her clothing. Feeling vulnerable, she grabbed a bar of Ivory soap

from her suitcase and, after an uneasy glance about
her, made a dash for the lake.

The water was freezing. She shuddered as the cold
bit into her skin, then braced herself before plunging
into the icy depths.

Brrrr. The chilly waters took her breath away. Teeth
chattering, she pulled the last of the hairpins from her
hair. Her hair floated behind her as she quickly
worked the soap across her shoulders and lathered
her arms.

Overhead, gray-white clouds skimmed across a
bright blue sky. She closed her eyes and ducked her
head beneath the water. Lord, love an orphan what
she wouldn't give for a hot bath—or even a tepid one!

She kept a wary eye on the shore as she scrubbed,
making certain she was still alone. She wondered what
Jimmy was doing.

Jimmy. If he hadn't looked a sight, his handsome
face all but hidden by feathers. Why, she hadn't seen
anything so ridiculous in her life. Her anger giving
way to amusement, she giggled. If he didn't look like a
furry monster that had been dragged out of a swamp!

His brilliant blue eyes had positively flashed with
indignation. Just thinking about the look on his face
turned her giggles to laughter. Jimmy was just going
to have to strip himself naked and . . .

The soap stilled in her hand as a startling vision
came to mind. Rather than the trepidation that such
a thought would normally evoke, she was strangely
fascinated. Her body suddenly glowed with a warmth
that was puzzling, given the frigid temperature of the
water. Could it be that she found Jimmy . . . well . . .
vaguely attractive?

Absolutely not! Sheesh! What could she be thinking? The idea was absurd! Ridiculous! Jimmy was to
blame for their present predicament. Feathers and molasses, indeed! Who else would think of such a stupid,
ridiculous idea? She wasn't attracted to him. She was

furious at him. Even if he did have the most intriguing blue eyes and crooked smile she'd ever set sight on.

She knitted her brows together and quickly scrubbed herself from top to bottom until every last feather, drop of molasses, and wayward thought had been thoroughly washed away.

*That's it,* Jimmy fumed. *Take your own sweet time.* She'd been gone for what had seemed like hours, though common sense told him it was probably closer to a half hour. Still, a half hour was enough time to bathe a passel of dirty youngsters. How dare she leave him by the side of the road looking like a swamp monster, with no means to clean himself or Old Ironsides.

At one point, he'd been forced to fight off a hungry hound who'd obviously mistaken him for a fowl. Bees buzzed around him; flies hovered. He felt like the main course at an outside banquet.

His ill temper increased when car number four approached. That annoying man Staggs jumped out with his ever-present camera in tow.

"Haven't seen anything like it since Uncle Ben's distillery blew up the chicken house," he shouted excitedly. "Would you stop shaking? I'm trying to take your photograph."

Jimmy didn't want his picture taken. What he wanted to do was smash the camera over Staggs's head.

No sooner had Staggs taken his picture and driven off than Billy Joe drove by in car number two, blowing his horn and waving his Stetson over his head.

Never in his life had Jimmy felt so humiliated. Never had he met such an annoying woman. Enough was enough! This was definitely it, the end of the road. He was finished, through! Kaput!

Angrily, he pulled off his clothes. Maybe he could sneak into the water without Elizabeth seeing him.

Just as he pulled off the last of his garments, he

heard a growling sound. The mangy hound was back
and somehow managed to look even more starved
than before. "Shoo. Go away!"

The dog growled and licked his chops.

"Go home, boy."

The hound growled again, showing its teeth.

Cursing beneath his breath, Jimmy grabbed his
towel, shot through the thick growth, and made a flying leap through an opening that led to the lake.

He burst out of the bushes only a few feet away
from where Elizabeth stood on the shoreline, drying
herself off. By the time he saw her nude glistening
body, he was running too fast to stop. He plowed into
her and the two of them plunged into the icy waters.

Elizabeth's screams practically pierced his eardrums.
Arms and legs flailing, she splashed about in the
water, sputtering with rage.

In a desperate attempt to save her from drowning,
he grabbed her. She fought like the dickens, and it
took every bit of his strength to contain her in his
arms. She stilled for a moment, her firm round breasts
pressing against his bare chest.

Their gazes locked for an instant before she pushed
him away. "Don't you touch me, you ... obnoxious
brute. . . . You're nothing but a rapist!"

Rapist? She couldn't be serious. He dropped his
hold on her, his face turning red. Of all the ungrate-
ful . . .

He tried to rescue her and what thanks did he get?
Despite his irritation, he was nonetheless taken aback
by the look of horror on her face. By gum! She honestly thought he was capable of doing the things she
accused him of.

"It's all right." He spoke with a calmness that belied
the confusion he felt, though he was forced to raise
his voice over hers. "I never meant ... I mean, I was
trying to escape ..." It wasn't until he swam a short
distance away from her that she finally stopped her
screeching, though she continued to call him every

name in the book. He was beginning to understand why she'd spent time in jail on an obscenities charge.

What a fetching sight she made. Her wet hair streamed around her lovely face and fell down her back. She held her arms modestly crossed in front, but she still couldn't hide the lovely full mounds of her breasts. "How dare you?" she cried accusingly, her eyes flashing blue fire. "I could have you arrested for assault and indecent exposure."

He rubbed his sore cheek where she'd hit him, his gaze resting on her creamy smooth shoulders. "Assault and indecent exposure would be a good place to start."

*"Ooooooh."* Her face red, her eyes snapped with renewed fury. "If you would be kind enough to turn your head."

"I won't look," he said, letting the current pull him farther away from shore. "But I think you ought to know there's an unfriendly dog out there."

"I'll take my chances!"

The growing distance between them seemed to have a calming effect on her, though it did little for his own peace of mind. Had it not been for the icy waters . . .

Wasn't this just peachy! Here he was, waist-deep in an icy lake, trying to escape a wild dog and a maniacal road hog, and what was he doing? Thinking carnal thoughts, that's what! Thinking about dragging her to that strip of beach and having his way with her, that's what. Thinking about what it would feel like to bury himself in that full-breasted, soft white body of hers!

Damn! Was he in trouble! BIG trouble! Admittedly, it had been a while since he'd last been with a woman, but he had no idea it had been *that* long. As soon as he got to Hogs Head—*if* he got to Hogs Head—he vowed to bed the first woman who would have him.

For now, he faced the grim prospect of calming his own rampaging male hormones while trying to convince the maddening woman in front of him that he had no romantic interest in her.

She eyed him as if trying to decide whether or not he could be trusted. What a glorious sight she made! He gave a ragged sigh and covered his eyes with his hand.

At last she turned and waded back to shore. "If you look, I'll know."

Despite her threat, he couldn't keep from watching her. His gaze swept down her smooth white back and lingered on her beguiling behind before dropping down to take in her shapely legs. After she wrapped the towel around her, he sucked in his breath and ducked beneath the icy-cold water.

# Chapter 10

"The only time a man willingly says 'I do' is when a woman asks him if he wants to drive."
*Women at the Wheel*
Circa 1915

Shivering, Jimmy searched for his towel, wrapped it around his waist, and walked barefooted back to the car.

Elizabeth, dressed in clean overalls, her hair neatly braided and pinned atop her head, pointedly ignored him. That was just jim-dandy as far as he was concerned. He was in no mood to get into another argument.

She had carted everything out of the backseat of the car and was busily clearing off the running board. Molasses and chicken feathers dripped down the side of the car. What an unbelievable mess.

Worse. The mangy dog was eating the last of Jimmy's Oreo biscuits. Jimmy reached for the carpetbag that Elizabeth had dumped on the pile with their supplies, and the dog bared its teeth.

"Hush now, doggie," Elizabeth said. She glared at Jimmy but said not a word to him. Holding his all too inadequate towel firmly in place, he disappeared into the bushes.

By the time he emerged, dressed in clean trousers and a blue chambray shirt, the dog was gone. And so was every last bit of dried ham, beef jerky, and Oreo biscuit. Wasn't that just great? Her attempts on his life having failed, she was now trying to starve him to death!

Feeling hungry and cold and more than a bit sorry for himself, Jimmy carried the canvas bucket down to the lake to fill it. Cleaning the sticky mess off Old Ironsides was going to be a bigger chore than he'd anticipated. He had no idea what to do about the tires.

He heaved the bucket back to the car and watched Elizabeth from the corner of his eye. Ah ha! He knew it. She was blushing!

The lady had protested too much, as they say—damn near acted like a wildcat—but she was definitely interested. *Wild on the road, wild in bed.* Maybe Crankshaw was right. Not that it mattered, of course. This last day or so was enough to convince him that a woman with a milder disposition would be more to his liking—and would certainly be kinder to his nerves.

Jimmy sighed in regret and Elizabeth looked up. She moistened her lower lip as their eyes met, her cheeks growing redder. She quickly looked away and Old Ironsides was afforded the most vigorous scrubbing imaginable.

Amused and unable to take his eyes off her, Jimmy set the bucket of water on the running board. Even her overalls struck him as more intriguing now that he'd glimpsed the luscious firm body that lay hidden beneath. Desire unlike anything he'd previously experienced flared like a bonfire within him, and his body shuddered in heated response.

Heart pounding, he sucked in air and forced himself to concentrate on scrubbing the square-topped rear fender.

The chug-chugging sound of an engine broke the strained silence between them. He wondered if it was one of the other racers, though he doubted it. Unless one of the other drivers had gotten lost or had major repairs, they had in all probability reached the next checkpoint by now.

The car rumbled into view and Jimmy tossed his rag into the bucket. Having learned his lesson about standing in the middle of the road, he stood to the side.

Jimmy identified it as a Model T touring car, but it was not one of the racers. Built before Henry Ford issued his renowned "Give them anything as long as it's black" mandate, the car was green with a wooden frame.

The motorist was a farmer whose deeply lined face was shaded by a straw hat. Next to him a middle-aged woman wore a veiled "beekeeper" bonnet to keep the road dust off her hair. The farmer pulled his car behind Old Ironsides and turned off the engine.

"Suffering catfish! What happened here?"

Jimmy walked up to the side of the farmer's car, grinning. "We had a dispute with a chicken."

"By the looks of things, I'd say the chicken won." The farmer climbed out of his car and shook Jimmy's hand. "Name's Parker. Leroy Parker. This here is my wife, Mabel."

"Jimmy Hunter." Jimmy shook the farmer's hand and tipped his flattened Panama hat toward Mabel. "And this is Miss Elizabeth Davenport."

The farmer's wife raised the hem of her bright floral dress and lifted a firm, sturdy leg over the door. Her lisle stockings puddled around her thick ankles as she lowered her heavy bulk onto the running board and stepped to the ground. "Glory be, aren't you the woman driver?" she asked, and then, spotting the placard on the side of Elizabeth's car, still dripping with molasses, she clapped her chubby square hands together. "You *are* the woman driver."

Elizabeth blushed. "How did you know?"

"Glory be, child! Your name has been in all the newspapers. Yes, indeed, right on the front page." The woman's excitement grew, her voice rising along with her eyebrows. "I never met a woman driver. I must tell you it's quite an honor to meet a celebrity like yourself."

"I'm afraid after today I won't be much of a celebrity," Elizabeth said ruefully. "We have two flat tires and no spares. It looks like I have no choice but to drop out of the race."

"Oh, dear." Mabel walked around Old Ironsides. "My, my, my. That had to be a pretty big chicken." She stared at what was left of the back tires. "Leroy will help you. He's very good at this kind of thing."

Leroy scratched his head. "It's going to be a little hard to do. I'm down to one spare myself."

Mabel refused to be discouraged. "We'll just have to take a tire off our own car."

"Oh, we couldn't allow you to do that," Elizabeth protested. "Why, you'd be stranded."

"Now don't you worry about a thing," Mabel said, her mind obviously made up. "It's for a good cause." She took Elizabeth's hand and patted it. "This isn't just for you, dearie. Why . . . you could well become the patron saint of women drivers."

"Oh, I don't think that's possible. . . ."

Jimmy noted the worried look that flitted across Elizabeth's face and sighed in relief. Obviously she found the notion of being a patron saint overwhelming, if not downright intimidating. Maybe now she would give up this harebrained scheme of hers to win the race. Nothing would please him more.

"Course it's possible," Mabel argued. "Fact is, it's necessary. Every woman in the country is counting on you to win the race."

"Really?" Elizabeth's eyes widened in surprise. "Women are really counting on me?"

His hopes dashed, Jimmy sighed and pushed his hands into his pants pockets. Judging by the look of "divine vision" that crossed Elizabeth's face, Mabel had effectively squelched his last hope of Elizabeth giving up the race.

"Absolutely. Why, that's all we talked about at our

last quilting bee," Mabel declared. "Now don't you worry about a thing. My Leroy will have you on the road in no time flat."

Jimmy rubbed his hand across his chin. "That's mighty kind of you both, but it's really not necessary to put yourself out like this. We've lost a lot of time and I'm not sure we can make it up...."

"Of course we can make it up!" Elizabeth exclaimed, nodding her head in determination.

He frowned at her. It was one thing to think positive, but it was nonsense to continue this charade. "How can you think such a thing? Fastbender must be hours ahead of us by now, and his car is in much better condition than Old Ironsides."

Already, Elizabeth's car was missing a front fender and bumper from their rendezvous with that barn. At the rate they were dropping parts, there'd be nothing left of the car by the time they reached Seattle.

"I don't care," Elizabeth said stubbornly. "You're absolutely right, Mabel. I owe it to every woman in this country to win this race."

Mabel clapped her hands together. "Spoken like a true saint. I can hardly wait to tell the members of the Tuesday Morning Quilting Bee I met you in person. Why, they might even see fit to make me president."

Since Elizabeth's mind was set, Jimmy wasted no more time. The sooner they were on the road again, the sooner he could wash his hands of the whole affair! He and the farmer set to work, pulling the front tire off the farmer's car.

While the men changed tires, the two women scrubbed Old Ironsides.

As much as Elizabeth enjoyed Mabel's company, she couldn't seem to concentrate on what the woman was saying. She was too busy trying to ignore Jimmy—and failing miserably. Her eyes seemed to take on a life of their own. No matter how much she tried to concentrate on cleaning the car, she inadvertently found herself following Jimmy's every move.

Changing tires was no easy task under normal conditions, but today it took the strength of both men to pull the shredded rubber tubes off the rims and install the replacements.

Now that she knew what Jimmy looked like without clothing, she had a new appreciation of the muscles in his back, muscles that rippled and bunched beneath his shirt as he worked, like the waves in a mighty sea.

She recalled in vivid detail every line, every plane of his strong yet well-proportioned body, all the way from his bare chest down his washboard-straight abdomen and strong, sturdy legs. Ah, but that wasn't all she recalled, and no matter how hard she tried to control herself, she inadvertently found herself staring at the front of his trousers.

Catching herself, a fast burn sprang to her already hot cheeks. What in the world was the matter with her? Why, she had no interest in Jimmy. Not in that sense. It was pleasant, of course, to meet up with a childhood friend, but if she never saw him again after the race, it would be no skin off her nose. None!

Feeling somewhat relieved, she went back to her scrubbing, only to find herself gazing at the image of him reflected in the beveled side mirror.

Mabel leaned toward her and whispered in her ear, "You don't know how lucky you are that your nice young man lets you drive."

Embarrassed, Elizabeth quickly averted her eyes and rubbed her wet rag across the hood. Was she really so obvious? "What? Oh, he's not my young man. He's my mechanic."

"Really?" Mabel glanced at Jimmy, then back to Elizabeth. "Are you sure that's all he is?"

"Of course I'm sure," Elizabeth said stiffly, and when Mabel looked unconvinced, she felt obliged to explain. "He's not nearly so nice as you might suppose. He doesn't approve of my driving."

Mabel gasped in horror. "You don't say!"

"Absolutely. He complains all the time I'm behind the wheel. You should hear him. He calls me a road hog and a speed demon."

Mabel looked properly appalled. "Oh, my." She gave Elizabeth a motherly pat on the back. "Well, don't you let him discourage you."

"Nothing's going to discourage me." Elizabeth glanced toward Jimmy and nearly fainted upon discovering he'd taken off his shirt.

"Your, eh . . . what did you call him? . . . mechanic, isn't the only one who disapproves of women drivers. My Leroy's a good man, but he won't let me drive. He says women have no business driving machinery."

"It's not any harder than driving a horse and wagon," Elizabeth said. She scrubbed the leatherette seat, purposely keeping her eyes focused on the task at hand.

"That's what I told Leroy. But do you think he'll listen? If you finish the race, you'll inspire more women to take the wheel. That's the only way some of us will ever get our men to cotton to the idea."

Elizabeth jumped to the ground and squeezed the older woman's arm. "I promise you I'll finish the race, Mabel. No matter what happens. You wait and see."

Mabel folded her hands together and gave a determined nod, as if the two of them had ratified a secret pact.

It was almost dark by the time Elizabeth and Jimmy were ready to hit the road again.

Jimmy carried the acetylene supply canister around to the front of the car and filled the two headlamps with the gas. He then added solid carbide and pulled out a box of Bryant and May's motor matches.

"Stand back," he warned, and Elizabeth, Mabel, and Leroy stepped away from the car. Elizabeth kept a worried eye on Jimmy. Acetylene lamps were known to explode and required constant maintenance, but they were infinitely more practical than candle lamps.

It took only a quick touch of the match before a hissing sound escaped, signaling that the water was dripping properly onto the carbide. After the front lamps were lit and burned brightly, Jimmy repeated the process with the single red-glass lantern in back.

Elizabeth breathed a whole lot easier when at last Jimmy carried the brass canister back to the sideboard of the car and strapped it in place. The carbide would have to be renewed in four hours, but with a little luck they should reach their destination long before then.

"Ready?" he called to Elizabeth.

She nodded and gave Mabel a hug. "I can't tell you how much I appreciate what you've done for us. I won't ever forget your kindness."

"Don't mention it," Mabel said. "You win that race, you hear?"

"I'll give it my best." Elizabeth didn't feel right about leaving the Parkers stranded. "Are you sure we can't drive you back to your farm?"

"Don't be ridiculous," Mabel said. "You've lost enough time, already. Besides, you'll never get Leroy to leave his automobile. Now don't you go worrying about a thing. When we purchased the horseless vehicle, we made a rule: If we don't show up by suppertime, our sons have to come lookin' for us."

Mabel gave them the milk and cheese she had planned to deliver to a neighbor, along with some freshly baked bread. Jimmy moved to the front of the car to start the engine, then the Parkers stood by the side of the road and waved as Elizabeth drove off.

The steady white light of the acetylene headlamps illuminated only a small portion of the road, making it difficult to drive much faster than five or six miles an hour without missing a curve or crashing into a tree.

Jimmy had been uncharacteristically silent since leaving the Parkers. Other than an occasional warning to slow down, he said nothing about her numerous near misses.

Feeling strangely nervous in his presence, strangely

shy, she slid a quick glance in his direction. Never had the cab of the Model T felt so confined.

Since the episode on the beach, she was utterly aware of his maleness. This heightened interest in Jimmy stimulated an alarming, though no less intriguing, new awareness of herself. The protective shell she wore like armor had taken her a lifetime to perfect. Now suddenly it felt as fragile as a broken vase.

The previously dormant womanly part of her responded to his presence as if answering an urgent call.

It was too dark to see much more than his profile outlined by the headlamps, and for that she was grateful. If she couldn't see him clearly, then he couldn't see her. Her burning cheeks wouldn't give her away, nor would the alarming fact that she couldn't keep her eyes off him.

She had thought him handsome, but had never noticed his splendid profile. It was rugged and well-defined, with a straight nose and a strong jaw. Of course nothing could top his manly splendor as he came flying out of the bushes earlier that day.

Naked as a jaybird.

Just thinking about it made her feel all shivery and warm inside. True, his nakedness had startled her at first. Frightened her. But amazingly enough, she'd felt no revulsion. In retrospect, she realized that that fact was what had frightened her most, what had sent her senses reeling.

She'd never thought to see a naked man without shame or fear and maybe even disgust. But today, after the first initial shock, she'd felt none of the usual feelings of degradation. Instead, a tingling warmth had washed over her that was in many ways more frightening because of its newness. It wasn't Jimmy she'd fought off in that lake. It was her own confused feelings.

She glanced at him again, and in the white glow of the gaslights met his heated gaze for an instant before turning her head to watch the road. Her heart beat so quickly she was hardly aware of the jolting, rocking motion of Old Ironsides as it barreled through the night.

*He's thinking about me, about seeing me naked.* She knew this as surely as she knew her name. She tried to calm herself—think rationally. Jimmy wasn't Mylar Carson. He wasn't going to force himself on her.

This statement became a chant that she repeated over and over in her head as they drove along that dark deserted road. Eventually, she believed it, but having put the one fear to rest, she was assailed by another.

What if by some remote chance they grew close to one another? Not that she had any intention of letting such a thing happen. But what if they did? Would he find her body unattractive or otherwise lacking?

She recalled with chilling clarity the humiliation of being pinched and poked as a child by all those farmers and their wives. She'd been denounced as skinny or weak more times than she cared to remember.

Those memories, along with the horror of what Mylar had done to her—and the terrible lack of privacy in jail—had had a grueling effect on her. As a result, she'd guarded her body against further invasion by wearing mannish clothes and hiding behind eyeglasses and goggles and, in some cases, an acid tongue.

She considered this necessary for survival and never thought much about her appearance. Until now. Now she wished with all her heart she wasn't skinny or plain.

She recalled the moment Jimmy came flying out of the trees as naked as the day he was born. For one brief and painful moment, she had wanted to be beautiful, just for him. Embarrassed and disconcerted by the revelation, she pushed the memory away, along with her unsettling thoughts.

She didn't care a mule's ass what Jimmy Hunter thought. He was a man, and as much as she didn't want to believe it possible of Jimmy, she knew from painful experience that men were capable of doing terrible, terrible things.

It was ten-fifteen that night before Elizabeth pulled into checkpoint number two. She was tired and bedraggled, her eyes gritty as sandpaper. Every muscle in her body screamed with pain. Her head throbbed, and even though she knew it wasn't possible, even her eyebrows seemed to ache.

Jimmy stirred awake as soon as she turned off the engine. Old Ironsides shuddered and groaned, its lights growing dim as the last of the carbide melted away.

Jimmy climbed out of the car, stretched, and reached for his carpetbag. "I'm sorry, Elizabeth. This is where we part company." He looked exhausted, and the glow of a nearby arc light emphasized the lines of weariness etched in his face.

She gave the steering wheel a frustrated shake before sliding across the seat and hopping to the ground after him.

The poor man was tired, but dammit, so was she! "You can't quit now," she pleaded. "Please, Jimmy, say you'll stay. You heard Mabel. This isn't just about me anymore. This is about women everywhere."

"If you think for one moment I am going to spend one more day in that . . . that rattletrap while you try to kill me, you best think again."

"Jimmy, please . . ."

He searched her face in the silver glow of the streetlight, and she instinctively shrank back in the shadows as she had learned to do during all those times she'd been scrutinized during the orphan auctions.

What was he looking for, anyway? The gentle, quiet, and naive little girl of long ago? Well, he wasn't going to find her. Not now. Not ever. For that little girl no longer existed.

"Forget it!" she bit out. "I don't need your help."

Expecting an argument, she was surprised and more

than a little disappointed when Jimmy spun on his heel without another word and stormed away.

Hands at her waist, Elizabeth watched until he'd disappeared through the brass-framed doors of the hotel. *You'll be sorry, Jimmy Hunter. You wait and see!*

# Chapter 11

"Some states have traffic laws!"

*Women at the Wheel*
Circa 1915

It was the morning of day three. Dressed in a fresh pair of overalls, her hair braided and pinned neatly, Elizabeth paced impatiently, wearing a path in the ground around her Model T.

The hours had gone by all too quickly. Her twelve-hour stopover was due to end in twenty minutes and she was still without a mechanic.

The driver of car number nine, Cabbie O'Brian, had been taken to the hospital with stomach pains and was reportedly too ill to continue the race. She tried to convince the driver's mechanic, a man named Moe, to work for her.

Moe's pencil-thin mustache twitched and his beady eyes kept darting back and forth as they talked, as if he feared lurking eavesdroppers. "I can't work for a woman," he exclaimed, looking insulted. "Why I'd be the laughingstock of my profession."

Why Moe considered dropping out of a race more noble than working for a woman was a puzzle, but no matter how much she pointed out the flaw in his reasoning, he refused to change his stubborn fool mind.

One car was scratched and two cars had failed to make it out of New York. That left seven cars in the race. Her competitors, for the most part, were at least a couple of hours ahead of her. How could she make up that much time? Without a mechanic, she couldn't even race.

For the love of an orphan, what was she going to do?

As much as she hated to admit it, she needed Jimmy Hunter. Still, she had her pride. If he didn't want to be with her, she wasn't going to beg!

Not knowing what else to do and unable to remain idle for long, she cranked up the Tin Lizzie herself. It required a strong arm and a quick foot and today she managed both without missing a beat. Strangely comforted by the chugging rhythm of the engine, she patted the fender like she would a faithful old dog. "Don't you worry, Old Ironsides," she said, surprised to find herself using Jimmy's pet name for the vehicle. "I'll find someone to take care of you—you just wait." Suddenly, she had an idea. Positive it would work, she eagerly climbed behind the wheel.

She swung a wide U-turn in the middle of the street and pulled the car in front of the official checkpoint. A robust race official wearing a plaid suit stepped forward with an unbearable air of importance, carrying a clipboard.

He walked around the car before reaching Elizabeth's side. "Where's your mechanic?" he asked, a cigarette dangling from his thick lips.

"He . . . eh . . . Mr. Hunter will no longer be riding with me."

The official blew smoke in her face. "You can't race without a mechanic."

She coughed and fanned the smoke away with her hand. As much as she hated the thought of having to ask such an obnoxious and arrogant man for anything, she had no choice. "I have a problem I'd hoped you could help me with." The man looked interested, and feeling encouraged, she continued. "I don't have a mechanic, but it's terribly important I finish the race. You don't happen to know anything about engines, do you?"

"Me?" The man gave her a leering smile. "I know a thing or two. Whadaya want to know?"

"I thought perhaps you might like to be in the race. You know, as my mechanic."

The man thought for a moment. "Perhaps we could make a little deal."

Elizabeth didn't like the way the man was looking at her. She didn't like it at all, and she fought against the panic that began to rise inside. Swallowing hard, she forced herself to respond in a calm voice. "What kind of a deal?"

He touched her arm with his fingertips. Startled, she pulled away. He didn't look fazed in the least. "I'll take care of your engine if you take care of mine."

Sickened and repulsed, Elizabeth reached for the fuel lever. "I'm not interested."

"Now wait just a minute." His hand clamped onto her steering wheel and his eyes seemed unnaturally bright. She glanced across the seat, searching for something to use as a weapon. She wasn't sure if she could reach the umbrella in back.

"You and I could have ourselves a good time," the official said, smirking. He tossed his cigarette onto the ground. "A real good time."

"If you would kindly let me proceed," she said icily, "I'll forget that you and I had this discussion."

"I don't want you to forget." His hand dropped from her wrist to her lap. "What's the matter, Miss Davenport? You too good for me?"

Elizabeth tried pushing his arm away, but he sank his fingers deeper into her leg and held on relentlessly, taunting her. "You want a mechanic, you got one. The first thing a good mechanic does is check out the engine parts." He literally lifted her from the seat and dragged her kicking and screaming out of the open car.

Her vision blurred and suddenly all the memories

of the past came back to haunt her. The squeezing of
arms and legs. The trips to the barn. The shameful
horror. Not again!

She absolutely refused to let another man have his
way with her. Lashing out, she swung her leg and
kicked her attacker in the groin.

His eyes bulged. Releasing her, he grabbed his
crotch. "Why, you little . . ." He advanced toward her,
his fleshy face red with anger.

He grabbed her by the wrist and she fought him off
with every bit of strength she had, realizing as she did
so that in the past it had never been enough.

Jimmy had dragged himself out of bed that morning
with the greatest reluctance. Every bone in his body
ached. Every muscle screamed. He hadn't slept a
wink, but it wasn't the physical pain that had kept him
pacing the floor at such ungodly hours. It was
Elizabeth.

The darn fool woman had slept in her car. Again!
It wasn't safe for a woman to spend the night alone
parked on a deserted street in an unfamiliar town.
He'd stood by his hotel window for the better part of
the night, watching the flivver, just to make certain
she was safe.

In the wee hours of the morning, Jimmy glimpsed
a moving shadow. He'd twisted his back trying to hang
on to the windowsill while craning his neck to see
through the branches of an overgrown tree. Fortunately, it was only a cat. Still, he was lucky he hadn't
fallen out of the second-story window altogether and
broken his bloody fool neck.

After his morning ablutions, he headed for the hotel
dining room. With a little luck, he would be back in
Hogs Head that night, where he could put this unfortunate experience behind him.

Of course he hated the idea of abandoning Elizabeth, but who could blame him? She was, as the old
saying went, an accident waiting to happen. Actually,

he was doing her a favor by quitting while they were both still alive. If she had any sense in that pretty little head of hers, she'd hightail it back to where she came from and forget about the race.

She had the easy job; his would be considerably harder. For not only did he have to renege on a childhood promise, he was also faced with the difficult task of forgetting her all over again. Hell, if he hadn't been able to forget her after twenty years, would he have any better luck now, after what had happened yesterday at the lake?

The vision he had carried of her all through his childhood and adult years was gone forever. She was now a woman in every sense of the word and it would be a long time—a very long time—before he could forget how beautiful she'd looked standing in the light of day, her naked loveliness outlined against the magnificent expanse of sky and water.

The sight of her pretty pert breasts and nicely rounded hips had filled him with an aching need that refused to go away. Even when he managed to think of other things, the strange hollow aching remained. He sighed and stepped into the hotel dining room.

The driver of car number one, Sir Higginbottom, sat by the window.

"I see you made it, young man," Higginbottom called over to him in his clipped British accent. "Come and join me."

"Thank you." Jimmy walked over to Sir Higginbottom's table and sat down opposite him.

Sir Higginbottom wore a full-length duster to protect his street clothes from road dust. "I must say that young woman driver puts on a bloody good show. Saw her taking off like one of those newfangled flying machines the other day. Would you like a spot of tea?"

Though he would have preferred a strong cup of coffee, Jimmy nodded.

Sir Higginbottom signaled for the waiter, then lifted

the teapot and filled Jimmy's cup. After the waiter took Jimmy's order, the Englishman cleared his throat and glanced around. "I hope you don't mind me asking, but I can't help but be curious. Has she tried anything?"

Jimmy lowered his cup. "I beg your pardon?"

"Miss Davenport. Has she tried anything?"

Jimmy decided he really did need that coffee. "I'm not sure I understand your meaning."

The Englishman looked down his long narrow nose. "You do know she served time on an obscenities charge?"

Jimmy set his cup down with a clink. "So I heard. Eh ... you wouldn't happen to know what she was accused of doing, exactly, would you?" Obscenities was rather a vague term. It could mean anything from disrobing in public to performing illicit sexual acts. Judging by the way she overreacted when he'd inadvertently touched her breast in the lake, neither seemed likely. What then could she have possibly done to warrant time in jail?"

Sir Higginbottom stroked his mustache. "If I recall, it was a book she wrote. A shockingly scandalous and obscene book."

Jimmy couldn't believe his ears. "Elizabeth ... eh ... Miss Davenport wrote ... eh ... Do you know what the book was about?"

"I have no idea. I was in England at the time it was published. But my mechanic's brother's best friend's sister knows someone who read it. From what I gather, it was quite graphic in content. Heard it was the most shocking book written by a woman since *Jane Eyre*."

"You think *Jane Eyre* shocking, do you?"

"Of course it's shocking. Now I ask you, what's a woman doing writing about love and passion? Next they'll be writing books describing the act of procreation."

The waiter brought two plates stacked high with

flapjacks, and Jimmy fell silent. What in heaven's name was his Elizabeth doing writing obscene books? Not that she was *his* Elizabeth, of course, and he supposed she could write anything she damned well pleased. Still, he felt betrayed, and more than a little foolish, for holding on to a vision of his childhood sweetheart that apparently had nothing to do with reality.

Sir Higginbottom wiped his mouth with the edge of his linen napkin. "I say, young man, we need to do something about that Billy-Joe chap. He's been pulling too many pranks. Crankshaw caught him trying to change the road signs yesterday. In the name of King George, if the man had gotten away with it, we'd all be in Kentucky.

"What do you propose we do?"

"I have no idea, but—" He stopped and glanced out the window. "Good heavens, what is all that racket?"

"It sounds like a fight." Jimmy rose to his feet and peered through the lace curtains for a closer look.

Sir Higginbottom nodded vigorously. "By thunder, it *is* a fight. And if I'm not mistaken, it appears to involve your driver."

Jimmy's heart sank faster than an anvil in a rain barrel. Sir Higginbottom was not mistaken, and if Jimmy could believe his eyes, Elizabeth fully intended to wallop one of the race officials senseless with her umbrella.

Jimmy backed away from the window, almost falling over his chair, and tore through the dining room and lobby with the Englishman close at his heels.

By the time they ran out the front door of the hotel, a riot had broken out. Jimmy pushed his way through the crowd, ducking flying fists and stepping around two men rolling on the ground.

Jimmy grabbed hold of the race official's collar, pulled him away from Elizabeth, and sent him sprawling in the dirt.

"Come on!" He reached for Elizabeth's hand.

She raised what was left of her tattered umbrella as if to clobber him, then dropped her arms. "Oh, thank God, Jimmy. I thought you were *him*." She was gasping for breath and Jimmy feared she was going to faint.

Lord, she looked like she'd been to war and back. Her overalls were ripped in several places, the straps hanging down her arm. Her hair had come unpinned and had fallen to her shoulders in tangled strands. Her face was pale.

"Let's get out of here," Jimmy said. "Get in."

"What?"

"Get in the car!"

He boosted her into the seat and quickly started the engine with a few swift turns of the crank.

By now the official had managed to pull himself up on his feet. Holding on to an iron hitching post, his forehead bleeding, the man shook an angry fist at her. "Stay right where you are!"

Jimmy hopped into his seat. "Go!" he shouted.

Elizabeth turned on the gas lever and jammed her foot down hard on the gas pedal. Old Ironsides sped ahead with squealing tires and blaring horn.

Grabbing on to the door, Jimmy opened his mouth to complain, but upon seeing the excited mob chasing after them, led by the angry official, he decided against it. As unlikely as it seemed, there were worse fates than driving full speed ahead with Elizabeth at the wheel.

He waited until they were several miles out of town before he insisted she slow down. His arms folded across his chest, he glared straight ahead, not trusting himself to talk.

They drove in silence for several more miles. Though the dirt road was fairly smooth, with hardly any ruts, she drove with less than her usual exuberance.

"Would you mind telling me what ever possessed you to beat up on a race official?" His voice held a cold, hard edge, but he couldn't help it. He was angry, dammit, and for good reason. He fully expected to be on the train to Hogs Head by now.

"He deserved everything he got and more."

The fury and hatred in her voice surprised him, and forgetting his own anger, he studied her pale face. "Did you know him?"

"Never met him before in my life."

"Did he . . . try something? Elizabeth?"

"It doesn't matter."

*Dammit, Elizabeth, look at me. Talk to me. Make me understand.* She wouldn't look at him and he felt as if a door had closed between them. "It matters, Elizabeth," he said with none of his earlier rancor. "Of course it matters. A man has no right to force his attentions on a woman." Her lips trembled and he knew he had hit upon the truth. Sickened with outrage, he drove a fist into his palm. "No right at all!"

She looked at him, her mouth open in surprise, and he could swear that behind the amber glass of her goggles her eyes glistened with tears. "Elizabeth?"

She turned to survey the road ahead. "How far to the next town?"

Sighing, he reached for the map. "We'll report him at the next check-in."

"No!"

Jimmy glanced at her sharply. "We can't let him get away with that. He had no right."

"No one will believe me, Jimmy."

"They'll believe me!"

"The only thing they're going to believe is what he tells them."

"What he did was wrong and he should pay the consequences!"

"What consequences, Jimmy? I'm the one with the bad reputation. Chances are he'll tell everyone I'm the one who made improper advances. Heaven help us if the newspaper gets hold of this. The last scandal caused me enough problems. If it hadn't been for all the negative publicity, the orphans' house would have been built by now. Another scandal and I'll never accomplish my goal."

Jimmy slapped his palm on the rim of the door in frustration. What she said was undoubtedly true, but he didn't like it. He didn't like it one bit. He felt a powerful, almost fierce need to protect her. "I think we should make a formal complaint to Mr. Ford at the end of the race."

She turned her head toward him. "At the end . . . ? Does this mean you're still my mechanic?"

"No! I mean yes. Hell, I don't know what I mean. Pull over."

"What?"

"You heard me. Pull over."

She steered to the side of the road and screeched to a stop. Peeling his face away from the dashboard, he fought for control. He didn't have the heart to yell at her, not after what she'd gone through that day. Not after seeing the tears that she obviously hadn't wanted him to see. Feeling strangely at odds with himself, he made a quick decision. "I'll be your mechanic until we reach Hogs Head, but that's as far as I'm going."

"But . . ."

"Let me finish." He cleared his throat. "When we reach Hogs Head, I'll help you find another mechanic. Agreed?"

She nodded, though it was obvious she did so with a great deal of reluctance. "Agreed." She looked about to take off again.

"Wait. We're not done yet."

"Well, say your piece, Jimmy Hunter, and be done with it. I haven't got all day."

"Very well," he said, relieved to see her old fighting spirit return. "As long as I'm your mechanic, you will obey my rules. You'll stay on the road and you'll not go one notch above thirty-five miles an hour on country roads and eight miles in town. Is that clear?"

"How do you expect me to win a race crawling along like an injured snail?"

"How do you expect to win the race when you keep driving off the road?"

"You don't have to yell."

"I'm not yelling," Jimmy yelled. "But so help me, Elizabeth, if you even think of speeding, I'm through. Do you understand? Finished! Kaput!"

It was a tough bargain, but Elizabeth had no choice but to agree to his terms. The rules of the race required her to travel with a mechanic. Like it or not, he was the only mechanic available. Suddenly, an idea occurred to her. Maybe if she did everything he told her to do, he'd change his mind and stay with her all the way to Seattle.

She glanced at him sideways. It was obvious from the way he was holding on to the door frame that he meant business. She would have to be careful. If he suspected the real reason she had so much trouble staying on the road, she would lose him for certain.

Squinting through her goggles, she pulled away from the side of the road ever so slowly. The goggles were designed to keep the road dust and glare out of her eyes, but did nothing for her poor vision. She felt sick at having broken her tortoiseshell spectacles. With their saddle bridge and full riding-bow temples that fit snugly around her ears, they had been as comfortable as they were functional, as long as she wasn't driving a car.

She chanced a glance at Jimmy, who was watching the speedometer with a look of approval. Stifling the smile that played on her lips, she held the steering wheel straight, so as not to weave, and prayed the road didn't make any unexpected turns. She could just barely make out the needle on the speedometer and it was pointing at the thirty-miles-per-hour mark.

Oh, yes, she could do this. It would be hard, but if she could get Jimmy to stay with her for the remainder of the race, it would be well worth the effort.

# Chapter 12

"Ignore a red light at your own peril."
*Women at the Wheel*
Circa 1915

Jimmy couldn't believe it; they had actually driven for an hour with only a few close calls. Elizabeth had nearly missed a turn—and had pretty near wiped out a flock of sheep—but for the most part she'd stayed on the road and maintained a reasonable speed.

Jimmy found himself actually beginning to enjoy the ride, even though his backside ached from the constant jostling and his long legs felt cramped.

The Model T race had been mapped out to take the drivers off the main road through countryside resplendent with rolling green hills. Patches of yellow and purple wildflowers dotted the hills like colorful scraps of fabric spread across a dressmaker's floor. Dazzling whitewashed farmhouses were surrounded by flowering peach trees and the air was fragrant with the sweet smell of spring.

Full-leafed sycamores and liquidambars stood on either side of the road like watchful sentinels. The car traveled along a dirt road, but it was graded and well-maintained.

Jimmy filled his lungs with the clear fresh air and lifted his face toward the sun that filtered through the overhead branches. Yes, indeed, he'd been right to put his foot down.

"See, what did I tell you?" he said at length. "Easy does it. Stay on the road and keep to a respectable speed and everything will work out just peachy."

"You were absolutely right, Jimmy. I should have listened to you from the very start."

Thinking she was perhaps a bit too compliant for his peace of mind, he cast a wary eye in her direction. Due to the ever-present goggles and driving helmet, he couldn't see much more than her upturned nose and her pretty, pink, bow-shaped mouth, but her chin seemed less stubborn than usual. Perhaps she really was sincere about following the rules he had set down. Lord, he hoped so.

When she glanced his way and caught him staring, he quickly turned his attention to the map, but he couldn't contain his curiosity. He wanted to know everything about her, from the moment he'd last seen her at the age of seven to the present day. He had so little to go on. The rumors he'd heard coupled with the fleeting, but no less disturbing, glimpses of anger that seemed to simmer just below her surface made him more curious than ever.

Many authors had written scandalous books and had not spent time in jail. What in the world could she have written to justify being treated like a criminal? Did she write about illicit sex? He watched her from the corner of his eye. *Deviant* sex? What was it?

Was Crankshaw right? Could it really be true that a brazen, fearless driver was also a wild lover?

He glanced at Elizabeth—and she at him. Something—some electrical spark—exploded between them, like fireworks on a summer night, before they quickly turned away to stare at the road ahead.

He vowed to purchase a copy of Elizabeth's book at the very next town. Then he'd know without a doubt what exactly she had written.

In his mind's eye, he could still see her standing in naked splendor, her lovely slim body outlined by the

sea, her glorious hair highlighted by the dazzling rays
of the sun.

Grimacing against the aching need that such memories incurred, he forced himself to focus on the map
in his lap, following the line that ran the width of
Ohio and into his home state of Indiana. A lot of help
that was! Rather than help him block out the disturbing thoughts that continued to plague him, the
map only made matters worse.

He'd lived in Indiana for twenty of his twenty-seven
years and never knew there were towns with such *interesting* names. A dot marked the town of French
Lick. He pulled his gaze to another part of the map
and noticed a town named Sexton. He was shocked
to find himself poring over the map, studying each
state in turn, searching for towns with names that had
sexual overtones.

Damn Elizabeth and her book! Disgusted with himself, he folded the map and slid it into its leather index
case. He didn't trust Elizabeth to drive unless under
his watchful eye, and it was for this reason that he
fought the drowsiness that threatened to overcome
him. But lack of sleep made it nearly impossible for
him to keep his eyes open. Finally, not even the terrible jolting motions of the Model T could keep him
awake.

He awoke with a start and checked the watch he'd
purchased in the last town. It was after four. Why
hadn't they arrived in Wheeler by now? He studied
the passing scenery, looking for a familiar landmark.
"Where are we?"

"Don't you know?" she asked. "You have the
map."

He spotted a sign and almost fell off his seat. It
couldn't be. He sat up straight in his seat. "What the
hell are we still doing in Ohio?"

"What makes you think we're still in Ohio?"

"That's Cincinnati ahead and the last time I looked
that was in Ohio."

She stared at him in confusion, unaware apparently that she was weaving from one side of the street to the other. "All I did was follow the road."

"You couldn't have followed the road." He pulled the map out of the leather case, but he didn't need a map to tell him they were going south, not east. They drove by a signpost that confirmed his suspicions and headed down Euclid Avenue. "Turn right at the next street."

"I'm not going down that street," she said, looking self-righteous. "It's a red-light district."

"A red ...?" He looked up as they drove beneath two wooden crossarms rising at least fifteen feet above the intersection. Bright red lights were attached to the arms. He'd never seen anything like it before. Most towns hid their red-light districts, but Cincinnati was unabashedly advertising theirs for all the world to see. "Turn down the next street."

Upon reaching the next intersection, she slammed on her brakes. Jimmy had grown accustomed to her abrupt stops and had braced himself accordingly.

The policeman who had been following directly behind them on his two-wheeled bicycle, however, wasn't so lucky. The front of the bicycle plowed straight into the back of Elizabeth's car with a gut-wrenching thud.

Elizabeth and Jimmy watched with openmouthed horror as the poor officer sailed over the handlebars of his bicycle and into the backseat of Elizabeth's flivver, headfirst.

"Good heavens!" Jimmy exclaimed. He quickly scrambled over his seat to assist the unfortunate lawman. "Are you all right, officer?"

The officer sputtered as he fought his way into a sitting position. "No, I'm not all right!" He glared at Elizabeth. "You drove through a red light."

Elizabeth and Jimmy exchanged glances. "Is that against the law?" Jimmy asked.

"Of course it's against the law! You're supposed to stop for a red light. Do you hear me? Stop!"

Elizabeth frowned. "But why?"

The policeman stared at her in exasperation. "To let the traffic flow on the crossroad. When the light turns green, two long buzzes will sound and that means traffic is permitted to proceed down Euclid. Traffic wishing to cross on One hundred and fifth Street must wait for one buzz."

"I didn't hear any buzzes, did you, Jimmy?"

"That's because you had the red light. You were supposed to stop and wait for your buzz."

"That's a pretty interesting system." Jimmy was impressed. His mind immediately jumped on the possibilities. Why, it wouldn't be all that difficult to install a similar light in his hometown of Hogs Head. He pulled a notebook out of his pocket to scribble down notes. It would certainly solve the problem of those endless traffic jams that occurred whenever an argument broke out over right of way. "I think this buzzer light is a damned good idea. You and your town should be commended."

"You think so, eh?" The shiny brass buttons on the policeman's blue uniform shone in the sun. "We're the first town to have such a light, you know. Not even New York or Washington has one yet."

"The first, you say?" Jimmy gazed back at the light which had turned green. If he had his way, Hogs Head would be the second town with such a light.

"Yes, indeed." The policeman climbed out of the backseat, surveyed his mangled bicycle, and strolled over to Elizabeth's side of the car. "And your name is . . . ?"

"Davenport," Elizabeth said. "Miss Davenport."

The policeman gave no indication of having heard of her. "Pleased to meet you, Miss Davenport. You might be interested to know of another first." He pulled out a pad and made notations on it with a magic screw pencil. He then tore out a sheet of paper and handed it to her. "You're the first driver to get a citation for failing to stop for the light."

Elizabeth's face lit up in a brilliant smile. "Why, officer, I'm truly honored."

"As well you should be. That'll be twenty dollars."

"We'll be honored to pay the fine, won't we, Jimmy? I can't believe it." She fingered the citation as if it were made of gold.

"Speak for yourself," Jimmy grumbled. He reached for his money clip and handed the officer two crisp ten spots.

The police officer carefully folded the money. "You'll have to come back after we paint safety stripes down the center of the road."

"Every street should have safety stripes," Jimmy said. Such a stripe might prevent the many head-on collisions that were now becoming so prevalent.

"They certainly should," Elizabeth agreed. "But only if they've earned it. If you ask me that red light is a menace. This street doesn't deserve a safety stripe or any other such honor."

The policeman gave her a strange look, then grabbed his hat from the street. "I'm sure the City Council will be happy to hear of any recommendations you might like to make."

"If I think of any, I'll let them know." Elizabeth tucked the citation into her pocket and drove off.

It was at least two hours later that they finally left Cincinnati, having had to pay fines for *three* traffic citations in all. One for running a red light, one for sideswiping a trolley car while making a U-turn, and another for stopping when the light turned green and causing an accident.

In an effort to avoid crashing into them, a horseless milk truck had swerved and overturned. Fortunately, no one was injured, but the street was littered with broken glass and dozens of cats had sprung from every tree and alleyway to lap up the spilt milk.

"Another first," the same policeman had said, glowering at Elizabeth for a third time. He'd looked so incensed that even his brass buttons seemed to have lost their luster. "This time you got yourself a citation for *stopping* on a *green* light."

Elizabeth might have felt honored at receiving the first citation, but even she recognized there was no honor in receiving a second or even a third one. "I forgot what I was supposed to do when the light turned green," she'd argued. "How do you expect me to remember all your rules and regulations? Sheesh!"

Jimmy was greatly relieved when at long last they left Cincinnati behind.

# Chapter 13

"Hand signals are useful, but most men can't tell a 'no' from a 'yes.' "

*Women at the Wheel*
Circa 1915

It took hours to backtrack and find their way to the northern part of Ohio. They finally found the road they were looking for, but they'd have found it a lot sooner had Elizabeth not persuaded Jimmy to ask directions.

A man walking along the road with a mule told them to take Rosemary Lane, but after they'd driven for miles without finding the main road, Jimmy finally discovered there were *two* Rosemary Lanes, one going north and south, the other going east and west. The roads had been named by two rivaling brothers who, according to the locals, were once in love with the same woman. Naturally, Elizabeth had turned up the wrong lane.

They were further delayed by a total of three flat tires. Fortunately, they found a farmer with a Model T Ford that was used as a power source. The farmer had jacked up the rear of the car and attached a leather belt to one of the wheels, which enabled him to churn his butter, saw firewood, and do an amazing number of other chores. Since the farmer had no use for the rubber tires, he was more than happy to let Jimmy take what he needed.

The following morning, Jimmy spotted yet another puzzling road sign, this one pointing the way east to Cincinnati, rather than south. Jimmy was almost positive that the cowboy driver, Billy-Joe, had turned the sign. Of all the underhanded tricks!

Determined to report the cowboy to the next race official, Jimmy examined the sign. The wood was warped and weather-beaten, the chiseled letters worn thin by wind and sand. Jimmy would have sworn the sign hadn't been touched in years. If Billy-Joe had indeed moved the sign, he'd left no incriminating evidence.

A farmer came rattling down the street in his horse-drawn wagon and pulled up behind Elizabeth's car. "Got a problem, young man?" he called to Jimmy.

Jimmy walked over to him. "I was just curious about the sign. It's turned wrong."

"Yep."

Puzzled by the farmer's lack of concern, Jimmy persisted. "I think someone must have turned it."

"Nope. It's always been that way."

Jimmy frowned. "Always?"

"Yep. Ever since my grandpappy put it up." The farmer glanced over his shoulder as if he suspected someone might be spying, then spit a yellow stream, of tobacco onto the dusty road. "My grandpappy fought in the South during that great War Between the States. His job in the war was to change road signs to confuse them Yankees. He never stopped, even after he moved his family to Ohio. Most of the signs he put up have been changed over the years. But not this one." He gave a toothless laugh. "Ain't no one around here wants to change this one."

"Why not?" Jimmy said. "It's got to be a nuisance."

"Ain't no nuisance," the farmer argued. "The locals plumb know their way round the area blindfolded. Strangers keep goin' straight, thinkin' they're headin' for Cinc'nati, and end up in Cotterville instead. Usually by then they're hungry and out of fossil fuel. Old

Gus sells them sandwiches and fuel and the rest of us sell produce and other goods. We told Gus he was a fool when he first talked about openin' up one of them there petroleum stations. Dang it if he ain't the richest man in town. It's enough to make a man change 'is trade."

Jimmy started to tell the man exactly what he thought of Gus and the town of Cotterville, but his voice was drowned out by the loud roar of automobile engines. Sir Higginbottom drove up from the road leading to Cincinnati and right behind him were Staggs and that fool undertaker, Stonegate. Apparently, Elizabeth wasn't the only driver confused by the sign. Staggs jumped out of his car and, shouting orders to his mechanic, set to work arranging his tripod and camera.

Sir Higginbottom pulled off his goggles and wiped his forehead. "I say, Hunter, did you happen to notice the sign is turned wrong? Looks like Billy-Joe has been up to his old tricks."

"Billy-Joe isn't at fault this time. This man's grandpappy is the culprit." Jimmy then explained how the sign had been misdirecting travelers for over fifty years. "Ever since the War Between the States."

Sir Higginbottom walked over to the sign to check for himself. "I do believe you're right. This sign hasn't been touched in years."

Mr. Stonegate got out of his car, his craggy and usually somber face lit with a smile. "This man's grandpappy did us a favor. Did you check out the graveyard in Cincinnati? Everything laid out nice and neat. We should all be so lucky as to die in Cincinnati."

"Dying there is easier said than done," Jimmy said. "We had two accidents in Cincinnati, and as you can see, we're still alive and kicking."

Mr. Stonegate slapped Jimmy on the back. "Don't feel bad. There're worse fates."

Staggs stood in the middle of the road, his camera

resting on its tripod. He checked the location of the sun. "All right, everyone. Gather around the sign."

"Dammit, I don't want my photograph taken!" Sir Higginbottom growled, but the farmer was more than happy to pose and stood by the sign, glaring into the camera lens until Staggs had captured his picture.

Jimmy was anxious to get started, but Sir Higginbottom insisted upon giving the farmer a piece of his mind. "I say, sir, do you realize the inconvenience your sign has caused me?"

Staggs nodded. "You aren't the only one who was inconvenienced. I fully expected to reach Wheeler yesterday! Now the light will be all wrong by the time I get there. Have you ever tried to take a photograph in bad light?"

Jimmy was in no mood for an argument. The last twenty-four hours had been hell. Worse! Starting with a brawl and a fast escape, they'd collected three traffic citations, had two accidents, three flat tires, and had driven in more circles than a horse on a carousel. The last thing Jimmy wanted was more trouble.

Leaving Sir Higginbottom and Staggs to argue with the farmer, Jimmy jumped into his seat and signaled for Elizabeth to go. Elizabeth pulled away with her usual lead-footed, horn-blowing, death-defying spurt.

Not wanting a lady to gain the advantage, the other drivers reacted quickly. Staggs grabbed his camera and made a wild dash for his car. Sir Higginbottom ran around in circles yelling to his mechanic, who had chosen an inopportune moment to answer a call of nature. Mr. Stonegate reached his car first and quickly pulled behind Elizabeth's.

Low on fuel, the four Model T's barely made it into Cotterville. As much as Jimmy resented having to give the man named Gus his money, he had no choice.

What irritated Jimmy the most was how Gus stood waiting for them as they rolled into town. A tall, thin man with a scraggly beard, Gus leaned next to the brightly painted ten-gallon pump. He waited until all four cars had come to a full stop before reaching for the hose, then taking his own sweet time, he stretched it toward Old Ironsides.

Old Gus soon managed to redeem himself, however, with his fuel dispenser. The glass tank was marked like a measuring beaker. Instead of having to rely on guesswork and the integrity of the fuel company, customers could clearly see how much gasoline they were purchasing. Intrigued with the modern tank, the drivers stood next to their mechanics watching Gus pump.

Gasoline rose, filling the cylinder glass globe completely before running down the hose and into the car. Sir Higginbottom's mechanic, Mr. Chin, nodded his approval. "That iz somethin', all right."

Sir Higginbottom agreed. "Old Gus might be a crook," the Englishman whispered, "but he's an honest one." No sooner had Higginbottom made this declaration than he discovered that Gus's fuel was about to cost him fourteen cents a gallon, a full penny more than the going rate. "That's highway robbery!"

"The cost of living keeps going up," Staggs complained.

"So does the cost of dying," Stonegate added.

Staggs set up his camera and allowed no one to leave until he'd captured the momentous occasion. Jimmy scowled into the camera and resisted the urge to wring the man's neck.

Driving in a pack, the four Model T's arrived in Wheeler late that afternoon with Elizabeth in the lead. No sooner had she pulled into town than mobs of people spilled into the street, forcing her to slow down to little more than a crawl.

Sir Higginbottom and Staggs fell behind as the mob closed around Old Ironsides. Elizabeth made her way slowly through town while the crowd cheered. Frantic hands reached out to touch the fenders and hood of Elizabeth's rumbling Tin Lizzie.

Jimmy scanned the sea of faces, puzzled by the number of women. "What do you suppose is going on?" He lifted his voice to be heard over the roar of the crowd.

Elizabeth looked every bit as puzzled as he was. She shook her head. "Maybe somebody important is coming to town." The cheers grew louder, then changed into a singsong chant. "Go, Liz, go!"

One woman jumped on the running board and, trying to get as close to Elizabeth as possible, practically heaved herself on top of Jimmy. "You saved my life!" Tears running down her cheeks, she gazed at Elizabeth and shouted in Jimmy's ear. "If it wasn't for you I'd be a sex slave."

Jimmy's eyes popped open as he battled to keep the peacock feather on the woman's hat away from his face. Good heavens! What was this woman talking about? Sex slave? Never had he heard such a shocking thing in his life. What kind of town was this?

The woman was pulled away from the car by a group of screaming women who quickly took her place. Crowding onto the running board until Jimmy feared they would tip the car over on its side, the women shouted the most outrageous and shocking statements he'd ever heard.

One heavyset woman ran beside Old Ironsides, peeling off layers of clothing and tossing them to the crowd. "This is my body. . . . My body."

Jimmy pulled a lady's lacy petticoat from his lap and tossed it back to her.

"I don't believe it," Elizabeth said, her lips quivering with emotion. "They came for me, Jimmy, me!"

The petticoats were bad enough, but suddenly he was bombarded with lacy bloomers and corset covers. "Good heavens, Elizabeth!" He shouted to be heard above the din. "What is all this business about sex slaves and . . . bodies?"

"They read my book, Jimmy. They read my book!"

"Your book?" He stared at her in disbelief. *The famous book that practically everyone in the whole damn world had read but him? That book?* He'd heard it was shocking, but nothing had prepared him for this! Well, by George, he had some reading to do, all right. Just as soon as he got his hands on a copy, he intended to read every single word for himself. Sex slave, indeed!

Bombarded with all manner of intimate apparel that would make the most worldly man blush, he didn't notice that Old Ironsides was veering toward the sidewalk until he heard the cheers from the crowd turn into horrified screams. "Watch out!"

Elizabeth swerved. Wheels squealed; rubber burned. She missed the crowd, but when a woman threw a bouquet of roses onto the hood of the car, Elizabeth was so overwhelmed by emotion, she inadvertently pressed on the gas pedal instead of the brake.

Old Ironsides lurched forward, sending frantic spectators scattering in every direction. The automobile jumped across the boardwalk and rumbled up the concrete steps of City Hall.

Bouncing up and down like the needle on a fast-speed sewing machine, Jimmy could barely speak. "S-s-s-stop!" By the time he'd found his voice, they had indeed come to a stop. Miraculously, no one had been hurt, nor had the car incurred any damage. But since the Model T was now perched on the steps of City Hall like a tipsy crow, its front grille less than two inches from the brass doors, Jimmy was in no mood to count his blessings.

For several moments a stunned hush settled over the crowd. Finally a voice called out, "No more sex slaves!" As if responding to an army officer's cry of "Charge!" the frenzied mob pushed and shoved their way up the steps of City Hall.

Jimmy stared at the fast-advancing crowd in horror, not sure whether to run or surrender. Meanwhile, Elizabeth stood up in her seat and waved, acting as if she were some damned performer on stage.

The crowd loved it and showed their approval with thunderous applause. Not even the half-dozen policemen, whose bungling attempts to restore order resembled a Keystone Kops flicker, nor the trapped mayor banging on the glass door of City Hall, seemed to dampen the crowd's enthusiasm.

Elizabeth looked radiant. Her cheeks were flushed pink and her eyes sparkled. Watching her, Jimmy forgot the crowd, forgot the precarious position of the car, forgot he and Elizabeth were probably going to be hauled off to jail. He was even oblivious to Staggs, who kept sticking his confounded camera in Jimmy's face and shouting things like, "Look this way! Great! The petticoat's a nice touch."

All Jimmy could do was stare at the look of disbelief on Elizabeth's face and wonder about the sudden surge of pride he felt swelling in his heart.

# *Chapter 14*

"The shortest distance between two points is sometimes a U-turn."

*Women at the Wheel*
Circa 1915

Hours after Jimmy had hoped to reach Toledo, their
car rolled to a sputtering stop on a dark, lonely road.
He estimated they were still well over a hundred miles
away from their destination. He couldn't believe it. It
had taken four days to drive a little over four hundred
miles from Buffalo. At this rate, Elizabeth would
never reach Seattle.

They had followed the Lincoln Highway for quite a
few miles and had been forced to follow one detour
after another. Earlier, they had passed through the
same town three times before heading in the right
direction. But this took three U-turns and what Jimmy
could only describe as a WXO turn.

Now it appeared yet another problem would further
delay their progress. The motor sputtered and died
and the car rolled to a stop. They were out of fuel.

Jimmy held his tongue. After the hell of a day she'd
put him through, he didn't dare open his mouth for
fear of what he'd say. He was in no mood to be civil.

Heaving a sigh, Jimmy climbed out of the car and
grabbed the lantern from the sideboard. Gasoline va-
pors were extremely volatile and more than one hap-
less driver had lit a lantern or cigar and been sent to

kingdom come. Not wanting to take a chance on throwing business Stonegate's way, Jimmy made Elizabeth step back before he lit it.

The light was dim, but combined with the headlamps it proved adequate. He lifted the driver's seat to reach the gasoline tank, and after carefully lining a funnel with chamois, lifted the five-gallon can of fuel off the running board and unscrewed the cap.

He'd emptied the can and, not wanting to chance anything more preventing their long overdue arrival in Toledo, poured oil into the engine crankcase through the breather pipe.

The oil level had dropped low and he checked to make certain the front bearing was properly lubricated.

A cool northerly wind was blowing and the air held the smell of wet dust. Rain was definitely on its way. The thought filled Jimmy with dread. That's all they needed.

Lord, if he had one sensible bone in his body, if he had a lick of sense in his head, he'd get as far away from Elizabeth and Old Ironsides as was possible.

What a day this had been!

It made his head swim just to think about it. He shuddered at the memory of Elizabeth nearly plowing down that group of suffragettes who had come to town to cheer her on and almost wiping out City Hall. Still, nothing irritated him more than that damned citation—their fourth in two days. It wouldn't have been so bad had Elizabeth gotten a ticket for reckless driving. But, no! *He* was given a ticket for contributory negligence.

He was still irked that Elizabeth had complained to the policeman about him. The nerve of her. Blaming him. She was the one who drove up the steps of City Hall. What gall she had to tell the policeman *he* had made her nervous. Nervous! She was lucky that's all he'd done.

He glared in Elizabeth's direction. She looked cold

and tired, and as much as he resisted the urge, he couldn't help but feel sorry for her. Maybe it wasn't entirely her fault. The crowd *had* been distracting. He wouldn't have minded paying the hefty fine so much had those crazy women not escorted them out of town, waving apparel that was never meant to see the light of day and chanting "It's my body." It was damned embarrassing. Nothing his eccentric aunt or his suffragette mother had done in their battle for women's rights could compare.

Jimmy straightened, wiped his hand with a rag, replaced the front seat, and strolled over to where Elizabeth stood holding the lantern.

"Is everything all right with the car, Jimmy?" Her face looked pale and dark shadows skirted her big blue eyes.

Much to his chagrin, he felt another wave of sympathy wash over him. Still, he could no longer contain his curiosity. He walked around in a circle, looking up at the dark starless sky. "Would you mind explaining to me what all that business was about back there? What was that nonsense those women kept shouting about their bodies? And what is this about you freeing sex slaves?"

Elizabeth didn't look the least bit taken aback by his questions. "I told you, Jimmy, they read my book."

"Ah, yes, the famous book." The book he was going to read as soon as he got his hands on a copy.

"Yes, and I plan to write another. I didn't want to, but now that I know all the good my first one has done, I'm anxious to get started on it. I don't care if they *do* put me in jail again. Let them!"

"You're going to write another obscene ... eh ... book?"

"A woman's body is not obscene." In the flickering light of the lantern, her eyes gleamed like black jade. "No matter how much some men might try to make it so."

"I never thought a woman's body was obscene, Elizabeth." Certainly not hers. Lord, not even those damned oversize overalls she insisted on wearing could make the soft curves of her shapely hips and tiny waist look anything but feminine. "I just don't think women should be running through the streets waving their unmentionables and yelling 'sex slaves.' "

"I don't see what you're all upset about, Jimmy. This is 1915. A woman's underwear is no longer unmentionable. You can open up any mail order catalog and you'll see how mentionable it is."

"That's not the same as having it waved in your face, Elizabeth, and you know it." Lord, he couldn't believe it. They were standing in the middle of nowhere in the cold night air, arguing about women's underwear. "I resent you implying that I have no respect for a woman's body. If that were true, I wouldn't be so upset about women running around flaunting themselves."

She bit her lip and glanced away. "I wasn't talking about you, Jimmy."

He frowned. "Then who?"

"Never mind. It's not important." She shoved the lantern into his hand and walked back to the car. He quickly extinguished the light and chased after her.

"It must be important if you brought it up."

"I don't want to talk about it."

"All right, then don't. But it's true, isn't it? You were sent to jail because of the book you wrote."

"Yes, and I'll probably be sent to jail again with my future books. But I don't care. Right is right. And a woman should have a say over her own body. Now would you please crank the engine so we can get started? I'm cold."

He replaced the lantern and walked to the front of the car. He wondered what she meant about women having a say over their bodies. Whatever it meant, it didn't sound good. It sounded to him as if a man would have to gain permission before he kissed a woman. And what if a man wanted to do more?

Would he have to get something in writing? Pay for a permit? What? He cranked up the car, but the engine didn't sound right.

"I think we better stay the night in the next town," he said. It made no sense to break down on the road somewhere at this time of night.

Upon arriving in a little town that wasn't even on the map, Jimmy checked the engine. "Hold the light still," he muttered. When the light continued to move, he reached out and took the lantern from her. His fingers inadvertently touched hers, causing his heart to race. His eyes met hers for an instant before she glanced away.

Holding the lantern over the motor, he checked the hoses. As far as he could tell, no leaks existed. He set the lantern on the running board. "You go to the hotel," he said. "I'll stay with the car."

"You're going to stay . . . ? Her eyes swam with gratitude. "Oh, Jimmy, thank you." He felt a warm glow wash over him. All the anger and frustration of the day disappeared in the brightness of her smile.

He lifted his hand to her cheek, meaning to wipe away a smudge of oil, but he inadvertently became distracted by the softness of her skin and his finger lingered. He regretted the angry words that had waged between them, the hostile looks. "Elizabeth, I . . ."

She pulled away from him, looking like a frightened child. Before he had a chance to apologize or even explain his intention, she bid him a crisp good night, then turned and hurried—ran, more like it—to the hotel.

Feeling crushed, he debated whether or not to follow her. He wanted her to look at him with trust in her eyes. Damn! Every time he touched her, she had the same pained look on her face, like she was stepping into a tub of icy water. Did she really expect him to ask her permission before touching her? Was that it?

If he ever got his hand on that book, maybe then he'd understand what she expected of him.

Heart heavy, he watched the doors of the hotel long after she'd disappeared, debating whether to follow her and demand an explanation or to wait until after he'd read the book.

Shivering, he stuck his hands in his pockets. His fingers touched something soft and satiny. It was the pink ribbon that had fallen off Elizabeth's car on that very first day.

Running his thumb along the ribbon's smooth surface, he was reminded of all that was soft about her, all that he longed to touch. A strange aching loneliness washed over him. Sighing, he glanced around him.

Since this was not an official check-in point, Elizabeth was the only automobile racer in town. Laughter drifted from a nearby tavern. A dog barked in the distance. Somewhere a shutter banged in the chilly breeze. Though the town was too small to have one of the newer movie palaces that were springing up across the country, it did have a nickel theater and a sign bearing a picture of Theda Bara saying "Kiss me, my fool."

Damned if he hadn't been tempted. Had Elizabeth not pulled away, who knows what might have happened?

He noticed a tiny bookstore opposite the hotel, sandwiched between a pharmacist and a dry goods store. All three businesses were closed, but the buildings had a second floor and he suspected the bookstore proprietor lived upstairs. It was late, almost midnight, too late to wake someone simply to buy a book. He'd have to wait until morning.

Curious as to whether or not the bookstore even had a copy, he stuffed the ribbon back into his pocket and reached for the lantern.

Moments later, he stood in front of the window, the lantern held high, reading the names of the books displayed. All the popular books of the day were propped in the window, plus a few boxed parlor games, including everyone's favorite, How Silas Popped the Question.

Dime novels with garish covers were stacked haphazardly. *Tarzan and the Apes,* written by a former lightbulb vendor by the name of Edgar Rice Burroughs, was stacked twice as high as Robert Frost's *North of Boston. Deadwood Dick* competed with *Buffalo Bill* and *Jesse James.* Elizabeth's book was nowhere in sight.

He jumped up on the window ledge and held the lantern high over his head. Pressing his nose against the dusty glass, he could barely make out a few titles on the books lining the back wall, but it was too dark to read the rest.

He jumped down and searched for a sign that listed opening hours. Overhead came the sound of a window sash being raised. Ah ha! Now he was getting somewhere. He stepped away from the shop, hoping to persuade the proprietor to open the store.

Without warning, icy cold water hit him square in the face. "Yeow!" Jumping back, he shook himself. "What the . . . ?"

A woman wearing a ruffled nightcap hung out of the second-floor window. "That'll teach you to go prowling around at night, you scoundrel. Now git, before I call the sheriff."

Drenched to the bone, and feeling utterly cold and miserable, he hurried back to the flivver, his teeth chattering.

He dried himself off, but because he and Elizabeth had escaped that morning in such a hurry, he'd left his carpetbag with all his clothes at the hotel.

He pulled off his soaked shirt and felt in the darkness for something dry to put over his shoulders. He found a ruffled petticoat that had been tossed into the car earlier. At the moment, he was too cold to care what he looked like and he gratefully wrapped the flimsy lace unmentionable around his shoulders.

Determined to get some sleep, he crawled into the cab. He tried every position possible. He let his feet dangle over the car frame, on the floor, and finally decided to sit upright. He was tired, exhausted to the bone, and still he couldn't sleep. But his insomnia had nothing to do with the cold night or the cramped quarters of the car.

He couldn't stop thinking of Elizabeth. As much as he wanted to deny it, that was the full and puzzling truth. Her blue eyes and determined smile seemed to hover in the black of night, turning the darkness into light.

Even when he closed his eyes, he wasn't safe. For the vision of her standing naked in the sun continued to plague him. Never would he forget how beautiful she looked, her full breasts bathed in sunlight, the wind in her hair. His blood pumped through his body in a heated rush, until even the silk petticoat felt too warm.

His hand literally ached to hold the breast his fingers had previously only grazed. He longed to savor every part of the full, curving mounds to his heart's content. The aching need to kiss her pretty pink lips almost overwhelmed him. The desire to stroke her gloriously long, gloriously blond hair was too much to bear.

"Oh, Elizabeth." He whispered her name in the dark and it seemed to echo in the lonely cab of the car. Was it really true? Were a woman's wild driving habits really an indicator of what a man could expect in bed?

What if it was true? Lord almighty, what if it was! Wouldn't that be something?

She could have all the say she wanted over her body, but he wanted it, dammit, wanted her more than he'd ever wanted any woman in his life, and no book was going to change that!

# Chapter 15

"Nothing cools down an overheated 'motor' faster than a cold woman."

*Women at the Wheel*
Circa 1915

Elizabeth couldn't sleep. It was well after midnight, but she was too restless with excitement to settle down. She couldn't stop thinking about the crowd of cheering women who'd greeted her as she'd driven through Wheeler.

The warm reception had taken her by surprise. Surprise could be a dangerous thing, especially to a person with something to hide. But for one magical moment she'd lowered her guard and her heart had swelled with unbelievable joy.

It had been so long since she'd allowed herself to feel, she'd almost forgotten how. She'd learned at an early age to block the pain, hide the feelings, pretend they didn't exist, until eventually she had succeeded in numbing herself into cool indifference. The only problem with this particular solution was that feelings of pain and joy came from the same source; to numb one meant to numb the other.

How surprised she'd been by the genuine outpouring of approval and acceptance from the crowd. Shocked, really. She'd almost come to expect the same rejection and criticism that had followed the publication of her book. Never once had she stopped to consider that the so-called moralists and politicians who had declared her book wanton spoke for only a portion of the population.

Everything had happened so quickly, she'd not had time to brace herself. Caught off guard, the women's tears had touched her unlike anything had touched her for years. Their gratitude revitalized her. Their fervor filled her with new determination.

She was going to finish this race, if for no other reason than to free the spirit of women who were still constrained by old-fashioned thinking and outdated expectations.

If only Jimmy would stay with her to the end, everything would be perfect. But he was still determined to bail out once they reached Hogs Head. She would give anything if only he'd change his mind. *Oh, Jimmy, even if I did win the race, it wouldn't mean a thing to me without you by my side!*

For the third time that night, she climbed out of bed and stood shivering in the dark in front of her hotel window. Wishing she had her eyeglasses, she squinted her eyes until she could pick out the dark shape she knew was Old Ironsides.

Jimmy was surely asleep by now, and she had no reason to think he would break his promise about staying with her automobile. No, it wasn't Old Ironsides that kept her glued to the window; it was the aching desire to make Jimmy understand why she had pulled away from him.

Mortified at her earlier behavior, she fought to ward off the shudder that began with a cold knot in her stomach and traveled throughout her body. He'd wanted only to rub the grease off her face and look at how she'd reacted! What must he think of her? She couldn't bear to guess!

She wanted so much to go to him, to apologize for pulling away, to make him understand it had nothing to do with him. *Oh, Jimmy, if only I could bring myself to relax next to you. Would you put your arms around me? Kiss me? Could I really let you?*

She wouldn't blame Jimmy if he hightailed it back to Hogs Head on the very first train. Considering all that she'd put him through, she could only wonder why he'd stayed this long.

Sometimes he treated her as if she were still the little orphan girl who'd sat in that old baggage car crying her eyes out. Well, she wasn't that little girl. Not anymore. Nor was she the woman she saw reflected in his eyes on occasion, though Lord knows she wanted to be.

He saw her as both a girl and a woman. Which image, she wondered, had kept him from leaving? The one she'd outgrown or the one she was too frightened to embrace?

She crossed her arms in front of her aching breasts and ran her hands along her arms in an effort to bring warmth to her chilled flesh.

What would he think if he knew that the little girl had stopped existing at the age of twelve?

Mylar Carson had called her *little girl* the first time he took her to the barn, as if depersonalizing her made what he did less reprehensible. *Well, now, little girl . . .*

She quickly clamped down on the memories, but not soon enough. Feeling sick to her stomach, she bent over at the waist and hugged herself tight, trying to make herself stop shaking.

The little girl was gone, but the woman had never really been allowed to take her place. She had no way of knowing if it was possible to be held by a man in a way that was gentle, not violent; loving, not crazed.

And until she met Jimmy she had had no desire to find out. But now the need to know was as threatening as the look she had seen on Jimmy's face earlier, and she shrank back into the shadows, grasping the draperies much like a drowning swimmer reaches for a life preserver. But nothing she did kept the disturbing memories at bay.

She narrowed her eyes in the darkness and managed to pick out the fluttering strips of satin tied to the back of her flivver. Soothed by the ribbons blowing in the wind, she took a deep breath and tried to calm her racing heart.

Gradually, the terror subsided and the shaking stopped. She tiptoed across the room and climbed back into bed.

The rain began that night, and by the next morning, the road to Toledo had already turned into a river of mud.

Jimmy had never seen such a downpour. Both he and Elizabeth were dressed in rubber raincoats and hip boots, but they could barely see the road for the mud and water.

Elizabeth was forced to drive less than ten miles an hour, and in some spots considerably slower.

A bridge had collapsed, forcing them to take a fifty-mile detour. It rained so hard at one point, they sought shelter in an old deserted barn until the downpour subsided.

While Elizabeth drove, Jimmy worked the hand-operated windshield wipers, but they did little good. They stopped at a little roadside café that had red-checkered curtains at the window and the best coffee Jimmy had tasted since leaving home. Before they left, Jimmy was able to obtain a raw potato from the cook. He smeared the potato across the windshield, creating a film that made the water run off quicker.

By the time it grew dark, they were both exhausted. "I think we better stop and wait till the rain lets up," Jimmy said. Twice, flooded roads had forced them to take another route and they'd lost more time.

The canvas top was up and the leather window curtains fastened tightly, but Old ironsides was about as waterproof as a bucket full of holes.

"Toledo can't be that much further ahead," Elizabeth said. "Please, Jimmy. We can't stay here."

Jimmy relented, but only because he was anxious for a hot meal and a warm bed. Lighting the lamps was a chore. Even though his matches were protected, they were damp.

No sooner had they pulled back onto the road than a loud *Ah-ooh-ga* sounded behind them. Jimmy glanced out the little square window built into the canvas top. He could see the headlamps behind them, but it was hard to see much else.

"Why doesn't he just pass, Jimmy?"

Jimmy unsnapped the curtain on his side and flung his arm through the opening, motioning the driver on by. The driver kept honking, the nose of his car on the tail of Elizabeth's. "Better pull over," Jimmy said. "There might be a problem."

Elizabeth slowed down. It wasn't until the other Model T Ford pulled alongside them that Jimmy recognized Fastbender and his mechanic.

"He's going to push me off the road," Elizabeth exclaimed.

Jimmy cursed. "Dammit, Fastbender. Go!"

Suddenly, the right front tire of Elizabeth's Ford flew off the edge of the road. The saturated ground gave way and Elizabeth's car rolled down the side of a fourteen-foot embankment before coming to a jolting stop at the edge of a fast-moving stream.

Only a miracle had kept them from rolling into the sloshing torrents. An uprooted tree floated into view, its branches scraping the front grille of their car. The tree spun eerily in the muddied waters like a dancing skeleton, then disappeared downstream.

The engine sputtered and died, but the roaring sound of rushing waters filled the void. The rank odor of mud and vegetation permeated the air. It smelled worse than a swamp.

Jimmy vaguely remembered banging his head against the windshield during the descent. With an impatient nod, he fought off the hazy fog that made thinking a chore, and gave Elizabeth an urgent shake.

"Elizabeth?" He frantically eyed her up and down in the dim light of the headlamps and sighed in relief upon feeling her stir. "Are you all right?"

She raised her head off the steering wheel, her hand on her brow. "It's just a little bump.... It's nothing...."

"I'll be the judge of that. Let me see." Only one headlamp remained lit, but it was enough. He lifted the goggles off her face and gently touched her forehead. She winced slightly and he frowned in worry. "Do you feel dizzy or faint?"

"No, I told you. I'm fine." She wet her lips and smiled, setting his mind at rest and doing so much more. The heated desire that had smoldered within him for far too long now flared into flames of passion.

He was tempted to kiss her until she was consumed by the same fiery need, the same fiery desire that had kept him on edge these last two days. Normally, that's exactly what he would have done. But Elizabeth seemed to have her own rules as to how a man went about making his intentions known. And, dammit, he wanted her so much he was willing to play by those rules—even if it meant asking permission to do something he considered as natural as breathing. "Elizabeth, would you mind if I ...."

Her eyes, luminous in the dying lights of the car lamps, grew wide. "If you what, Jimmy?"

He knew what he wanted to do; he just couldn't get the words out. Some things weren't meant to be spoken. "Go outside and see if any damage has been done to the car?"

She looked at him for a full minute before responding. "I don't mind."

Reluctantly pulling his gaze away from her trembling lips, he reached for the rubber raincoat in the backseat, unfastened the leather curtain, and opened the door. Rain dripped inside and he quickly climbed out of the car and slammed the door shut.

He leaped to an area above the waterline, his boots

sinking into the mud. It was still raining hard, with no sign of letting up.

The rain felt cold, and that was fine with him. Something had to cool down his heated body.

Jimmy surveyed the area around them. The water was rising quickly. Whether or not they'd have to bail out before dawn was anyone's guess.

Something told Jimmy it was going to be a very long night.

# Chapter 16

"Driving in the rain or fording a river are not nearly so difficult as folding a road map."

*Women at the Wheel*
Circa 1915

Elizabeth sat huddled in the car, the cold damp air chilling her to the bone. Rain pelted the canvas top and ran down the windshield in thin watery sheets. She wiped the fog off the glass with her glove, her anxiety increasing with each passing moment.

Dear God, where was he? And what if something had happened to him? She cried out in fright when the last headlamp went out. "Jimmy?" She strained her ears, but all she could hear was the relentless sound of rain beating against the canvas top and the rapid flow of the river.

She breathed in relief when at last the car door opened and Jimmy slid into the seat next to her. An odd, almost giddy feeling washed over her.

He pulled off his dripping raincoat, spreading it across the backseat to dry, and wiped his wet face with a towel. "I'm afraid there's not much we can do until it stops raining."

It was too dark to see his face, but Elizabeth heard the worry in his voice and shivered involuntarily. "It's all my fault." Much to her dismay, her eyes filled with tears, but she was too tired and too cold, not to mention too worried, to hold back, and one muffled sob escaped. "You must hate me."

"Aw, come on, Elizabeth. Don't cry now. Please don't cry. Things aren't that bad."

"Don't you try and make me feel better, Jimmy Hunter. I know when things are bad and when they're not. And I'm telling you, this is bad."

"It's not as bad as it could be," Jimmy said. "If that river overflows its banks ..."

"Do you ... do you think it might?"

"It's raining pretty hard."

She grabbed hold of the steering wheel. "Oh, Jimmy! What are we going to do?"

"We'll keep our eye on it."

"But ..."

"If the water rises too high, we'll abandon the car and seek higher ground. Meanwhile, we're going to sit tight and see what happens."

She leaned her head against the back of the seat. "Jimmy, I'm scared."

He reached for her hand and she stifled the gasp that rose to her lips. *It's only Jimmy. He's not going to hurt me or make me do something I don't want to do.* She forced herself to calm down, to concentrate on the warm sensations that flowed from his hand and traveled the length of her arm.

Lord, she wanted this. Wanted him to hold her hand. Hold her. She wanted so much to trust him, trust that he was every bit as kind and gentle as he appeared to be. *Trust him like I once trusted Mylar Carson.*

It occurred to her that it wasn't so much the danger inherent with the rising waters that frightened her as much as the knowledge that even nature could betray her and let her down. In the past, rain had made her feel safe. Rain and snow and sleet—any harsh weather—for such inclement conditions would rule out trips to the barn.

She thought of all the times she'd stared out of her

bedroom window at the sky, praying for bad weather and trying to convince herself how lucky she was to have a home. Many children were pulled off the orphan trains at harvest time, and when the work was done, sent back to the orphanage. But the truth was, she'd envied those children. Living on the streets—anywhere—would have been preferable to what she had suffered in Oregon.

As much as she'd hated the indignity of having her arms and legs squeezed, hated hearing how thin she was, how plain, how inadequate, she would have gladly gone through the torment again, just to escape Mylar.

Lord, what a fool she'd been. Her heart had sung with gratitude when at last a man had stepped forward and, without touching her, announced to the agent he was taking her home. How ironic that the man who'd at first treated her with the most dignity would later treat her with the least.

The thought filled her with panic. She tried pulling her hand away, but Jimmy tightened his hold.

"Don't be scared, Elizabeth." He squeezed her trembling fingers as if he never meant to let her go, no matter how much she fought or otherwise protested. "I promise you, we'll make it out in time. I'm not going to let anything happen to you."

His thumb moved across her skin like velvet over silk, and the desire for his touch superseded any need to pull away. Circling her skin, he began a sensuous exploration of the valleys between her knuckles.

Her heart pounded; her body grew so warm it felt flushed. She let out a long, lingering sigh. Jimmy, apparently taking this as a sign of encouragement, leaned closer, and his warm breath caressed her cheek.

She closed the distance between them, but when his lips brushed against her forehead, she was jolted back to reality.

Pulling her hand away, she faced the front of the car and stared at the curtain of rain sliding down the windshield. She was painfully aware that Jimmy made no further move toward her.

Tormented by the agony of loss, of loneliness and despair, she blinked back fresh tears.

She yearned to reach out to him, to seek the comfort of his arms. She wanted to rip a hole in her world and escape into his.

Desperate to break the invisible chains holding her back, she sought for a way to be close to him without touching him physically. "Tell me about Hogs Head."

"There isn't much to tell." He sounded hesitant, confused, maybe even hurt. She regretted having pulled her hand away and was greatly relieved when, despite his claim, he started to talk about his home.

"Hogs Head is a great place to live. Everyone knows and cares about everyone else."

Curious as to whether such a place really existed, she probed further. "Do you like living in a small town?" After she had been released from jail, she'd fled to New York City to escape the narrow-minded thinking of her own small town in Oregon.

"I love it. But I didn't know how much until the week I spent in New York. It was the first time in my life I knew what it meant to be lonely in a crowd."

"The first time?" It was an astonishing thought. She'd always felt alone, even while in school. She never dared let anyone get too close or know her too well, for fear of giving away her shameful secret. New York City, with its mass of indifferent faces, made her feel anonymous and therefore secure. It might have been a false security, but it was no less a comforting one.

"My parents live outside the town in an old rambling house," he continued, the fondness for his family and hometown evident in his voice. It gave her a warm feeling to know his home had been happy and full of love. It wasn't just a dream of hers; it really *was* possible, and knowing this made her more determined than ever to build her shelter and put her plan into action.

"I have my own apartment, next to the electrical works where I work."

"You said your parents are inventors?"

"They are." His laughter touched her like warm sunshine. "If my mother and father were here, I daresay they'd already be busy inventing some machine to miraculously lift us up the embankment."

"Were you the only child?"

"Not by a long shot. I have five brothers and three sisters."

"Did you ever feel . . . different, like you didn't belong? Because you were adopted?"

"Never. My parents treated me as if I were their very own flesh and blood."

"It must have been wonderful growing up with so much love and acceptance."

Jimmy absorbed the sadness in her voice before he replied. "It *was* wonderful." Cursing himself for losing the tenuous trust that had been building between them, he tightened his hands into fists.

He wanted to kiss her—was desperate to kiss her—to bury his face in that glorious hair of hers, to bury himself in that glorious body—and she wouldn't even let him hold her hand!

She gave him no choice but to respond only to that part of her that she couldn't control. If only his senses weren't so focused on her. Lord, he was aware of her every breath, her every sigh. The delicate fresh scent of her hair and skin titillated him. The warmth of her body played with his senses. But this was no time to lose his head. Not with the rain still falling and the water still rising . . .

"What about you, Elizabeth?" he asked, his voice coming out in a grating, almost harsh, whisper. He cleared his voice, determined to earn her trust—one way or another. "Tell me about the family that adopted you."

She held herself so still and took so long to reply, he thought perhaps she'd fallen asleep. When at last she spoke, her voice sounded distant, hollow, as if it came from a part of her that had never known sunshine or light. "Maybe some other time. Not tonight."

Not wanting her to slip away from him altogether, not wanting to lose the rapport of moments earlier, he searched for something, anything, to restore it. "Then tell me about you. What is this orphanage idea of yours?"

This time she answered freely, and he smiled at her enthusiasm as she outlined the details of her plan. "Oh, Jimmy, don't you think this is a wonderful idea? Just think! I'd be building a home for children in the same circumstances the two of us were in all those years ago. I want these children to have all the love and security that's possible while waiting for suitable families to adopt them."

"Do you plan to help find families for these children?"

"Absolutely. Anyone interested in adoption would have to come to the home and go through a thorough investigation. If the couple can adequately prove they are capable of providing a safe and loving home, they'll be introduced to the child in a warm, friendly environment." Her voice rose. "Believe me, they won't be allowed to pinch or probe the child!"

Her sudden outcry was followed by a moment of awkward silence before she cleared her throat and continued in a quiet, controlled voice. "Once I prove my home a success, I'm convinced others will see this as a more humane way to place children. When that happens, I'm certain we can start to work for reforms."

"Making the couple go through a screening process is an interesting concept."

"It makes sense, don't you think?" Elizabeth fell silent.

"I was one of the lucky ones," Jimmy said. "The woman who was to become my mother pulled me off the train, crutches and all, and said she would find me a proper home." He chuckled softly. "The problem was, her standards were so high, no one in town could live up to them. After she married a fellow inventor named Jonas Hunter, the two adopted me."

"You were lucky, Jimmy."

"I feel terrible, Elizabeth. I was so lucky, it never occurred to me what a terrible, heartless system the orphan trains really are."

"Don't get me wrong, Jimmy. The Children's Aid Society does more good than bad with this system. Most of the children they place do find good homes. And don't forget they've rescued many children from the streets over the years."

"But there were abuses."

"Yes, Jimmy," she said slowly. "There were abuses." For a time she fell silent.

"It's going to be difficult to change the system," Jimmy said at length. "The society has been placing orphans for sixty-five years." He laid his hand on her shoulder, but feeling her cringe beneath his touch, he pulled his hand away. *Dear God, what could have happened to make her so fear a man's touch? Or is it simply that she fears me?*

For hours, it seemed, Jimmy sat by her side, battling the urge to touch her. It wasn't easy. In the cramped confines of the car, the slightest movement meant brushing against her shoulder or arm. There was no way to avoid it. So he held himself perfectly rigid, not moving an inch, and told her about all the wonderful people he'd grown up with. Elizabeth seemed fascinated and made him describe his family members down to the last detail.

From time to time, he'd open the door a crack to measure the height of the water. Just when the water reached the top of the running board and it looked as if they would have to seek higher ground, the rain slowed to a drizzle and finally stopped altogether. Then the wind picked up, whistling through every possible opening of the flivver.

At last, after so many hours together, unable to continue sitting close to her without touching her, he decided to do the very thing he'd told himself he wouldn't do. "Elizabeth," he whispered softly. "Would it be all right . . . you know . . . if I kiss you?" There, he had done it. Done what he thought he could never do. Relieved that he'd managed to say the words aloud, he inhaled and waited.

And waited. She said not a word. Nothing. "Elizabeth?"

He leaned closer and her soft even breathing told him she was asleep. Grimacing, he laid his head back against the seat. Wasn't this peachy? He was burning up with desire and she was sound asleep!

If he had any sense, he'd sleep too. If only his blood wasn't boiling inside with the need to take her in his arms and make love to her. But he didn't dare give in to his impulses. The few times he'd as much as touched her, she had either tightened up or pulled away. Never had he known a woman to react so.

Perhaps he'd been too harsh with her. Maybe that's why she seemed so fearful of him. He regretted having lost his temper during the course of these last few days, and though he'd had good reason for doing so, he swore never again to raise his voice or otherwise show anger—no matter how recklessly she drove.

He would do anything—anything at all—to rebuild her trust in him. He never wanted to feel her tremble at his touch again.

She stirred, gently at first, then began to move her head frantically from side to side as if having a bad dream. "Elizabeth?" he whispered. He hesitated to lay so much as a finger on her for fear he would bring her more distress.

Thrashing about in her seat, she muttered, but he couldn't understand the confused, almost feverish words she uttered. Then suddenly she stilled and her voice grew clear as a crystal bell. "It's raining. We can't go to the barn today." Her breathing returned to normal and she slept peacefully.

Questions about her past nagged at him. Her words repeated themselves over and over in his mind. It was as if he'd witnessed a horrible crime and couldn't stop thinking about it. But this was crazy. Lots of people had nightmares, and she'd said nothing alarming. If anything she sounded bright, almost happy about the rain. So why was he so certain that a deep and abiding anguish lurked behind every word?

He stared into the darkness and tried to concentrate on the wind and the constant sound of rushing water, but it was her soft breathing he heard, her soft breathing that wrapped around him like the words of a beautiful song. "Oh, Elizabeth," he murmured, "why do you always pull away?"

# Chapter 17

"Driving at night can scare the living daylights out of you!"

*Women at the Wheel*
Circa 1915

It was still dark when Elizabeth woke. "It's cold," she whispered. The little square of blanket they shared barely covered their laps.

"Move closer," Jimmy said. "We can keep each other warm."

It made sense; Elizabeth knew it made sense and still she couldn't bring herself to move.

"I'm not going to hurt you, Elizabeth. Dammit, we can't sit here and freeze to death!"

Feeling foolish, she moved away from the steering wheel. A bolt of electricity shot up her spine the moment his arm slid around her shoulders. "There," he whispered softly, pressing his head next to hers. "Isn't that warmer?"

Panic rose inside like a volcano about to explode. She wanted to pull away, run, hide. But a part of her responded to the warmth he offered, to the soothing words he whispered, to the protective shield he provided. Slowly the panic began to subside, fading away like angry clouds at the end of a violent storm. Gradually, her muscles relaxed.

She felt like she was floating on a warm cloud, like she was a fragile blossom held by a sturdy stem. Was this how love felt? Not knowing the answer saddened her and made her realize more than ever how much was missing from her life.

"Your hair smells like orange blossoms," he whispered.

Her eyes flew open. Fear pressed its ugly sharp claws into her as the past came hurling toward her like a runaway train. *Your hair smells so good.*

Pushing away the memory, she swallowed the sob that rose in her throat.

"Is something wrong?" Jimmy asked, apparently sensing her apprehension.

"No," she lied, forcing herself to relax. "Nothing's wrong."

"Elizabeth," he whispered. "Don't worry. I'll take care of you."

Lord, how she wanted to believe him. Wanted to believe in love and all that went with it. But it was hard—so terribly, terribly hard to overcome the habits of a lifetime.

Hard and maybe even impossible.

She awoke the following morning still sheltered in Jimmy's arm, the gray light of dawn pushing back the night. She moved her head ever so slightly to study his face. He was still asleep. A sprinkling of dark whiskers covered his handsome, strong jaw.

His brilliant blue eyes usually commanded her attention, but with his lids lowered, the soft, sensitive curve of his mouth captured her interest today. She traced a visual line around his lips and felt her own mouth tingle with a strange and unfamiliar need. God love an orphan! If she wasn't tempted to kiss him on the lips!

Her heart skipped a beat, then raced like an engine. Warmth and safety had been her main concerns during the night, but in the dim light of day the nearness of him made her heart pound and her body feel shivery in a way that was both threatening and pleasurable.

She'd grown up fearing the part of men that turned them into brutes; today she feared the womanly part within her that was tempted to unleash Jimmy's maleness.

He stirred and his eyes opened. For a moment he looked confused, but the startled look left his face as soon as his gaze settled on her face. He lifted his head off her shoulder and smiled. "Good morning."

Afraid he could guess her thoughts, and more than a little disconcerted by them, she looked away.

He pulled his arm from around her shoulders. "The rain's stopped." He unfastened the curtains and climbed outside, stretching his long, lean body with a yawn.

Walking around Old Ironsides, he captured her eyes through the windshield. For a breathless moment, his heated gaze locked with hers, then he nodded in the direction of the road above.

"I'll hike to the road. See if I can flag down someone. Stay here. I won't be long."

She lifted her hand in a half-wave, then watched him slip and slide his way up the embankment before disappearing over the crest. The automobile seemed empty without him and she felt very much alone.

Worried about his safety, she stood on the running board and waited anxiously. The water level had dropped, but the ground was saturated.

It seemed like an eternity before he returned, with the photographer and undertaker trailing behind.

Staggs, holding a box camera firmly in hand, looked like a young reporter eager to catch a news event. " 'Morning, Miss Davenport. Wow! No one will believe the fix you got yourself into this time." He gave her a reassuring smile. "But they will after they see these photos."

She scowled at him. She felt like a wreck, her body so stiff, she could hardly move. Lord knows what she must look like. "I did not get myself in a fix! That fool Fastbender ran me off the road!"

Staggs stared through the viewfinder of his camera. "That's perfect!" he called. "Shake your fist again! That's the way."

"If I ever get my hands on him I'll—"

"Hold it! Perfect!"

His camera clicked and he moved around to the front of the car, spreading his legs across a puddle so as to get a closer shot at the front wheel.

"I thought you'd be on your way to Chicago by now," she said irritably.

" 'Fraid not. The road's washed away up yonder and me and the other drivers were forced to spend the night in our vehicles. Can't complain, though. We're all in the same boat."

Elizabeth couldn't believe her good fortune. "Are you saying that no one made it to the next checkpoint?"

"Not a one. Daresay we won't make it till dark."

While Staggs took his photographs, Stonegate and Jimmy set to work digging Old Ironsides out of the mud.

After a while, Stonegate shook his head in disgust. "Mud!" he spat out. "It's an undertaker's worst nightmare."

Elizabeth nodded in sympathy. "I appreciate your helping us."

"Don't mention it, ma'am. Your mechanic, here, said this race is mighty important to you."

"I'm sure it must be important to you, too. To both of you."

Staggs snapped another photo. "Actually, a friend of mine was scheduled to race but he was thrown from his horse. So I said I'd race in his place. It gives me a chance to see the country, take some photographs." He pointed his camera at Stonegate. "So why are you in the race?"

Stonegate lifted his head in a classic pose. "For the money, of course, like everyone else. I plan to buy me a fine piece of land with a great view. Someplace peaceful and serene."

Staggs snapped his photograph. "Do you plan to build a house?"

"A house? Oh, no, nothing like that. I plan to build a cemetery." He leaned on his shovel, a faraway look on his face. "I've always wanted to own my own cemetery. I tell you, with the way people drive nowadays, we're going to need them."

Jimmy stopped digging and walked to the other side of the car where Stonegate had dug an enormous hole. "We're trying to dig Old Ironsides out, not bury it."

A sheepish grin spread across Stonegate's face. "Sorry, I got carried away. I can't seem to stop digging a hole until it's six feet deep. It's an occupational hazard."

"That's why I like photography," Staggs said, lifting his camera for another shot. "There aren't any occupational hazards."

Jimmy tossed a shovelful of dirt in Stonegate's hole. "If you don't put that camera away, there will be!"

They reached the outskirts of Jimmy's hometown of Hogs Head after dark that night—two days behind schedule, but not as far behind the others as Jimmy had originally feared. The rain had turned out to be a blessing in disguise.

Elizabeth hadn't said much during the last few hours and he could guess why. Hogs Head was where they parted company.

"Elizabeth, I'm going to find you a good mechanic, I swear."

"I'm not worried," she said lightly.

"You're not?"

"Not at all. You said you'd find someone to take your place and I believe you."

Frowning, he stared at the dark road ahead. Couldn't she sound a bit more regretful? They had gone through hell and high water together. That had to count for something. "It might not be that easy," he bit out. "Mechanics don't exactly grow on trees, you know."

Arms folded, he glowered in the dark. Normally, he loved coming home, but tonight he felt little joy in knowing Hogs Head was just ahead. If anything, he grew more irritable with each passing mile, knowing his hometown was that much closer.

He was just tired, he decided. And exhausted. After a good night's sleep, he'd be his own good-natured self again.

They approached the town limits, and knowing how tricky the turn ahead was, he sat forward. "Watch out for the curve. Take it nice and easy. . . ."

Just as Elizabeth was halfway through the curve, the bright lights of the electrical plant blinded her.

"Easy does it!"

Instead of braking, Elizabeth pressed down hard on the gas pedal. Old Ironsides plowed through the fence of the Hunter Electrical Works and headed straight for the power plant.

Faster than a wink, Jimmy reached for the steering wheel, giving it a quick jerk. "Hit the brake!" he yelled. "The brake!" They missed the plant, but rammed into the steel tower. Old Ironsides came to a jolting stop, throwing Jimmy forward and back like a rag doll.

A loud boom shook the Model T. Sparks danced around the car, snapping and crackling like fireworks. A brilliant flare exploded, lighting the sky with a series of bright flashing lights. Then, suddenly, it was pitch-black.

"What was that?" Elizabeth asked, her voice shaking.

Jimmy spoke in a low, hoarse voice that was barely more than a whisper. "You just blew up the Hunter Electrical Works."

# Chapter 18

"The backseat driver is the only motorist who never runs out of fuel."

*Women at the Wheel*
Circa 1915

Jimmy climbed out of the car in a daze. He couldn't believe it. The electrical works!

Not a single light was visible for as far as the eye could see. Fortunately, nothing had caught fire, but the smell of burning wires permeated the air.

Fire bells clanged in the distance, calling the Hogs Head volunteer fire brigade into action. Jimmy dreaded the task of explaining how the head of the electrical works happened to be a passenger in the horseless vehicle that had rammed into the transformer.

"Jimmy?"

Under any other circumstances, her plaintive voice would have melted him. Tonight, he gritted his teeth and fought back the urge to wring her pretty little neck. She'd gone too far this time with her reckless driving. Way too far.

"What?"

"I didn't mean to cause you so much trouble."

He was saved from having to respond by the arrival of the fire brigade's horse-drawn hook and ladder and the recently purchased gasoline-powered Model T fire truck.

The shiny fire truck had been used for only one fire so far, with disastrous results. The gleaming machine had arrived promptly, but it had drawn so much attention from the crowd—and the firemen had been so eager to show off the truck's modern equipment—that the Hogs Head Brewery had burned to the ground, unnoticed.

Now, sirens blared and lights flashed as men dressed in yellow rubber coats and black leather helmets poured out of their vehicles like an army of ants.

Hot on the trail of the firemen were numerous citizens in their automobiles, followed by a line of horse-drawn buggies.

The fire chief, a congenial man by the name of Walt "Smoky" Hampton, walked up to Jimmy and shook his hand. "It seems you have a problem."

"Yes, well . . . eh . . . This is Miss Davenport. She's new to these parts. That's why she missed the turn."

"That's right," Elizabeth agreed, looking strangely subdued. "Had it not been after dark, I'm sure I wouldn't have missed the turn."

Smoky hooked his thumbs on to his bright red suspenders and scraped the ground with the toe of his rubber boot. "Didn't see it? The electrical works is lit up brighter than the Great White Way in New York City. It's hard to believe you didn't see it, ma'am."

"Oh, I saw it all right," Elizabeth said. "But the lights blinded me so much I didn't know which way was up. . . ."

"Jimmy! Is that you?" Before he had time to reply, his aunt Hattie had thrown her arms around his neck, practically knocking him over in the process.

Rumor had it that Jimmy's aunt was in her late seventies, though no one could prove it. She claimed she was on the sunny side of sixty, and anything that did not support her contention had mysteriously disappeared years ago, including the family Bible where births and marriages had been recorded for generations.

She'd gone to great lengths to hide her true age and in recent years had scrupulously avoided apparel or hairstyles she thought made her look old before her time. From her painted bow lips to her mop of shocking red hair, she was a presence to be reckoned with.

Shouting orders to Smoky, with whom she'd been at constant war since he'd declared the general store she'd owned and operated for close to forty years a fire hazard, she glared at him when he ignored her. "Damn fool!" she muttered. "He don't know nothing about nothing."

Ignoring the fireman, she fluttered around Jimmy like a fussy old hen. "Oh, my poor dear boy. Are you all right?"

"Of course he's all right," Jimmy's uncle Barney said from behind her. A tall, stately man with snow-white hair, he leveled his faded eyes on Jimmy with a look of affection. "He's standing, isn't he?"

"Uncle Barney's right," Jimmy said, gently pulling himself out of his aunt's arms. "I'm fine. And now I want you to meet someone." He reached for Elizabeth's hand and pulled her into the glare of light. "Uncle Barney, Aunt Hattie, everyone, this is Elizabeth Davenport."

A gasp of surprise rose through the crowd. "That's the automobile driver," Hank Bolter, the town mechanic, called out.

"It looks like it ... ," replied Sheriff Williams, who had just driven up in his Reo runabout.

Then everyone started talking at once. "Hold your horses!" the sheriff yelled. "I can't hear myself think." He turned his attention to Elizabeth. "Is this true, ma'am? Are you the woman driver?"

"Yes, I am," Elizabeth replied.

Aunt Hattie gave Elizabeth a thorough visual check. "You don't look big enough to scare a fly, let alone drive a car across the country."

"I have help," Elizabeth explained. "Jimmy's my mechanic."

All eyes swung to Jimmy, then everyone began talking at once all over again.

"It can't be."

"I don't believe it."

"Jimmy ain't no mechanic." Bolter's voice rose above the rest. "The town ain't big enough for two of us. Besides, who's going to run the electrical works?"

"If Jimmy says he's a fanatic, then he's a fanatic!" Aunt Hattie scolded.

Jimmy raised his voice so his hard-of-hearing aunt could hear. "You better change the batteries in your hearing aid, Aunt Hat."

"Oh, dear." She reached for the hearing device she wore tucked in her ear and gave it a good shake. "Why, I never dreamed that our dear sweet Jimmy was in that race."

"Don't worry, Aunt Hat. My racing days are over. I agreed to help out until we reached Hogs Head and that's it. Would it be all right if Miss Davenport stayed with you for the night once she's checked in with the race officials?"

"Of course she can stay with me," Aunt Hattie declared. "Don't you worry about a thing."

He pecked his aunt on the cheek. "Now if you'll excuse me, I've got work to do." He glanced at Elizabeth, who was the center of his aunt's attention. She looked pale and exhausted, but knowing Aunt Hat, she was in good hands.

Since the danger of fire was no longer a concern, he walked stiffly to his office. The old injury in his leg was acting up, his back felt like it had been rammed with a steel rod, and he had a king-size headache. He'd give anything to climb into the nearest bed and sleep for a week. But as the head of the electrical works, his job was to restore electricity to the town as soon as possible.

What a disaster! Of course, since Elizabeth Davenport had kidnapped him, it had been one disaster after another. He'd been shot at twice, fined, and nearly

eaten alive by a wild dog. He'd been run off the road
and pretty near drowned. Now he'd been embarrassed
in front of his own family and friends. There was no
way in hell he would continue as Elizabeth's mechanic,
and she could beg and plead all she wanted.

The next morning, he awoke to the sound of his
aunt's strident voice coming from downstairs. With the
power out, and his own small apartment having been
closed up in his absence, he'd decided to spend the
night at his parents' house, which was equipped with
a dynamo for just such electrical emergencies.

He cocked his ear upon hearing his name. Whatever
it was that had his aunt riled up so early in the morning obviously had something to do with him.

He glanced at the clock. It was only seven a.m. He'd
had less than three hours of shut-eye. Rubbing the
sleep out of his eyes, he rose, and after attending to
his morning ablutions, hurried down the stairs.

His mother and aunt fell silent as he walked into
the kitchen. It was another indication he had been the
topic of their conversation. "Good morning," he said,
forcing a cheerfulness he didn't feel.

His aunt sniffed, but his mother returned his greeting. "Good morning, Jimmy. Your aunt was just telling me about that poor dear woman driver."

*Poor dear woman, indeed!* He walked over to the
gas stove and poured himself a cup of coffee. Judging
by the look on their faces, though, he was going to
need something stronger than coffee to brace himself.

He held up his hand, palm side out, and took a long
sip of the hot brew. The last few days on the road
had made him appreciate the simple things in life, like
hot coffee. Not sure he was ready to handle whatever
his mother and aunt had on their minds, he finally
signaled with his hand he was ready, and right on cue,
they both started talking at once.

"One at a time," he pleaded. His head still ached.
He had a mess at the electrical works and he was

feeling guilty as hell, though there was no logical reason for him to feel anything but justifiable anger. Elizabeth had brought on her own troubles. In any case, he felt like hell, and the last thing he needed was to face his mother and aunt when they were wearing their righteous expressions.

Aunt Hattie folded her arms in front of her heaving bosom. "How can you leave that poor sweet girl stranded?"

"Poor? Sweet?"

"Aunt Hattie means Elizabeth," his mother explained. Kate Hunter regarded her son with a look of displeasure. "Your aunt's taken quite a liking to her. We all have."

He stared at his mother. "You've met Elizabeth?"

"Your father and I met her last night, and I must say, we were very impressed."

"That's because you never had to ride in an automobile with her."

"But she's written an excellent book," Kate said, as if this justified whatever else Elizabeth might do.

Jimmy almost dropped his coffee cup. "You *read* her book?"

"Of course I have," Kate said. "And I agree with her fully. Women should have a say over their own bodies."

"You're damned tooting they should!" Aunt Hattie exclaimed. "Women are tired of being sex slaves!"

Jimmy groaned and rubbed his forehead.

"To think you, my own nephew, my own flesh and blood . . ."

Jimmy started to remind her he was adopted, but thought better of it. Knowing Aunt Hattie, she'd probably destroyed any legal papers having to do with his adoption just so she could hold on to her stubborn claim that they were blood-related.

". . . to think you would refuse to continue as her mechanic," Aunt Hattie moaned. "Where are your manners? Where's your sense of responsibility?" She threw her hands up and gazed at the ceiling. "Dear God, where have we gone wrong?"

Unable to reason with either his mother or aunt, Jimmy gulped down the rest of his coffee and stomped out of the house. He didn't have time for female hysterics. He had work to do.

He drove his electric runabout through town on the way to the electrical works. Compared to Old Ironsides, the hum of his electric car was as pleasing to the ear as a cat's purr.

Emergency crews had worked through the night, and their vehicles were still parked next to the office when Jimmy pulled up.

A crowd of curious onlookers stood around Old Ironsides, and judging by the querulous sound of their voices, a full-fledged controversy was in progress. Jimmy scanned the sea of faces looking for Elizabeth, but she was nowhere in sight.

He wished the same could be said of Miss Irma Wannamaker. He'd hoped to reach his office unnoticed, but no such luck. No sooner had he parked his car than the prune-faced spinster whirled around and leveled a stony stare at him. A second-generation suffragette, she never missed an opportunity to stand on her soapbox. "Jimmy Hunter! How dare you leave that poor woman stranded."

He groaned inwardly and climbed out of his car, aware that he was now the center of attention. He clenched his fists and stood his ground. "I'm not leaving anyone stranded." Not wanting to get into an argument, he disappeared into his office and summoned his foreman, a mild-mannered bespectacled man by the name of Randy McGillis, to his office.

McGillis brought him up to date on their progress and assured him the electricity should be restored within the next few hours. Jimmy nodded. "Keep me fully informed." After his meeting with McGillis, Jimmy drove over to the Hogs Head Bank where his childhood friend, Cecil Dunkirk, worked as a bank teller.

Jimmy strolled up to the window and pretended to be making a deposit. Cecil's father owned the bank and Cecil insisted he had to work harder than anyone else so the other employees wouldn't accuse his father of showing favoritism.

"I need to talk to you."

Cecil flashed a crooked-toothed smile, then quickly composed himself in a businesslike manner so no one could accuse him of socializing on the job. Still, for all his business airs, he didn't look like a banker. He was too tall, for one thing, and no matter how conservatively he dressed, nothing could tone down his shock of red-orange hair. The only difference between his hair and Aunt Hattie's was that his was natural.

In recent years, Cecil seemed to sprout more freckles than good sense. He had wanted to be an automobile mechanic but had gone into the banking business to please his father.

"Can't it wait until after I get off work?" Cecil asked, barely moving his lips. He made a show of counting out a stack of one-hundred-dollar bills.

"It's important." Keeping his voice low, Jimmy told Cecil about Elizabeth and the race. Following Cecil's lead, he moved his own lips as little as possible.

"So what do you want me to do about it?"

"I want you to be her mechanic."

Cecil lost track of how much money he'd already counted. "What?"

"You heard me. Cecil, this is the chance of a lifetime. You've wanted to be an auto mechanic ever since Aunt Hattie drove her horseless carriage through the Methodist Church."

Cecil's hands stilled. "I thought it was a sign ... from, you know ..." He glanced upward. "If your aunt hadn't disrupted worship, Mr. Humbinger would have announced my engagement to his daughter. All because he caught Mary Jo and me petting on the

front porch." Aunt Hattie had caused so much damage when she crashed through the wall, the church
couldn't be used for the next three Sundays. By then,
Mary Jo's father had cooled down.

"It *was* a sign," Jimmy said.

"Maybe it was and maybe it wasn't," Cecil said.
"But I can't just walk out on my job."

Forgetting the need to be discreet, Jimmy's voice
rose. "If you don't do this, you'll never forgive yourself. Come on, Cecil. For once in your life stand up
to your father."

"Shhh." Cecil glanced around anxiously, and when
it appeared no one had noticed the personal nature
of the conversation, he replied, "If I don't follow in his
footsteps, it would kill him. Is that what you want?"

"Once you win the race, your father will have to
accept the inevitable."

"Win the race?" Cecil's face held the look of someone who had just been given three wishes from a
magic genie. But almost as soon as it appeared, the
light went out of his eyes. "What if the lady driver
doesn't win the race? I'd look like a fool in my father's eyes."

"Listen to me, Cecil. There're no guarantees. But
if you don't do this, you'll spend the rest of your life
stuck in this bank. Is that what you want?"

"No. . . ."

"Then what do you say?"

Cecil stuffed the money back into his drawer. After
a while, he looked up. "You're right, Jimmy. If I don't
take a chance, I'll be stuck here forever." He locked
the drawer, then hesitated for a full minute before
hanging the key ring on a nail. "You talked me into
it."

Jimmy sighed in relief, though his spirits were still
low. He had the utmost confidence in Cecil's mechanical ability. No question. Even so, Jimmy felt like he
was deserting Elizabeth. "Do you understand your responsibilities as a mechanic?"

"What do you take me for, Jimmy? Of course I understand my responsibilities. The mechanic keeps the engine running."

"Yes, well ..." Jimmy tried to choose his words carefully. "It's a little bit more than that."

Cecil's brows knit together. "What do you mean, more?"

"You have to navigate—you know, read maps, check the road signs. Make sure Miss Davenport stays on the ... eh, you know, right road."

"Doesn't sound too hard."

"And you have to make certain all the laws are obeyed."

"Laws? You mean like traffic laws? I thought that was the driver's responsibility."

"Normally it would be. But in this case ..."

Suspicion flashed in Cecil's eyes. "Are you saying that Miss Davenport is a reckless driver?"

"No, no, no! Nothing like that. She just gets ... distracted at times. It can happen to anyone." Jimmy pressed his face closer to the iron bars separating them. "Promise me you'll take care of her."

Cecil studied him closely. "You're really worried about her, aren't you?"

Jimmy shrugged. "No more than I would be about anyone else. One day you'll thank me for this, Cecil. Mark my words."

"I better."

Jimmy waited for Cecil to find another clerk to take over his window, then drove him to the electrical works. This would be great for Cecil, great for him. Hell, it would even be great for Elizabeth. She had only one thing on her mind: She wanted to win the race. She'd made that abundantly clear, and if anyone could help her achieve her goals, it was Cecil.

So why did he feel so miserable?

He knew why. It was because Elizabeth had no interest in him personally. However, he couldn't deny his own feelings; he was attracted to her as he'd never been attracted to any other woman in his life. And if he spent one more day alone with her in the small, crowded confines of Old Ironsides, he would make a fool of himself, he was sure of it. Better by far to bail out now, while he still could.

# Chapter 19

"Motorists who drive down the middle of the road don't know whether to turn right or left."

*Women at the Wheel*
Circa 1915

*Jimmy wouldn't leave me, would he?*

It was a question very much on Elizabeth's mind as she sat at the table in the warm, cozy kitchen of his childhood home and watched Jimmy's mother pour boiling water into a brown crock teapot.

In her midforties, Kate Hunter was still a beautiful woman, with only a few silver strands threaded through her reddish-blond hair. She had a youthful, trim body and an easy smile. Her clear blue eyes glowed with warmth and kindness.

Elizabeth had taken an instant liking to her. Since arriving in town last night, she had met Jimmy's mother and father, his aunt and uncle, and an amazing assortment of his brothers and sisters. She envied Jimmy for belonging to such a warm, loving family. How different her life might have been had she been half as fortunate.

Kate carried the teapot to the table. Blue Willow china was spread across an oil-boiled cloth. A vase of fresh flowers stood in the center of the table.

"I don't understand why Jimmy's being so stubborn about this. He started the race. I think he should finish it."

Elizabeth helped herself to a freshly baked brownie. "Don't blame Jimmy. It's been a very difficult race. And I'm afraid I'm not the best driver in the world, as my little mishap last night proves."

"Nonsense! Anyone can have an accident. No one should know that better than Jimmy. I can't tell you how many times he's blown out the windows of the house with his experiments. And once he electrocuted the chickens. Fortunately none of them were seriously injured, but their feathers fell out. You never saw such a sight in your life. People came from miles around to see our naked chickens."

Kate smiled and her eyes got that faraway look that mothers so often get whenever they recall their grown children's childhood antics. After a moment, she poured the brewed tea into two cups.

"I'm afraid I've had more than my share of accidents," Elizabeth explained.

"Why do you suppose that is?" Kate asked.

Elizabeth took a sip of the fragrant herbal tea before she replied. "For one thing, I have myopic eyes. I can't see more than a few feet in front of the car."

Kate stared at her in horror. "Good heavens. That could be dangerous. Why don't you wear eyeglasses?"

"Normally I do. But it's impossible to wear eyeglasses on the road. If I don't wear driving goggles, the road glare is terrible. And dust flies in my eyes until I can't see a thing. It's quite a nuisance, I must admit."

"Oh, dear, this *is* a problem." Kate stirred a teaspoon of sugar into her cup. "Does Jimmy know about your vision difficulties?"

"Oh, no! I didn't want to worry him. I've not told anyone but you. It's not as if I'm blind or anything; it's just hard for me to see the road clearly or to read the signs."

"Dear me." Kate watched Elizabeth over her teacup. "I wish there was something I could do."

"You've done enough already. Really you have."

Kate regarded Elizabeth thoughtfully. "Jimmy used to talk about you as a child. He always wondered what had become of you."

"He was a good friend to me when we were in the orphanage together—and later, on that train. Somehow he always seemed to make the day brighter and the night less dark. It seems fitting, somehow, that he grew up to be an electrician."

Kate nodded. "He was always fascinated by electricity, even as a boy. I'm sure you must know that Jimmy's parents were killed in a train accident."

"No, I didn't know. Jimmy never talks about the years before you adopted him."

"It was a terrible accident. The train plunged off a trestle and hundreds of people were killed. It's a miracle Jimmy lived."

"Is that how he injured his leg?" Elizabeth recalled Jimmy using crutches as a child, but she'd never known why. Since they'd met again, on occasion she'd noticed Jimmy limping or rubbing his leg.

"Yes. We were lucky to find a doctor in Boston who made it possible for Jimmy to walk without crutches." Kate sipped her tea before continuing. "We contacted the railroad for a report of the accident. That's when we learned that it had taken hours for rescue crews to reach the train. Jimmy was the sole survivor in his railroad car."

"How awful!"

"It *was* awful. Thank God the accident happened at night. It was so dark, Jimmy couldn't see the mangled bodies around him. His parents . . ." Kate took a deep breath. "I think he associates darkness with death. He was only a child when he first told me he wanted to grow up and make the dark disappear forever."

Elizabeth recalled the long-ago day when they were seven and Jimmy had climbed into her bedroom window with a gunnysack filled with candles he'd stolen from the orphanage pantry. Together they had lit every candle—and there must have been several dozen. Her room was as bright as sunlight by the time they'd finished, and it was truly a glorious sight.

Kate smiled to herself. "My Jimmy's done that, you know. Filled almost every house in Hogs Head with light. Because of him, this town is lit brighter than a bonfire at night. You're not the only one who's been blinded upon driving into town."

"You must be very proud of him." As they talked, Elizabeth helped herself to another brownie and had a second cup of tea. She was sorry when it was time to leave. "I best get started. I need to purchase supplies before I leave town. I also want to check out the eyeglasses in Aunt Hattie's General Store. I broke mine." She dreaded shopping for spectacles as it was such an ordeal to buy eyeglasses. Sometimes she'd have to try on countless numbers before she found a pair of ready-mades that improved her vision without eyestrain.

"I hope by now Jimmy has come to his senses and agrees to help you finish the race," Kate said.

"Oh, so do I, Mrs. Hunter. So do I."

Later, after she'd purchased her eyeglasses and a few necessities, including a box of Oreo biscuits in the hope Jimmy would change his mind, she rode with Aunt Hattie and Uncle Barney in their horse and buggy, Jimmy's parents following behind in their Buick touring car. They drove through town and headed for the electrical works.

Jimmy was standing near Old Ironsides when she arrived, and for a joyous moment, she dared to believe he intended to finish the race with her.

Seeing her nephew, Aunt Hattie gave an exasperated tutting sound. "It's a shameful day when one's very own flesh and blood walks away from his responsibilities."

"It's really not Jimmy's fault," Elizabeth said, surprised to find herself defending him. "He wouldn't have been my mechanic in the first place had I not kidnapped him."

Rather than looking shocked by such an outrageous confession, Aunt Hattie gave an approving nod. "And if you had any sense in that head of yours, you'd kid-nap him again!" With that she lifted the picnic basket filled with homemade baked goods from the back of the wagon and headed for Elizabeth's Model T.

Jimmy stood in the shade of an old oak tree, talking to a man with a mop of curly carrot-orange hair the likes of which she'd never seen outside the town of Hogs Head. Jimmy motioned for her to join them.

"Elizabeth, I want you to meet Cecil Dunkirk. He's agreed to be your mechanic for the rest of the race."

She tried with all her heart not to show her disappointment. "How do you do?" she said politely, hoping her voice didn't give her away.

Cecil grinned. "I'm doing just fine, ma'am. I checked your automobile over, and as soon as I finish fueling it, we can leave. I did have a hard time, though, straightening out that front bumper. Never saw a car with so many dents. If you ask me, you should write to Mr. Ford and complain."

"I don't think it's Mr. Ford's fault. . . . We drove on some rough roads."

"That's what Jimmy said. I hope this race succeeds in drawing attention to that particular problem. Next year, I plan to drive all the way to California. I hear there's a redwood tree in one of those national parks with a tunnel right through the center that's big enough to drive your car through. Must be something. Driving through a tree."

"I would say driving through a tree is considerably better than driving up one," Jimmy said.

Elizabeth's gaze collided with Jimmy's, and for a second she thought she saw something flicker in the depths of his eyes—a softening, perhaps, maybe even regret. But all too soon the look was gone, replaced by stubborn censure.

Cecil scratched his head. "I don't think it's a good idea to drive up a tree."

Jimmy ran his hand over a dented fender. "Cecil is an excellent mechanic and I've filled him in on the rules of the race."

"I'll do my best to keep your vehicle in good running condition," Cecil said, obviously sensing her reluctance to accept him as her mechanic.

"I'm sure you will," Elizabeth said kindly. The man looked so earnest, she didn't have the heart to hurt his feelings. "I'm ready to go when you are." It made no sense to prolong the agony.

Cecil pushed a portable fuel dispenser over to the car, leaving her and Jimmy alone. Jimmy looked tired, his thoughts kept hidden by the rigid mask of his face. She swallowed hard, not wanting him to know how much she wanted him to stay with her. "Then it's true. You're going to desert me, just like you said?"

"I'm not deserting you. I told you I'd find someone to replace me and that's what I've done."

Blinking back tears, she could no longer keep her feelings to herself. Cecil would probably be a fine mechanic, but he couldn't hold her like Jimmy had held her, couldn't make her feel as safe and secure as she had felt with Jimmy. "Jimmy . . . I . . ."

"Come along, girl," Aunt Hattie shouted. "Why are you lollygagging about? You've got a race to win!"

One by one his family members rushed over to hug her. Aunt Hattie pulled a hand-knitted shawl off her shoulders and handed it to her. Kate and Jonas gave her a recently patented gasoline gauge.

"Just put this end into the gasoline tank," Jimmy's father explained, "and this little gauge will indicate how much gasoline is left."

"How clever." Elizabeth smiled and thanked everyone. She pretended everything was as it should be, but in reality her heart was breaking. Whenever she could manage a glance Jimmy's way without seeming obvious, she chanced it, keeping her head lowered.

If his stoic face was any indication, he had no intention of changing his mind. She told everyone goodbye and, mustering as much dignity as she could, walked with grim determination to her car. Though moments earlier she had almost made a fool of herself, she would now rather die than let Jimmy know how she felt.

Jimmy stood next to Old Ironsides, holding the door open for her. "Good luck, Elizabeth."

She kept her fists jammed into her deep pockets and her chin held high. "Thank you for your help."

"It was my pleasure."

They were so polite to each other. So distant.

"You better go," Aunt Hattie said, scowling at Fastbender, who zoomed past them the second the required twelve-hour layover had been satisfied, shouting jeering remarks at Elizabeth.

"Oh, no, not again. The lady road hog!"

Aunt Hattie placed her fists on her hips. "You bloody, fool-mongering hypocrite," she yelled at the top of her considerable lungs. "Your father looks funny and your mother's a ..."

"Aunt Hattie!" Kate scolded, tugging on the older woman's arm.

"Well, it's true!" Aunt Hattie declared, not looking the least bit apologetic. "Mercy me, I don't know what the world is coming to. Imagine talking to a lady like that."

"It's the Sunday supplements," Miss Wannamaker said with a look of disdain. "I tell you those comics are ruining our youth."

Jimmy put his arm around his aunt's robust shoulders. Watching the love that passed between them—and recalling the night those same arms had held her—Elizabeth felt a stabbing pain in her heart. Swallowing hard, she spun around, fighting for control. She stepped on the running board and scooted across the seat until she was behind the wheel.

She managed to put her goggles in place before anyone could see her tear-filled eyes. The sooner she left the warm and friendly town, the better. She wished to God she'd never come to Hogs Head. She wished she never knew how wonderful a town could be. For it only made her past seem that much more empty and her future that much more bleak.

Adjusting the pillow at her back and putting on her gloves, she waited for Cecil to crank the engine and take his place in the companion seat. For the love of an orphan, she would do this. She would finish the race, build her orphan home, and forget she ever met the likes of Jimmy Hunter.

With a final wave, she took off, horn blaring, wheels screeching, leaving a wake of dust and fumes—along with a piece of her heart—behind her.

# Chapter 20

"Nothing is more irritating than a temperamental mechanic."

*Women at the Wheel*
Circa 1915

Electricity was restored in Hogs Head before dark, but Jimmy was convinced the arc lights on Main Street were not as bright as usual. His exhausted foreman insisted the power station was working at full wattage. "I tested the lines myself." McGillis was a good man and Jimmy had no reason to doubt him. Still ...

"There's nothing wrong with the lights," his father said that night as Jimmy sat around the dining room table with his parents and siblings. "It must be the mood you're in."

"I'm not in any mood," Jimmy protested. His father had been the third person in the last hour to accuse him of being in a mood. There was nothing wrong with his mood. Nothing wrong at all that a simple telephone call wouldn't cure.

After having supper at his parents' house and driving back to his own one-bedroom apartment, he marched into his small though orderly kitchen, picked up the handset on the wall phone, and turned the crank. Overly anxious, he was nonetheless surprised to find himself barking at the operator. Tempering his voice, he explained in a quieter but still terse voice,

"I'm telling you something is wrong with the telephone lines."

Miss Pinckney harrumphed into his ear. As the one and only operator for the Hogs Head telephone company, she considered it part of her job to know everyone's business. Lord help the man or woman who did something without letting her know in advance. When Flossie Cartwright eloped without first informing Miss Pinckney, it was a full six months before the incensed operator allowed the new bride to place a telephone call.

"Don't you think I'd know if there was a problem with the lines, Jimmy Hunter?" she said in that annoying pinch-nosed voice of hers.

"Are you sure there were no calls for me while I was at my parents' house?" He had kept the telephone operator informed of his every whereabouts, calling her faithfully whenever he left his apartment, calling her again upon arriving at the electrical works, and later when he was leaving. Still, it was possible something had slipped her mind.

"I'm going to tell you one more time," she huffed in his ear. "No one called you!"

He slammed the handset into the holder and paced back and forth in front of the telephone. It was a straight shot to Chicago from Hogs Head. Elizabeth should have checked into the Chicago Automobile Club, the next official check-in station, hours ago.

In an effort to take his mind off his worries, he sat down in his favorite chair to read Elizabeth's book. He had borrowed this copy from his aunt's library.

*The Wisdom of Family Limitation* was an impressive-looking book, with the name Miss Elizabeth Davenport inscribed on the cover. The book turned out to be lively and shocking, but hardly obscene.

Elizabeth minced no words in getting her message across that women owed it to themselves, their families, and society as a whole to have control over their bodies. "The odd notion that women are sex slaves creates poverty and despair."

Doctors who refused to educate themselves in women's matters were, in her opinion, ignorant. "The common belief of the day that birth control is synonymous with prostitution is outrageous." Blaming society's refusal to face facts, she cited the number of children living on city streets, "Many of whom die from starvation or end up living in abusive homes."

*Like Elizabeth.* The thought did nothing to relieve his guilt and even less for his peace of mind.

It was irrational to feel guilty for something over which he'd had no control. His promise to protect her had been a childish fantasy. For all he knew, it was still a childish fantasy. That sad realization filled him with remorse, and shaking his head, he continued reading.

The book was written specifically for women, but Jimmy absorbed every word. He felt both a sense of awe and relief at what Elizabeth had written. Awe for the sheer logic behind what she had to say. Relief because she said nothing about women giving up sex altogether. Only that women should control the number of births according to their own particular circumstances.

The way she had reacted to his touch, he'd naturally assumed . . .

He jumped to his feet, sending the book flying across the room. It didn't matter what he'd thought. She was gone and what was he doing? Waiting around like a lovesick schoolboy, that's what!

And it was all because of Cecil! Dammit! Was it asking too much for the man to make a simple telephone call? Just one telephone call was all it would take, and Jimmy would put her out of his mind and go to bed.

He *could* put her out of his mind. Of course he could.

As the hours crept slowly by, his imagination began

to get the best of him. Maybe Elizabeth hadn't made it to the next checkpoint. That's why Cecil hadn't called! Maybe they were at the bottom of a ditch somewhere. In the dark!

Or maybe that fool cowboy had pulled one of his practical jokes. For all he knew, Fastbender had run her off the road again. Hell, knowing her, she could be halfway to Alaska by now. To the North Pole! At the bottom of Lake Michigan!

The more possibilities that occurred to him, the more depressed and worried he became.

What was he thinking to send someone with Cecil's inexperience along? Maybe all that time spent in the bank counting money had adversely affected Cecil's brain. It was possible, wasn't it?

The grandfather clock struck nine, then ten, and still Cecil hadn't called. Jimmy debated about calling it a night, then decided to wait another hour.

The clock struck eleven. He'd wait till midnight.

At two o'clock in the morning, he reluctantly came to the conclusion that Cecil wasn't going to call. He finally turned off the lights and went to bed.

Instead of pacing the floor, he took to twisting and turning until his sheets were knotted and the blankets ended up in a heap on the floor. Abandoning any thought of sleep, he turned on the light and lay staring up at the ceiling.

Why the hell didn't Cecil use the damned telephone?

Elizabeth and Cecil had had car trouble some two hours after leaving Hogs Head and it had taken Cecil the rest of the day to repair it. Unlike Jimmy, who was not opposed to doing whatever was necessary to get the car running again, Cecil was a perfectionist.

"I'm not riding in a car held together with chewing gum!" he announced when she suggested Jimmy's trick for handling hose leaks. It was the first of many arguments they were to have that day. Cecil was horri-

fied when she wanted to drop eggs into the radiator—
and Jimmy's habit of pouring paraffin into the fuel
tank to make the fuel last longer nearly sent him into
a frenzy.

Still, nothing compared to the shouting match that
occurred after she'd driven through the front window
of the Automobile Club of America.

Cecil had been livid and he didn't mind letting the
entire city of Chicago know it.

"Of all the reckless things to do!" he screamed at
her.

"Reckless?" Elizabeth shouted back. "How do you
expect to drive through a redwood tree if you can't
even drive through a glass window?"

It took several hours to straighten out the mess with
the Automobile Club. The other drivers were furious
because they weren't allowed to check in, and the police threatened to haul the lot of them to jail if order
wasn't restored.

Today, things hadn't gone much better. After leaving Chicago, the road was worse by far than any she'd
driven since leaving Buffalo. Old Ironsides rose and
dipped so violently it was all Elizabeth could do to
keep from bouncing out of her seat.

Next to her, Cecil held on to the door and recited
the Lord's Prayer. Earlier, it had been the twenty-
third psalm. Elizabeth shook her head in disgust.
Sheesh. What was it with these mechanics?

"Are you sure we're not lost?" he asked somewhere
between *the valley of death* and *beside still waters.*

"You have the map," she said irritably. So far he'd
offered little help. For one thing, he suffered from
motion sickness, and she had to keep stopping to let
him out. When he wasn't sick he recited the Bible.

Cecil checked the compass he kept in his shirt
pocket, but the car was bouncing up and down, making the instrument worthless. "Something doesn't
seem right with the sun," he said at last.

Elizabeth glanced up. There wasn't any sun; thick

gray clouds covered the entire sky. Cecil might be a mechanic and have the entire Bible memorized, but he sure didn't know dinky-do about navigating.

"Stop!" Cecil shouted, sounding more like Jimmy every minute. Letting out another exasperated "Sheesh," she braked, but only because she didn't want to chance his throwing up in the car.

He climbed out of Old Ironsides and walked around in a circle, staring down at his compass. "We seem to have veered off the road," he called to her.

"What do you mean, veered off?" she asked. She climbed out of the car to join him, her boots sinking into the newly overturned soil.

"Do you see a road anywhere?" he asked.

Hands on her waist, she glanced around. It was darn annoying the way farmers kept plunking their fields down in the middle of the road. There ought to be a law against such careless placement of crops. "No, I don't. Where do you suppose the road went to this time?"

"There's a sign over there on the fence post." He pointed to the far side of the field, but without her eyeglasses, Elizabeth saw only a blur. "Maybe it will direct us back to the road. Stay here."

She climbed back into the idling car and waited. She wished with all her heart that it was Jimmy she waited for, not Cecil.

Jimmy. Just the thought of his name filled her with such longing, she could hardly breathe. But she would never forget the hard, unforgiving, and unrelenting look on his face as she drove away.

Her thoughts were interrupted by Cecil's frantic cries. She turned her head in his direction and strained her eyes, but she couldn't see much. She searched for her eyeglasses. *Dammit, what did I do with the eyeglasses I bought?*

"Cecil? Are you all right?"

By the time she found her eyeglasses, he was only

a few feet away, running full speed with a black bull at his heels.

"Oh, dear God," she cried. "Do hurry!"

He took a flying leap, landing in the seat by her side. "Go! Go!"

Needing no further incentive, she stepped on the gas pedal and raced across the field. The bull charged after them, its steaming snout mere inches from their rear bumper. With a mighty thud, it rammed against Old Ironsides.

"Faster!" Cecil screamed. He was huddled on the floor, his red head bopping up and down like a rubber ball.

"I'm going as fast as I can!" She glanced back at the bull. Jumping Jupiter! Wouldn't you know? One of her streaming satin ribbons was red!

In all the confusion, she inadvertently turned the wheel, and Old Ironsides spun around in a wide arc to face the bull. The confused beast came to a sliding halt, the dirt literally flying out from beneath its skidding hooves. The wide-eyed beast and Old Ironsides faced each other like feuding foes. Elizabeth honked her horn and the bull took off in the other direction, with Old Ironsides giving chase.

Cecil lifted his head and peered over the backseat. His eyes were so wide, mostly white could be seen. "Where's the bull?"

"In front of us!"

Cecil's head spun around. The bull was in front, all right, frantically trying to escape. The bull and the Model T were heading straight for a deserted barn. "Yeow!"

At the last possible moment, the bull veered in one direction, Elizabeth in another. She followed an old wagon trail that was heavily rutted with tracks, but at least it wasn't furrowed.

Cecil reclaimed his seat and mopped his forehead with a handkerchief.

"What did the sign say?" she asked. "Did it say where the road was?"

"It said 'Beware of Bull.' "

It took them another hour before they found a farmer who pointed them in the right direction. Thanking the man profusely, they started on their way again. Suddenly the car sputtered and the motor died.

"Now what?" Elizabeth groaned, slamming the steering wheel with her open palm.

"We're out of gas," Cecil said.

"How could we be out of gas? We just filled the tank this morning."

Fortunately for them, the farmer was still in sight. Cecil chased after him and got a lift into town. It was a full two hours before he returned, hauling a gasoline can.

"Hurry up," Elizabeth said. "We'll never make it to the checkpoint by nightfall."

After filling the tank, Cecil put the seat back and cranked up the motor. But instead of climbing into the companion seat, he walked around to the driver's side and leaned his arm on the dummy door. "I hate to tell you this, Miss Davenport. Being that you're a friend of Jimmy's and all. But I've made a momentous decision. I've decided to go back to Hogs Head where I belong."

Elizabeth stared at him in disbelief. "What do you mean, go back to Hogs Head? You can't leave me. You promised Jimmy."

"I tried my best to do right by that promise, but I can't stand it anymore. I've been chased by a bull and was nearly scared out of my wits when you drove through the window of the Automobile Club."

"But we checked in before car number three," she argued. It was a close call; Crankshaw was walking through the door when she accidentally stepped on the wrong pedal and crashed through the window. The last she saw of Crankshaw, he was diving beneath a desk.

"I tell you, Miss Davenport, my bones have been rattled so much, I swear they're about to turn to jelly. And my stomach ... I can't take this no more. I thought I wanted to be a mechanic, but now I realize that banking is far less nerve-wracking. My pa was right. I'm not cut out to be a mechanic."

"Sheesh! How do you expect to drive through a redwood if you let a little thing like a bull and a glass window rattle you? Do you think driving through a tree is going to be a picnic?"

"I'm not driving through any tree and I'm not getting back in your car. I'm finished. I'll never touch another automobile as long as I live. That nice farmer over there is going to drive me back to the train station. I'm sorry." Without giving her a chance to respond, he grabbed his suitcase from the back of the car and hurried toward the wagon.

Elizabeth jumped out of the car and chased after him. "You can't do this. You can't desert me. You're supposed to be Jimmy's friend."

"I'm sorry, Miss Davenport, really I am." He heaved his pack into the wagon and swung himself onto the seat next to the driver.

Hands at her waist, Elizabeth watched the wagon pull away. Now what was she going to do? What a fine kettle of fish this was. And it was all Jimmy's fault!

# Chapter 21

"Love is blind, but no more than a motorist in a dust storm."

*Women at the Wheel*
Circa 1915

Jimmy had deserted her. And now, so had Cecil.

Cecil abandoning his job was a nuisance, but it didn't affect her emotionally. In some regards, she was glad to be rid of the man. He was a worse fuddy-duddy than Jimmy!

Jimmy.

She drew a ragged breath. Just thinking his name brought a lump to her throat and tears to her eyes. Lord, she'd done too much crying lately. Irritated at herself, she wiped away the tears with the heels of her hands and forced herself to take deep breaths.

He didn't care a fig about her. So why should she care even half a fig about him?

Oh, but she did. She cared for him with her heart and soul, with the entire essence of her being. No matter how hard she tried to deny it, her love for him was like a knife cutting her into little tiny pieces.

Nearly overwhelmed by the deep and abiding pain that threatened to pull her into a dark abyss of loneliness, she tried to assert some authority over her thoughts. It was her own fault. She should never have let a man get close to her. She should never have let him touch her. Kiss her.

Never!

And she never would again!

Feeling worse than before, she nonetheless recovered enough to consider her options. If she drove into the next checkpoint without a mechanic, she'd be disqualified. Somehow, she had to make certain that didn't happen.

Refusing to give in to the depression that was like a weight on her shoulders, she pulled around the farmer's wagon and hit the open road at full speed.

From Chicago the route had turned south to St. Louis and traveled past fields of newly planted corn. Cattle grazed on the flat prairie land; numerous rivers and streams crisscrossed it. It seemed to Elizabeth she was forever having to brake in order to cross a narrow bridge or ford a shallow stream.

The skies were fairly clear, but the wind began to blow, whipping up dust from newly plowed fields and flinging it into the air. Grit filled her nostrils and eyes, making it difficult to breathe or even see the road. She missed a signpost and had to turn around. She would still be lost had it not been for Staggs, who happened to find her and insisted upon taking her photograph before pointing her in the right direction.

The towns were spaced farther apart than they had been previously, and accommodations were becoming more difficult to find. She hadn't seen so much as a tourist camp or a roadhouse since leaving the Chicago area.

The wind had died down, but as the sun set in the west and purple shadows began to settle over the landscape, Elizabeth realized she'd have to grab whatever sleep was possible in her car. Dust no longer blinded her; her tears did. The lonely road that stretched ahead of her seemed endless, but her tears had nothing to do with the road and everything to do with Jimmy.

Angry at herself for giving in to her emotions, she

blinked her eyes furiously, and only succeeded in making her vision more blurred than before.

*Elizabeth Davenport, if you aren't the world's biggest fool!* She wasn't going to cry. Not for Jimmy. Not for anyone. She'd find herself another mechanic and finish the race—even if it killed her.

Still, no matter how hard she tried, she couldn't hold back the tears. They came fast and furious now, forcing her to pull over or risk driving into yet another planted field.

Damn Jimmy! How dare he come into her life and make her feel things she never meant to feel, want things she never meant to want. What gave him the right to turn her world inside out, upside down, then abandon her like an old shoe? If she never saw him again, it would be too soon!

That night after work, Jimmy rushed to his parents' house and ran down the stairs to the basement. He found his mother bent over her workbench, working with quiet intent.

She looked up upon hearing Jimmy, her face soft. "What are you all fired up about, son?"

"Did I receive any phone calls?" he asked.

She looked puzzled. "No. But why would your calls come here?"

"Because they didn't come to my house or office. My calls must be going somewhere."

Kate gave her son a look of sympathy. "Oh, dear. I'm sure either Cecil or Elizabeth would have called if anything was wrong."

"You don't understand, Mother. When Elizabeth is at the wheel, something is always wrong."

"Now don't you worry, dear. If she survived her mishap in Chicago, I'm sure she'll survive anything."

Jimmy stared at his mother aghast. "Mishap? What mishap?"

Kate covered her mouth with her fingertips. "Oh, dear. I thought you would have read about it in the

*Hogs Head Gazette* by now. This morning's paper is over there, on your father's workbench."

*My God, why didn't I think about the newspaper?* Jimmy dashed across the basement, grabbed the paper, and hastily scanned the bold headlines on the first page. *Woman Driver Crashes Through Window.* Heart standing still, he quickly read the accompanying article until he found what he was looking for: Elizabeth was not injured. Neither was Cecil. What a relief; he still had the option of killing Cecil himself.

He tossed the paper aside. "Isn't this just peachy? I have to wait until I read the newspaper before I know what's going on."

"I don't know why you're so upset," Kate said soothingly. "The paper said no one was hurt."

"This is yesterday's news. Anything could have happened to her since then." He picked up a pair of driving goggles from his mother's workbench and turned them over in his hand. They looked similar to the ones Elizabeth wore.

"What are these doing here?"

"Elizabeth told me she was having a difficult time seeing the road clearly."

"If she would drive slower, she wouldn't have so much trouble," Jimmy muttered, his ill temper growing worse by the minute.

"Speed has nothing to do with it. You do know she has myopic eyes, don't you?"

"Myopic eyes? Elizabeth?" He slapped his palm across his forehead. "Of course! Now I remember! She wore eyeglasses as a child." A chill shot through him as he considered the implications. "No wonder she kept driving off the road. She could have killed us both." Lord, she almost had! "My God!" he exploded. "What in the world is she doing driving without her eyeglasses?"

"Do calm down, Jimmy. This is so unlike you. . . ."

"Calm down? Do you know how dangerous it is out there?"

"Yes, that's why I got to thinking there had to be other people with myopic eyes. Do you realize what a serious problem we would have if all these people took to driving fuel-powered vehicles?"

Jimmy shuddered at the thought.

"I took the lens from a pair of eyeglasses and placed them in these goggles. Then I tinted the glass and . . ."

He took the goggles from her and held them up to his eyes. Everything was a blur. "Will Elizabeth be able to see through these things?"

"She should," Kate said. "The eyeglasses match the pair Elizabeth purchased from Aunt Hattie's store. It's a pity she left before I came up with the idea of changing the lenses in the goggles. . . . Wait, Jimmy. Where are you going? Jimmy!"

# Chapter 22

"Nothing tests character or vocabulary like a roadblock."

*Women at the Wheel*
Circa 1915

At the first crack of dawn, Elizabeth climbed out of the car and stretched her weary limbs. The early morning air was cool and damp, swirling about her in a ghostly gray mist. But an occasional glimpse of blue sky picked up her spirits. Hard as it was to believe, things could be worse.

She reached into her suitcase for soap and a towel and followed the sound of trickling water to a little creek that ran along a pebbled bed. The cold clear water revitalized her and turned her skin pink. Shivering, she quickly dressed in fresh clothes and, though she had no appetite, forced herself to eat some of the dry cheese and stale bread left over from the day before.

After straightening out the backseat and washing the dirt and grime off the windshield, she cranked up the car. The temperature had dropped during the night, and Model T's were notoriously difficult to start in cold weather. Her arm ached by the time the engine finally gave a reluctant sputter, then grumbled to a start.

The car rolled forward and she jumped out of the

way in the nick of time. Damn! She'd forgotten to set the emergency brake. Again.

Old Ironsides rumbled across the meadow as if it had a mind of its own, picking up speed as it started downhill.

"Come back here, you crazy old car. You're not leaving me, too!" Running as fast as she could, she was finally able to jump onto the running board. Steering the car away from a tree, she then heaved herself behind the wheel.

Heart racing in her chest, she pulled on the emergency brake, and taking a moment to catch her breath, donned her goggles and gloves.

Ready at last, and making certain her road map was handy, she stepped on the gas pedal and drove back up the hill and onto the road.

The stretch of road was paved in broken stone and asphalt, a mixture called macadam. The hard, smooth surface enabled her to drive a steady thirty-five miles per hour for most of the morning, with only a few detours along the way to slow her progress. Some of the detours had been planned by Mr. Ford to take the drivers through certain towns, but most of the circular side trips were made by accident. Either she had misread the map, missed a turn, or lost track of the road altogether.

She could well understand why Mr. Ford was pushing for legislation to provide funds for paving roads. It was her opinion that a few more road signs wouldn't hurt, either.

Between the long hours on the road and the little sleep she'd had the previous night, she couldn't stop yawning. The few times she had drifted off in the night, she was haunted by dreams of Jimmy. On several occasions, she'd woke in a confused state, expecting to find herself in his arms.

Oh, Jimmy! She gripped the steering wheel so tight, her knuckles ached. Never did she think it possible to miss anyone as much as she missed Jimmy. Just thinking about his deep blue eyes and easy smile filled her with such a terrible longing, she could hardly think about anything else.

How could he abandon her? Let her drive off without him? Pretend as if nothing had happened between them?

*Nothing had happened, you fool.* She pressed a foot against the gas pedal. *He tried to kiss me and I pushed him away.* A lump formed in her throat. Who could blame him for turning his back on her? *Oh, Jimmy . . . how I wish things could be different. . . .*

By noon the fog had disappeared and the sun was shining, bright as newly polished brass. But she hardly noticed; never had she felt so depressed in her life. She'd run the whole gamut of emotions from regret to anger. From blaming herself to blaming Jimmy.

Well, he was gone now and what did she care? She didn't need anyone in her life. She'd never had anyone in her life. Not really. Not anyone she could trust or depend on, and what did it matter? She was doing just dandy, thank you very much. Just because there were times when she'd see a loving family like the Hunters and wonder what it would be like to have a family of her own didn't necessarily mean she couldn't be happy without one.

Of course she could be happy! She'd build her children's home and write her books. What more could she possibly want? Certainly not the likes of Jimmy Hunter!

Around one that afternoon, Elizabeth parked the car beneath a large shade tree and took a break. She'd stopped for a late breakfast at a roadside café. That was only two hours ago, but it seemed longer. How lonely the road was without someone at her side. How desolate.

Sighing, she checked her map and then continued on her way. If she didn't find another mechanic before reaching the next checkpoint, she would be disqualified. Time was running out.

A few scattered towns lay ahead. Her chances of finding a mechanic looked slim, but at this point she was willing to settle for anyone, even someone who had never seen the inside of a self-propelled vehicle. *Just don't let him try anything!*

She drove for another fifty miles without passing a single soul. The paved road had ended and the road was now dirt, but well-maintained. A southbound passenger train ran parallel to the road, black smoke curling from its engine.

Normally, the sight of a train would bring back such unpleasant memories, she would inevitably slow down to let it pass unchallenged. Today, however, she welcomed the company.

When it appeared as if the train was about to leave her behind, she stepped on the gas in a desperate attempt to keep up.

Something white fluttered from one of the passenger cars. Squinting to no avail, she pulled off her goggles and reached for her eyeglasses.

She was now able to pick out the form of a man waving at her from the door of a Pullman car. Probably a friendly conductor, she decided, or one of the passengers who, seeing the placard on the side of her vehicle, was cheering her on.

She waved back and the man kept waving. Curious, she picked up speed until she was able to pull alongside the coach. Something about the man made her heart skip a beat.

She could hardly breathe. "Jimmy?" His name trembled on her lips. Not certain if she could believe her eyes, she wiped away the road dust that had already stuck to the lenses of her eyeglasses. "Jimmy?" This time she shouted his name at the top of her lungs. "Jimmy!"

She drove off the road and onto the gravel bed next to the tracks, forcing the gas pedal all the way to the floor.

Dear God in heaven, it *was* Jimmy, and he appeared

to be holding on to the railing for dear life, one foot in midair.

"Come closer!" he yelled.

"Oh, my God!" she gasped. Surely he wouldn't do anything crazy. "Don't jump!" she pleaded. "It's too dangerous."

"Closer!"

"Jimmy, no!"

"Then I'll jump to the ground."

Jimmy tossed a carpetbag and his Panama hat into the car, practically scaring her to death. *Ooooooh,* she didn't like this. Didn't like it at all. She considered slowing down and letting the train go ahead of her. But fearing Jimmy might be foolish enough to jump to the ground as he threatened, she had no choice but to make it as easy on him as possible.

Her mouth dry, her heart pumping as fast as it could, she steered the car as close to the train as she dared. Biting her bottom lip, she forced herself to concentrate. One mistake on her part and ... Pushing the thought away, she managed to keep the car running a straight course next to the tracks.

He motioned her to drop back, and timing his jump to accommodate the speed of the train, he let go. She screamed and closed her eyes tight. It wasn't until he shouted in her ear to watch out that she dared look. Swerving the car at the last possible moment, she managed to miss a telegraph pole.

Jimmy sat in the seat next to her, grinning like a naughty schoolboy. She slammed on the brakes. Jimmy was jolted forward and back, but for once he didn't complain about her erratic driving.

"Jimmy Hunter! Don't you ever, EVER do anything so foolhardy again! You could have broken your neck. You could have killed yourself, you could have ..."

Jimmy listened to her rant on about all the horrible things he could have done and his grin grew broader. "So you missed me, eh?"

She sniffed. "This isn't funny. I don't know what I'd have done if something had happened to you."

For the longest moment he stared at her—and she at him—as if neither could believe their eyes. "Where's Cecil?" he asked finally.

At the mention of Cecil's name, she made a face. "He decided he preferred banking to being a mechanic."

"He what?" Jimmy threw back his head and laughed. "Who would have thought it?" His smile faded and his eyes brimmed with tenderness as he gazed at her. "It just proves that a person doesn't always know the value of something until he almost loses it."

"Oh, Jimmy." She was so happy to see him, she could hardly find her voice. "What are you doing here?"

"I brought you something." He reached into his carpetbag and drew out a pair of driving goggles. "A gift from my mother."

"What?"

He reached for her eyeglasses and gently pulled them off her nose. "Try these new goggles on."

Elizabeth took the goggles from him and slipped them in place. She glanced in one direction, then another. It was amazing. She could actually see past the hood of the car. Could, in fact, see quite an impressive distance down the road. Amazingly enough, she could see just as clearly as if she were wearing her eyeglasses.

"Oh, Jimmy, I can't believe it." She pulled the marvelous goggles off and gazed at him. He gazed back, his eyes warm with approval as they lingered on her lips.

Her stomach fluttered in nervous anticipation. Everything about him, from the gold flecks at the end of his eyelashes to the laugh lines around his mouth, filled her with wonder.

It was obvious by the look in his eyes he wanted to

kiss her. Obvious by the nervous knot in her stomach that she had every intention of letting him.

Forgetting all the reasons why his kiss was forbidden, she held herself in rigid anticipation, and promised herself that this time she wouldn't pull away.

"Elizabeth," he whispered, and the warm, sensuous sound of his voice sent a thrill of excitement coursing through her veins. He cupped his hand beneath her chin and lifted it upward. *He's going to kiss me.* He slid an arm slowly around her shoulder, his eyes never leaving her face. *HE'S GOING TO KISS ME!*

As much as she anticipated the event, she couldn't ignore her stomach. What had started as a flutter of butterflies now felt like a whole flock of birds. *Dear God, help me through this. Don't let me pull away or get sick or . . .*

His lips brushed her mouth and she instinctively pulled back. He looked startled, then hurt. "Don't you want me to kiss you, Elizabeth?"

"Of course I do," she said, her voice hoarse.

"Well, you sure have a funny way of showing it. The way you act, you'd think I was trying to make you one of those sex slaves you women keep screaming about."

A look of horror crossed her face. "I never thought that!"

"Then what is it? Tell me."

"I wasn't ready."

"How will I know when you're ready?"

She took a deep breath, closed her eyes, and puckered her lips. *I'm going to do this!* "I'm ready now."

"Good heavens, Elizabeth. That's not how you show a man you're ready to be kissed."

She opened her eyes. "It's not?"

"Haven't you ever been kissed before?"

Embarrassed and humiliated, she pulled away from him. "Of course I've been kissed before. I've been kissed lots of times. Why, I was even kissed by the mayor of San Francisco."

He looked at her closely. "Was that the same mayor you pushed into the mud?"

"*Ooooooh.*" Her cheeks flaming red, she climbed over her door and jumped to the ground.

Jimmy practically fell out of the car in his rush to chase after her. A pain shot through his leg. Apparently, he'd injured his leg when he'd made that foolhardy jump from the train. Lord, what had gotten into him lately? He was acting reckless and crazy. Heaven only knows he was ready to jump over the moon for one of her kisses. "Damn!"

He grimaced as he tripped over a fallen log, but his loud curse brought her to his side.

"Jimmy, are you all right?"

He scrambled to his feet. "Yes, I'm all right." He grabbed her by the arm. "No, I'm not! Dammit, Elizabeth! What's the matter with you?" They were both breathing hard. "You said you wanted me to kiss you and then you act like I'm doing something wrong!"

"I do want you to kiss me, Jimmy. It's just . . ."

"What, Elizabeth? Tell me."

She lowered her lashes as she looked away. "I can't tell you."

"Why not?"

"I just can't." She looked up, her eyes dark with pain. "Please don't make me."

Jimmy made no attempt to stop her when she pulled away. Not knowing what to do, what to say, he walked in a circle with his fists pressed deep into his pockets. He hated being made to feel guilty for wanting to do what the good Lord surely must mean for him to do.

Maybe he'd misunderstood the look on her face earlier. The look he would have sworn said she wanted him as much as he wanted her. Could he really be that wrong? Had he been so preoccupied with his own needs and desires that he'd projected feelings on her that were simply not there? It was possible, of course, but he didn't want to believe it.

"Is it someone else?" he asked. "Are you betrothed or . . . married?"

The question seemed to increase her misery. "There's no one."

Wasn't that just fine and dandy? She wasn't even going to offer him a way to save face. "All right, then say it. It's me."

"No, Jimmy, it's not you." She gazed at him through tear-filled eyes. "Believe me, it's not."

"Then what?"

She opened her mouth to speak, but her soft, trembling voice was drowned out by the sound of a fast-approaching automobile. Car number seven rambled by and Fastbender's mechanic tossed a bucket of icy cold water on them.

Drenched, Elizabeth cried out, "*Ooooooh,* if I ever get my hands on that man, I'll . . ." Shaking with fury, she stormed back to the car.

Frustrated, Jimmy angrily kicked a rock and followed her. Angry at her, angry at Fastbender, angry at himself, he snatched a towel from the backseat and dried his face. Fool! How many times did she have to push him away before he got the picture?

He tossed the towel back into the car and cranked the engine. So she wanted it to be business only between them, did she? Well, by George, she wouldn't get any further argument from him. "Let's go!" he shouted curtly over the roar of the engine. "If it's Fastbender you want, then it's Fastbender you'll get!"

# Chapter 23

"All is fair in love, war—and driving in traffic."
*Women at the Wheel*
Circa 1915

For the next few hours, Jimmy sat in the car next to her and never uttered a sound. Now that her new goggles allowed her to see the road, Jimmy no longer had to warn her of any stray livestock or slow-moving buggies. Amazingly enough, she drove all afternoon without so much as a close call.

Though they were making good time, Elizabeth felt little joy. Her heart felt so heavy, it was like a brick in her chest.

She didn't like this. Didn't like the terse silence that stretched between them, or the way he avoided her eyes. The tension was so great, she feared her nerves would snap. She was tempted to drive off the road just to hear him speak, and was greatly relieved when at last they arrived in St. Louis.

A cheering crowd greeted them as Elizabeth reached the town limits. They were the last of the drivers to cross over the Illinois/Missouri state line and check into the Hotel Jefferson.

St. Louis was considered by some the start of the actual race. Drivers would no longer be required to honor the twelve-hour layover rule that had been established to encourage towns to cooperate with race officials.

Elizabeth considered the layover rule a clever ploy by Mr. Ford. By requiring the racers to stay a certain number of hours, the town benefited from the publicity and the business that was generated by the tourists pouring in to see the racers for themselves. Hotels were booked, restaurants packed.

Elizabeth knew that from this point forward it would be a whole new race. From St. Louis to Seattle, drivers could drive as they pleased, following whatever route they chose and driving for however many hours they could stay awake. They would no longer be required to detour off the main roads to little out-of-the-way communities. The only requirement was that drivers had to have their passports stamped at each official checkpoint. A missing stamp would mean the driver was disqualified.

Elizabeth pulled up in front of the hotel and stopped. For several moments, she and Jimmy sat side by side, neither of them moving. She glanced at his profile and wished with all her heart she knew how to erase the confusion and hurt that was so clearly etched on his face.

She bit her lower lip and tried to catch his eye. Somehow she had to make amends. She couldn't bear the thought of spending the remaining days of the race with this terrible strain between them. "If you take care of the car, I'll stock up on food. If we hurry we can be on the road before dark."

Jimmy folded his arms across his chest. "First, we're going to get some sleep."

"What?"

Finally, finally, he looked at her, but his eyes were hooded with indifference, his face remote. "We're both exhausted. After we leave St. Louis, towns are few and far between. This could be the last chance for sleep and a hot bath for days."

"Are you out of your mind? Everyone else is going to get a head start."

Jimmy glanced at the field across from the hotel

where the other drivers and their mechanics were working feverishly on their cars. Sparky was having a sneezing fit, as evidenced by a handkerchief over his mouth. Mr. Chin and Sir Higginbottom appeared to be having another disagreement. The Chinaman's hands were hidden in his sleeves.

Staggs stood a short distance away, taking photographs of Billy-Joe, who straddled the hood of his car, pretending it was a horse.

"Leave it to me." He climbed out of the car and, dodging horses, motorized taxis, and trolley cars, ran across the busy cobblestone street.

"May I have your attention for a moment?" he called to the others.

Fastbender leaned against his car, his cigarette dangling carelessly from his mouth. Crankshaw finished cleaning his windshield, and Stonegate brushed the road dust from his stovepipe hat.

"Speak up, lad." Sir Higginbottom lifted a china teacup to his mouth and made a face. "In the name of the king, don't ever let a Chinaman make tea."

Jimmy waited until he had everyone's attention before he began. "As you know, once we leave St. Louis, we're on our own. None of us will want to stop for any length of time, let alone for a good night's sleep."

"So what are you saying?" Crankshaw impatiently pulled his pocket watch out of his vest pocket.

"I'm saying—rather I'm asking—that we make a pact to spend the night here in St. Louis so we can all get a fresh start in the morning. This could be our last chance for hot baths or a good night's sleep until we reach Seattle." He glanced at each road-weary face. "What do you say?"

Sir Higginbottom tapped the bowl of his silver spoon against his cup. "I say it's a splendid idea."

Staggs nodded in agreement. "Hunter is right. We don't know what problems we're going to face once we hit the open road."

Crankshaw glowered at Fastbender, who ground his

cigarette out with the heel of his boot, and said nothing. "Can we trust everyone to keep their word? What if someone gets a head start while the rest of us are sleeping?"

"We'll post a guard," Jimmy said. "I'm sure we can find someone in town willing to watch the cars for a fee."

"I say, by jove, let's do it," Sir Higginbottom said. "Anyone want a crumpet?" He passed around a plate of round unsweetened bread. Crankshaw took one and stuffed it whole into his mouth. Sir Higginbottom looked taken aback by such a display of bad manners, but said nothing.

"Everyone look this way," Staggs called out. A collective groan rose from the group as he squeezed the bulb of his camera.

"All right," Jimmy said. "All those in favor of staying the night in St. Louis say aye."

"Aye!"

Jimmy pulled his watch out of his pocket. "Let's synchronize our watches. It's now four-forty-five. I say we meet here at six a.m. sharp."

Everyone agreed to the plan and Jimmy walked across the street to break the news to Elizabeth.

"Oh, Jimmy! That's wonderful."

"Why don't you check into the hotel? I'll meet you at, say, eight for dinner in the hotel dining room. That'll give me a chance to fuel up and check the tires and engine."

Anxious to rid herself of road dust, Elizabeth grabbed her suitcase from the back of the car. "Eight will be fine."

Jimmy drove Old Ironsides to where the others were parked. Meanwhile, Elizabeth stopped to look in the window of the shop next door to the hotel. The shop had one of those French names that she didn't dare try to pronounce. Madame Bouvier's something or other spelled with a Q. Boutique.

In the window was a mannequin dressed in a fashionable hobble skirt and tunic. The outfit was a vibrant peacock-blue in color. Never had Elizabeth worn anything so elegant or feminine—and for good reason. Such an outfit would only call attention to the feminine curves she tried so hard to hide.

The last time she had dressed like a lady was at the age of twelve. She'd taken such great pains to make herself a frock. How stylish it was, hugging her waist and showing off her still-developing breasts. The gown had been a mistake—a terrible, terrible mistake. She still remembered how shy she'd been, modeling her outfit for Mylar. Despite her shyness, she'd felt so grown-up. How happy it had made her when he'd heartily approved.

But the happiness soon turned to terror and horror. The day she wore that gown marked the first trip to the barn. Later, she ripped the gown off and threw it into the fireplace and watched as angry flames devoured it. Never had she worn such a gown since.

Pushing the memory away, she gazed up at the beautiful outfit, surprised to find herself tempted to go into the store and try it on. She longed to see how she looked in something that was soft and feminine. Something that wasn't baggy or ugly.

Wouldn't Jimmy be surprised if she showed up for dinner in such a beautiful outfit? Oh, yes, indeed he would. She could just imagine the look in his eye. Sighing with regret, she turned from the window.

A woman came rushing out of the store. "Mademoiselle?" The woman, whom she presumed was Madame Bouvier, was dressed in an elegant black silk suit and moved in a fragrant cloud of perfume.

Madame Bouvier's eyes widened as she gazed in horror at Elizabeth's overalls. As if suddenly remembering her manners, the Frenchwoman quickly recovered. "I couldn't help but notice how the color matches your eyes," she said with a thick French accent. With a graceful sweep of an arm, she indicated the outfit in the window. "You simply must try it on."

Elizabeth blushed. "Oh, no, I couldn't."

But Madame Bouvier was apparently used to reticent customers. With polished ease, she led Elizabeth into the little dress shop. "The French have a saying." She spoke in her native tongue, then quickly translated. "Never interfere with things that are meant to be."

Once she had coaxed Elizabeth into the shop, Madame Bouvier pulled a dress off a hanger that was identical to the one in the window and held it up. "Perfect," she said, allowing the *r* to roll off her lips as easily as a ball rolling downhill. "Now, mademoiselle, you mustn't—absolutely mustn't—interfere with Providence."

Later that evening, her head still spinning with rolling *r*'s and heady perfume, Elizabeth soaked in the bathtub for nearly an hour. Normally, such a luxury would relax her, but tonight her nerves were stretched taut as a rubber band about to snap.

She couldn't stop thinking about Jimmy. A warm wave of pleasure swept through her as she recalled the heated look of desire in his eyes when he tried to kiss her. Pleasure turned to anguish and despair as she remembered the look of confusion and hurt in his face when she'd pulled away.

Grimacing, she lowered her body even deeper into the water. "Oh, Jimmy," she sighed dreamily. "If only you knew how much I had wanted that kiss." *Still want it.*

She toweled herself off and reached for her newly purchased dress, her fingers trembling as she caressed the soft fabric. She could still remember with startling clarity the vision of herself in the shop's beveled mirror.

Madame Bouvier had floated gracefully about the shop, gathering the necessary accessories and talking about Providence until Elizabeth began to believe what she said was true.

From the moment Elizabeth had donned the dress

and stood gaping at herself in the mirror of that shop, she felt like she was living in a dreamworld. She'd looked ... well, beautiful. Confident. Confident enough to let a man kiss her. To let the *right* man kiss her. And Jimmy was the right man, she was certain.

Now, Elizabeth examined the fitted bodice and waist, and the slight flaring skirt that showed off her trim hips. A blue satin ribbon formed a band just above the hemline of the fashionable hobble skirt. It was the most beautiful dress she'd ever laid eyes on.

Normally, she could not have afforded such luxury. But upon learning Elizabeth was the woman driver everyone was talking about, the owner of the shop insisted upon reducing the dress to less than half its original cost if Elizabeth agreed to wear it when claiming her prize. "Naturally, everyone will want to know where you purchased your dress," the woman had said, then handed her a card printed with side-by-side photos of her shop. The card was designed to be viewed through the prismatic lenses of a stereoscope.

Elizabeth suddenly felt overwhelmed. Now she was obligated to win the race for Madame Bouvier. The list of people to whom she was indebted kept growing. How would she ever repay them?

Nervously, she pulled on her undergarments. She then carefully donned the silk stockings Madame Bouvier had insisted must be worn, along with the pair of dainty kid shoes.

Surprised at how nervous she was at the thought of having dinner with Jimmy, she arranged her hair and finished dressing, taking pains to get everything exactly right.

She then walked back and forth a couple of times to practice taking the small steps a hobble skirt required.

She stared at herself in the mirror and hardly recognized her reflection. Her hair waved softly around her face and was pulled back into a roll at the back of her head. The peacock-blue of the dress matched her eyes perfectly, the color complementing the pink tones of her skin.

A smile playing at the corner of her mouth, she again dusted her nose lightly with Freeman's face powder for the sheer pleasure of doing something ultimately feminine, then stepped back for another look in the mirror.

Satisfied, she picked up the kid-leather clutch purse that Madame Bouvier insisted no lady should be without and slipped her hotel key inside. Now that face powder was so popular, nearly every woman carried a purse. Elizabeth supposed purses were useful, especially now that pockets were becoming so rare. Still, purses took some getting used to. The few times she'd carried one in the past, she'd managed to leave it behind and was forced to make special trips to retrieve it. Perhaps in the future, one of those purses with a chain designed to hang around the wrist would be more practical.

Head held high, heart pounding, she took one more quick glance in the mirror, then started for the hotel dining room. *Dear God, help me be every inch the woman Jimmy wants me to be ... if only for tonight.*

# *Chapter 24*

"Only an enterprising woman can wrap a man around her finger while keeping her hands on the steering wheel."

*Women at the Wheel*
Circa 1915

Jimmy was already in the dining room when she arrived. He sat quietly at a table in a secluded corner, but it seemed to Elizabeth as if the very room revolved around him.

The room was aglow with flickering candles and softly lit chandeliers. The steady hum of voices competed with the sound of music.

Jimmy glanced at his watch, then looked toward the entrance. Upon seeing her, his mouth fell open. His eyes wide with astonishment, he rose slowly to his feet. His mouth curved upward in approval. His gaze smoldered with admiration.

The seductive look he gave her made her pulse race. She moistened her lips and took a deep breath.

Sir Higginbottom, Crankshaw, and the others were gathered around the bar. Their lively banter died as she strolled past them. Billy-Joe jumped from the stool, clutching his Stetson to his chest. Crankshaw nearly choked on his cigar, and Sir Higginbottom's eyes practically popped out of his head. Even that morbid undertaker, Stonegate, sounded more cheerful than usual. "You look pretty enough to wake the dead, Miss Davenport."

She smiled politely. "Thank you, Mr. Stonegate."

Staggs practically fell over his own feet trying to get a photograph of her, and Fastbender licked his lips.

Resisting the urge to give Fastbender a piece of her mind, she walked toward Jimmy and tried to concentrate on taking small steps. Tonight, she didn't want to think about her opponents or the race. She didn't want to think about anything but Jimmy.

"You look ... beautiful," Jimmy said when she reached their table. His warm, appreciative gaze slid down the length of her, leaving a hot, blazing trail, before he lifted his eyes to her face.

Her cheeks burned with pleasure. "Thank you, Jimmy. You look very nice yourself." Handsome was how he looked. Tall and handsome. He was dressed in blue serge trousers with a plaited bosom shirt, lisle hogskin suspenders, and a four-in-hand necktie. An elastic garter circled each arm, keeping his shirtsleeves the perfect length.

She sat down in the chair he held for her and laid her clutch bag on the table.

She smiled up at him, and when it looked as if he intended to stand by her chair staring at her for the rest of the evening, she picked up the bill of fare.

Jimmy took his place across from her and fingered his own menu, but his gaze remained on her face.

Tango music floated from the flared flower horn of a gramophone, and a young couple tried out the new and controversial Latin American dance rage with uncertain steps and self-conscious laughter.

Embarrassed by the couple's suggestive moves, Elizabeth quickly lowered her eyes so as not to stare. She couldn't imagine anyone dancing the tango in public or anywhere else.

Jimmy cleared his throat and tugged at his tie as if it were choking him, but his warm eyes never left her face. "I think I'll try the chicken pot pie, but I know it won't be as good as Aunt Hattie's."

She looked at Jimmy through the thick fringe of her lashes. "I really loved your family."

The corner of his mouth lifted and a soft light touched his face. "They took quite a liking to you, too."

"It must have been wonderful to grow up in such a loving family."

Jimmy studied her for a long moment before he replied. "I don't have much to complain about."

Something in his voice alerted her. "They adore you," she said tentatively, sensing his unease.

He grinned. "I know."

"But?"

He sat back in his chair. "But nothing. I love them and they love me."

"And you had no problems growing up with such illustrious parents?"

"Problems? Why would there be problems?"

"I would imagine that Kate and Jonas Hunter cast a very large shadow."

He arched an eyebrow as if surprised by her observation. "You're right. Having such well-known and successful parents was hard at times. Not just for me, but for all us kids. Our teachers expected more from us because of who we were. It's hard to live up to that kind of pressure."

"I can imagine."

"I'm not complaining. None of this was my parents' fault. It's just I always hoped that one day . . ." He stopped midsentence, and for a shivering moment, she felt his gaze touch her very soul. It was as if they connected in a way that defied physics. As if they communicated in some newly discovered way. "Never mind." The flickering candlelight bathed his face in a warm orange glow, but a shadow danced in the depths of his eyes.

"Tell me, Jimmy," she pleaded softly. She wanted

to know everything about him. "What do you hope for?"

He hesitated for a moment before replying. "I hope that someday people will see me as my own person, and stop thinking of me as the son of two famous inventors."

"I don't think of you that way," Elizabeth said.

Jimmy's eyes softened. "You're the exception, believe me."

"Am I?"

He nodded and leaned his arm on the table. "I admire you because you don't live in anyone's shadow."

She searched his face. Was he mocking her? She was used to being derided, had learned to live with it. It was the price a woman paid for daring to step beyond the perimeters established by society. A woman had her place, and if she insisted upon wearing pants, entering races, or pursuing other manly endeavors, she paid the consequences. Oh, yes, Elizabeth was used to being ridiculed and mocked. But it would hurt more coming from Jimmy. "I'm not sure what you mean."

"Look at you. You don't sit back and complain about the hand you were dealt. Instead, you plan to build an orphan's home and change the system. And look at this race. No matter how awful the other drivers treat you, you persist."

"Some people would call that stubbornness," she said, feeling self-conscious. She wasn't used to compliments, and tonight they were falling like raindrops.

"Some people would be right," he said, a smile playing on his lips.

Meeting his smile with one of her own, she rearranged the silverware.

"Then there's your writing career."

She blushed modestly. "One book hardly constitutes a writing career."

"I found your book very . . . interesting. Especially the part about a woman's body being her own."

She stared at him. "You . . . *read* my book?" Never

in a million years would she have dreamed he'd do such a thing. Though she was secretly pleased, her cheeks flamed red. "But it's about limiting family size."

He leaned back in his chair. "You don't think a man would be interested in such a topic?"

"They should be. But most men don't care a fig about getting a woman in a family way."

"What about you? Have you got something personal against having children?"

"Not at all! But as I wrote in my book, I'm against a woman having more children than she can adequately care for. If more women practiced family limitations, we wouldn't have any need for orphan trains."

"I don't understand what one's got to do with the other. Children are put on those trains because they have no parents, not because their parents have too many children."

"That's not true, Jimmy. Did you know that almost half of those so-called orphans have at least one parent?"

Jimmy's eyebrow lifted in surprise. "Really?"

She nodded. "Some were born to unmarried women, but there are many whose parents simply can't afford to feed another mouth. I know of at least three families who gave up children for this reason. One family has already given up two children and yet they're expecting another child. I'm telling you, Jimmy, it's criminal. That's one of the reasons I've agreed to write another book on the subject. Even if it means I'll probably have to go back to jail."

Jimmy's eyes grew wide. "You're writing another obscene . . . eh, book on family planning?"

She lifted her chin stubbornly. "Yes, and I'm going to keep writing books for however long it's necessary. No child should ever have to go through what I—" She stopped.

"What did you go through, Elizabeth? What happened to you after I got off the train at Hogs Head?"

"I don't want to talk about it. What happened, happened. And nothing's going to change it."

"Sometimes it helps to talk about things." He moved his hand across the table, resting his fingers only a few inches from hers.

She stared at his strong, firm hand and fought against the burning tears that threatened to mar her evening. "I can't talk about this."

He wrapped his fingers around hers. His hand felt warm and protective. Safe. She wondered what it would feel like if he should touch her elsewhere.

"We don't have to talk about anything you don't want to talk about. I just want you to know that if you change your mind . . . I'm here for you."

His touch sent shivery sensations up her arm. "I know, Jimmy, and I can't tell you how much it means to me. But there's nothing to talk about. I'm just tired. You're right about us needing a good night's rest." His gaze settled lazily on her mouth, and feeling a heated response, she inadvertently wet her lips. Their eyes met and locked, and they might have spent the rest of the evening gazing at each other had the wine steward not stopped at their table.

After their glasses had been filled with the best red wine the house had to offer, Elizabeth glanced down at her menu. Her road-weary eyes had trouble focusing on the words. "I think I'll try the chicken pot pie, too."

After dinner, Jimmy checked his watch. "I think I'd better walk you back to your room. We need to get all the rest we can."

She nodded, feeling a sense of disappointment. The evening had been wonderful, everything she could have hoped for, and she wanted more, much more. "I'd like to check on Old Ironsides. You know, just to make certain everything's all right."

"Good idea. I'll go with you. Your purse," he added, when she got up without it.

"Thank you." She tucked her purse beneath her

arm and waited for him to sign the check. Ignoring the other drivers, who were still watching her in disbelief, she led the way out of the dining room, her heart pumping in anticipation.

Outside it was cool, and millions of stars sparkled like white diamonds against a black velvet sky. A gentle breeze rustled the trees, and Elizabeth caught sight of the ribbons on the back of her car fluttering in the darkness.

The young man Jimmy had hired to keep watch over the vehicles greeted them. A tall, skinny youth with buckteeth and a friendly smile, he had agreed to watch the cars for the privilege of being allowed to drive one. Earlier, he had driven Crankshaw's motor car around the block.

"Everything all right?" Jimmy asked.

"Perfect, sir."

Jimmy's fingers brushed the small of Elizabeth's back, sending shock waves up her spine. "Watch your step," he cautioned. Together they walked over to Old Ironsides, and when it appeared that everything was closed up and secure, she thanked him, her voice shaking.

"I think I can sleep now."

He smiled down at her. The light from the hotel danced in his eyes. "That's good to hear." He peered at her intently and she felt a warm tingling sensation.

"I enjoyed our evening together." His voice was as soft as the music that played in the background—but it held an intensity that mesmerized her. She stood perfectly still on the outside, but on the inside everything was working full speed. Currents of desire raced through her so that she could hardly breathe.

Slowly, his head moved closer. His lips were but a whisper at first, brushing against hers ever so lightly before he finally captured her mouth.

Succumbing to the delicious sensation of his lips on hers, she stood on tiptoe and shyly slid her arms around his neck. Her confidence building, she drew his head closer until their lips melted together in a heated flame.

Raising his mouth from hers, he gazed into her eyes, warm approval radiating from his face.

"Oh, God, Elizabeth!" Crushing her to him, he reclaimed her lips, his kisses more heated and more urgent than before. She had one second of panic when the voice she fought to mute momentarily caught her off guard. *Watch out. This is a man and men do terrible things to women.*

Had it not been for the sight of the ribbons fluttering in the dark she might have pushed him away. Not because she wanted to—dear God, never that. But because a deeply ingrained belief could not that easily be wiped out by a pair of warm lips, no matter how much she wished it were so.

Pulling his head back, Jimmy studied her with curious intensity. She smiled tentatively and stroked his cheek with her hand. Oh, dear God, she wanted this, wanted him. *Please don't let me ruin what we have— could have.*

Apparently reassured, he lowered his head again, this time his lips staking out her mouth in a wonderful and all-encompassing kiss that touched her very soul. Enthralled by the wondrous sensations, she absorbed the sweet essence of his kiss. Of him.

Lord love an orphan! This was unlike anything previously experienced. Those hadn't been kisses in her past. They'd been assaults. Brutal and cruel assaults!

By contrast this kiss was sweet and loving and intoxicating. Having separated the present from the past, she kissed him back with equal fervor, her arms wrapped firmly around his neck, the last glimmer of shyness falling away like a discarded garment. She could do this!

Her senses spinning with heated sensations, she was totally unprepared for the intrusion of his tongue. Struck by a surge of panic, she stared hard at the ribbons, and forgetting it was Jimmy who was kissing her—and feeling all at once confused and dazed—she willed her mind to take flight as she kept her lips clamped firmly shut.

He drew away so abruptly that for a moment she feared she had inadvertently pushed him away out of habit. "I got the message this time," he said gruffly.

She stared up at his angry face, dumbfounded. She tried to speak, but the words came out in a confused muddle that made no sense. Finally, she stopped trying to explain and a terrible tortured silence stretched between them.

He stood waiting for something—denial, probably. "I do want your kisses, Jimmy," she managed at last, her voice shaking.

"That's what I thought at first. But ..." He drew his fingers though his hair, looking totally frustrated. "You run hot and cold. One moment you're kissing me ... the next moment ... Hell, how am I supposed to know what you want?"

"You're a fine one to talk," she said defensively. "A girl shows a little resistance and you give up."

"A little ..." His astonishment increased. He grabbed her by the shoulders, and because she was suddenly reminded of the many times Mylar had grabbed her so, she stiffened. Just when she thought Jimmy was going to kiss her again, he suddenly let her go with a muffled curse. His back toward her, he stood with his hands on the hood of the car, his head low.

Devastated, she could only stare at him. She had been so certain that this time would be different. She'd wanted so much to forget the past, forget everything but her feelings for Jimmy. Tonight, she honestly and truly thought she could be the woman he wanted, the woman he so deserved. But now that she knew how very impossible that dream was, she was overcome with anguish.

Dammit, it wasn't fair. She had failed Jimmy, failed

herself, and there was nothing—absolutely nothing—
she could do about it.

During all those years of abuse, she'd fought to hold
back everything that couldn't be physically taken away
from her. No man but Jimmy had ever touched her
mind, her heart, or her spirit. Now she realized she'd
been a fool to think these things mattered.

She'd held on to her soul with her entire being and
what good had it done her? If she couldn't give willingly of her body, what did the rest matter? What
would Jimmy care if she loved him with her entire
being if she couldn't love him physically? She was no
more a woman than Old Ironsides was human.

She couldn't bear to look at him for fear he'd see
her deepest, most secret shame.

He looked up finally and turned to face her. "Elizabeth . . ." He wanted to try again, to recapture the
ecstasy they'd shared only moments earlier; she could
see it in his eyes.

And she was tempted—so tempted.

But the warning voice clamored in her head and
she knew the monster inside was ready to pounce
again. *He's a man and men do . . .*

"No, Jimmy, I can't!" She moved away from him,
unable to bear the stricken look on his face. With an
anguished sob, she ran to the hotel as quickly as her
hobble skirt would allow, leaving him to stand alone
in the dark.

# Chapter 25

"No one drives as slow as the car ahead or as fast as the one behind."

*Women at the Wheel*
Circa 1915

At exactly ten minutes to six the following morning, Elizabeth strode out of the hotel. Without looking left, right, up or down, she charged across the street, threw her suitcase in the back of the car, and took her place behind the steering wheel.

Jimmy kept his head bent over the engine, trying his damnedest to ignore her. Ha! He'd have better luck ignoring a gun at his head. Not only could he not ignore her, he noticed everything about her, from her pale face to the whiteness of her knuckles as she gripped the steering wheel.

It was obvious by the blue shadows skirting her haunted eyes that she hadn't slept that much. Well, that made two of them. Not once during the long, lonely night had he been able to stop thinking of her, thinking of the evening they'd spent together, of the precious few seconds when he'd held her in his arms and she had returned his kisses with as much fervor and passion as he had bestowed on her.

Damn! What had he done wrong? Had he pushed too hard? Misread her lips? What? His troubled thoughts had kept him tossing and turning all night long.

Never before had a woman interfered with his sleep like Elizabeth Davenport had. Never had he wanted to kiss a woman more. Never had a woman put up more of a resistance.

Had she only allowed him to kiss her because she thought he would no longer be her mechanic if she denied him? Was that it? And then when things got too heated, she ran scared.

Dammit! Did she think he could be so easily bought? If that was the case, then it would be a cold day in hell before he ever tried to kiss her again! From now on, it was strictly business between them.

He slammed down the hood and wiped his hands on a rag.

"Good morning, Jimmy," she said finally.

He greeted her with a cool indifference that had nothing to do with his actual feelings and everything to do with hurt pride. "Good morning, Elizabeth."

Inside, he felt anything but cool and he certainly was not indifferent, no matter how much he wanted to be. He gave the car one last cursory inspection before cranking up the engine.

Old Ironsides jumped to life and the car nuzzled against him like a horse looking for sugar. "Whoa, there," he said.

Rivulets of water ran down the windshield to the hood. He knew it was dew, but damned if it didn't look like Old Ironsides was shedding a tear or two. It was easy to understand why some owners swore their cars had personalities.

Jimmy pulled a rag out of the back pocket of his trousers and wiped the windshield. His eyes locked with Elizabeth's for a split second, but she quickly looked away.

So that's how it was going to be. Cursing beneath his breath, he stopped to pat the only fender that remained like a man petting a dog. "Cheer up, pal. There's worse things than being spurned by a woman." Though he sure as hell couldn't name one.

Realizing he was actually talking to a car, he shook his head in disgust. Wasn't this just peachy? He was acting crazy and it was all Elizabeth's fault. She was doing this on purpose. He was sure of it!

Overhead the sky changed from orange to yellow as the rising sun spilled over the treetops like warm melted honey. For now, at least, the skies were clear, but some of the hotel guests traveling from the west had reported rain on the road ahead and there were rumors that one or two of the main bridges had been washed away.

Jimmy took his place in the companion seat. "Ready when you are."

"Ready," she said, matching the cool, detached tone of his voice.

He tightened his jaw. He'd hoped for something more from her, hoped she would offer some rational explanation as to why she had suddenly pulled away from him. But there was nothing forthcoming, not even a smile or a friendly word. Nor the slightest sign of regret.

Fine and dandy. Now that he knew where he stood, he wouldn't make the same mistake twice. After finishing the race, he intended to hightail it back to Hogs Head and forget he ever knew her. Forget he ever kissed her. Forget everything about her.

He studied the face of his watch. One by one, the other drivers pulled onto the road in the order they had arrived. The lead changing from one minute to the next, they drove in a pack as far as St. Charles.

Staggs finally settled into the lead, followed by Crankshaw, Fastbender, Billy-Joe, Stonegate, Sir Higginbottom, and, finally, Elizabeth.

Just before the drivers reached Columbia, Fastbender and Crankshaw pulled ahead of Staggs, leaving the other five cars to jockey for position.

No sooner had they left Columbia than trouble started. Elizabeth had two flat tires, got lost twice, and broke a wheel. The wheel caused a five-hour delay.

They spoke only when necessary and then with an amazing economy of words.

When Elizabeth grew so tired she could hardly keep her eyes open, she finally relinquished the wheel to Jimmy.

Exhausted, she fell asleep immediately, but the nightmares that had plagued her for years came back to haunt her as never before. In her dreams she could see the old barn, smell the hay, hear the soft flapping sound of ribbons tied to the snow post. The ribbons grew more faded and frayed with each passing month. The last bit of color was generally faded out by July. Judging from the color, Elizabeth knew it had to be March or April, and she felt a sense of despair as she realized that it was spring and there would be few rainy days left to protect her. A songbird sang, filling the air with its musical trill, but it gave her no joy. Suddenly, a shadow fell over her. A hand grabbed her arm. She screamed.

She woke suddenly, her body drenched. Her heart beat so fast she could hardly breathe.

"Are you all right?" It took her a moment to make sense of her surroundings and to recognize Jimmy's concerned voice. "Elizabeth?"

"Yes," she said grimly, staring at the misty air illuminated by the headlamps. Waking up during a nightmare was a mixed blessing. She woke before the bad part, but an interrupted dream was more likely to keep repeating itself in her thoughts than a dream left to run its course.

Jimmy slowed down and pulled over to the side of the road. "That must have been some dream. You cried out. You sounded so ... afraid."

She bit her lower lip. *Dear God, what did I say?* "It was just a dream, a nightmare."

"These nightmares ... you seem to have them a lot. Maybe if you talk about them ..."

"No!" She rubbed her head and regretted being so

harsh with him. He was only trying to be kind. "I'm sorry, Jimmy; I didn't mean to snap at you."

He turned back to the steering wheel. "Go back to sleep."

"I'd rather not. At least for a while. I think I'm ready to drive. It helps to keep my mind off things." Despite the long grueling hours on the road, she feared sleep at the moment more than she needed it.

"Are you sure?"

"I'm sure."

Without another word they exchanged seats. She drove for the remainder of the night, and gradually the horror of the nightmare faded away and the warm, sweet memories of Jimmy's lips took its place. It was dangerous, she knew, to think about such things. Even if they were pleasant.

It would be better for all concerned if she simply forgot his kisses altogether. But how could she, when her body, her heart, the very essence of her soul wouldn't let her forget, not for a single moment, how it felt to be kissed by a man in a way that wasn't hateful or brutal? *Oh, Jimmy, will I never again feel your heated kisses?*

Dawn broke and a silvery gray light touched the cloudy sky. She glanced over at Jimmy. He was asleep, his head turned toward her and his lips pressed together in soft, velvety folds. She envied his ability to sleep so peacefully, as if he hadn't a care in the world, and she wondered if she would ever know such luxury.

The lighter the sky grew, the harder it was to keep from looking at him. Every time her gaze wandered in his direction, her heart turned over in response.

Dear God, never had she thought it possible to want a man like she wanted Jimmy. He had kissed her not once but twice in a way that went beyond anything she'd ever imagined.

Maybe it had been a mistake to judge all men based on her experiences with one brutal man. Occupied with her thoughts, she inadvertently turned the wheel

too far to the right. The car bounced onto the rough
shoulder and Jimmy's eyes flew open.

"Dammit, Elizabeth. Watch where you're going!"

"I *am* watching!" she snapped back, but only because it seemed better to argue with him than to endure one more minute of awkward silence.

So, as if by mutual agreement, they spent the day
bickering about her speed, the way she oversteered,
his taking so long to refuel, her failure to put the
emergency brake on, and whether or not the dark
clouds ahead meant rain.

"Of course it means rain!" he yelled, the dark
clouds reminding him of the look on her face when
he'd tried to push his tongue between her lips. "It
sure as hell doesn't mean fair weather!"

"You don't have to shout!" she shouted back, reminded of the ominous look in his eyes when he'd
pulled his lips away from hers.

Finally weary of fighting, they fell silent late that
afternoon, each lost in their own thoughts. Fortunately
the road, though mostly unpaved, was fairly level, with
only a few rough spots. They traveled over rolling
hills, past fertile farmlands, and through wooded wil-
derness. A few sprinkles dampened their windshield,
but by the look of the ominous clouds ahead, the
worst was yet to come.

# Chapter 26

"The meek shall inherit the earth, but the road belongs to the driver with the loudest horn."

*Women at the Wheel*
Circa 1915

Just after nightfall, Elizabeth pulled off the road. Jimmy raised the canvas top while Elizabeth set out the picnic basket the hotel had provided for them. They ate, seated on the running board, and spoke only when necessary.

"Please pass the bread," he said.

"Please pass the cheese."

And neither one said what was really on their mind.

After they'd had their fill, Jimmy refueled and cranked up the car. With Elizabeth at the wheel, they started out again, both staring out the windshield at the dark road ahead and refusing to look at anything else, least of all each other.

An occasional light from one of the farmhouses provided a welcome beacon in the shroud of blackness that surrounded them, and Elizabeth found herself slowing the car as they drove by each house, as if by doing so it was possible to capture a bit of homey warmth to take with them.

They reached Glasgow at five-thirty the next morning. Sir Higginbottom and Staggs were sitting in their cars, waiting for the ferry to return to carry them across the Missouri River.

Elizabeth's headlamps picked out Sir Higginbottom's mechanic, Mr. Chin, waving his arms over his head. After she'd braked, Sir Higginbottom hurried over to greet them, juggling his teacup and saucer. "Those bloody fools, Crankshaw and Fastbender, arrived here first. I drove up just as the ferry took off. It left well over two hours ago. I wouldn't put it past them to have bribed the captain not to return."

"Is there another way across?" Jimmy asked.

"Not that I can tell. The water's pretty deep."

"Have you seen Billy-Joe or Stonegate?"

"Billy-Joe had to be towed and I haven't seen Stonegate since late yesterday afternoon."

"Can't we cross on that?" Elizabeth asked. She pointed to the Union Pacific Railroad trestle that spanned the river.

"Good heavens!" Sir Higginbottom exclaimed, spilling his tea. "You can't be serious."

"Have you got any better ideas?" Elizabeth asked.

"No, but . . ."

"Well, then . . ." Elizabeth pressed her foot on the gas pedal, and before Jimmy could say a word, whipped the car into a sharp two-wheeled turn and headed straight for the river.

Jimmy grabbed hold of the door with both hands. "What the . . . ?"

She swung a wide circle until the two front wheels were lined up with the railroad tracks, then jammed on her brakes.

"Dammit, Elizabeth! You nearly scared the life out of me." He pulled his handkerchief out of his pocket and mopped his brow. Lord, he'd actually thought she meant to cross the tracks. Well, she'd had her fun. Now it was time to get serious. He narrowed his eyes across the river, spotting a faint light from the ferry on the other side.

"Hold on!" Elizabeth shouted.

Before Jimmy could utter a syllable, Old Ironsides

lurched forward like a mechanical frog leaping onto a steel-plated lily pad.

"Dammit! Are you out of your cotton-picking . . . Yeow!"

Clutching the door, he gaped down at the thunderous roar of water beneath them. The railroad ties were set eighteen inches apart, and as far as he could tell, the tracks were not ballasted. Old Ironsides's wheels spanned thirty inches, which meant they hit every damned tie. The motor car bounced up and down like pebbles in a tin can.

Without warning, she stepped on the brake and stopped in the middle of the trestle. "*Ooooooh,* Jimmy, I don't like this."

"It's a hell of a time to decide that." He glanced over his shoulder to determine whether they should keep going straight or back up.

Incredibly, Sir Higginbottom and Staggs were in hot pursuit and were only a short distance behind. In the name of God, they were all crazy!

"Go! Before a damn train comes!" Elizabeth didn't move. He threw up his arms in exasperation. He would never understand her, not even if he lived to be a hundred. "You've driven like a maniac for days. You've driven up stairs, through glass windows, and into more ditches than a ditchdigger. Why are you balking now?"

"It was different before."

*Damn, was that a train ahead?* "Different?" His voice had risen so high, he sounded like a soprano. "How?"

"I couldn't see. Now that your mother has made these wonderful driving goggles, I see everything as clear as a bell."

"Is that the problem? Hell, why didn't you say so?" He reached over and undid her goggles. "Now drive!"

"I can't see, Jimmy."

"I know."

"But . . ."

"Go, dammit!"

Elizabeth held on to the steering wheel and squinted, her mouth set in a stubborn line. "*Ooooooh, I don't like this.*"

Neither, dear God, did he. "Drive!"

Elizabeth stepped on the gas pedal and the car moved forward in an alarming bumpity-bump motion and she immediately slammed on the brake.

"Don't stop!" he yelled. A single glaring light confirmed his suspicions. A train was heading straight at them.

Elizabeth drove forward, faster than was safe, but a hell of a lot slower than was prudent. "That's it. Now keep the steering wheel straight. Straight! You can do it." He kept his voice calm so as not to alarm her, but he never took his eyes off the beaming light ahead. He strained his ears and heard the faint sound of a train whistle.

"What was that, Jimmy?"

"Nothing. Keep driving. We're just about at the end."

"But it sounded like a train."

Much to his horror, she began to slow down. "You're right, Elizabeth, it is a train. And it's about to hit us from behind." He hated lying, but desperate situations called for desperate measures.

Her face paled, but she stepped on the gas and Old Ironsides catapulted off the tracks like a rock in a slingshot before bouncing onto the road.

Jimmy turned in his seat and held his breath until Sir Higginbottom and Staggs drove safely off the trestle and onto the road behind them, mere seconds before an eastbound freight train thundered across the river.

He dabbed at his forehead with his handkerchief and handed Elizabeth back her goggles.

Crankshaw and Fastbender were parked on the side of the road. Apparently thinking their leads were secure, they had stopped to catch up on sleep.

Laughing gaily, Elizabeth beeped her horn as she drove by. *Ah-ooh-ga!* The heads of the sleepy drivers and their mechanics popped up from the depths of the parked cars like four jack-in-the-boxes. Fastbender raised a fist over his head in a curse.

"We're ahead, Jimmy." She rapped one hand against the steering wheel. The exuberance of the moment all but erased the tension between them. "Do you see that? We're ahead."

His forehead still wet with beads of perspiration, Jimmy laid his head against the back of his seat and grinned. Elizabeth was a maniacal driver who should be banned forever from the road, but what the hell? It felt good to get the best of Fastbender for a change. "Ya-hoo!"

Jimmy beat out a tune on the cherrywood dashboard and broke into song. "Be my little baby bumblebee ... do-di-do, do-di-do," he sang, his rich, full voice rising above the sound of the motor for mile after mile. "Sing with me," he pleaded each time he changed tunes.

Elizabeth, clamping her lips together, stared at the road and didn't utter a word, not a word.

"Sing with me!" he pleaded again. "Come on, you know the words. "Gasoline Gus and his jitney bus . . ."

Lord, he knew all the popular tunes of the day, from Irving Berlin to Gershwin. He also knew an amazing number of songs she'd never heard of, but no amount of pleading on his part could convince her to join him.

She'd loved to sing as a child. But that was years ago, before she learned that singing was yet another form of degradation. Singing was just one of the many ways orphans tried to make themselves more appealing to prospective families.

She still recalled standing on the platform of a train station in Oregon and singing her heart out. She was only seven years old at the time, but her whole future seemed to depend on how well she sang. She'd actually thought if she sang well enough, no one would notice how skinny she was—or how plain.

The Children's Aid agent in charge had told her if she didn't find a family, she would have to go back to New York. Everyone knew what a terrible disgrace it was to be sent back to the orphanage. That's why on that long-ago day, she'd stood on a nearly deserted platform singing all the popular songs of the day. Her knees shook from stage fright and her young voice quavered, but she hoped and prayed that one of the stragglers would take pity on her and take her home.

When Mylar Carson had walked over to the agent in charge of Elizabeth's "little company," as groups of orphans were called, and offered to take her home, she thought it was a miracle. She thought herself the luckiest child in the world, and she promised herself to be the best little girl any man could want.

At Mylar's request, she sang for him every night, after the chores were done. He'd sit in front of the fire, staring moodily into the dancing flames as she sang. She tried so hard to make him smile and never understood why he wouldn't. Once, she even attempted to dance for him.

In those early years, she worshiped the man. But that was before the first trip to the barn, before she knew what dastardly deeds he was capable of. Before she was robbed of her childhood.

After that, she never sang again.

Pushing her thoughts away, she tightened her grip on the steering wheel. By her side, Jimmy continued to croon. "By the light . . . do-di-do . . . of the silv'ry . . ."

The Model T Fords, led by Elizabeth, drove in a pack all the way to Bates City. Everyone stopped for fuel, then drove together for several miles outside of town before Fastbender and Crankshaw pulled ahead again.

Jimmy leaned forward in his seat and cocked his head. The engine was making a strange noise.

"You'd better pull over."

Elizabeth pulled to the side of the road. By now, the last of the racers had shot past them and the Model T's looked like little black beetles in the distance. For as far as the eye could see, not a farmhouse was in sight.

Jimmy climbed out of the car and folded back the hood. His worst fears were confirmed. The dented transmission case had caused damage to the flywheel. Fortunately, the flywheel was one of the few parts that could be replaced during the course of the race without breaking the rules, but it had to be ordered from the Ford Motor Company.

Jimmy kicked a rock in frustration. Of all the bad luck.

"Jimmy? What's wrong?"

He took a deep breath. He would have given anything—anything at all—not to have to break the news to her. She joined him in front of the car, looking worried.

"We have a problem," he said. "See this . . ." He pointed to the dented transmission. "The flywheel's cracked."

"How long will it take to fix?" She had such confidence in his ability as a mechanic, he dreaded having to break the news.

"It can't be fixed. I'm sorry, Elizabeth, really I am."

She wrinkled her forehead, her eyes blue as the sky. "What are you saying, Jimmy?"

"I'm saying we're out of the race. It's over."

# Chapter 27

"A motorist who signals one way and turns another has an open mind."

*Women at the Wheel*
Circa 1915

For the longest while, Elizabeth said nothing. She simply stared at the transmission case in disbelief. Jimmy felt like an utter failure. Damn, he hated having to dash her hopes.

"I'm sorry, Elizabeth. I can't tell you how sorry. I know how much this race means to you."

"It's not just me, Jimmy. The women of America are counting on me. The Parkers and the orphans are depending on me. So is Madame Bouvier."

Jimmy raised an eyebrow. Madame Bouvier? Since when had Elizabeth's winning the race become of international concern? "You gave it your best."

"My best isn't good enough, Jimmy. It's got to be your best, too."

"My best?" He was completely taken aback. Never had anyone accused him of not doing his best.

"I know if anyone can fix it, you can."

"Dammit, Elizabeth. I'm not a magician with a magic wand, and we're not exactly in the hub of technology."

"But you're a mechanic. . . ."

"Electrician."

"That's even better. Anyone who can make a few

wires light up an entire room should certainly be able to fix a little old flywheel."

He glanced around, looking for God only knew what. Flat prairie land stretched for as far as the eye could see. The rippling waist-high grass hissed at the wind like an angry snake.

A single road and the railroad tracks were all that sliced through the wide expanse of grass. He turned to face the tracks, a slow grin inching across his face. "By George, maybe we can whip up a little magic." He took her by the hand and pulled her through the grass.

"Where are you taking me?" she asked, running to keep up with him.

"You'll see." Next to the railroad tracks stood a little hand wagon designed to ride over the rails. "Look what we have here." He released her hand. The wagon was a bit rusty, but otherwise in good condition. He pushed it onto the main track.

"You're not going to ride that thing, are you?" Elizabeth glanced up and down the track. "It could be dangerous."

"Dangerous?" Her sudden concern for his safety struck him as odd. "Driving across a trestle wasn't dangerous? What about all those other tricks you pulled? Besides, I'm not going to ride it. *We* are."

"Oh, no you don't, Jimmy. I'm not getting in that thing."

"Now, now, Elizabeth. Remember what you said? The women of America and all those little homeless children are depending on you. And don't forget the Parkers, and what was the name of that woman? Madame somebody? Think what harm you could to our national security if you offend the French. President Wilson's already in trouble with Europe."

He circled his hands around her waist, lifted her off the ground, and carried her kicking and screaming over his shoulders.

"Put me down, Jimmy!" she shrieked. "You heard me! At once!"

He obligingly set her down—inside the hand wagon—and hopped in beside her.

'I'm not doing this, Jimmy. I don't care what you say." Her leg over the side, she looked about to jump, but Jimmy had already begun to pump. The rusty gears made a grinding sound that pierced the ears and sent shivers down his spine, but the hand wagon quickly picked up speed.

Elizabeth held on to the side with both hands. "*Ooooooh*, I don't like this!"

"You'd better start pumping," he called. His hands firmly on the rusty T bar, he pushed down hard, extending his arms the full distance, then pulled the bar up. Up and down, up and down he pumped.

Elizabeth glanced back at him and he was struck anew by her beauty. The wind and sunshine were in her hair; her eyes were bright with blue fire. Only the stubbornness on her face kept him from crushing her to him and having his way with her. *As if she'd let me.*

"And if I don't?"

"Then that train's likely to run us over."

"What train?" Elizabeth gave him a mocking look before letting her gaze wander behind him. She squinted as she stared over his shoulder. She didn't have her glasses on, so she couldn't see. That was to his advantage and he decided to make the most of it.

He glanced over his shoulder in an effort to prove he was telling the truth and got an unpleasant surprise. He blinked, not wanting to believe his eyes, but there was no denying the column of dark smoke that had suddenly appeared in the distance. It was the kind of smoke that came from a train—a very fast train. Muttering a curse, he pumped harder. "Don't just stand there. Help me. It *is* a train, Elizabeth, I swear!"

Elizabeth scrambled opposite him and grabbed hold of the other handle. Following his lead, she pumped furiously.

The handcar glided along the rails at a rapid speed, but it wasn't fast enough and the train rapidly gained on them. A whistle pierced the air and a flock of protesting crows rose from the cornfields and took to the skies in a single black mass.

Jimmy glanced over his shoulder. This time the engine was clearly in sight. "We're going to have to jump!"

"What?" Elizabeth's eyes widened as she glanced at the ground racing by. "Over my dead body."

"Dammit, Elizabeth. This is no time to make demands." He abandoned the pump and grabbed her around the waist.

She tried pulling away. "I'm not jumping, Jimmy!"

"Now, now, Elizabeth. Remember the orphans? The women of America? Madame what's her name? Where's your sense of duty?" He crushed her to him and she buried her head in his chest.

"Jimmy! No!"

"Close your eyes."

"Don't make me do this!" She held on to his neck so tight, if the train didn't kill him first, he'd die anyway—of strangulation.

Trying to loosen her hold on his neck, he eyed the advancing train. Hell, it was close enough to chuck a rock at. He tightened his hold on her. "One . . ."

"Jimmy, no!"

"Two." He didn't wait for the count of three. There wasn't time. Holding Elizabeth tight, he jumped. His feet hit the ground hard. With a jolt that knocked the wind out of him, he rolled like a barrel to the bottom of an incline.

The scream of grinding metal pierced the air as the train collided with the handcar and pushed it several feet along the track with its cowcatcher.

Lying facedown in the grass, Jimmy fought the dazed fog in his brain. He moved a leg and then an arm and finally regained enough of his senses to ascertain he was neither dead nor seriously injured.

Shaking away the fog, he pushed himself up. Elizabeth lay motionless next to him. Filled with dread, he frantically crawled to her side and shook her. Nothing.

"Elizabeth! Talk to me. Dammit, Elizabeth, say something!"

She moaned softly and he rolled her over onto her back to check for any signs of injury. "Elizabeth!"

She blinked, then opened her eyes. He watched her struggle to focus, and then suddenly she smiled, a smile so open and giving, with none of the usual sadness or reserve, that his heart skipped a beat. "Jimmy?"

Overwhelmed with relief, he collapsed in a heap by her side, his breathing still labored. A sharp pain pierced his right shoulder and his confounded leg felt like someone had driven a stake through it, but he didn't care. Elizabeth was all right and that's all that mattered. He massaged the crick in his neck and the ache in his leg.

Elizabeth was fully conscious now, and the color had returned to her cheeks.

"You sure you're okay?" he asked.

She nodded, then giggled. Jimmy forced his breath between his lips. How beautiful she looked when she laughed so freely, how utterly desirable. Sunshine lit her face and her eyes danced with merriment. Her hair tumbled around her head in a golden halo. Beguiled, he was unable to take his eyes off her. "What's so darn funny?"

"Do you realize how funny you looked trying to outrun a train?"

He grinned. "What about you?" He lifted his voice to imitate her. " 'I'll jump over my dead body.' "

She laughed again, and he wanted so much to believe that the laugh was for him. It wasn't until she grew serious and glanced away that he realized he was still staring at her.

Kneeling by her side, he drew a clean handkerchief out of his pocket and wiped the smudge of dirt away from her cheek. She looked up at him, her eyes smoky with nameless emotions.

On impulse, and despite his earlier vow, he dropped

a kiss on her pert little nose. She bit her lip and quickly turned away, refusing to look at him.

He drew back, cursing himself. How many times did she have to reject him before he would learn his lesson? How much hurt must he endure? What made him keep coming back for more? Was it an inflated ego? Or an inflated heart?

"Elizabeth . . . I . . ." Surprised to find himself about to apologize, he stopped. He'd done many things in his life he'd come to regret, but kissing Elizabeth wasn't one of them. He'd be damned if he'd apologize for doing something that was perfectly natural. She's the one who should apologize. Ha! She should get down on her knees and beg his forgiveness for refusing to allow nature to run its course!

She grew still as a statue, her stony face etched in pain. Worried, he turned her chin and examined her head. Her cheeks flared red and she quickly averted her eyes.

It occurred to him that perhaps it wasn't an injury that was causing her so much distress, but his nearness.

"Don't worry," he said curtly. "I'm not going to kiss you again. I know how much you hate it."

Her eyes opened wide and he could see the look of desperation in their depths. "That's a lie, Jimmy. I . . . like when you kiss me."

He stared at her, frowning, his confusion made worse by a deep and yearning need to believe she spoke the truth. *Please don't do this to me. Tell me you don't want me, tell me you hate me, but don't tell me you want my kisses unless you mean it.* "You sure have a funny way of showing it."

"I don't mean to. It's just new for me."

"New? How do you mean new?"

"No one's ever kissed me like you, Jimmy."

Now he was really confused. This last kiss had been nothing more than a peck on the nose, the one prior to that little more. Neither kiss represented anything near to the kisses he was capable of if given the proper encouragement. "That's hard to believe."

"But it's true." She bit her lower lip. "Jimmy ... if you kiss me again, I promise I won't pull away or ... or ... get sick to my stomach."

Her words were like a slap in the face. He blinked. "Suffering catfish, Elizabeth! I've never made a woman sick in my life!"

"Oh, I didn't mean ..." Her lips pressed together, she gazed at him with eyes dark from pain. Under most circumstances he would have felt sorry for her. But at the moment he was too busy trying to ignore the heaviness in his groin, second only to the heaviness in his heart.

Fearing he was about to walk into a trap, he hesitated. But the prize was too great to resist and any fear of rejection faded away as he searched her face for a reassuring sign. "Do you mean it, Elizabeth? Do you really want me to kiss you?"

Her lips trembled and her gaze grew luminous with emotion. "I really do, Jimmy."

His heart skipped a beat. He closed the distance between them and lifted his hand to her cheek. He heard her intake of breath and hesitated. She lowered her eyes and looked away. He narrowed his eyes and tried to keep his rising anger at bay. "What the hell! Do you want me to kiss you or don't you?"

"I told you I do." She kept her eyes averted, but her trembling lips belied her words.

Furious now, he jumped to his feet with a muttered curse. He gave her a look of contempt and turned away. He staggered from her, battling the tall grass like a man fighting off demons.

He didn't have time for games. They were stranded in the middle of nowhere and somehow he had to find a way out of this predicament. Guessing the direction of the nearest town, he tramped through the tall grass to the road. As far as he was concerned, he was through. Finished. Kaput! This time he really meant it. He wanted nothing more to do with Elizabeth—or the race!

# *Chapter 28*

"Backseat driving has its advantages, but don't try
it unless you're prepared to walk."
*Women at the Wheel*
Circa 1915

Jimmy stood by the edge of the dirt road, trying to
ignore the muffled sounds coming from the depths of
the prairie grass. Damn! He hated it when she cried.
He spun around, but only the top of her head could
be seen in the tall wind-blown grass. Heaving a sigh,
he traipsed back.

She didn't look like she was playing games; she
looked for all the world as if her heart were broken,
just as it had been all those years ago on that orphan train. . . .

"Elizabeth?" He moved closer, but she pushed
him away.

"Don't you touch me, Jimmy Hunter. You made it
perfectly clear you don't want anything to do with
me."

He drew back in astonishment. "Dammit, Elizabeth,
you're the one who doesn't want anything to do with
*me*. Not the other way around!"

She looked up with big liquid eyes. "What difference does it make how I feel?"

"What difference?" He dropped down on the grass
beside her. "Why, it makes all the difference in the

world. When a man and woman kiss, it's because they both feel something. . . . Something special."

Her body rocked by a choking sound, she stared up at him. "Both of them?"

"Of course both of them." His gaze followed the silvery tear rolling down her cheek, but he resisted the urge to stop its progress. "Don't cry, Elizabeth. Please don't cry."

He longed to kiss away her tears, kiss her pretty pink lips until they trembled with desire, kiss her until she melted in his arms. But he knew he would only meet more disappointment if he tried. And so he made no move toward her. Nor she toward him, though pools of smoldering emotion swam in the depths of her tear-filled eyes.

Damn, if she didn't look like she wanted to be kissed! She said one thing and did another. She enticed him with her smoky looks, then pushed him away. It was enough to drive a man to drink.

More curious than angry, he settled by her side. "All right. Let's start again. You said you wanted me to kiss you."

"I do . . . Jimmy . . . I really do."

Dammit, he believed her, which only made matters worse. "All right . . . ," he repeated, his mind working quickly. He wanted to kiss her and she wanted to kiss him. What could be more simple?

He thought for a moment, then decided to try a different approach. He lifted his hand and held it close to her cheek without touching her. She followed his hand with her eyes, and when he made no motion to close the distance, she glanced up at him, questioning.

"I'm not going to touch you," he whispered. "You have my promise. If you want me to kiss you, you're going to have to kiss me first."

She clasped her hands and held them to her chest. "I don't know if I could."

"Then I guess there won't be any kissing," he said grimly.

"I guess not," she said, sounding utterly miserable and looking equally so.

He cupped his hands around her face without touching her. "So we're just going to sit here and look at each other." He moved closer, close enough to feel her warm breath, smell her sweet scent. Talk about torture ... Nevertheless, he meant to keep his word. "You're at the wheel," he said softly. "If you want me to touch you, you're going to have to beg."

Her eyes grew round. "You want me to beg?"

"Just a little." His gaze riveted upon her lips, he moved his head slightly as if their mouths were actually touching. It was difficult. His lips burned with the need to kiss her; his arms ached with the need to hold her. His face was less than an inch or so away from hers, so close and yet so terribly far. Her warm, sweet breath mingled with his, and it was all he could do to control the urgent driving need inside him.

Inadvertently, he touched her cheek. She pulled back so quickly she startled him. But she didn't look scared this time, or, thank God, even sick. She looked soft and inviting and oh, so desirable.

She stared at his lips as if mesmerized, then swooned closer to him. This time her mouth brushed slightly against his, sending a heated response shooting through him. It took every bit of self-control he possessed not to grab her on the spot and take her then and there. But he didn't dare. If he and Elizabeth were to have a chance together, he had to let her take the lead, however long it might take.

Elizabeth gazed at his delectable soft lips, so temptingly close. Surprised at herself for allowing their mouths to touch, she still felt the dizzying effects. Her senses were jolted at first, but a pleasurable warmth followed the initial shock. Braver now, she brushed his lips again.

His eyes flared in heated desire and he grimaced when she pulled away, but he made no move to stop her. She held her breath, waiting, knowing that she'd

waited a lifetime for this. She waited, knowing somehow that no mere kiss could fill the deep and urgent
craving that trembled deep inside her. She waited,
knowing this time there would be no turning back.

But Jimmy, apparently meaning to keep his word,
made no move toward her. A softness filled her heart
that could only be love. Love! Was there any man
on earth more patient than Jimmy? More forgiving?
More trustworthy?

"Oh, Jimmy." She feathered his lips again.

And again.

He gave her full control over him, over them, and
heady with the knowledge that nothing would happen
that she didn't want to happen, she ignored the inner
voice that told her to pull away, succumbing instead
to the seductive feel of power that drew her to him.

She brushed his mouth with hers again, and this
time her lips stayed firmly attached. Mmm, he tasted
so delicious, so utterly and wonderfully delicious. His
manly scent filled her head as she pressed against
his mouth.

He was breathing hard now. He sighed in content-
ment when she wrapped her arms around his neck,
moaned with pleasure when she ran her lips across his
cheek, trembled with desire when she nipped his ear;
but true to his promise, he made no move to touch
her or even return her kisses.

She felt a wonderful release with each kiss, as if one
by one the chains of the past had come undone. She
felt free as a bird. Free as the wind and the sun and
the stars. Laughing out loud, she threw herself at him,
pushing him into the grass and smothering him with
kisses. *Ooooooh,* she liked loving Jimmy. Never had
she felt more alive!

*She'll be the death of me yet.*

Jimmy's body felt like it was about to explode. The
exquisite pain of desire and passion burned inside like
a powder keg about to ignite. Blood pounded through

his veins. His arms ached to hold her; his groin screamed with his need to be buried in her depths. Never had a woman excited him more.

God help him.

He was determined to keep his word; he wouldn't touch her until she begged him. But her kisses grew so searingly heated, he could no longer hold back. Without any effort on his part, his lips melted against hers of their own accord.

She drew back, and for a horrified moment he feared he'd scared her away again. But she gazed deep into his eyes. "Kiss me," she whispered. "Please kiss me."

His heart hammered against his ribs. It sure sounded like begging to him. Forcing himself to move slowly, he lifted a hand to her silky smooth cheek, and when she covered her hand with his, he caressed the other side of her face.

"All right," he said, his voice husky with emotion. His gaze dropped to her mouth. "I'm going to touch your mouth with my finger." His eyes met hers. "Just my finger." He lifted his hand and slowly began to trace her lips, following the gentle curve with a single searing fingertip.

"Now I'm going to do the same thing with my mouth," he explained. He touched her mouth with his, kissing her as lightly as a feather. Her response was a little teasing nip of his lip and he widened his eyes in surprise. "Why, you little . . ."

His instinct was to throw all caution to the wind and give full rein to the force inside him that was hammering to be let out, but he didn't want to move too quickly or otherwise do anything to break her trust.

He lowered a hand to her waist and pulled her close, her breasts pressing against his chest. "Are you okay?" he whispered.

"Oh, yes, Jimmy. Yes!"

He smiled to himself. If that wasn't begging, he

didn't know what was. He kissed her tenderly, his lips demanding nothing, but promising everything.

He pulled back between each kiss to give her time to prepare for the next one—and the next. He discovered that by telling her in advance what to expect, she was much more receptive, more likely to respond. Finally he told her what he meant to do with his tongue.

She shivered slightly, but her mouth rounded like it did when she found something interesting or to her liking.

"Are you ready?"

She nodded and he covered her lips with his mouth. He pressed gently with his tongue, and after the third attempt, her lips softened and parted for him. Filling the sweet, warm recesses of her mouth, he felt a thrill run down his spine when her tongue met his in a heated dance.

"Oh, Jimmy," she whispered. She surprised him by grabbing his shirt, thus preventing him from moving away. Their foreheads pressed together, his breath mingling with hers, they gazed at each other. "That feels so good."

It saddened him to hear the amazement in her voice. Dear God, what could have happened in her past that made her fear a man's touch?

Resolving to make her forget everything that had happened before that very moment, he gently, patiently brushed her hair away from her pretty pink cheeks and hoped to God he was man enough not to demand more than she could offer.

He wanted to protect her from anything threatening, but he wanted her so much he didn't think it possible to hold back much longer.

He cupped her face in his hands and kissed her again. "We don't have to go any further. Not unless you want to."

He saw the shadows of indecision play on her forehead, but only for a fleeting moment. "What's next?" she asked, and damned if she didn't sound eager!

A tender joy washed over him as he gazed into her eyes. "Next comes the touching," he said. "I want to feel you all over." He picked up her hand and kissed each fingertip in turn. "I want you to feel me."

Her nod took so long in coming, he suspected she still didn't know how much or how little she was ready for. "All right. We'll take it nice and easy." He wanted to do right by her, right by them. But it was hard to hold back when he wanted her more than life itself. His trousers cut into his male member, but he dared not loosen the buttons. He could control his kisses, even control his hands, but there was only so much a man could control.

"Anytime you feel uncomfortable, let me know and I'll try to stop, Elizabeth. I swear." He touched his lips gently to hers as he ran his hand across her shoulders and gradually dropped down to the swell of her breast. A moan that sounded like a sob escaped her lips.

Cursing himself for moving too quickly, he pulled his hand away, but not soon enough. Already the apprehensive look had returned to her face. He took a deep, steadying sigh, then held up his hand. "Take it."

Her eyes widened as she searched his face. "What?"

"Take my hand. Make it do what you want it to do." He waited for her to wrap her fingers around his, and only when she had full command of his hand did he kiss her again. "Show me, Elizabeth. Show me how to make love to you."

She pressed his hand to her cheek and dropped a kiss across each knuckle. She then drew his hand to her chest, and he could feel her rapid heartbeat beneath his open palm.

His head leaning against her forehead, he closed his eyes, content for now to let her lead him. She felt warm and soft and utterly feminine. His eyes flew open when she moved his hand to her soft, rounded breast and his fingers curved slightly around the lovely firm mound. She pressed his hand against her and he sighed with relief when the tiny peak beneath his palm began to pebble.

Gradually, the fear and confusion left her eyes and he saw the look of trust return. At last, she guided his hand to the strap of her overalls and, without saying a word, dropped her own hand to her side, thus freeing him to proceed on his own.

"Are you sure, Elizabeth?" He couldn't bear the thought of doing something she wasn't ready for.

She looked him straight in the eye, her face determined. "I'm sure, Jimmy."

"All right, then." Suddenly feeling self-conscious and inadequate, he glanced around just to make certain Staggs and that confounded camera of his were nowhere in sight, then worked a strap down her arm.

Keeping her gaze locked in his—and watching for the least bit of resistance on her part—he slipped his hand inside her shirtwaist and lace corset cover. She didn't protest, and encouraged, he cradled her naked breast in his palm, giving her time to adjust to his touch before reaching for the other.

Elizabeth closed her eyes to better concentrate on the wonderful sensations. His touch was as soft and warm as the sunshine and it felt heavenly, so heavenly! She squeezed her eyes shut to hold back the tears of relief. But the feelings of happiness and joy, wonder and thanksgiving, were so overwhelming, she needed the release the tears offered.

Never had she known a man so gentle, so patient, so giving. His kisses filled her with sweet ecstasy; his touch sent flames of desire across her flesh. Oh, dear God, she had no idea a man could be this loving. Never had she thought a woman could actually want to be touched by a man. Long to be touched by him. Need to be touched.

As incredible as it seemed, she needed his touch every bit as much as she needed air or sunshine.

"I hope these are happy tears," Jimmy said, swiping a tear away with a flick of his tongue.

"Oh, yes!" she exclaimed, lifting her face upward to be fully kissed by him.

"Take my hand," he whispered in her hair. "Take my hand before I do something you don't want me to do."

There was nothing she didn't want him to do, but he was so insistent she covered his hand with her own and guided it down her hips and, feeling an almost unbearable need between her thighs, moved his hand toward the tingling, heated spot with only the slightest hesitation.

"Are you sure, Elizabeth?" he whispered in her ear.

"I'm sure," she said, and to prove it, she released his hand.

As if testing her, he ran his hand down the length of her, then began working her overalls down her body.

Stripped of her overalls, she lay before him dressed in only her underwear. "You're so beautiful, Elizabeth. So feminine and soft." He ran his finger along the lacy edge of her white batiste corset cover. He untied the blue satin ribbon at her waist and undid the pearl buttons, freeing her breasts to his view.

Feeling suddenly vulnerable, she crossed her arms in front of her naked breasts. "Don't hide from me," he pleaded. He traced the swell of her breasts with the tip of his finger.

She turned her head and stared at the blue ribbon on her chemise. "Elizabeth," he whispered, "come back to me." When she didn't respond, he captured her chin and turned her head toward him. "Help me."

His plea was a sword stabbing her heart. "I'm afraid if you look at me, you might find me wanting."

He stared at her in astonishment. "How could you think such a thing? You're beautiful!"

"A lot of people found me ... not acceptable."

He narrowed his eyes. "People? What people?"

"Everyone said I was too skinny and . . . Jimmy, I'll understand if I'm not what you expected and . . ."

He frowned. "Everyone? You mean when you were a child?"

She nodded.

He took her in his arms and held her tight. "Elizabeth, you're everything I've always wanted in a woman, and so much more."

"Oh, Jimmy, when you look at me I . . . I almost believe it when you say I'm . . . I'm not lacking."

"You're perfect!" he said fervently. "Perfect in every way. Perfectly beautiful." He pulled her chemise from her breasts and gazed at her with warm, loving eyes. "I want to touch you and I want to taste you." He looked deep into her eyes as if to make certain she understood his intentions before covering one quivering pink tip with his mouth.

She hardly recognized the cry of pleasure as her own. She arched her back to meet him. Smiling softly, he released the tie to her ruffled drawers and gently worked the garment down her hips.

Seeing herself mirrored in his eyes, she actually did feel beautiful and feminine. His hands moved slowly, sensuously over her hips, and finally his fingertips touched the golden crisp hair between her thighs with great tenderness.

A moment of uncertainty passed between them, but this time she didn't pull away. Her flesh grew warm and tingly and she writhed beneath his touch.

Something like fireworks flared in his eyes when at last she reached for the button on his trousers.

Moving with unprecedented speed, he drew his suspenders down his shoulders and pulled off his trousers. He lowered his body onto hers and captured her face between his hands. "Elizabeth Davenport, I want you so much," he said, kissing her.

"Oh, Jimmy." She gazed up at him and moved her hips seductively. "I want you, too."

"You better want this, Elizabeth, because I'm not sure I can stop."

His body, hot and tense, quivered as he entered her. She thrilled to the feel of him inside her. He nuzzled his head into her neck, but she cupped his face, wanting to look into his face and into his eyes. She needed to see the look of love.

His face radiated warmth and tenderness; his eyes shone with love and admiration. Memorizing every line, every nuance, she moved her body with his as he gradually increased the tempo.

At first she was frightened by the throbbing intensity she felt. Was it normal to feel such a powerful and urgent need for another human being? Soon, however, such thoughts fell by the wayside and she surrendered herself fully to the whirlwind of new and wonderful sensations.

Digging her fingers into his back, she drew him ever deeper inside until it seemed as if they were but one entity. His mouth came down on hers as his thrusts increased. Flung to the heights of ecstasy, she matched his frantic tempo until she felt his body stiffen and heard him cry her name. Explosive waves ripped through her, filing her with liquid fire. A cry of joy slipped through her lips as she shuddered with releasing waves.

She held on to him until the last tremor had faded away and a peaceful glow like a warm blanket settled over her. Still breathing hard, he rolled onto his back, pulling her with him until she was on top.

Elizabeth ran her hand over his face, his chest, telling herself over and over this wasn't a dream. How wrong she'd been all these years, how terribly, terribly wrong, to believe she could never make love to a man. How wrong to think she was forever cursed to live a life of loneliness and despair.

She pressed her body against his, not wanting to let him go. Feeling empowered by her newly found freedom, she shamelessly nuzzled his chest, flicked her tongue in his ear, and ran her hands all over him.

Jimmy grinned. "I'll give you twenty-four hours to stop."

She grinned mischievously. "That sounds like begging to me."

"It is, believe me, it is." He moaned with pleasure as she ran a series of kisses up and down his chest. "You're not only a road hog, you're a love hog."

"A love hog?" she asked, nuzzling his skin.

"What else would you call a woman who takes unfair advantage of a man?"

"Me? Taking unfair advantage? I've never done such a thing in my life."

"Oh, no? You're driving me wild and you know it." Flames of desire burned in his eyes. "Come to think of it, you've been driving me wild since the day we first met." He kissed her on the mouth, pressing his entire body the length of hers until he was fully aroused again. "Hold on, baby. We're going for another ride."

Her pretty lace chemise lay in the grass next to them. The blue satin ribbon blew in the gentle afternoon breeze, but Elizabeth was too busy to notice.

# *Chapter 29*

"A speedometer records mileage but won't reveal how far a man and woman in a motorcar have gone."

*Women at the Wheel*
Circa 1915

Later, Elizabeth lay in Jimmy's arms. They were hidden from anyone's view by the tall sweet-smelling grass. Her hand in his, she savored the feelings that radiated from her sated body. Not even the dark clouds gathering in the west like a flock of black sheep could dampen her spirits.

The breeze that had blown across the prairie earlier was now a brisk wind. Dust began to rise, turning the blue sky a muddy brown.

The wind was as worrisome as it was annoying, an unwanted intruder they both tried to ignore. Elizabeth ran her hand over Jimmy's chest, letting the light sprinkling of golden hair tickle her palm, and sighed with happiness. She couldn't quite explain it; it was as if a terrible dark weight had been lifted from her shoulders.

She never knew a man and a woman could be so happy together. It was as if someone had suddenly shined a light in the darkest corners of her heart and soul.

Only one thing marred her happiness. "Jimmy, what are we going to do about Old Ironsides?" Their automobile had to be at least three or more miles away, the closest town another five.

With a reluctant sigh, Jimmy rolled away from her, then sat up. "I've got an idea."

Elizabeth groaned. "I hope it's not like your last one."

His mouth lifted in a teasing grin. "I thought my last idea was a winner." He tossed her overalls to her and reached for his trousers.

"I was talking about the railroad handcar."

"This one can't fail." He pulled on his trousers, his hair blowing in the wind, his naked chest gleaming in the hazy glow of the dust-veiled sun. He leaned down and dropped a kiss on her lips, lingering a moment longer than was prudent. With a reluctant sigh, he pulled away from her. "I'll be back."

She watched him run up the incline toward the railroad tracks, his long, agile legs carrying him swiftly despite his slight limp.

Curious as to what he was planning to do, she quickly pulled on her clothes. Her tangled hair blew about her face, but having lost her hairpins during the tumble down the incline, there wasn't much she could do about it.

Blinking against the dust, she searched for Jimmy, but her myopic vision wouldn't let her see that far. She chased through the grass, calling his name.

"Over here!"

Reaching his side, she watched him struggle with the remains of the rail car. "You're not going to ride the tracks again, are you?" she asked, horrified.

Jimmy pushed the boxy vehicle next to a telegraph pole. "Nope." He climbed on top of the unsteady cart, balancing his weight with wide-spread arms before grabbing hold of the pole. He then wrapped a weathered piece of rope around his waist and began to shin upward.

"Jimmy Hunter, come down from there this minute before you break your neck."

He grinned down at her. "Don't worry. I've done this before. I'm an electrician, remember?" His legs wrapped around the pole fireman style, he pulled himself upward.

"*Ooooooh,* I don't like this." Anxiously clasping her hands together, she watched him fiddle with a box at the top of the pole. "What are you doing, Jimmy?"

"Shhh."

Elizabeth waited at the bottom of the pole with her arms stretched upward, ready to catch him should he fall. Not that she had much chance of saving him, but it made her feel better, just the same. Finally, he started down, empty-handed, and she tried not to show her disappointment.

"Don't feel bad, Jimmy," she said when he reached the ground. "You gave it your best."

"Why should I feel bad? I accomplished what I intended. Now all we have to do is wait."

"Wait?" She glanced around her. For as far as the eye could see, there was nothing but flat prairie land.

Jimmy grinned and slipped his hands around her tiny waist. "I tapped out a message in Morse code on the telegram relay box at the top of the pole. It should reach the dispatcher in the next town. If everything goes as I hope, someone should be along pretty soon to pick us up."

"Why, Jimmy, you're a genius." She slipped her arms around his neck and gazed at him adoringly. "I do believe you are the handiest man a girl could ever have around."

He grinned, glanced around, and not seeing any sign of Staggs, once again pulled her down into the grass. "We have time for me to prove just how handy I can be."

It was forty-five minutes later before a whirling dust cloud in the distance signaled help was imminent. "Better get dressed." Jimmy jumped up and scrambled about for their clothes.

By the time the sheriff drove up in his Buick coupe,

Jimmy and Elizabeth were standing by the side of the road, a carefully measured distance between them. So proper they looked, so chaste, like a couple expecting to meet each other's parents for the first time. Like a couple who'd never exchanged so much as a secret kiss.

The sheriff, a large, rugged man with wild long hair that fell around his massive shoulders, looked them up and down. "Howdy, folks. Are you the ones who telegraphed for help?"

Jimmy stepped forward, his hand outstretched. "Yes, we are, Sheriff. I'm Jimmy Hunter and this is Miss Davenport."

"Davenport, eh?" The sheriff shook Jimmy's hand, but he studied Elizabeth. "You wouldn't happen to be the same Miss Davenport who's racing across the country in that race, would you?"

"One and the same," Jimmy said.

"Well, who'd ever think I'd drive out here to meet me a celebrity. Read about you in the paper. Hop in and I'll take you back to town."

Elizabeth climbed into the front seat, leaving Jimmy to take the rumble seat in back.

The sheriff drove them into a little town called Scooterville and pulled up in front of his office. Using the candlestick phone on the sheriff's desk, Jimmy had the operator put him through to the Ford Motor Company in Michigan. The connection was poor and he had to yell to be heard over the static, but he managed to put in a request for a repair man.

He hung up. "A mechanic will arrive on tomorrow's train."

Elizabeth bit back her disappointment. Even if the mechanic managed to get Old Ironsides up and running again, they had little chance of catching up to the other drivers.

She hated having to admit defeat. Especially now that she knew so many people were counting on her to finish the race. She hated knowing she was going to let a lot of people down. But what choice did she have?

The Ford representative arrived in town the following day. A small, skinny man with a nervous tic, he stepped off the train with a toolbox in hand and introduced himself as Mr. Littleton.

A parade of horseless carriages were parked at the train station, waiting for him to arrive, and one of the drivers, a farmer named Manny Porter, whisked the mechanic to the blacksmith's shop where Old Ironsides had been towed.

Elizabeth and Jimmy rode in the sheriff's car. They were followed by the string of motorcars that had come from as far away as the next county to cheer on the woman driver. One vehicle was filled with the newspaper reporters who had bombarded her with questions earlier as they waited for the train.

Main Street was completely blocked. Horns blared and tempers flared. One horse was so frightened by the commotion, it pulled free from the hitching post in front of Abigail's Dry Goods Store and ran into Millie Nestlebrook's Beauty Salon. Screams pierced the air as the horse pranced by the row of startled women seated beneath steaming asbestos tubes, their hair wrapped in rods.

At noon, Mr. Littleton signaled Jimmy to crank up the engine, and a hush settled over the crowd. It took Jimmy three complete turns of the handle before the engine jumped to life and Old Ironsides took to rattling and heaving, grunting and hiccuping like an old man on his last leg. It was music to Jimmy's ears.

The crowd went wild. Cheers filled the air and hats shot into the sky. Horns blared and church bells rang out.

"Listen to her purr," the sheriff said.

It was more of a roar than a purr, but no one corrected him. Certainly not Elizabeth, who was too grateful that her motorcar was running again to complain.

Everyone had been so warm and friendly, Elizabeth seemed reluctant to leave, but Jimmy urged her on. "Hurry!" he called to her. "Let's go!"

A long parade of vehicles followed them all the way to Boonville before dropping behind.

Later, they pulled into Kansas City and had their passport stamped at the Baltimore Hotel. A sleepy-eyed desk clerk did the honors.

"Could you tell me what time the other cars left Kansas City?" Jimmy asked.

The clerk slid the check-in log across the counter so Elizabeth and Jimmy could read it. Elizabeth wasn't as far behind as he'd thought. According to the log, Fastbender and Crankshaw had been towed into Kansas City after the two had collided. Billy-Joe Mason was caught speeding through Warrington and had to spend the night in jail. Sir Higginbottom had burned his hand trying to heat his tea water on the engine and had been rushed to the hospital. Staggs had checked in less than an hour ago. Stonegate had not yet checked in.

"Well, what do you know?" Jimmy said. "Fastbender and Crankshaw are only three hours ahead of us."

Elizabeth couldn't believe it. "Three hours!" At this point in the race, three hours was nothing. "Oh, Jimmy! Maybe we still have a chance to win." It was a pretty big maybe, and she was grateful to Jimmy for not pointing this out.

Jimmy checked his watch. "If we hurry, we should reach Lake Madison in about an hour. I just hope the ferry runs through the night or we're stuck till morning."

"Maybe there's a railroad trestle we can cross."

Jimmy's face darkened at the thought. "I've had my fill of riding the rails for a while."

It took two and a half hours to make the one-hour drive. Elizabeth somehow made a wrong turn and

Jimmy didn't discover the mistake until they'd reached Kansas City for a second time. Now he pointed to the lights in the distance. "It looks like campfires along the riverbank."

Elizabeth pulled next to the lake, her headlights shining on a familiar face.

"What the ..." Jimmy hung out over the door. "Crankshaw, is that you?"

A dark shape broke away from a campfire and moved toward Elizabeth's car. "It sure as hell is. And what, might I ask, took the two of you so long?"

"We had car trouble," Jimmy explained. "But what do you care how long it took us?"

"That fool ferry captain refuses to take us across the lake until we're all together. Said there was no point in making several trips across the lake when one trip would do the job."

"I'll be." Jimmy grinned. He hopped out of the car. "Sounds like a sensible man to me." He walked over to the campfire and warmed his hands. "Looks like we're all here now. Let's get started."

"We're not all here," Crankshaw muttered. "Car number two's missing."

Jimmy glanced around the campfire, trying to remember who drove car two. "Billy-Joe!"

Stonegate sprinkled tobacco on a small square of paper. "Took off in that direction." His stovepipe hat nodded in the southerly direction. "Said he was going to find himself another way across the lake." He rolled the paper to form a stick-thin cigarette and wet the edge with his tongue. "I told him it was a grave mistake."

"Dammit, Stonegate, must you always talk about graves and cemeteries?" Sparky complained, coughing. His wheezing and coughing had grown worse since the start of the race. "It's damned morbid."

"A cup of hot tea would cure that cough," Sir Higginbottom said.

"I'm not drinking any damned tea," Sparky growled.

Staggs handed Sparky one of those new hard candies with a hole in the middle. "Have a Life Saver."

Crankshaw threw the butt of his cigar into the fire and grabbed his walking cane. "We're not waiting for Billy-Joe. It took us forever to get out of Missouri. I'm not about to hang around all night just to cross a river." He turned on his heel and headed for his car.

This started a stampede, but Elizabeth, who was already behind the wheel with her engine still idling, had an advantage. No sooner had the others started toward their vehicles than she stepped on the gas pedal and drove straight for the dock. Jimmy had no choice but to chase after her on foot.

Elizabeth was the first to drive across the ramp and onto the ferry.

# Chapter 30

"Fight fire with fire if you must, but a fast car is better."

*Women at the Wheel*
Circa 1915

"We're ahead!" Jimmy banged out a tune on the dashboard with his hands. "We're ahead! We're almost at the halfway mark and we're ahead!" Elizabeth smiled and he grinned back at her.

It had taken almost all night to make the ferry crossing. The captain had refused to budge until a red-faced Billy-Joe had returned just after dawn. As irritating as the delay had been, it had been a blessing in disguise, allowing each of the drivers and their mechanics to catch up on sleep.

"We're going to do this, Jimmy. We're really going to do this."

Her enthusiasm made him smile and he didn't have the heart to tell her how slim their chances really were. He doubted that Old Ironsides could make it over the Rockies. The way the engine was clattering, he was beginning to wonder if they'd make it to the next state.

Overhead, the Kansas sky was brown with dust, and an occasional flash of lightning streaked toward the western horizon.

The wind had followed them all the way from Missouri, and powerful gusts swept across the landscape, kicking up dirt and pounding against Old Ironsides like an angry mob trying to overturn the car. Elizabeth was forced to slow to a crawl to keep the car on the road.

Jimmy sat with his head back against the seat, his eyes closed. Not even the ungraded road, the worrisome wind, or the rough sound of the engine could mar his pleasant thoughts. His head filled with the memory of making love to Elizabeth, he allowed himself to hover somewhere between sleep and wakefulness.

"Jimmy."

"Yeah."

"What's that ahead?"

He opened one eye to survey the road ahead. What he saw brought a chill to his bones. Both eyes wide open now, he sat forward. The gray cloud he'd seen earlier stretched across the entire plains ahead from one horizon to the other. At first he'd thought it was a dust storm, but now he knew otherwise. "Damn! It's a prairie fire."

"Oh, no! What are we going to do?" Already the air was thick with the rancid smell of burning grasslands. Strong gusts of wind sent whirlwinds of dust sweeping across the road, blocking their vision.

"We're going to have to turn back." He glanced behind and quickly realized his mistake. Turning back was no longer possible. The high winds had spread the fire at an amazing speed. Bright orange flames raced across the landscape, sending pillars of gray smoke spiraling upward. They were surrounded by fire.

Coughing, Elizabeth let Old Ironsides roll to a stop.

Jimmy climbed out of the car and surveyed the landscape. Smoke and dust blew into his watery eyes. Already his throat felt scratchy and raw.

He grabbed the flask from the backseat, which they kept filled at all times. "Have some water." He waited for Elizabeth to drink before wetting his own lips.

The low-growing buffalo grass next to him caught fire and he stomped out the smoldering sparks with his foot. But orange flames flared up behind them as a clump of tall grass caught fire close enough to burn the paint off the back of the Model T. A short distance away, a dry cedar tree burned like a torch.

Jimmy poured what little water remained onto a clean handkerchief and handed it to Elizabeth.

"Here, put this over your mouth." He lifted his voice to be heard over the wind and the turbulence created by the quick-moving flames.

Elizabeth fitted the handkerchief over her mouth and nose and tied it in back of her head. Her face was hidden by the handkerchief and driving goggles.

"Oh, no, Jimmy, look!"

One of Elizabeth's ribbons had caught fire. Jimmy made a quick decision. He leaped back into his seat and slammed the door shut. "Give it some gas!" he yelled.

Without argument, Elizabeth pushed the hand lever forward and the car shot down the road faster than a mule with its tail caught afire. Flames leaped up directly in front of them and Elizabeth did one of her quick stops, practically throwing Jimmy over the hood.

"Why the hell did you stop?"

Elizabeth studied him through her goggles. "Do you want me to drive through that fire?"

"No, I want you to roast beans. Dammit! What choice do we have?"

"You don't have to yell!"

"I'm not yelling! Just drive!"

Elizabeth eased the car forward like she was out for a Sunday drive. He couldn't believe it. The one time he wanted her to drive like hell, she drove like a little old lady in a horse and carriage. "Go, dammit!"

She slammed on the brakes. "I'm not driving through that fire. It's dangerous."

Without further argument, he reached over and undid her goggles.

"I can't see, Jimmy."

"I know."

"But . . ."

"Drive, dammit, drive!"

Elizabeth held on to the steering wheel and squinted, but she threw the lever forward and the car took off like a tin can kicked by a schoolboy.

"You better hurry," he said. "Our rear end is about to turn into a fireball." It was a slight exaggeration, but it did the job. Elizabeth pressed hard on the pedal and Jimmy's teeth began to rattle as they hit the thirty-miles-an-hour mark on the speedometer.

Smoke blocked Elizabeth's already myopic vision and she drove off the road. Over trenches and gullies they flew, all four wheels leaving the ground at times.

Holding on for dear life, Jimmy prayed no traffic came from the opposite direction. He didn't even know which way they were heading. It was impossible to see anything for the thick gray smoke. It was harder still to breathe.

Bright orange flames lapped at the sides of the flivver, and the smell of burning paint mingled with the acrid smell of burning grass. Jimmy kept his eyes on the side of the car closest to the gas tank.

"Keep going!" His voice was drowned out by the deafening roar of fire and wind coupled with the sputtering chug of the engine.

"*Ooooooh*, I don't like this!"

And, dear God, neither did he.

At long last, they shot out of the thick blanket of smoke like a man out of a cannon. For miles around them, the land lay barren except for a few charred trees. Smoke curled from smoldering ashes and the air was thick with soot.

"We made it, Jimmy. We made it!"

"Don't stop yet." He waited until they were out of danger before telling her to pull over. He climbed out of the car to check for damage. The wind had died down and the sky ahead looked relatively clear.

The intense heat had caused the paint on Old Ironsides to bubble and peel. Only one charred ribbon remained, the others having burned away. Otherwise Old Ironsides had escaped remarkably unscathed. Jimmy patted its sooty fender. " 'Atta girl."

He wiped the black away from his hands and helped Elizabeth out of the car. "Are you all right?"

She smiled up at him, her liquid eyes shining. "I think so."

He wrapped his arms around her and held her tight. "Sorry about the ribbons. We'll replace them at the next town."

She pulled away from him. "I don't need the ribbons anymore," she said. He watched her yank the last of the ribbons away from the back of the car. The grim look on her face brought a chill to his bones. He'd seen that same look after each of her nightmares. He placed a firm hand on her shoulder. "Are you sure you're all right?"

For a long while she said nothing. Finally she met his questioning gaze and forced a smile. Her face was streaked with ashes, but he suspected the tears she quietly shed had nothing to do with the fire. "I've never been more happy in my life." She squeezed his hand and walked away from the car, and because he sensed her need to be alone, he stayed back, but he was tremendously relieved when at last she called to him. "Oh, look, Jimmy. There's a creek over here. Bring the soap and towels."

Jimmy reached into the backseat and grabbed what they needed, along with two drinking cups. His lips were parched, and his throat dry.

After washing away the soot and ashes, they drank their fill of the cool water, filled their flask, and started back.

A half-burned sign by the side of the road told him they were only five miles east of the little town of Manhattan, Kansas. "See that sign?" he said. "We're halfway to Seattle." Elizabeth was in the lead. The lead!

Judging by the thick wall of smoke behind them, he suspected the other drivers would have a difficult time getting through the fire. Talk about luck.

He slipped his hand around her waist, and humming a tango, he pressed his cheek next to hers.

"I can't tango," Elizabeth said.

"Sure you can. Just pretend you're a panther stealthily stepping through a torrid jungle," he said, quoting Vernon and Irene Castle, the famous dance team whose ballroom antics filled the society pages of newspapers across the country.

Holding her hand in his, he extended his arm forward and danced her up and down the lonely stretch of road.

At first she resisted, but in no time at all she had the panther exactly right, and the musical sound of her laughter filled him with pleasure. "That's it, Elizabeth. Come on, now, think torrid jungle."

They danced until they were out of breath and then collapsed on the ground, laughing. But no matter how much he made her laugh, he couldn't forget the look of desolation on her face as she'd pulled the last of the ribbons off Old Ironsides. It was almost as chilling as the stormy clouds that suddenly appeared in the sky ahead.

# Chapter 31

"Never cross your bridges until you get to them."
*Women at the Wheel*
Circa 1915

The weather changed quickly, and by late that afternoon it was bitterly cold. Elizabeth pulled over to the side of the road, and Jimmy plugged the holes in the canvas top and spread the woolen lap robe over their legs.

Dark, angry clouds swept across the sky like an invading army. After driving through Abilene, they were hit by a hailstorm. Icy stones the size of grapes pelted them, forcing them to take cover under a tree. The hail doubled in size and would have riddled the hood full of dents had Henry Ford not built his car out of heavy-gauge sheet metal.

The hail was followed by torrential rains that pelted the windshield and washed away the road, leaving dangerous ruts and overturned trees in its path.

By the time they reached Ellsworth, the mud was as thick as gumbo soup. Elizabeth parked the car as close to the hotel entrance as possible. Jimmy lifted her from the car and carried her to relatively dry ground. Together, they dashed inside the hotel. Even so, they were dripping wet and chilled to the bone by the time they entered the lobby.

Though they had no intention of staying the night, Jimmy rented a room with a bath and handed her the

key. "You'd better change out of those wet clothes.
I'll fetch your suitcase."

Elizabeth took full advantage of the four-legged
bathtub before donning dry overalls. Later, she sat
in front of the blazing fire in the lobby and sipped
hot tea.

The door flew open and Sir Higginbottom blew into
the lobby, dressed in a slick mackintosh, his hand still
bandaged from his burn. After his passport was
stamped at the desk, he walked over to the fire, spread
his raincoat out to dry, and lowered himself into an
upholstered chair. "It's a bit wet out there," he said
with typical English understatement.

Elizabeth offered him a cup of tea. "As far as I
know, it's English tea."

"Don't mind if I do." He watched as she poured
his tea. "Ah, perfect. Thank you." Balancing the cup
and saucer in his hand, he moved closer to the fire.

Jimmy joined them, dripping wet. "How far behind
are the others?" he asked Sir Higginbottom.

"Crankshaw should be arriving any minute. Staggs
and Fastbender are about fifteen minutes back. None
of us have seen Billy-Joe or that bloody undertaker."

"Oh, dear," Elizabeth said. "I do hope they're all
right."

"It's still raining cats and dogs outside," Jimmy said.
"Do you think the others will agree to stay the night?
We could start off in the morning in the same order
we arrived. I don't see any sense in risking our necks."

Sir Higginbottom studied Jimmy over his teacup.
"Can't speak for the others, you know. But you have
my vote." He called over to the desk clerk. "I say,
young man, would it be possible to arrange for some
bread and cheese and perhaps some smoked meat to
be brought to us?"

"Very well, sir."

By the time Crankshaw and Fastbender walked into
the hotel, a plate of sandwiches had arrived. Crankshaw headed straight for the public telephone.

"What have we here?" Fastbender mocked. "I do believe it's the lady driver."

"The lady driver is in first place," Jimmy said.

Fastbender cast a glaring look at Jimmy before turning back to Elizabeth. "Is that so? Well, enjoy it, little lady. The real test is about to begin. How are you at navigating rivers?"

"As good as any man."

Fastbender laughed. "This I gotta see."

She jumped to her feet. "You'll see it, all right. Just don't expect me to send you a life saver when you go floating downstream."

"You're the one who'll need a life saver. . . ."

"Is that so? Well, let me tell you something, you . . ."

Jimmy stepped between them. "We need to work together. It's raining harder and the roads are getting worse. I say we spend the night here and start off in the morning."

Fastbender's lip lifted in a dismissing sneer. "You and the lady driver can do anything you want. I'm heading out."

Jimmy regarded the man with disdain, but he kept his temper in check. "It's dangerous."

"I guess that means chickens and lady drivers should stay inside where it's safe." Fastbender walked across the lobby and practically ran into Stonegate, who had arrived in time to hear the end of the discussion.

"Hunter's right. It's time we buried the hatchet," Stonegate said, sounding more cheerful than usual.

"Get out of my way, Stonegate! I'm not burying anything with you!" Fastbender disappeared through the door.

Jimmy swore beneath his breath. "Fool."

"How far is it to the next checkpoint?" Sir Higginbottom asked.

Before anyone could answer, Crankshaw yelled into the telephone. "What do you mean, you have no intention of marrying me? I'm telling you, Myra, you won't find better!"

Staggs rolled his eyes, then returned to the map spread across his lap. "In this rain, I'd say it'll take us about four hours to reach Dorrance."

Sir Higginbottom put down his cup. "I guess we'd better get started then, hadn't we?"

Elizabeth started for the door, but Jimmy caught her by the arm. "We don't have to do this, Elizabeth."

"I'm not quitting, Jimmy."

She could tell by his face how much he disapproved, but he dropped his hands to his sides. "Do you want me to drive?"

She glanced out the window. Rain drove hard against the diamond-shaped panes. Jimmy's offer was tempting, but she wanted to be in the driver's seat.

All her life, starting from the time she was hauled across the country in the baggage car and made to parade in front of strangers, it seemed that her destiny was out of her hands. It gave her great satisfaction to pass each of those train stations now, twenty years later, behind the wheel of her very own motorcar. "I'll drive," she said.

"But the rain . . ."

"I'll drive, Jimmy." Strange as it seemed, she felt safe in the rain. It wasn't all that long ago that it had been the only time she'd felt safe. "This is my race."

"Don't shut me out, Elizabeth. It's my race, too."

Surprised, she studied him. It had never occurred to her that the race had come to mean anything to him other than an aggravation. "Oh, Jimmy, I'm not shutting you out. I could never shut you out. But I have to do this. Please understand."

He didn't understand. She could see it in the eyes that pleaded with her, the face that beseeched her. "Stay here with me tonight where it's safe and warm."

She was tempted, so terribly, terribly tempted, but she'd come too far to give up now. "I'm sorry, Jimmy."

Pulling the hood of her rain gear over her head, she dodged outside into the driving rain. She had no way of knowing if Jimmy would follow, but she prayed with all her heart that he would.

Rain hammered down on her, and the cold, muddied waters rose to her ankles as she waded to her car. She sat in the dark cab of her Model T staring at the doors of the hotel. Jimmy was nowhere in sight.

Her spirits plummeting, she gripped the steering wheel and closed her eyes against the hot tears. He wasn't going to come. That part didn't surprise her. What surprised her was finding out she couldn't leave without him.

Suddenly, she heard a tapping sound on the windshield. Her eyes flew open. Her vision was blurred with tears, making it more difficult than usual to see, but she knew without a doubt it was Jimmy.

Her heart danced with joy as he struggled to light the headlamps. At last, he cranked up the engine and hopped inside the car.

"I told you. It's my race, too," he said by way of explanation.

Smiling, she pulled out onto the road behind Sir Higginbottom. It was raining so hard it was impossible to see the road, and at times she could see only the red light from the back lantern on the Englishman's car.

When Higginbottom's light ran out of carbon, Jimmy hung out the open window trying to navigate by the telegraph poles. "Stay to the right. Now left. Left! That's a girl. Now keep going straight."

Lined up like black shiny beetles, all six Model T's chugged through the night. No one had seen hide nor hair of Billy-Joe.

One after another, the weary drivers and their mechanics traveled through Blackwolf and Wilson, reaching Dorance at eight in the morning. The rain turned into a drizzle outside of Bunker Hill and they picked up speed, but only as far as Hays when they met with torrential rains once again.

She was barely going five miles an hour. Elizabeth's eyes burned from lack of sleep. Next to her, Jimmy pounded out tune after tune on the dashboard and sang at the top of his lungs. Though he acted with the best of intentions and had succeeded in keeping her awake, she thought if she heard one more song, she would scream.

Just outside of Ellis, Fastbender took advantage of a lull in the weather to shoot around Elizabeth's car and take the lead. His advantage lasted for only a few miles, until he missed a turn in the road and sank into a mud hole.

Elizabeth pulled over to the side of the road and stopped her car. Crankshaw and Staggs drove by, honking.

"Why are you stopping?" Jimmy asked.

"We can't leave him in the mud."

"Are you crazy? He tried to kill me. And look how he's treated you. Fastbender is your main competitor. Without him, you can win this race."

"I want to win this race with him," she said, her voice sharp with grim determination. "What fun will it be to win the race if he's not there to see me do it?"

"But . . ."

She laid a hand on Jimmy's arm. "Please. Do this for me."

Jimmy shook his head. "This is crazy, Elizabeth."

"I know, Jimmy. I know."

It took Jimmy a little over an hour to pull Fastbender out of the mud, but did he get a word of thanks for his efforts? Not a one! If anything, Fastbender was downright surly as he sped off. Watching the tail of Fastbender's car, Jimmy swore it would be the last time he raised a finger to help the man, and Elizabeth could plead all she wanted.

"Don't worry, Jimmy," Elizabeth said, guessing the

reason for Jimmy's dark look. "Fastbender will get what he deserves."

"He better," Jimmy growled. Hearing a strange hissing sound coming from the rear of the car, he turned and groaned. "Meanwhile, he's on the way to Oakley and we're stuck here with a flat tire."

It was the first of two flat tires that day, which is why they didn't arrive in Oakley until after ten that night.

They found Crankshaw in the hotel lobby, trying to use the telephone. The distressed clerk tapped him on the shoulder. "Excuse me, sir, but the phone lines are down."

Crankshaw brushed him away impatiently. "So you said." He spoke louder, his voice booming into the mouthpiece. "Myra! Can you hear me?"

Famished, Elizabeth and Jimmy headed for the hotel dining room, where Sir Higginbottom, Staggs, Fastbender, and their mechanics were enjoying a hot meal. It appeared that every resident in town had turned out to greet the weary drivers.

A tall man with a droopy mustache and a Billy-Joe drawl brought out his ukulele, and a woman named Mary-Dee, who was wide enough to cast a shadow the width of a barn, insisted that Sir Higginbottom join her on the dance floor for a rousing two-step.

Around eleven, Fastbender headed for the door. Jimmy blocked his way. "Where do you think you're going?"

Fastbender's eyes were bloodshot from lack of sleep. "I'm heading for Limon, Colorado. I believe that's our next checkpoint."

"Well, you're about to change your plans," Jimmy said. He nodded toward the bar where Higginbottom and Staggs were entertaining a small gathering with their road adventures. "We took a vote and decided to spend the night here."

"You can spend the night anywhere you damn well please. I'm leaving."

"That's going to be a bit difficult," Jimmy said, biting out each word. "First you're going to have to get through me. Then you're going to have to get through Staggs and Sir Higginbottom. Then you'll have to get by Miss Davenport." He winked. "That's when it's going to get real tough."

The air between the two men snapped with tension, and the room fell silent as all eyes turned to Fastbender.

Next to him, his mechanic sighed. "Come on, Fastbender. We can all use a good night's sleep."

Fastbender studied each driver in turn. Although Elizabeth was directly responsible for hauling him out of that mud hole a ways back, he showed no more regard for her than before, and blatantly ignored her. "All right, Hunter, have it your way."

Satisfied, Jimmy turned to address the others. "I suggest everyone get some shut-eye. We'll meet downstairs at six in the morning for breakfast and we'll pull out in the order we arrived."

It was still raining the following morning when Elizabeth and Jimmy started off. Mud was everywhere. The six cars drove caravan-style through muddied fields to avoid roads that were under water. Winning the race took on less importance than survival, and even Fastbender seemed reluctant to pull ahead of the others when given the chance.

Following each other like ants at a picnic, the Model T Fords were practically bumper-to-bumper when Crankshaw pulled over to the side of the road to answer a call from nature. Instead of leaving him behind, the other five drivers waited patiently and the cars remained in the same order as they pulled back onto the road.

Outside the small town of Phillips Valley, the men worked together to pull a metal roof off an old barn and used it to ford an overflowing creek. Just as Elizabeth was driving across the makeshift bridge, an uprooted tree floated downstream, catching beneath Old Ironsides's frame.

Sparky helped Jimmy pull the branch free, but a

strong smell of gasoline confirmed Jimmy's worst fear. "The gas tank is punctured."

Elizabeth grimaced. "Oh, Jimmy, what are we going to do?"

Jimmy checked his map. "We're about six miles from the closest town."

"Will we make it?"

Jimmy shook his head. "At the rate we're losing fuel, I doubt we'll make it another mile."

Elizabeth felt her already low spirits sink. Was there anything else that could go wrong?

Fastbender took off, followed by Crankshaw, Sir Higginbottom, and Stonegate. But Staggs walked back to her car. "I'll stay with you if you like. It's bloody dangerous out here."

Elizabeth smiled her gratitude. "I'm much obliged to you, but there's no point in us both losing the race. You go on ahead and give Fastbender a run for his money."

"If that's what you want. Good luck to you." Staggs snapped a photograph of her before making his way back to his automobile.

"I've got an idea." Jimmy lifted the portable gasoline can from the running board and worked to free the fuel line. Attaching one end of the rubber hose to the carburetor, he fed the other end around the windshield.

Jimmy cranked up the car and took his seat. He then stuck the end of the hose into the gasoline can. The idea was to feed the engine with fuel directly from the can, bypassing the damaged tank. "Let's hope this works."

Elizabeth drove slow at first, giving Jimmy a chance to regulate the fuel until it flowed smoothly through the hose before picking up speed.

They drove through raging waters and over muddied fields. Sometimes Elizabeth had to drive miles out of the way before she could find water shallow enough to drive through.

At long last, the high plains of western Kansas fell behind them and the road began to ascend as they crossed over the Colorado state line.

It was obvious from the amount of water still on the ground that a heavy storm had hit the area earlier, but for now, at least, the rain had stopped.

By the time they reached the little speck of a town called Limon, they had climbed over five thousand feet.

The deserted street flanked by a few rundown buildings was lit by a single arc lamp.

Elizabeth parked in front of a general store that advertised gasoline for sale. The store was closed, but Jimmy banged on the front door to wake the owners.

A light flicked on in an upstairs window and soon an elderly man dressed in a white nightshirt and a nightcap opened the door of his shop. Jimmy explained his problem and the man stepped outside to fill Jimmy's fuel can with a portable wheel cart gasoline pump.

"Cain't repair the gas tank, but I can give you an extra fuel can and a thinner hose."

"I appreciate your help," Jimmy said. "Sorry to wake you."

"No problem."

With that the owner turned off the lights and went back to bed. Shivering against the cold, Jimmy climbed back into the car.

Elizabeth was asleep, her head against the seat. Feeling sorry for her, he ran his knuckle down her velvet soft cheek, and dropped a tender kiss upon her forehead.

He'd done all he could do in Limon, but he didn't have the heart to wake her.

He doubted it would make any difference either way. With the fuel tank damaged, they had little hope of making up lost time. The most he could do was to nurse the fuel into the carburetor until they reached Denver.

He stared at the black void that stretched out in front of them for as far as the eye could see. *If they reached Denver.*

# *Chapter 32*

"Never pick up a hitchhiker—unless he can read a map."

*Women at the Wheel*
Circa 1915

Jimmy was just about to doze off when Elizabeth suddenly cried out. Reaching for her in the dark, he pulled her close. Her body trembled next to his, filling him with alarm. "It was just a nightmare," he said soothingly. *Another nightmare.*

She clung to him, and though it was freezing in the car, her forehead felt warm, almost damp to the touch. "Oh, Jimmy, hold me," she whispered.

He held her close, and telling her of his intentions, he kissed her until she stopped trembling and relaxed against him. "Tell me about the dream," he whispered. "I want to understand, Elizabeth. I want to know what it is that makes you so afraid."

"I'm not afraid. Not anymore. You've helped me not be afraid."

"But you still have nightmares."

She pulled away from him and grabbed hold of the steering wheel. He'd lost her again. He could feel an invisible block between them, a block that made the cold and the dark seem almost hospitable in contrast. "We better go," she said with firm resolve. "What about the fuel tank?"

Disappointed and hurt that she refused to confide

in him, he tried not to let his feelings show. "I couldn't get it fixed. We have ten gallons of gasoline. That should get us to Denver."

"Let's go, Jimmy."

He climbed outside to crank up the engine. The air was brisk and a full moon spun magical threads of silvery light through the branches of the tall pines.

He watched Elizabeth through the windshield. It was too dark to see her face clearly, but it didn't matter. Every inch of her face and body would forever be etched in his memory. He only wished he knew her heart as well.

He did know that she wasn't trying to win the race as much as she was running away from something. He had his suspicions, of course, as to what that something was. But he wouldn't know for sure until he heard it from her own lips.

"What's taking so long, Jimmy?"

"Nothing," he said, reaching for the crank. Not a darn thing.

They drove for the remainder of the night. Just before dawn, Jimmy insisted they stop and take a break.

Climbing out of the car, he stretched his weary bones, replaced the carbon in the headlamps, and read the road map. Despite their fuel tank problems, they seemed to be making good time, though it was hard to know for certain.

They hadn't seen hide nor hair of the other drivers for hours.

A light, hazy fog swirled in front of the headlamps. To the east, a pencil-thin silvery light signaled dawn. He folded his map and climbed back into the car. Elizabeth said nothing and he sensed she was still feeling the lingering effects of her nightmare.

"We're a little over twenty miles from Denver," he said, trying to offer encouragement.

She stared straight ahead, looking downhearted. "Aren't you forgetting something?"

"I sure hope not."

"Look at the mountain we still have to get over."

"After everything we've been through, what's a little mountain?"

"It's not just the mountain, Jimmy. It's the fuel tank. . . . It's . . ." Once she'd started, all the frustration and exhaustion that had been building for days poured out of her like water from a spigot.

"Don't fret, baby. We'll get all those things fixed. Just as soon as we reach Denver."

"And after we leave Denver, we've still got the badlands and who knows what else? I'm through."

"Let's not make any rash decisions, Elizabeth."

"This is not a rash decision. I'm no longer in the race and that's the end of it." She climbed out of the car and almost stepped into a pool of quicksand. *"Ooooooh."*

She marched off with only the dim glow of the headlamps lighting her way. Worried, Jimmy chased after her. "Elizabeth! You're tired and don't know what you're saying."

"I know exactly what I'm saying, Jimmy. I'm quitting. You're right. I should have quit long before now. I made a respectable effort. No one can say I didn't!"

"You've done magnificently," Jimmy said sincerely. He fell in step beside her. Unwilling to believe she would give up, he decided to play along with her. He only wished she would slow down. It was still too dark to see much. For all he knew, they were about to walk off the mountain.

"Certainly with all the publicity I've generated, I shouldn't have any trouble finding backers for my children's home."

"I daresay you're right. Who needs this old race?"

At last she stopped and faced him, her face barely visible in the dim morning light. "You're absolutely right. I'll concentrate on writing my books, and if that's not enough to help me build my orphan home, I'll write another and another—and I don't care if I have to go to jail!"

"That'll keep you out of trouble," Jimmy said.

"And you can go back to Hogs Head and run your family's business."

He creased his forehead in alarm. This was beginning to sound serious. "You can't quit now, Elizabeth. You'll never forgive yourself."

"I'll forgive myself just fine. I've proven that I'm in control of my destiny. What do I need to win the race for?"

Jimmy raked his hair with his hand, surprised at his own sense of loss. He'd told Elizabeth it was his race, too, but until that very moment, he'd had no idea how important it had become to him.

That was a surprise. He cared nothing for money or fame. Still, he had no desire to quit. He'd put too much into this race, both physically and emotionally. Old Ironsides's peculiarities still confounded him, but no more than its pint-size driver. Besides, keeping that old machine in repair after what Elizabeth had put it through was every bit as satisfying as heading the electrical works. Maybe more so. For once in his life, he didn't have to live in his parents' shadow.

While he would have gladly given up the race in the past, he no longer wanted to quit. "Some people might think twenty-five thousand dollars is a good reason to keep going."

"There're more important things in life than money."

"Granted, but I never thought you were a quitter."

"Don't think you're going to shame me into continuing, Jimmy Hunter. I said I'm finished and I mean it!"

"All right, we'll compromise. You finish the race and I won't complain about your driving."

"You can do all the compromising and bribing you want. My mind is made up. And I'm not one of those women who changes her mind easily."

"I know," he said dryly. He studied her determined face. He had no right to talk her into something she didn't want to do. It was her race, no matter how much it had come to mean to him. Still, it was hard to believe she could give up now, after everything she'd been through. Maybe she was just tired. Or discouraged. Maybe she was just testing him. "I guess that's that, isn't it?"

"I guess so." Her eyes locked with his. "Thank you, Jimmy, for everything. I couldn't have cóme this far without your help."

The sky lightened, revealing pools of quicksand around their feet. One misstep and they could both be in serious trouble. "I'm not sure I did you any favors."

"Well, you did, and to show you how much I appreciate your help, I plan to dedicate my next book to you."

"Your next ... book?" Horrified at the idea, he tried to think of a way to discourage her without hurting her feelings. "People will think ... I mean ..."

Her face blank, she stared at him, then suddenly she laughed aloud. "Not my family limitation book, Jimmy. My *next* one. I'm calling it *Women At the Wheel*."

Relief rushed through him, but the idea struck him as incredible. "You're writing a book about women drivers?" It was his turn to stare—which he did for a full several seconds before bursting into laughter. "This I gotta see."

A frown settled on her forehead. "And indeed you shall. I'll even inscribe a copy to you." She studied him, annoyance written on her face. "I know you have a low opinion of my driving but I didn't think you were opposed to limiting births."

"I'm not opposed. It only makes sense. No one should have more children than it's possible for them to take care of."

"I see. You just don't want your name attached to a book on the subject. Is that what you're saying?"

"It's not something that a man ... I mean ... it

seems to me a woman would have far more credibility on this topic than a man."

"In other words you think babies are only a woman's concern."

He wasn't sure what he believed. Other than taking necessary steps to protect any young woman he'd kept company with in the past, he'd not really thought much about the subject. He'd always assumed, of course, that once he settled down and got married, he'd father a whole houseful of children, just like his parents.

"I suppose limiting births is a good idea," Jimmy conceded, "for some people." His statement obviously did nothing to appease her. Hell's bells, the tension in the air was as thick as the stillness before a storm. How in the world did they get into such a discussion? Trying to prevent the argument that was brewing between them, he quickly changed the subject. "I think our best bet is to drive back to Limon and catch a train."

"Do you mind driving back?" she asked, her voice lacking its usual exuberance.

The offer surprised him. In the past, she'd seldom relinquished the steering wheel, and then only after a great deal of persuasion on his part. Any hopes he had of her changing her mind were squelched. Obviously, she was serious about quitting. "Elizabeth, are you sure about this?"

"I've made up my mind, Jimmy." She carefully stepped around a pool of quicksand and headed back to the car.

Shoving his hands in his pockets, he followed, feeling depressed. It was *her* race, he told himself. *Her* decision. No matter how much he wished it weren't so.

The sound of an engine shattered the early morning stillness. Jimmy narrowed his eyes, trying to determine if he knew the driver. "It looks like Fastbender!" he called out. "How in heaven's name did we pass him?

We better tell him we're turning back. That way he can notify the race officials."

"You tell him," Elizabeth said, sounding like a shadow of herself.

Jimmy stood by the side of the road and waved. "Stop, I have something to tell you!" Fastbender beeped his horn and drove though a puddle, splattering Jimmy and Elizabeth with mud. "What's the matter, Miss Tin Lizzie? Got a problem?" He whizzed by and disappeared around a bend in the road, raising his hand over his head in a victory sign.

Elizabeth stood staring at him with her hands tight at her side, mud dripping off her pretty pert nose. "*Ooooooh*, I don't like that man." She spun around, tore open the door to the car, and grabbed her goggles. "Crank her up!" she shouted. "If we hurry, we'll reach Denver in time for breakfast."

Jimmy scratched his temple. One moment she was despondent, and the next, yelling out orders. "I thought you were quitting. I thought you didn't care about winning the race."

"This isn't about winning."

He eyed her suspiciously. "If it's not about winning, why the hell are we going to Denver? Just so you can get even with Fastbender?"

"This isn't about winning and it's not about Fastbender," she said earnestly. "I can't quit now. People are depending on me."

"That's right. People like Mr. and Mrs. Parker. Like those women in Cleveland. And don't forget Madame what's-her-name."

"I wasn't thinking about them, Jimmy. I was thinking about you."

He studied her earnest face. "Me?"

"You were the only one who really believed I could do this, Jimmy. You said I couldn't drive, but you never once said I couldn't win the race. If I quit now, I'll let you down."

"Nothing you do is going to let me down." He

grinned, relieved to see her old spirit back. "Unless you drive me off the side of the mountain."

She slipped on her goggles and reached for her driving gloves. "Oh, Jimmy . . ." She lovingly kissed him on the lips, then heaved herself inside the car. "Let's go!"

In Denver, they found an official Ford repair shop, and Jimmy decided to have the entire car overhauled. The last thing he wanted to do was to break down in the notorious Wyoming badlands.

He and Elizabeth walked the short distance to the Savoy Hotel to get their passport stamped.

The clerk was a tall, skinny man wearing a Stetson cowboy hat. He took the passport from Elizabeth. "Welcome to Denver. You're the last to arrive."

"Last?" Jimmy scratched his head. There had to be a mistake. No one had seen or heard from Billy-Joe in quite some time. "Does that include car number two?"

The clerk glanced down at his notebook. "Car number two was first." He then listed the order in which the others had arrived.

Jimmy frowned. How in hell did Billy-Joe always manage to sneak past them unseen? The man was slippery as a snake.

The clerk stamped Elizabeth's passport with the Ford emblem and handed it back to her.

Despite the discouraging news, he decided to go forward with his plan to have the engine overhauled and the gas tank repaired. As it would probably take six to eight hours to do the job right, it would cost them dearly in time. Still, the hardest drive was still ahead, and the stopover would give them time to do their laundry, stock up on supplies, and catch up on some much-needed sleep.

For all Jimmy knew, this could be their last chance.

# Chapter 33

"Mountain driving requires a steady hand, steel nerves, and a lot of luck."

*Women at the Wheel*
Circa 1915

It was nearly five that afternoon before they were ready to leave Denver.

"So what do you think?" Jimmy asked when Elizabeth met him by the car, looking rested and like her old self. He referred to the brand-new silk taffeta ribbons he'd purchased from a local department store and tied to the back of Old Ironsides. Ribbons in every color of the rainbow fluttered in the late afternoon breeze.

Upon seeing the ribbons, Elizabeth froze. A look of bleakness flashed in her eyes, but it was gone so quickly, he wondered if he'd imagined it. "Oh, Jimmy, they're beautiful!"

"Do you like them?" he asked, studying her closely.

"Of course I like them." She smiled up at him, but it seemed to him something was lacking in her eyes, some sparkle. Shrugging the thought away, he cranked up the car. Old Ironsides roared like a lion with rusty insides. It was a great improvement over how the engine had sounded before the overhaul.

It had rained off and on for most of the day, but for now at least, the rain had stopped.

By the time they reached the Interocean Hotel in

Cheyenne nearly ten hours later at three o'clock in the morning, Elizabeth was exhausted.

The lobby of the hotel was deserted, with not a hotel clerk or bell captain to be found.

"Damn!" Jimmy banged on the bell to no avail. It looked as if they had no choice but to stay at the hotel longer than planned. Jimmy turned away from the registration desk and found Elizabeth curled up on the brocaded sofa in the lobby, already asleep.

Feeling sorry for her, he pulled off his coat and covered her. Maybe it·was just as well that the desk was empty. He sank into a chair opposite her and yawned.

Sometime later he was awakened by a woman's screams. His eyes flying open, he jumped to his feet. Elizabeth thrashed about on the sofa, kicking and screaming.

"Let me go!"

Jimmy rushed to her side. "Elizabeth, wake up!" Protecting himself against her flailing arms and legs, he tried to calm her down. She blinked her eyes, looking dazed and confused.

"It's me, Elizabeth. Jimmy."

She stared up at him, and looked utterly distressed upon seeing the bloodied scratch on his left cheek where she had dug her nails into his flesh. "Oh, Jimmy, I'm so sorry." She covered her mouth with her hand and looked about to burst into tears.

"It's all right, Elizabeth. After what I've been through these last few days, a little scratch is nothing. That must have been some dream. I hope it wasn't about me," he said lightly, trying to make her smile. "I've been known to cause a woman trouble, but never nightmares."

"It wasn't about you. Oh, Jimmy, I would never have nightmares about you. It was ... nothing."

He knew better. Something or someone had hurt her, hurt her so bad that he feared she would never recover. At times, her pain was so evident to him, it was like a brick wall keeping them apart.

He knelt on the floor by her side and cradled her head in his arms. "Talk to me, Elizabeth. Tell me what happened to you after we separated as children."

"That has nothing to do with this, Jimmy. It was just a dream. Haven't you ever had a nightmare? Just don't . . ."

"Don't what, Elizabeth? Don't touch you without giving you time to brace yourself? Don't kiss you without first announcing my intention? Who was he, Elizabeth? Who was this man who made you so afraid to be touched? Afraid to love? Who?"

"Don't, Jimmy," she pleaded. She beseeched him, "Please don't do this to me."

He touched the silky strands of hair that framed her lovely pale face and couldn't in good conscience deny her request. At least not tonight. But he made a silent vow to eventually find out who or what it was that haunted her. "All right. We'll play it your way. For now."

Just before dawn, the clerk returned to his desk, whistling a tune. Jimmy stood and helped Elizabeth to her feet. "Let's get your passport stamped."

The rain started again that morning and it continued to pour steadily all day. Water rushed down canyons, causing landslides and washing out bridges. Elizabeth was constantly forced to backtrack or take an alternative route.

They reached Cheyenne at noon, and after pulling into the filling station, bumped into Crankshaw having a broken wheel repaired.

"Heard the Fort Steel bridge is down," Crankshaw announced grimly. He stuck his cigar in his mouth.

Jimmy frowned at the news. According to his map, the Fort Steel bridge was the only way across the Platte River. "What do we do now?"

"According to the mechanic, we could cross on the

Fort Steel trestle, but not without permission. I just wired Union Pacific and I suggest you do likewise."

"Thanks." Jimmy narrowed his eyes. "Why are you helping us?"

Crankshaw's face took on a sheepish look. "Now don't go getting me wrong, here. I have every intention of winning this race. It's my only hope of getting Myra to marry me. But should somethin' happen so that I don't, I'll be pulling for the little lady to win."

Crankshaw's change of heart surprised Jimmy. "That's mighty generous of you," he said warily, still not sure whether to trust Crankshaw.

"Don't get the wrong idea. The truth is, I'd rather see a mule win than that fool-headed Fastbender." Crankshaw glanced around. "You won't say anything, will you?"

"Say anything?"

"To the others. It wouldn't look good, you know, if word gets out that I'm rooting for a lady."

"Your secret's safe with me." Jimmy turned to go, then stopped. "By the way, if something happens that Elizabeth doesn't, you know, cross over the line first, I'll be rooting for you."

"That's damned decent of you, Hunter. Damned decent. I'll make sure you get an invitation to my wedding."

Elizabeth and Jimmy met up with Sir Higginbottom and Fastbender at the trestle. The two drivers stood in the driving rain arguing with a Union Pacific employee, who refused to let them cross without permission from the proper officials.

Grinning to himself, Jimmy joined them and introduced himself to the trainmen. Upon hearing Elizabeth's name, the man nodded. "I received permission an hour ago. You can cross when you're ready."

Jimmy thanked him, then turned to the two open-mouthed drivers. "See you around."

He climbed back into the car, grinning.

"What's so funny?" Elizabeth asked.

"See that trestle?"

"Yes."

"As soon as you drive over it, you'll be number one again."

"Oh, Jimmy! Really?" Her smile touched his heart like sunshine, and not even the driving rain or the biting cold wind could penetrate the warmth that radiated from her.

Elizabeth was number one for the next three days, but neither she nor Jimmy took much comfort in the fact. They were too busy battling rain and mud. The road from Cokeville to Pocatello led through rugged mountains. The road was nothing more than a narrow shelf hanging precariously from the side of a sheer cliff. Jimmy estimated that the road was only six inches wider than the wheels. One slip and they would drop hundreds of feet into Bancroft Canyon.

The dismay on Elizabeth's face grew by the minute. Both hands on the steering wheel, her eyes riveted to the narrow ribbon of a dirt road, she navigated one dangerous curve after another, complaining all the while. "*Ooooooh,* I don't like this, Jimmy. I don't like this at all."

Jimmy considered having her drive without her goggles. To see or not to see, that was the question. With Elizabeth it was hard to know which was more dangerous. He'd offer to drive, but there was no room to change drivers. He decided to let her continue with her goggles.

"Don't look down." For once he didn't have to remind her to drive slow, but he did have to tell her to stay clear of the mountainside. She was driving so close to the rough, rocky cliffs, Old Ironsides's entire right hand side was scraped and dented.

They reached American Falls, Idaho, at eight that night. Since there was still no sign of the other drivers, Jimmy decided they could afford to spend the night at the hotel. It was chancy, but both he and Elizabeth were exhausted.

After a good night's sleep, they started out early the following day, reaching an unmarked crossroads around noon. Elizabeth stopped the car and stretched while Jimmy studied the map.

The land lay barren for as far as the eye could see. Somehow, they had veered off course and had ended up in what could only be the Great American Desert.

The air was warm and Jimmy lowered the canvas top. After days of rain, the sun offered a welcome relief.

"Hi, ho. Do you need some help?"

Jimmy glanced in the direction of the male voice. A stranger waved and limped toward them. The bearded man was dressed in torn, ragged clothes that were at least two sizes too big, and a shapeless rawhide hat. "Howdy, ma'am." He gave Elizabeth a polite smile, his two front teeth missing. He squinted against the sun and ran his hand across his whiskered chin. He glanced at the map that was spread on the hood of the car. "Looks like you two are lost."

"Looks like you might be, too," Jimmy said.

"Not me. I know these parts as well as any man can. What are you doing out here?"

"We're in the Henry Ford cross-country race," Jimmy explained. "Perhaps you've heard of us? The driver's name is Elizabeth Davenport."

"A woman race car driver, eh? That's mighty interesting."

It struck Jimmy as odd that the man hadn't heard of the race. It had been in all the newspapers. Perhaps he couldn't read. "Your name is?"

"Wexler. Sam Wexler."

"We're mighty pleased to make your acquaintance," Elizabeth said.

"How is it that you happen to be in these parts?" Jimmy asked. There was no sign of a vehicle, or even a railroad, for as far as the eye could see.

"My horse threw me and ran off. I'm not lost; I'm stranded."

"You poor man," Elizabeth said. "We'd be happy to give you a ride."

The man glanced at the car and appeared to be trying to make up his mind about something. "I don't want to put you folks out any."

"If you can lead us to the National Old Trails Road, you'll be doing us a favor," Jimmy said. "We passed a couple of telephone poles a ways back, but none were marked with red, white, and blue stripes."

"The roads aren't marked as well as they might be. That's 'cuz the locals know where they're going and they don't care if anyone else does. Could I trouble you for some food and water?"

Jimmy handed Wexler a canteen and made room for him in the backseat. "Sorry about the mess."

"No problem." Wexler climbed onto the running board and settled down between the suitcases.

"Help yourself to what's in the picnic basket," Elizabeth said.

"I'm mighty obliged, ma'am." Wexler tipped his hat politely, then attacked the picnic basket with great gusto.

Jimmy and Elizabeth exchanged glances. It appeared the man hadn't eaten in quite some time. Jimmy folded the map, cranked up the engine, and took his place next to Elizabeth.

"Follow that trail to the left," Wexler said, his mouth full of food.

Jimmy glanced up at the sun. "Are you sure? It seems to me Seattle is the other way."

"We've had some pretty hard rains in the area. Washed out all the roads. I'm gonna have to take you the long way round."

Jimmy glanced back at Wexler and frowned as the man stuffed the last of the Oreo biscuits in his mouth.

Jimmy settled back in his seat. It was hard to believe the area had seen rain. The ground was covered with volcanic rock and it looked bleak and dry. But there wasn't any reason for this Wexler fellow to lie, was there?

"Whereabouts are you from?" Jimmy asked.

Wexler hesitated for a moment too long for Jimmy's liking before answering, "Laramie."

"What business are you in?"

"Banking."

"Just like your friend Cecil," Elizabeth said.

"Yeah," Jimmy said. Whoever heard of a banker who didn't read the newspaper? "Do you think the Federal Reserve Bank Act will help prevent another financial crisis on Wall Street?"

"Yeah, maybe."

Jimmy knew enough about bankers to know that one would never pass up the opportunity to debate the issue. Wexler was no banker, and if Jimmy's guess was right, he was not going to lead them back to the National Old Trails Road.

"Turn around, Elizabeth."

Elizabeth glanced at Jimmy as if she thought he'd lost his mind. "What?"

"You heard me." He felt something press hard against the back of his head and knew it was a gun even before he heard the metallic click.

# Chapter 34

"Never stand in front of a moving car or loaded gun unless absolutely necessary."

*Women at the Wheel*
Circa 1915

Elizabeth gasped at the sight of the gun.

"Shut up and drive!" Wexler yelled, any pretense at civility abandoned.

Elizabeth could never seem to concentrate on more than one thing at a time, and for now, the gun and the man in the backseat clearly had her full attention. She swerved back and forth as she headed straight for a deep dry gully left by an ancient river.

Both men let out a loud yelp as all four wheels left the ground and sailed through the air. The flivver cleared the chasm and landed safely on the other side, but it was several moments before the gunman had recovered enough to speak. By then, they'd had at least two more close calls.

"Stop the car," he squeaked out at last. Though his hand was shaking badly, he still held on to the gun.

Elizabeth glanced over her shoulder. "What?"

"You heard me. You and your mechanic are about to come to the end of the trail."

"*Ooooooh,* I don't like this."

"I don't give a damn if you like it or not," Wexler said, his eyes widening in horror as the car spun around and headed back to the ravine. "Stop the car!"

Afraid that Wexler would shoot, Elizabeth jammed on the brake. Unaccustomed to her driving, Wexler was thrown against the back of the front seat with such force he was momentarily stunned. Jimmy had braced himself and was ready. As soon as the car stopped, he twisted in his seat and grabbed hold of the gun. But Wexler wasn't about to give up his weapon that easily, and the two men struggled.

The gun popped into the air and landed on the ground. Wexler delivered a raw-knuckled fist to Jimmy's jaw. Dazed, Jimmy loosened his hold and Wexler jumped from the car. Recovering quickly, Jimmy took a diving leap and tackled Wexler to the ground.

Frantic, Elizabeth jumped out of the car and picked up the gun. Holding it with both hands, she turned toward the men, who were fiercely battling it out in front of Old Ironsides.

She pointed the gun, her finger on the trigger. The gun went off with a loud bang and a puff of smoke, sending Elizabeth flying backward and landing on her behind. The two battling men stilled and glanced in her direction. Their eyes round as saucers, they stared at the barrel of her gun.

"D-don't m-move," she said. Keeping the gun pointed at them, she stood up. "On your feet." Elizabeth was shaking so much, the gun wagged from side to side like the tail of a friendly dog. "On your feet," she repeated.

Wexler held his hands above his head. "Don't shoot, lady."

Winded, Jimmy shook the fog away from his head and rubbed his sore cheek. Lord almighty, Elizabeth held a gun like she drove a car. "That's Wexler, Elizabeth," he said, indicating with his hand. "Point the gun at him, not me." He climbed to his feet.

Elizabeth made a strange gasping sound. The hand holding the gun began to shake so badly, the weapon was almost a blur. Finally, she blurted out a warning. "Watch out!"

Jimmy turned not a moment too soon. Old Ironsides was rolling toward them, and because it was heading downhill, it was coming fast. "Yeow!" Both men took off running, the Model T close behind.

Jimmy veered in one direction, Wexler in another, and the flivver headed straight for a steep ravine. At the last possible moment, the front wheel clipped a jutting rock and the motorcar made a sharp turn.

Acting quickly, Jimmy managed to jump onto the running board and climb into the front seat. He brought the car to a stop a mere few inches from the edge of a dangerous drop.

Watching in horror, Elizabeth stood frozen in place, the gun still in her hands. Not until she knew for certain that Jimmy was safe did she allow herself to breathe.

She ran quickly toward the car, finding Jimmy slumped over the wheel.

"Jimmy? Are you all right?"

With a moan, he lifted his head. His right eye was already beginning to turn blue. "How many times do I have to tell you to put the emergency brake on?"

"You don't have to yell," she said.

"I'm not yelling. I don't have the strength to yell."

Shaken, he climbed out of the car, and Elizabeth threw herself at him, wrapping her arms around his neck. "Oh, Jimmy, I can't tell you how frightened I was when he ... when you ... I don't know what I would have done had something happened to you."

Actually, his life had only been in danger three times during the skirmish with Wexler. Once when Elizabeth flew over the ravine, a second time when she'd forgotten to set the emergency brake, and again when she'd pointed the gun at him. But rather than mention this, he grinned and slipped his arms around her. "Does this mean you care for me?"

"You know I do."

"Then you won't be needing this." He took the gun away from Elizabeth and tossed it away. The weapon fell next to a tumbleweed, sending a lizard skittering across the dry desert sand. Having disarmed her—and glancing around to make certain Staggs wasn't behind some rock, pointing a camera—he announced his intention to kiss her. As good as his word, he crushed her to him and covered her mouth with his own.

He pulled away reluctantly. Suddenly, he had the desire to do a lot more than just kiss her, but he didn't dare. It was getting hotter by the minute, and besides, Wexler was still on the loose. No doubt he was lurking behind the nearby rock formation, waiting for his chance to ambush them.

"Let's go!" Jimmy said. "We have to find our way back before dark."

"But what about Mr. Wexler?" she asked, scanning the rocks. "We can't just leave him here. He could die."

Jimmy glanced at her in disbelief. "Better him than us."

"I can't just leave him ... not again. ..."

He knitted his brow together. "Again?"

She bit her lip, her face dark as a thundercloud.

He touched her arm. "Elizabeth?" She looked so totally miserable, he wrapped her in his arms and held her close. Stroking her back, he murmured soothing words into her hair.

At last he felt her grow still in his arms, the trembling gone. He cupped her chin with his hands and gazed deep into her eyes. "Does this have anything to do with what happened to you in the past? The nightmares?"

She didn't answer him; she didn't have to. It was written clearly on her face.

Jimmy swallowed hard. He hadn't wanted to face what was so painfully obvious—had always been obvious. He had hoped, foolishly it turned out, to erase the past from her mind. During the times when they'd made love, he honestly thought he could. "This man ... he touched you, didn't he?"

She didn't move a muscle, but the color drained from her face.

"Dammit!" He dropped his hands to his side. His fingers curled into fists as the full horror of what she'd said hit him. It was far worse than anything he'd imagined. Not just any man had touched her; she was talking about the man who had adopted her, the man she called her father!

Fury coursed through him until his very blood seemed to boil. Blinded by rage and overcome with shock and horror, he was dangerously close to exploding. "I'll kill him!"

She paled and he immediately regretted his outburst. "I'm sorry, Elizabeth. But I mean it. I'll kill him; I swear I will. And if he ever comes near you again . . ."

"He won't, Jimmy. He's . . . dead."

"Dead?"

Tears swam in her eyes. "I killed him."

"Heavens to Pete!" He was so shocked by her admission, he could only stare in disbelief. "Are you serious?"

She nodded. "I pushed him. . . . He hit his head. . . ."

His hands caressing her arms, he brought her closer. "Oh, Elizabeth." She buried her head in his chest and he stroked her hair.

"I never meant . . . I didn't know he was injured . . . and I left him there." She was sobbing now, her tears staining the front of his shirt. "The sheriff ruled it an accident. No one knew I was responsible for his death."

"You have the right to defend yourself."

"I . . . I . . . left him!"

"You didn't know he was seriously injured."

Everything was suddenly so clear to him. He understood all those times she'd stopped to check on the other drivers, even when it made no sense for her to stop. He knew now why she was so reluctant to leave Wexler in the desert.

All the pieces of the puzzle fell into place: the night-mares, the feeling he had that she was running from something, the almost feverish desire of hers to build her safe haven for orphans.

He had an almost uncontrollable desire to protect her. To take her in his arms and keep her safe. "Oh, Elizabeth, I'm so sorry."

"I should have told you sooner. Before we ... I hope you don't hate me."

"Hate you?" He was so shocked by the very idea, he held her at arm's length. "How could I possibly hate you? I love you, Elizabeth."

"Oh, Jimmy. I never thought ... It never occurred to me that love could feel like this."

"If we ever get to Seattle, I hope to show you just how wonderful love can be."

She gazed at him, her eyes brimming with tears. "You don't know what it was like, Jimmy. Some people knew what he'd done and they blamed me."

"That can't be true," Jimmy said, shocked.

"It's absolutely true. I was so desperate I tried to get help. I told one of my teachers. She said I ... must have done something to make him touch me. Then when I confided in the pastor of our church, he said I was a sinner and would go to hell...."

Jimmy touched a finger to her mouth. "Surely you don't believe anything those people said, do you?"

"But why would they say those things if they weren't true?"

"They don't know any better. And they don't know you. Not like I know you. If they had, they would never have made such accusations."

"I tried to stop him," she whispered. "I even ran away once, when I was fourteen, but the sheriff found me and made me go back."

"You don't have to defend yourself to me. You were a child. A child! You had no control over what happened to you."

She studied him. "Oh, Jimmy, I always knew you were forgiving . . ."

"There's nothing to forgive. . . ."

" . . . and understanding. Please, we must find Wexler. He no longer has his gun. He can't possibly hurt us."

To waste one more minute in this desert than was absolutely necessary was foolhardy, but he didn't have the heart to deny her request. "One hour," he said. "If we don't find him in that time, we give up the search."

"Oh, thank you, Jimmy." She flung her arms around his neck without a moment's hesitation and showered him with heated kisses. *Wild driver, wild in bed.*

Grinning, he held her tight. "Thank *you*, Elizabeth."

Finally, he let her go and she scrambled behind the wheel. Jimmy grabbed hold of the crank. "Ready?"

"Ready!"

He glanced around at the vast shimmering desert. Finding Wexler was not going to be easy.

# Chapter 35

"Always signal your intentions—no matter how many times you change your mind."

*Women at the Wheel*
Circa 1915

They never did find Wexler. Once, Jimmy picked up his trail, but then promptly lost it. Even though Elizabeth had agreed to give up the search after an hour, she insisted they find the nearest sheriff's station and report Wexler missing.

That was easier said than done, especially since they had lost their only road map. It had apparently blown away earlier, during his scuffle with Wexler.

The sun began its descent and Jimmy grew worried. The last thing he wanted to do was spend the night in the desert with that crazy man, Wexler, on the loose.

He'd just about given up any hope when he spotted something in the distance. "Keep going," he said.

"What do you think it is, Jimmy?"

"I don't know. It looks like a crowd of people and ..." He couldn't believe his eyes. "That looks like Sir Higginbottom's car. And Crankshaw's and ..."

All the drivers were there, along with a group of strangers. Elizabeth pulled up alongside Crankshaw's car and Sir Higginbottom hurried to greet them.

"I say there, Hunter, we were wondering where you were."

Jimmy climbed out of the car. "What are you doing here?"

"We're all lost."

"All of you?" Jimmy glanced at the crowd of strangers dressed in long white robes. Damned if they didn't look like angels without wings. For one horrifying moment he feared Elizabeth had finally succeeded in driving him to his death. "Who are these people?"

"They're members of the Ultraview Society," Stonegate explained. "They believe the world is coming to an end at midnight."

"Oh, no!" Elizabeth gasped. "That's awful."

Staggs stood his tripod in the sand. "You can say that again," he complained. "What kind of photographs do you think I'm going to get at midnight?"

"Now Myra will never marry me," Crankshaw muttered.

"This is crazy," Jimmy said. "The world is not going to end. Now does anyone know the way out of here?"

"Not me," Billy-Joe said.

"Neither do we," Sir Higginbottom said. "But that priest over there said if the world doesn't end at midnight, he will personally escort us back to the road."

Jimmy pushed his hat back. "Well, isn't this just peachy?"

"Look this way, everyone," Staggs called out.

Behind them, the white-robed priests had dropped to their knees. With arms upraised, the group rocked back and forth, chanting loudly.

As the sun sank into the west, the air grew colder, and the chants grew increasingly louder. The drivers used the extra time to catch up on some sleep, while the mechanics worked on the cars.

Just before midnight, everyone gathered around the priests and a hush fell over the crowd. The torches had been extinguished and the light from the crescent moon cast dismal shadows around them.

"You don't by chance think they know something,

do you?" Elizabeth asked anxiously. She found the unnatural stillness more nerve-wracking than the chants.

Jimmy slipped his arm around her shoulders. "Let's hope they know the way back to the road."

At ten minutes past midnight, the drivers grew restless. Staggs, who hadn't left his camera for a moment, glanced at his watch. "I hope this isn't going to take all night."

At one o'clock, Jimmy walked over to the priest. "It's been a very interesting experience, but we really do have to go. We'd appreciate it if you would direct us back to the road."

The priest shook his head. "You young people are so impatient. The world should come to an end any minute now. You must learn patience, my son."

"Perhaps you made a mistake," Elizabeth suggested. The members of the Ultraview Society turned to face her and she gave a nervous smile. "Maybe you miscalculated."

The priest whipped out a piece of paper. "I did the math calculations myself." He shoved the paper into her hands, but she couldn't make sense out of the equations.

"It was just a thought," she said, handing the paper back.

"Oh, no! I did make an error." The priest looked horrified as he stared at the paper in his hand. "The world is going to end. But we're a thousand years too early."

Jimmy grinned. "Well, now, that's great news." He glanced at the circle of grim faces. "Isn't it?"

The priest glared at him. "I can see you have no understanding of these things at all. How can we go home and face people? Our credibility is gone."

"He's got a point there," Crankshaw said.

"Look this way," Staggs said, capturing the glowering priest with his camera. "Great shot!"

Jimmy walked in a circle, looking up at the sky. The

last thing he wanted to do was spend the rest of the night with these loonies. Suddenly, he had an idea. He stopped and faced the priest. "I don't believe you made an error. It's your prayers that have been answered. I think you should be treated as heroes for saving us all from total destruction."

"By jove, he's right," Sir Higginbottom said.

"Heroes?" The priest looked impressed, but not enough to give up the vigil. He did, however, agree to let one of the followers lead the drivers back to the main road.

The society member who volunteered rode a brown gelding across the desert, followed by the line of Model T Fords. In his flowing white robe, he looked like a sheik.

At last, Jimmy spotted a wooden post that was faintly marked with the red, white, and blue stripes of the National Old Trails Road. The engines roared as one by one the Model T's sped off, leaving the horseman in the dust.

It was still dark when Elizabeth rolled into Twin Falls on their last drop of gasoline. While Jimmy filled the gas tank, Elizabeth headed for the Perrine Hotel to have their passport stamped.

She disappeared into the hotel, but returned moments later, looking worried. "Jimmy, look at this." She shoved a day-old newspaper into his hands.

A picture of Wexler was on the front page. According to the article, Wexler was a convicted bank robber who had escaped from a Boise jail. "Well, what do you know? He really is into banking. I'm willing to bet the sheriff will be mighty pleased to know where he was last seen."

"Are you going to the sheriff now?" she asked.

"Yeah," Jimmy replied. "Just as soon as I replace the package of Oreo biscuits Wexler ate."

Upon reaching Boise some thirteen hours later, Jimmy checked the blackboard. It had been a day from hell. They'd had two flat tires, sprung a radiator leak that had required a full package of Wrigley's chewing gum to repair, and had to replace a bad spark plug. Fastbender had beat them by five hours.

"From now on, we're going to have to drive straight through," Jimmy said grimly.

Elizabeth didn't look the least bit fazed by this news. "Do you think we can catch him?"

"I don't know. Gaining ground is always harder than losing it."

That night, Elizabeth and Jimmy took turns driving while the other slept. They covered the distance from Boise to Olds Ferry in record time and crossed over the Snake River into Oregon.

Forcing the car as fast it would go, they pushed through Oregon and climbed over the Blue Mountains with less problems than Jimmy had anticipated. Low fuel had made it necessary for Elizabeth to drive up the mountain backward to allow what little gasoline they had left to flow properly.

Jimmy hung out the window yelling directions. By the time they had reached the summit, turned around, and started to coast down the other side, he was a nervous wreck. He'd also managed to shout himself hoarse.

Fortunately, they were able to purchase gasoline from the driver of a Model T they met on the road. It was one of the older models with a mother-in-law seat in back.

By the time they drove through hilly rangeland into the official checkpoint located at the Geiser Grand Hotel in Baker City, they had gained two hours on Fastbender and an hour on Crankshaw. The hotel clerk reported an unconfirmed rumor that Billy-Joe had broken an axle and was stuck in Walla Walla.

This is all Jimmy needed to hear. "Let's go!" he shouted, his voice ringing with excitement. He practically dragged Elizabeth out of the hotel.

They reached the western slope of the Cascades and

followed the winding road up toward Snoqualmie Pass just east of Seattle. Ahead, the uppermost peak of Mount Baker rose above the lofty pines, still wearing traces of its white wintry coat.

"Careful," Jimmy cautioned. "I see something through the trees." Elizabeth rounded a curve and Jimmy grinned. "Well, now. If it's not Fastbender. Looks like he's stuck. Pull around him."

Instead of doing as he said, she pulled up behind Fastbender's car and put on her brake.

Jimmy shook his head in exasperation. He didn't have to ask what she was doing. He knew, and as much as he wished she had it in her to leave Fastbender stranded, he loved her all the more because she didn't.

"We can't leave him stranded, Jimmy."

"Yeah, yeah, I know."

He climbed out of the car, but neither Fastbender nor his mechanic were anywhere in sight.

Elizabeth scooted across the seat and stepped out of the car behind him. "What do you think happened to them?"

"I don't know. Stay here. I'll take a look." Jimmy followed a narrow dirt footpath away from the road, and was surprised to find Crankshaw standing at the edge of a cliff staring down at the raging waters of the Matakie River.

"Well, what are you doing here?"

Crankshaw turned at the sound of Jimmy's voice, his walking cane in hand. "So you made it, Hunter."

Jimmy hiked the remaining distance until he reached the older man's side. The thunderous force of the waters racing down from the mountain peak to the valley below created a roaring sound. "Where's your mechanic?"

Crankshaw tossed the butt of his cigar down the cliff and it disappeared in the foaming waters below. "Sparky's along the trail somewhere standing on his head or something. It's supposed to clear the nasal passages."

"What's wrong with your car?"

"Nothing's wrong."

"Then what are you doing here?"

Crankshaw nodded downstream. "See that stump of a wooden post on the bank?"

"I see it."

"That's all that remains of the Matakie River bridge."

Jimmy felt sick. He couldn't believe it. To think they'd come this far only to have their dreams dashed because of one lousy bridge. "There must be another way across."

"Not unless you want to cross over on that." Crankshaw pointed to a log raft tied to a tree and bobbing up and down in the rushing waters. "Cheer up, Hunter. If we can't get across, there isn't anyone going to cross. Looks like the race ends here." He puffed on his cigar, his brows a dark thick line over his narrowed eyes. "Of all the blasted luck! Myra will never marry me now."

"Don't worry," Jimmy said. "If she really cares for you, she'll marry you no matter what."

"That's the problem. She doesn't care for me, not as much as I care for her. That's why I've got to do something wonderful, spectacular. Something that will make her marry me, no matter how she feels about me personally."

Crankshaw sounded so downhearted, Jimmy couldn't help but sympathize. "It's not a very good way to get someone to marry you."

"It's the only way. Listen, Jimmy, you don't know what I'm up against. Myra was married to some wealthy businessman who apparently was a saint. She says she's perfectly content spending the rest of her life honoring his memory."

"Then let her," Jimmy said. "Listen, women are a

dime a dozen. You don't have to put up with someone like that."

"That's easy for you to say. You're young and ... you're young."

"Youth has nothing to do with it. Listen, a woman is like a fiddle. You play all the right notes, and she'll say whatever you want her to. Flatter her. Tell her she's beautiful. Buy her pretty things." He pulled out the pink satin ribbon of Elizabeth's he kept in his pocket at all times and dangled it in front of Crankshaw's face. "In no time at all, you'll have her eating out of your hand."

"I don't know, Jimmy. I still say if I don't win the race I haven't got a chance in high heaven of getting Myra to be my wife."

Jimmy patted Crankshaw on the shoulder. "Trust me. Flatter Myra. Buy her something pretty. Make her feel beautiful. She'll drag you to the altar."

Jimmy's advice to Crankshaw had a chilling effect on Elizabeth. Neither man had noticed her standing behind them, listening to every word. So women were a dime a dozen, were they? A cold chill cut through her. Her stomach knotted and she felt physically ill. *Look at you; you make me sick,* Mylar had said after each abusive episode. *Whores like you are a dime a dozen.*

Stunned and confused, she staggered back down the narrow dirt path. She had believed Jimmy, believed he really cared for her. Now it turned out he thought no more of her than had Mylar Carson. She couldn't believe it! She felt used, her hopes and dreams for the future crushed.

She reached Old Ironsides just as Fastbender returned to his car.

"Well, now. If it ain't the lady driver." He raked her over with eyes filled with mockery, his mouth lifted in derision. "Those baby-blue eyes of yours have gotten you this far. Let's see them get you across the river!"

He laughed uproariously as he walked away, his laughter drowned out by the arrival of cars number one, six, and four.

At that moment, Elizabeth felt utterly alone. Just as she'd felt during her growing up years and during the time she spent in jail.

The three drivers parked their cars up ahead. Staggs, carting his camera and tripod, started up the path, followed by Sir Higginbottom. Mr. Stonegate followed close behind, carrying a shovel. Billy-Joe drove up next and chased after the others, waving his hat and leaving his mechanic to wander off in another direction.

Elizabeth waited until the others were no longer in sight. Fastbender's laughter continued to ring in her ears, but it was Jimmy's words that chipped away at her soul.

*. . . a dime a dozen . . . a dime . . .*

Something snapped inside her. The pain in her heart was like a deep, burning wound. She was used to being mocked, but finding out that Jimmy had used her was more than she could bear. Well, she'd show them. She'd show them all! Jimmy included.

She spit on her hands and rubbed them together. Her heart heavy as a boulder, she glanced anxiously at the fast-running river. Lord love an orphan, give her strength. Taking a deep breath, she reached for the crank of the car.

# Chapter 36

"The road to true love never runs smooth."
*Women at the Wheel*
Circa 1915

Jimmy led the other drivers along the river's edge until their way was blocked by a sheer granite wall.

Sir Higginbottom seated himself on a fallen tree and wiped the perspiration off his forehead. "I told you. There's no other way across."

As much as Jimmy hated to admit defeat, it was beginning to look as if Sir Higginbottom was right.

"We could try the other direction," Billy-Joe said hopefully.

Sir Higginbottom frowned with impatience. "The map clearly indicates . . ."

"I don't want to hear about your damn map!" Fastbender snapped.

Mr. Stonegate looked shocked. "Gentlemen! Life is too short for such squabbling."

"It's not *that* short," Billy-Joe said, nervously eyeing Stonegate's shovel.

"Everyone look this way!" Staggs sang out. All heads turned in his direction like spectators at a tennis tournament. Staggs squeezed the bulb of his camera.

Jimmy kicked a rock with his foot. He didn't want his photograph taken. He didn't even want to be here. What he wanted to do was to get the damned race

over so he could return to Hogs Head with Elizabeth
by his side.

Warmed by the idea, he started back, leaving the
others behind. As much as he hated to give up, he
saw little point in beating his head against a brick
wall. If they couldn't finish the race, maybe he could
convince Elizabeth to start back for Hogs Head today!
The sooner they returned, the sooner they could get
married.

Running now, he followed the meandering trail, his
feet barely touching the ground. He slowed his step
upon seeing Mr. Chin huffing and puffing his way up
the hill.

"Mr. Hunter!" The man waved his hand. "Come
quickly. Miz Davenport . . . she . . ."

Alarmed, Jimmy rushed to his side. "What about
Miss Davenport?"

"Miz Davenport drive across river."

"What?" He'd seen Elizabeth do some amazing
feats, but drive across water? Even Moses hadn't done
that! Hoping Mr. Chin had misunderstood something
or was otherwise mistaken, Jimmy tore down the path
as fast his legs would carry him. "Elizabeth!"

Racing around a cluster of thick trees, he froze in
his tracks as the river came into view. What Mr. Chin
said was true. Old Ironsides was straddling the log raft
and bobbing up and down in the water like a cork.
Standing on the raft next to the motorcar, Elizabeth
steered the raft around the rocks with a long
wooden pole.

"Elizabeth, no!" He ran the rest of the way to the
river, waving his arms over his head and yelling her
name. Damned if this wasn't the most foolhardy trick
she'd every pulled! If the raft was caught in the undertow, Elizabeth would never have a chance. She'd be
carried downstream toward the dangerous rapids.

Propelled by fear for her safety, he leaped over
fallen logs and crashed through thick brush. But by

the time he reached the river's edge, Elizabeth was too far out for him to reach.

The others came running up behind him. Huffing and puffing, Sir Higginbottom grabbed hold of a tree trunk, trying to catch his breath. "The woman's a bloody fool."

Jimmy stood poised at the edge of the river, ready to dive into the dangerous waters the moment trouble struck. Anything could happen. Elizabeth could fall off the raft. Old Ironsides could overturn, dragging Elizabeth along with it. He could lose her, dammit! Lose the one woman in all the world he loved more than life itself.

The men stood like sentinels along the water's edge, watching in speechless horror as Elizabeth guided the raft slowly across the river.

For the longest while, no one moved. Each man's gaze remained riveted to the boxy back of Elizabeth's Model T. The brightly colored ribbons danced gaily in the breeze as the car continued to pitch back and forth like a four-year-old on a rocking horse.

Staggs, realizing suddenly that a photo opportunity was about to slip through his fingers, quickly set up his tripod and camera. "I wish she'd look at the camera!"

"Look at the ..." Jimmy was incredulous. "Can't you see she's got her hands full just steering the raft?"

"My word!" Crankshaw exclaimed, lifting his walking stick up and down. "Look at her go! What courage."

Even Fastbender concurred. "I'll be damned! She's going to reach the other side."

Jimmy didn't dare utter a word until Elizabeth had cleared the midway point and reached calmer waters.

Finally the raft touched the opposite bank and she jumped onto dry ground. Ignoring the men, and apparently oblivious to the applause that greeted her successful crossing, she secured the raft.

The men watched as she calmly turned the crank, jumped into the driver's seat, drove off the raft and up the muddy bank. She disappeared through the trees, leaving the six drivers and seven mechanics watching in astonishment.

Stonegate stuck his shovel into the ground. "I swear that woman is going to send us all to an early grave."

"If it's all the same to you," Billy-Joe grumbled, "I'd prefer you wait until after the fact before you start making arrangements."

Sir Higginbottom edged away from the shovel. "I say, do you suppose we ought to follow her? She jolly well could win the race, you know."

"Not without a mechanic," Jimmy muttered miserably. He couldn't believe it. How could she do such a thing? How could she take off without him?

Staggs picked up his tripod and flung it over his shoulder. "If she's the only one who finishes the race, the officials might waive the mechanic rule."

"Good heavens!" Sir Higginbottom exploded. "I hadn't thought of that."

"I do believe Staggs is right," Crankshaw said. "If Miss Liz ... If Miss Davenport is the only one to finish the race, I don't see that the judges would have much choice, do you?"

Fastbender swore under his breath. "I don't know about the rest of you, but I'm not going to stand here all day. If a woman can cross on a flimsy raft, then anyone can do it. Help me with these logs."

Billy-Joe pushed his hat back. "What do you propose to do?"

"I'm building myself a raft." Fastbender started for his car and grabbed a length of rope.

Crankshaw chased after him, waving his walking stick. "Now just a darn minute, there. I was the first one here; I should be the first one to leave."

"Oh, yeah?" Fastbender spit out a stream of yellow tobacco juice. "I say the first one who builds a raft is the first one across."

A wild scramble ensued as the men raced about

gathering rope and rolling whole logs down to the river's edge.

"That's my log."

"I saw it first!"

"The cemetery is filled with people like you!"

"Look at the camera!"

Tempers flared, insults flew.

Crankshaw paced back and forth, stopping on occasion to beat his cane against a rock. "Where is that damned fool mechanic of mine?"

Jimmy hadn't moved from the river's edge. She left him! He couldn't believe it! Dammit, how could she do such a thing? Didn't she know how he felt about her? How much he loved her?

"If Sparky doesn't show his face in the next two minutes, I'll give Stonegate a reason to dig that hole he's itching to dig!"

Jimmy turned. "I think I saw Sparky head in that direction."

Jimmy and Crankshaw found Sparky a short time later, lying beneath a tree in a drunken stupor, reeking of whiskey.

"What a fine kettle of fish!" Crankshaw exploded. "Now what am I going to do?"

Jimmy walked in a circle, his face lifted toward the sky. *She left me. Dear God, where did I go wrong?*

"It's hard to imagine," Crankshaw said, "but you and I have something in common."

"Oh? What might that be?"

"You're without a driver and I'm without a mechanic. And it's all your fault!"

"My fault? How do you figure that?"

"If you had accepted the offer I made you on the train the day we met, I daresay you and I would have made it to Seattle by now."

Jimmy thought back to the first day of the race. It seemed like a lifetime ago. Never would he forget the moment he'd first set eyes on the pint-size bundle of fury who'd kidnapped him and then promptly stolen his heart. From the very start, even when she was her most reckless and outrageous—and before he knew she was his childhood friend—he had felt inexplicably drawn to her.

"Maybe you're right," Jimmy said miserably. "Maybe we would have reached Seattle by now. But it sure wouldn't have been as much fun." He stared glumly at the river through an opening in the trees, hoping she was waiting for him on the other side, but knowing, somehow, she wasn't. Lord, why had she left him?

"You've got it bad, eh?" Crankshaw asked, sounding strangely subdued. "For the lady driver?"

"Yeah," Jimmy admitted. "Real bad."

"What a damned nuisance. But don't blame yourself. The best of us have fallen under a woman's spell. Even me. Still, you have my sympathies."

"I need more than sympathy. I need a raft."

"By some strange coincidence, so do I. I can't believe how much you and I have in common."

"Yeah." Jimmy grimaced. "Amazing, isn't it?"

"Shall we?" Crankshaw picked up Sparky's feet and waited for Jimmy to grab hold of the mechanic's arms. Together he and Crankshaw hauled the unconscious man back to Crankshaw's Model T and dumped him into the backseat.

By the time they were ready to construct their raft, the best logs had already been claimed. "What do you say we do, Hunter? Cut down our own trees?"

"I've got a better idea." Jimmy raced to the river's edge and jumped on Staggs's raft just as it was drifting away from the shore.

"What the hell do you think you're doing?" Staggs yelled.

"Helping you across." Standing next to Staggs's mechanic, Casper, he stuck out his foot to push against a stubborn boulder. He struggled along with the other two men to guide the raft through the treacherous rocks. Battling the undertow was no easy task. Elizabeth had wisely crossed further upstream where there were fewer rocks. Even so, she'd made it look amazingly easy.

"Look this way!" Staggs yelled, holding up his box camera.

"Sheesh!" Jimmy said, unconsciously using Elizabeth's favorite term of disgust. Staggs wouldn't care if they all drowned as long as he got his damned photograph.

They had barely reached the opposite shore when Jimmy jumped to dry land and raced toward the raft Elizabeth had left behind. Untying the rope and grabbing the pole, he quickly started back.

Knowing what areas to avoid, Jimmy made the trip back with little trouble, reaching shore at about the same time Stonegate and Sir Higginbottom had finished tying the logs together on their own rafts and were about to embark.

Crankshaw waded out a few feet to grab the rope from Jimmy. Together Jimmy and Crankshaw secured the raft before racing back to Crankshaw's car.

Jimmy cranked up the engine and then jumped out of the way. Clamping down on his cigar, Crankshaw drove his flivver onto the raft.

It took little more than twenty minutes before they touched the opposite shore. Winded, Crankshaw leaned against the front of the car to catch his breath. "There's got to be an easier way to catch a woman."

"When you find out what that way is, let me know," Jimmy muttered.

Crankshaw climbed into the driver's seat and squeezed the bulb of his air horn. *Ah-ooh-ga.* With a gleeful shout, he guided the car onto the marshy bank, then stopped and waited for Jimmy to take his place in the companion seat.

"Seattle, here we come," Crankshaw warbled. With that, he sped away from the river in hot pursuit of Elizabeth.

# Chapter 37

"Driving is like courting; if you don't know when
to stop and go, you'll never get anywhere."
                              *Women at the Wheel*
                              Circa 1915

Snow in June! Jimmy couldn't believe it. Snowdrifts
were piled high on either side of the road, and the
mountain peaks glistened white. Snow was the last
thing Jimmy had expected this late in the year. The air
was brisk, and as the trees closed overhead, patches of
ice dotted the muddy road.

Where was she? Where was Elizabeth? It was a
question that took on chilling urgency when they
passed Sir Higginbottom and Fastbender frantically
trying to dig their way out of the snow.

The winding road grew so narrow in parts, Jimmy
swore the wheels of Crankshaw's car would go over
the edge. He had visions of Elizabeth lying at the
bottom of a cliff, her lovely body broken into a hundred little pieces. "Stop the car!"

"What?"

"I want to make sure no one's gone over."

"Dammit, Jimmy, we're ahead. I'm not stopping. I
don't care how bad you've got it."

"We haven't passed Elizabeth's car yet."

"And for good reason. She had a two-hour head
start."

"You don't know Elizabeth. She's probably taken a

few wrong turns along the way. She could be somewhere behind us."

"Not even Miss Davenport could get lost up here.
There're only two ways down this mountain. The road
or over the side."

Both men glanced at each other, and a look of mutual worry passed between them before they turned
their heads to judiciously watch the road.

*Dammit, Elizabeth! Where are you?*

*Where am I?* Elizabeth rubbed her eyes and gazed
out the windshield at the narrow dirt road that ran
through a mound of snow.

Then she remembered.

Exhausted by the difficult river crossing, she'd
pulled over to the side of the road to give herself time
to recover. She never expected to fall asleep.

The trip across the river had drained her. Stinging
blisters dotted her palms and fingertips where she'd
gripped the pole. The muscles in her shoulders and
upper arms ached. The back of her legs felt stiff.

Having no idea how long she'd slept or if any of
the other drivers had made it across the river, she
climbed out of the car. She grabbed a fistful of snow
and waited until the cold dulled the painful blisters
before pulling on her gloves. Still, it hurt to hold on
to the crank. Much to her relief, Old Ironsides required only a dozen or so cranks before it started up.

Scrambling back into the seat, she slowly eased the
car along the narrow road. Her heart pumped with
terror as she drove slowly across the narrow shelf of
a road hanging over a deep canyon. One tiny slip . . .

*Ooooooh*, she didn't like this. She fought the stinging moisture in her eyes. What was the matter with
her? Taking off like that. Running away from Jimmy.
She knew from past experience that running away
never solved anything. And here she'd run away again
rather than face the pain of yet one more rejection.

A patch of pure white snow told her she was the

first to pass this way. She was ahead! Dear God, if she found herself a mechanic before reaching Seattle, she could actually win this race.

But even knowing how close she was to winning didn't cheer her. Without Jimmy by her side, the race held no meaning for her. Not anymore.

Lord, how she loved him! Even now after hearing his cruel words. What a fool she'd been to think he loved her in return. Loved her the way she wanted to be loved. She'd given him everything. Everything! She loved him with her heart and soul—her very essence— and what did she get? *Women are a dime a dozen.*

The road straightened as it started downward, and she picked up speed accordingly. Seattle was less than a hundred miles away. A hundred miles to success and glory. A hundred miles of misery and loneliness.

A horn sounded behind her. It was one of the other Fords, but she didn't dare take her eyes off the road to look back. By the sound of the blaring horn, it was probably Fastbender. The car pulled up directly behind her.

"Elizabeth!"

Her heart raced at the sound of Jimmy's voice. Sheesh! Wasn't that a fine kettle of fish? He hurt her and humiliated her, but as soon as he chased her down, what did she do? Acted like a foolish schoolgirl with her head in the clouds!

The road straightened and she glanced at the rear-view mirror.

Jimmy rode in Crankshaw's car and she recognized Fastbender's horn farther back. Not wanting to drive faster than was prudent, given the condition of the road, she maintained her speed. The road grew more treacherous with each passing mile, narrowing to barely more than a few inches wider than the wheel span.

Crankshaw's car followed close behind, but Jimmy didn't call out anymore or otherwise try to distract her until the road grew wider. Then he started bellowing like a foghorn.

"Elizabeth! Pull over! We have to talk."

A hairpin turn enabled her to catch a glimpse of all six cars on her tail. Jimmy stood up in Crankshaw's open car, waving frantically. Sheesh, the fool man was bound to freeze to death.

The road widened to almost two lanes and Fastbender took full advantage, passing Jimmy and catching up to Elizabeth.

For a mile or so, Elizabeth and Fastbender drove side by side, neither able to gain the advantage. The last of Elizabeth's fenders came loose and fell by the wayside. And as she whizzed around a curve, the canvas top flew back and flapped up and down. The road narrowed again and Elizabeth was forced to choose between letting Fastbender pass or sticking to her guns.

A short distance behind her, Jimmy watched in horror as car number seven inched past Old Ironsides and Elizabeth boldly held her course. Hanging out the window, Jimmy slammed the side of the car with his hand. "Dammit! Is he out of his mind? He's going to get us all killed!"

"Calm down, Hunter."

How could he calm down with Elizabeth driving every which way she damned well pleased! Ignoring him! Acting as if they were strangers! What was the matter with her? Did she really think she could drive away and put an end to everything, just like that?

When it looked as if Elizabeth was going to go over the edge for certain, Jimmy practically climbed out of the speeding car. "Dammit, Fastbender! Get away from her." He cupped his hands around his mouth. "Elizabeth, let him pass!"

Crankshaw swerved and nearly sent Jimmy flying down the mountainside. "Would you sit down and shut up!" Crankshaw yelled. "I can't concentrate with you shouting."

"How do you expect Elizabeth to hear me if I don't shout?"

The road straightened and Fastbender zoomed by Elizabeth.

Jimmy fell back into the car, but sat on the edge of his seat, staring out the front window. He mopped his brow with his handkerchief. "Thank God."

For fifteen death-defying miles, the Model T's followed each other down the mountain like marbles down a chute. Horns blared, insults flew back and forth. At times, no more than an inch or two separated the front bumper of one car from the back bumper of another.

Crankshaw took advantage of a wide snow-free shoulder to pull his car alongside Elizabeth's. Jimmy hung over the side. "Dammit, Elizabeth. Pull over so I can talk to you!"

"I have nothing to say to you, Jimmy Hunter!"

"Well, I have plenty to say to you. For starters, I want you to know that I . . ." He never got a chance to finish what he intended to say. Ahead, Fastbender's car suddenly spun out and flipped over.

Elizabeth swerved, managing to miss Fastbender's car. A metal part flew across the road and she drove over it before stopping.

The remaining five cars came to a screeching stop directly behind her. Jimmy was the first to reach the crash site. Car number seven was tipped over on its side, its wheels spinning. The engine coughed, then died altogether.

Fastbender looked dazed, a trickle of blood oozing from a nasty cut on his forehead. With Crankshaw's help, Jimmy lifted Fastbender out of his car and carried him to the side of the road.

Jimmy covered Fastbender's forehead with his handkerchief, holding it firm to stop the bleeding.

"You fool. You could have gotten yourself killed and taken a couple of others with you."

Elizabeth ran up to them, followed by Sir Higginbottom and Stonegate.

Upon seeing Stonegate, Fastbender made a remarkable recovery. "Get that man away from me. I don't need no undertaker."

"That's no way to act," Elizabeth scolded. "Why, Mr. Stonegate is only showing concern."

"Well, he can show his concern to someone who needs it." Fastbender struggled to his feet.

Jimmy tapped Sir Higginbottom on the shoulder and nodded his head at Billy-Joe. "Give me a hand with his car."

Billy-Joe pushed his hat back and hung his thumbs from his belt. "Are you loco? The man could have gotten us all killed."

Crankshaw nodded. "I say we leave him here."

Jimmy was sorely tempted to do just that. "The problem is his car is blocking the road."

Sir Higginbottom agreed. "He's got a point there."

With a great deal of grumbling and even more complaining, the men stood by the overturned car and waited for Staggs to set up his confounded camera and take photographs. Sparky sneezed at an inopportune time and Staggs had to retake the picture.

Everyone worked together to push the dusty Model T Ford upright. Amazingly enough, except for a few dents in the side, Fastbender's vehicle appeared little the worse for wear.

As soon as the road was clear, Sir Higginbottom, Stonegate, and Billy-Joe raced back to their own cars. Jimmy spun around, looking for Elizabeth. He chased after her, but she had already driven away. Furious, Jimmy kicked a rock, and after jumping around on one foot, hobbled back to Crankshaw's car.

What was the matter with her? If she reached Seattle without a mechanic, she would be disqualified.

What was going on here? Did she hate him so much? What was this all about?

Elizabeth, once more claiming the lead, led the merry chase down the mountain. This time Fastbender drove at a respectable speed and, for once, made no effort to pass.

Suddenly Stonegate, who was trailing behind, honked frantically. Crankshaw cursed. "What the hell does he want?"

Jimmy glanced behind them. "Oh, no! It looks like he's lost his brakes. Pull over."

No sooner had Crankshaw driven to the side of the road than Stonegate zoomed by, leaving a trail of blue smoke behind him. At first it looked as if Elizabeth wasn't going to let him pass, but apparently she saw the smoke and at the last possible moment, pulled to the side of the road.

Jimmy, who had been holding his breath, slumped back in his seat. "That woman's going to be the death of me yet."

"I just hope she's not going to be the death of us all," Crankshaw grumbled.

Stonegate made it to the bottom of the mountain without mishap and was parked on the side of the road as the rest of the racers drove by. But it was obvious he was out of the race. That left just six drivers: Crankshaw, Fastbender, Sir Higginbottom, Staggs, Billy-Joe, and Elizabeth.

The hard-packed dirt road leading to Seattle was in good condition. They drove through woods so thick in places that only a narrow ribbon of steel-gray sky could be seen between the pointed tops of Douglas firs. They drove past lumber mills and paper factories. Somewhere along the way, Billy-Joe disappeared and then there were five.

Five cars racing toward a single dream.

Closer to the city the road was paved and well-wishers lined the sides, holding up banners and waving the racers on. Buggies and bicycles were parked next to shiny new automobiles, forcing the weary drivers to slow down almost to a crawl.

They followed what had once been an old Indian trail, but was now Seattle's busy Madison Street. Closer to town, uniformed policemen had managed to contain the crowds enough to let the drivers pick up speed again.

Jimmy ignored the cheering crowds. He was too busy watching Elizabeth. Damn, he couldn't believe it. She actually intended to cross over the finish line without a mechanic.

She waved to the crowds, and as was usual when she was distracted, began to weave erratically. Hanging out the side of the car, he shielded his eyes against the sudden appearance of the afternoon sun. "Step on the gas!" he yelled.

"I am stepping on the gas!" Crankshaw yelled back.

"Not you! Elizabeth!"

"See here!" Crankshaw argued. "A deal is a deal. You're my mechanic now."

"There's nothing in the rule book that says a mechanic has to root for his own car."

"Hell, if there isn't, there ought to be!"

"Keep the car straight!" Jimmy called. "You're oversteering." Jimmy was worried. Elizabeth's car appeared to be losing power. A closer look revealed fuel trickling from beneath her car.

Crankshaw's car inched up to Elizabeth's until the two cars drove side by side. The crowd went wild. Jimmy cupped his hands around his mouth and shouted, "You're losing fuel."

"Leave me alone!" she shouted back.

"I'm not going to leave you alone. I love you and intend to marry you!"

"What?"

"You heard me."

Elizabeth's car suddenly swerved into Crankshaw's. Metal hit metal and sparks flew.

"Damn!" Crankshaw jerked the steering wheel to

the left and veered toward the cheering spectators. The crowd scattered in all directions, but Crankshaw managed to regain control. Having lost valuable seconds, he raced to catch up to Elizabeth.

Jimmy straddled the door frame. Crankshaw glared at him. "You agreed to be my mechanic!"

"You've got a mechanic!"

"He's drunk."

"There's no law that said he has to be sober. Now, come on, Crankshaw. Be a sport. She hasn't got a chance of winning. She's losing gasoline."

Crankshaw cursed, but eased the car closer to Elizabeth's.

Elizabeth's mouth dropped open in horror. "Don't jump, Jimmy!"

"Steer the car straight, Elizabeth."

"*Ooooooh*, I don't like this."

Ignoring her warning, Jimmy waited until the front fenders of both cars were mere inches apart before making a spectacular leap and landing in the backseat of her car. The crowd went wild.

"Jimmy!" She hit one curb, then bounced toward the other. It was a brilliant move—for a billiard ball.

Up ahead, Crankshaw's tire blew and his car spun around and crashed into a telephone pole.

Fearing Elizabeth would insist upon stopping to help Crankshaw, Jimmy yelled, "Go, Elizabeth. Don't stop now!"

"I can't go any faster!"

Like an old woman at the end of a long walk, Old Ironsides slowed to a shaky crawl, then stopped altogether.

# Chapter 38

"The most difficult thing about driving is often the person sitting next to you."

*Women at the Wheel*
Circa 1915

Jimmy jumped out of the car. Elizabeth didn't have a chance in high heaven of winning the race now, but by George, he meant to see that she finished it.

"Steer!" He rolled up his shirtsleeves and pressed his palms against the back of the car. Gritting his teeth, he pushed the car toward the finish line. Suddenly, he was joined by Crankshaw.

Jimmy glanced at him in surprise. "What the . . . ?"

"I told you," he said, tossing his walking cane into the back of Elizabeth's car, "if I don't win, I'm rooting for the lady."

"That's mighty kind of you."

"Kindness has nothing to do with it. I'll be damned if I'll let that Fastbender win without a fight!"

Together, they pushed the car past the cheering crowds and across the finish line behind Billy-Joe, Sir Higginbottom, and Fastbender. Elizabeth was officially logged in at the number four position and Staggs came in fifth. Staggs would have placed higher had he not stopped to take a photograph of Crankshaw's car up the telephone pole. Billy-Joe was another story. No matter how many times Billy-Joe seemed to be out of the race, he always came out ahead.

"Damn, how does he do it?" Jimmy growled.

"Rye?"

At the sound of the woman's voice, Crankshaw spun around. "Myra!"

Moving incredibly fast for a man who walked with a limp, Crankshaw hastened toward a tall, slender woman and threw his arms around her, practically knocking one of the race officials in the head with his cane. Myra was dressed in a black hobble skirt and tunic, her gray hair pinned primly beneath a feathered hat.

Never had Jimmy seen Crankshaw act so socially inept. Rude maybe, but not inept. He actually stuttered as he introduced Myra and couldn't even seem to remember Jimmy's name. "This is the widow lady I told you about."

Jimmy tipped his hat. "I'm pleased to make your acquaintance, ma'am."

Crankshaw was as red-faced as a bride. "I didn't think you'd come."

Myra held her purse with both hands. "I changed my mind. A woman can do that, can't she?"

"Sure, but now that you saw me lose the race, you're probably more determined than ever not to marry me."

"That's why I came to Seattle. I decided if a woman is going to turn down a man's proposal, she ought to do it to his face."

"Ah, gee, Myra . . ."

"Now hear me out, Rye. I've had a change of heart. I saw you help that lady driver cross the finish line and I said to myself, Myra, that Rye Crankshaw has his faults, but he's a kind and honorable man." Myra gazed at Crankshaw with a loving smile. "I'd be a fool not to marry you, and if you still want me, I'd be proud to be your wife."

"Still want . . ." Crankshaw's mouth took to flapping up and down like an unhinged shutter. "You mean it,

Myra? You're going to marry me? Even though I lost the race?"

"I don't care about any old race," Myra said. "I care what's in a man's heart."

Crankshaw stared at her incredulously. "You're going to marry me because I helped Miss Liz ... eh, Miss Davenport cross the finish line?"

Myra looked uncertain. "You still want me, don't you?"

Crankshaw's face crumbled into a broad smile. "You bet I do!"

"It was nice meeting you, Myra," Jimmy said, but his words fell on deaf ears. The way Myra and Crankshaw were looking at each other, Jimmy doubted they knew anyone else was around.

Jimmy raised himself up to look over the crowd, searching for Elizabeth.

He spotted her, finally, surrounded by newsmen. He pushed his way through the crowd and stood watching from the sidelines while she fielded questions.

"How does it feel to be the only woman in the race?"

"Are you disappointed that you only came in fourth?"

"Only?" Jimmy glared at the newsman, a young mealymouthed kid who barely looked old enough to be out of school.

"I'm disappointed," Elizabeth admitted. "I had counted on the prize money to build my children's home."

"What a pity," a matronly woman said. She was dressed in the white skirt and blouse typically worn by many suffragettes. She handed Elizabeth a ten-dollar bill, and not to be outdone, the other women in her group did likewise. "This is for your home," the woman explained.

"Thank you," Elizabeth said, her eyes growing misty with gratitude. "Thank you, all of you. Thank you so much."

Later, after the crowd had dispersed to follow the winning drivers to the winner's circle, Elizabeth sat in Old Ironsides, thumbing through the bills in her hand.

Jimmy walked up to her side, trying not to show his anger and hurt. "Would you mind explaining why you took off without me? You could have gotten yourself killed."

She glared up at him. "What difference would that have made? Women are a dime a dozen, remember?"

A little bell went off in Jimmy's head and he muttered a curse. So Elizabeth had heard him talking to Crankshaw. No wonder she was so riled up. He climbed into the companion seat and slammed the door shut. "Crankshaw was depressed about his lady friend. What I said had nothing to do with you and me. I was simply trying to cheer him up."

"I hope you succeeded. Now would you please leave?"

He grabbed the door handle, then pulled his hand away. "No, I'm not going to leave, Elizabeth. Not until I've had my say. I've been through hell and back with you these last twenty-five days. The *Perils of Pauline* is nothing compared to what I've been through. Most men would have run the other way, but not me. Oh, no! I stayed by your side to the very end, and do you know why?"

"Because you wanted to win the race, and don't tell me you didn't."

He shook his head. "I thought I did. But you know what? I don't give a tinker's damn about winning. I stayed because I love you. Hell's bells, I've always loved you. I loved the little girl who cried her eyes out in the baggage car. And I fell in love anew with the irritating, mule-headed, stubborn woman who nearly drove me to my death. Now, you can accept that or not, Elizabeth. The choice is yours."

Having said his piece, he climbed out of the car and walked away.

"Jimmy."

He stopped in his tracks and allowed himself the luxury of smiling to himself before composing his features.

Slowly, he turned to face her. She was standing a short distance away. Dressed as usual in her overalls, her hair blowing in the breeze, she made a fetching sight.

"You said the choice was mine. What precisely does that mean?"

"You and I can part ways . . ."

"Or . . . ?"

"You can let me do the driving from now on."

She stood looking at him and said nothing.

"Dammit, Elizabeth, when a man proposes to a woman, he would like to see a little enthusiasm."

"Proposes? Is that what you think you did? Let me tell you something, Jimmy Hunter. That's not how a man proposes to a woman!"

"You're right. I'll try again. Elizabeth Davenport, will you . . ."

"No! I can't marry you, Jimmy. I'm a working woman. I have a book to write and a home to build."

"My mother and aunt have worked all their lives. I wouldn't know how to handle a wife who didn't work."

"I can't marry you, Jimmy, and that's that!" She turned and hurried toward Old Ironsides.

"Elizabeth?" He ran after her. "All right, I'll let you drive."

"Driving has nothing to do with this."

"I know what the problem is. I didn't ask you properly."

She stopped and turned. "The second time was a vast improvement over the first."

He grinned and dropped on one knee. "And the third will be a charm. Elizabeth Davenport, would you do me the honor of being my wife?"

She shook her head sadly. "I can't be your wife, Jimmy. I can't be anyone's wife."

"What are you saying? You're not a nun, are you?"

"What?"

"As far as I know, they're the only ones who can't wed."

"Certainly not."

"Then what? Tell me."

"I can't tell you, Jimmy."

"Dammit, Elizabeth. When a woman turns down a man's proposal of marriage, he has every right to know why. Is it something I did?"

"No."

"I know—you're still upset over what you overheard me say to Crankshaw, aren't you?"

"Jimmy, please ..." Her eyes filled with tears.

"I've got to know, Elizabeth. You owe me that much."

"You deserve a wife who is ... you know ... who hasn't been with another man."

"You mean a virgin?"

She blushed.

"Do you think I care a fig about that?"

"Every man wants his future wife to be ... He wants to be the first one."

"Elizabeth," he whispered. "I've had other women in my life. It's not something I'm proud of, but it's a fact I can't deny. But you're the only woman I've ever loved, and the day we made love in the tall grass of Missouri was unlike anything I'd ever experienced. As far as I'm concerned, that was the first time I ever made love. It was also the first time the sun ever shone and a bird ever sang."

"Oh, Jimmy, it was the same for me, but ..."

He stepped forward and circled his hands around her waist. "No buts," he whispered. "Just say you love me."

"Oh, Jimmy!" She flung her arms around his neck and melted against him. "I do love you. I truly, truly do!"

His mouth covered hers hungrily before he remembered he'd forgotten to warn her in advance of his intentions, but it didn't matter. For without a moment's hesitation, she kissed him back, and not so much as a shadow of the past interfered.

And that, too, was a first.

# Chapter 39

The following morning, Jimmy replaced the gas tank
in Old Ironsides. The tank had a huge dent in it and
Jimmy suspected it was a result of being hit by a part
from Fastbender's car. The dent had eventually sprung
a hole, which resulted in Elizabeth running out of gas
before she crossed the finish line.

Even with the new gas tank, there was no denying
that Old Ironsides was on its last leg. Its frame was
bent, its suspension shot, its once gleaming body dull
and dented. The canvas top was ripped and torn. The
car had more missing parts than a toothless man.

He ran his hand along its battered remains and
sighed. He and Elizabeth had decided to take the train
back to Hogs Head. The problem was, they couldn't
agree on what to do with the Model T Ford that had
served them so faithfully. He'd suggested they sell it
as a junker, but Elizabeth refused to even consider
such an option, and in all honesty, he couldn't
blame her.

Strangely enough, he'd grown fond of the old gal.
He was thinking seriously of getting rid of his electric
car as soon as he returned to Hogs Head and replacing
it with a Model T Ford. Maybe he'd splurge on one

of the newer models with an electric starter. Wouldn't that be something? He smiled to himself. It would make a perfect wedding gift for Elizabeth.

He glanced to the rear of the car where Elizabeth stood scrubbing away the dirt and the mud. "What do you say we put in an official complaint against Fastbender?"

"It would only look like sour grapes," Elizabeth said. "Besides, I wouldn't want to turn in one of my backers."

Jimmy drew back. "Backers? What do you mean, backers?"

"Fastbender is going to make a large donation to my orphanage."

"Holy smokes. How did you get him to agree to that?"

"I haven't. Not yet. But I will." She wiped her hands dry, reached into the car for an envelope, and pulled out a photograph. "Mr. Staggs gave this photograph to me this morning. As you can clearly see, it shows Fastbender nearly running Sir Higginbottom's car off the road. As soon as he sees this photograph, I'm sure he'll want to make a generous donation."

Jimmy took the photograph and studied it, then threw back his head and laughed. "That's damning evidence, all right. If Fastbender is wise, he'll pay up." Suddenly, Jimmy noticed something. He held the photograph up for a closer look. What he saw made his heart leap with joy. "Get in the car, Elizabeth! Hurry!"

"What?"

"Don't ask questions. Just drive back to race headquarters. I may have figured out a way to get you the rest of the money."

It was bedlam at the Henry Ford race headquarters in downtown Seattle. Reporters clutching yellow pads shouted out questions to anyone who looked the least bit official. Race officials ran around wringing their hands and shaking their heads.

A group of suffragettes waved signs that demanded women be given the right to vote, have a say over their bodies, and be allowed to win automobile races.

Elizabeth, dressed in her peacock-blue hobble skirt and tunic, stopped to talk to the leader of the group, a strapping woman with black hair named Isabel Pryor whom she'd met in San Francisco.

"Do you know what's going on?" Miss Pryor asked. "I've heard all sorts of rumors."

"We discovered some rule infractions," Elizabeth explained. "The race officials wouldn't listen to us, but Mr. Ford listened."

And he did listen, though it took Jimmy most of the day and almost all night before he was able to track him down. If it hadn't been for Staggs and his confounded camera, Billy-Joe would have gotten away with his dastardly deeds.

Henry Ford swept into the room and took his place at the podium. A tall, distinguished-looking man with white hair, he had an air of authority. His mere presence commanded attention, and a hushed silence fell across the room.

"Ladies and gentlemen," he began without preamble. "The Henry Ford Motor Company was built on integrity and honesty. The race was designed to call attention to the nation's disgraceful highways. As a result of this race, many cities and states have decided to do something about their roads."

Thunderous applause, echoing through the large hall, greeted his announcement. Mr. Ford held his hands up, commanding quiet. "We are grateful to every driver who helped us accomplish this noble goal. Because of them, people like yourself will be able to visit friends and family in distant cities and see our nation's glorious sights." More applause. "However, as grateful as we are, we cannot overlook the fact that some of our drivers committed serious rule infractions." The room was dead silent as Mr. Ford spelled out the violations.

Elizabeth clutched Jimmy's arm nervously. It was possible she would move up to the number three, or even two, position. That wasn't bad for a woman driver, and the money would allow her to hire an architect to begin drawing up plans. Surely this would give her more credibility in applying for bank loans.

Mr. Ford continued. "The driver of car number two, Mr. Billy-Joe Mason, has admitted to crossing three states by rail." A gasp of shock and disapproval traveled through the room as all eyes turned to Billy-Joe, who stood red-faced and hatless.

"Shocking!"

"Appalling."

Jimmy shook his head. He'd never been able to figure out how Billy-Joe always managed to pass them, sight unseen. It hadn't occurred to him that Billy-Joe was traveling by rail until he saw that photograph of Fastbender trying to run Sir Higginbottom off the road. In the background was a clear shot of a moving flatcar carrying Billy-Joe's car.

The next infraction involved Sir Higginbottom. All eyes turned the Englishman as Mr. Ford read the charges.

"It seems that Sir Higginbottom allowed a Ford company employee to temporarily take over the wheel when his car was stuck in quicksand. The rules clearly state that only registered crew members could drive."

Sir Higginbottom leaned toward Jimmy. "If that damned Chinaman could make a decent cup of tea, I wouldn't have gotten sick and driven into that sandtrap in the first place."

Mr. Ford still wasn't finished. "The third infraction is attributed to Mr. Fastbender, driver of car number seven."

Jimmy leaned toward Elizabeth and whispered in her ear, "He almost got away with this one."

"Mr. Fastbender replaced a part. As you know, the rules state that certain designated parts cannot be replaced."

Elizabeth looked at Jimmy. Jimmy looked at Elizabeth. Three drivers had been disqualified. *Three!*

Mr. Ford cleared his voice. "The official list of winners is as follows. In the number three spot, Mr. Rye Crankshaw."

Crankshaw grinned. His car had actually been towed across the finish line after being disengaged from the telephone pole. Next to him, Myra smiled proudly.

"In second place," Mr. Ford announced, "Mr. Roland Staggs, the driver of car number four."

"Yahoo!" Jimmy cried out. He couldn't believe he was actually cheering for the man, but if it hadn't been for Staggs and his confounded camera, they would never have caught Billy-Joe riding the rails.

"And in first place . . . Miss Elizabeth Davenport."

"Oh, Jimmy." She threw herself into Jimmy's arms and kissed him squarely on the mouth. The crowd went wild, and Jimmy, not accustomed to such a public display of affection, turned beet-red.

Having made his announcement, Mr. Ford left the podium and hurried through a back door flanked by Ford officials.

Mr. Stonegate ran up to shake Elizabeth's hand. "Congratulations, Miss Davenport. I couldn't be happier for you."

"How kind of you, Mr. Stonegate. I'm so sorry you weren't able to finish the race."

"Now don't you go worrying yourself into an early grave over me," he said. "As it turns out, the man who towed me into town owns a cemetery right here in Seattle and he's offered me half ownership."

"That's . . . wonderful!" Elizabeth exclaimed.

"Congratulations!" Jimmy said, shaking Stonegate's hand.

Stonegate blushed. "If either one of you ever needs . . . you know . . . I'll personally handle the arrangements myself.

"Thanks," Jimmy said, grabbing Elizabeth by the

hand and pulling her through the crowd. "But we wouldn't think of imposing."

"No imposition," Stonegate called after them. "That's what friends are for."

It was late that afternoon before Elizabeth and Jimmy finally managed to escape the crowd. Elizabeth drove while Jimmy sat looking at the bank draft in his hand, made out for twenty-five thousand dollars.

A four-foot-tall gold trophy took up the length of the backseat, engraved with Elizabeth's name, along with Jimmy's and Old Ironsides's. Elizabeth had insisted her entire crew be given proper credit.

"Oh, Jimmy, I can't believe it. I'm going to build the best home ever!"

"Do you think I can talk you into building your home in Hogs Head?" he asked.

"Hogs Head?" She lifted her head toward the sky to enjoy the sun and the wind on her face. "I think Hogs Head is the perfect place for my home."

He grinned. "And I'll personally handle the electrical wiring. By the time I'm finished, every corner will be brightly lit. Not one of your orphans will ever know a moment of darkness. Not if I have anything to say about it."

She gazed at him and her heart swelled with love. "Oh, Jimmy. It's going to be so wonderful."

The dirt road followed along the Puget Sound. The calm waters of the inland sea were dotted with fishing vessels, and only the low hum of internal combustion engines broke the peace and quiet. Stocky halibut schooners sailed past tuna clippers and gill netters. Farther out two boats flanked a squat-sterned purse seiner.

All that was left of an earlier rain shower were the orange-tinged clouds skidding across the sky. Without warning, Elizabeth pulled to the side of the road and slammed on the brakes.

"Look at the rainbow. Over there." She jumped out of the car and, lifting her hobble skirt above her ankles, followed a trail overlooking a bluff.

Jimmy pocketed the bank draft and chased after her, and together they stood in each other's arms gazing at the rainbow that spanned one of the many channels like a colorful bridge.

"I ordered that rainbow especially for you," Jimmy said. He lifted her chin and kissed her gently on the lips. "I love you, Elizabeth Davenport, and I can't wait to make you my wife."

"I love you, Jimmy Hunter, and . . . Oh, no!"

He frowned. "Now what? Elizabeth? Talk to me."

She flapped her jaw up and down, but nothing came out of her mouth. Unable to speak, she pointed frantically in the direction of Old Ironsides.

Jimmy spun around. "Oh, no!" Much to his horror, Old Ironsides was rolling toward the cliff.

"Do something!" Elizabeth cried.

Jimmy was too far away to do much of anything but watch as Old Ironsides disappeared over the edge. The Model T Ford made a spectacular dive into the calm blue water below, taking the Henry Ford cross-country race first-place trophy with it.

Elizabeth and Jimmy ran to the spot where Old Ironsides had gone over. Standing arm-in-arm at the edge of the cliff, they stared down below.

The old flivver floated nose-down, then gradually disappeared into the watery depths until all that remained were Elizabeth's colorful ribbons floating on the surface.

Soon, Old Ironsides sank deeper, taking the ribbons with it, until every last piece of satin disappeared, and nothing was left of the noble old car but a few oily bubbles.

Jimmy threw up his hands in exasperation. "Isn't this peachy! If I told you once, I've told you a thousand times, you must use the emergency brake."

"Sheesh! Blame me, will you?"

"If you would just learn how to drive!" He stomped away, but didn't get far before a most unladylike raspberry sound brought him to a halt. He whirled about to face her, then burst out laughing.

The next thing he knew, they were in each other's arms.

"Oh, Jimmy, what are we going to do?"

He slid his arms down to her waist. He hated to see Old Ironsides go, but somehow this end seemed far more fitting than selling the car to a junk dealer. "Just as soon as we arrive in Hogs Head, we're going to buy a brand-new Model T Ford and I'm going to invent an alarm that goes off if the emergency brake isn't set right."

"What a wonderful idea!" Her eyes glowed with happiness. "I can see myself now, driving through Hogs Head."

Jimmy shuddered at the thought. "I've got a better idea. We'll buy two Model T's. One for you and one for me. But for now, we walk."

"Walk?" Elizabeth glanced around. Behind them was nothing but thick woods. "But we're miles from anywhere."

"Don't remind me." He lifted his voice in song as he took her by the hand and led her toward the stretch of deserted road.

Struck by the humor in the situation, Elizabeth lifted her hand to stifle her giggles, then did something she never thought she'd do again: She sang. Her heart as light and free as the seagulls flying overhead, she lifted her voice with Jimmy's, and it seemed to her that it was the very first song that anyone had ever sung.

"She was a great flivver till she fell into the river ..."

> "Two people in love can live happily ever after, providing they share a single bed—and drive separate cars."
> *Women at the Wheel*
> Circa 1915
> By Mrs. Elizabeth Davenport Hunter

# *Author's note*

*Ribbons in the Wind* was inspired by the New York to Seattle Transcontinental Endurance Race of 1909. While my story is purely fictional, I strived to write an accurate account of what it might have been like to travel cross-country in a Model T Ford on roads "not fit for a mule" in the early part of the century. Those early motorcars really did ride the rails, ford rivers and travel "where no man (or woman) had business traveling." Cincinnati had the first traffic signal, though I have no idea who ran the first red light. For the purposes of my story, I bestowed this somewhat dubious "honor" upon my heroine.

Special thanks go to Cathleen R. Latendresse, Access Coordinator for the Henry Ford Museum and Jean Caldwell, Reference Librarian for the American Automobile Association.

**Watch for Margaret Brownley's
next book
*BUTTONS AND BEAUX*
in the fall of 1997**

# *WONDERFUL LOVE STORIES*

# WE NEED YOUR HELP

To continue to bring you quality romance
that meets your personal expectations,
we at TOPAZ books want to hear from you.
Help us by filling out this questionnaire, and in exchange
we will give you a **free gift** as a token of our gratitude.

- Is this the first TOPAZ book you've purchased? (circle one)

    YES     NO

    The title and author of this book is: _____

- If this was not the first TOPAZ book you've purchased, how many have
  you bought in the past year?

    a: 0 - 5     b 6 - 10     c: more than 10     d: more than 20

- How many romances in total did you buy in the past year?

    a: 0 - 5     b: 6 - 10     c: more than 10     d: more than 20 ____

- How would you rate your overall satisfaction with this book?

    a: Excellent     b: Good     c: Fair     d: Poor

- What was the main reason you bought this book?

    a: It is a TOPAZ novel, and I know that TOPAZ stands
        for quality romance fiction
    b: I liked the cover
    c: The story-line intrigued me
    d: I love this author
    e: I really liked the setting
    f: I love the cover models
    g: Other: _____

- Where did you buy this TOPAZ novel?

    a: Bookstore     b: Airport     c: Warehouse Club
    d: Department Store     e: Supermarket     f: Drugstore
    g: Other: _____

- Did you pay the full cover price for this TOPAZ novel? (circle one)

    YES     NO

    If you did not, what price did you pay? _____

- Who are your favorite TOPAZ authors? (Please list)

- How did you first hear about TOPAZ books?

    a: I saw the books in a bookstore
    b: I saw the TOPAZ Man on TV or at a signing
    c: A friend told me about TOPAZ
    d: I saw an advertisement in_____magazine
    e: Other: _____

- What type of romance do you generally prefer?

    a: Historical     b: Contemporary
    c: Romantic Suspense     d: Paranormal (time travel,
        futuristic, vampires, ghosts, warlocks, etc.)
    d: Regency     e: Other: _____

- What historical settings do you prefer?

    a: England     b: Regency England          c: Scotland
    e: Ireland     f: America     g: Western Americana
    h: American Indian          i: Other: _____

- What type of story do you prefer?

  a: Very sexy        b: Sweet, less explicit
  c: Light and humorous    d: More emotionally intense
  e: Dealing with darker issues   f: Other

- What kind of covers do you prefer?

  a: Illustrating both hero and heroine     b: Hero alone
  c: No people (art only)             d: Other_____

- What other genres do you like to read (circle all that apply)

  Mystery        Medical Thrillers      Science Fiction
  Suspense       Fantasy             Self-help
  Classics         General Fiction       Legal Thrillers
  Historical Fiction

- Who is your favorite author, and why?_____
  _____

- What magazines do you like to read? (circle all that apply)

  a: *People*            b: *Time/Newsweek*
  c: *Entertainment Weekly*    d: *Romantic Times*
  e: *Star*              f: *National Enquirer*
  g: *Cosmopolitan*      h: *Woman's Day*
  i: *Ladies' Home Journal*    j: *Redbook*
  k: Other:_____

- In which region of the United States do you reside?

  a: Northeast   b: Midatlantic   c: South
  d: Midwest     e: Mountain     f: Southwest
  g: Pacific Coast

- What is your age group/sex?    a: Female   b: Male

  a: under 18     b: 19-25     c: 26-30     d: 31-35    e: 36-40
  f: 41-45        g: 46-50     h: 51-55     i: 56-60    j: Over 60

- What is your marital status?

  a: Married      b: Single      c: No longer married

- What is your current level of education?

  a: High school       b: College Degree
  c: Graduate Degree   d: Other: _____

- Do you receive the TOPAZ *Romantic Liaisons* newsletter, a quarterly newsletter with the latest information on Topaz books and authors?

  YES            NO

  If not, would you like to?   YES      NO

  Fill in the address where you would like your free gift to be sent:

  Name: _____
  Address: _____
  City:_____ Zip Code: _____

  You should receive your free gift in 6 to 8 weeks.
  Please send the completed survey to:

  Penguin USA•Mass Market
  Dept. TS
  375 Hudson St.
  New York, NY 10014